THE ALPINE XANADU

AN EMMA LORD MYSTERY

THE ALPINE XANADU

MARY DAHEIM

THORNDIKE PRESS
A part of Gale, Cengage Learning

GALE
CENGAGE Learning·

Detroit • New York • San Francisco • New Haven, Conn • Waterville, Maine • London

GALE
CENGAGE Learning®

LIBRARY OF CONGRESS CATALOGING-IN-PUBLICATION DATA

Daheim, Mary.
  The Alpine Xanadu : an Emma Lord mystery / by Mary Daheim.
    pages ; cm. — (Thorndike Press large print mystery)
  ISBN-13: 978-1-4104-5823-0 (hardcover)
  ISBN-10: 1-4104-5823-7 (hardcover)
  1. Lord, Emma (Fictitious character)—Fiction. 2. Women publishers—Fiction. 3. Washington (State)—Fiction. 4. Large type books.
  I. Title.
PS3554.A264A88 2013b
813'.54—dc23   2013004859

Published in 2013 by arrangement with The Ballantine Publishing Group, a division of Random House, Inc.

Printed in the United States of America
1 2 3 4 5 6 7 17 16 15 14 13

To Tim Raetzloff, the leader of the Alpine Conservancy, and to all the Alpine Advocates who have revived a town that I thought was lost forever.

AUTHOR'S NOTE

The story is set in February 2005.

ONE

I was stunned by the letter from my old pal and *Oregonian* newspaper compatriot Mavis Marley Fulkerston. Not having heard from her in over two months, I worried. The reason for the lapse was valid, but the rest of the message upset me.

"Dear Emma," she began, "sorry for not thanking you sooner for the exquisite mother-of-pearl vase you sent for Christmas. Ray and I love it. Your backwoods gallery owner has surprisingly good taste.

"Ray and I took our usual post-holiday Oahu trip to escape Portland's gray skies. We had a great time — until we were waiting for the airport shuttle to take us home and Ray had a heart attack. One quadruple bypass later, he was pronounced viable (if ornery) and sent to rehab for two weeks. He's still grouchy and I may have to kill him.

"Your recent close call with death horrified me. Hope you've recovered by now. Hope you've also deep-sixed your zany idea about marrying the local sheriff. That shocked me more than hearing about the nut who tried to kill you both. The last time we talked about Milo Dodge was years ago, just before you dumped him. He sounded so unlike your kind of guy and about as exciting as meat loaf. Maybe you've spent too much time in Alpine. What happened to the independent, culturally aware, freethinking gal I knew on the *Oregonian?* I envision you atrophying like a petrified cedar stump in that isolated mountain burg.

"Okay, it's none of my business. I know you've been looking for a new man since Tom Cavanaugh died. I never met him, but when he abandoned you for his crazy wife and didn't help support your son until Adam was grown up, I thought he was a jerk. I'd hoped you had something going with the AP stud, Rolf Fisher, but then he retired and moved to France. He was civilized, single, and, according to you, good-looking. Maybe I'm venting, taking out my frustration with the Resident Grump, who doesn't even like the way I make toast these days.

"Go ahead, marry the dull and boring sheriff. Just hope he never has a heart attack and falls on top of your new designer luggage. I don't want to see you make another mistake when it comes to men. You're too good for that — you're too good for Alpine."

Mavis always sent her letters to *The Alpine Advocate* office instead of to my little log house. Maybe I'd complained too much about our often careless postman, Marlowe Whipp. It was the third Wednesday of February, post-pub day. I might have time to answer Mavis.

"Well?" my House & Home editor, Vida Runkel, demanded, startling me out of my gloom. "You look like the pigs ate your little brother."

"My *big* brother wouldn't appeal to pigs," I said, trying to shield the letter from Vida's probing eyes. "Ben's still on the Mississippi Delta getting reacquainted with his former parishioners."

Vida sat down in one of my two new, if used, visitor chairs. I'd replaced the originals after my former ad manager, Ed Bronsky, broke one of them just before New Year's. "Of course," she said testily. "He and Adam discussed their mission work on my radio show. Such hardships. So cold for Adam in that Alaskan village, so hot for Ben in Arizona. Are you going to Delia Rafferty's

11

funeral at the Lutheran church?"

I grimaced. "I forgot. It's at one, right?"

"Yes. Despite the Irish name, the Raffertys aren't Catholic."

"I went to Tim's service, remember?"

Vida adjusted the green bow on her wide-brimmed purple hat. "So sad when Tim was killed and their house burned down. Poor Delia had been gaga for some time. The baby's a year old now. Walking, according to Dot Parker. What kind of name is Ashley for a girl?"

It was better than Tank or Pewter, both of which had been given to recent local newborns. "Tiff's lucky her mom and grandmother babysit so she can work at the Grocery Basket," I said, aware of Vida's sharp gray eyes fixed on the letter I was trying to hide.

"Dot and Durwood enjoy their great-grandchildren," she said wistfully, probably thinking about her spoiled grandson Roger who'd finally disgraced himself. "Is that letter from an irate reader? It looks long."

As the *Advocate*'s editor and publisher, I'm the boss, but Vida is over twenty years my senior, and keeping secrets from her is futile. She sees all and knows all, and God help anyone who doesn't tell all. "It's from my friend Mavis. She's in a lather because

12

Milo and I are engaged."

Vida harrumphed. "What does Mavis know? She lives in Portland!"

"True," I said, accustomed to Vida's disdain for anyone who didn't call Alpine home. She was also a bit jealous of my other female friends. "Maybe she's off her feed because her husband had a heart attack."

"Many people have heart attacks," Vida asserted, "but their loved ones don't go around meddling in other people's affairs. Really, I cannot understand why she thinks she should give you advice. Has she ever met Milo? To my knowledge, Mavis has never been near Alpine."

"True on both counts," I agreed. "She thinks he's the wrong type of man for me. Face it, Vida, you used to feel the same way."

She bristled a bit, her imposing bosom heaving under her black vest and purple blouse. "That's because you had so little in common. Now it's obvious — too obvious sometimes — that you love each other. That trumps the rest. It would be nice, however, if you actually got married."

"You know we have to wait for an annulment of Milo's first marriage. Ben's started the process with the Seattle Archdiocese."

"Yes, yes." She pursed her lips and frowned. "I still say that given your high

13

profiles you should have a civil ceremony first. It simply doesn't look proper for you to live together without being married."

"We aren't living together. Tanya's been staying with him for over two weeks. I've hardly seen Milo. His daughter still has nightmares."

Vida grimaced. "I thought the Hawaii trip would've cured her of that. It must've cost Milo the world to send her and her mother, Tricia."

"It wasn't cheap," I said. "But I'm not unsympathetic to Tanya — or even Tricia. It was traumatic for them to be held hostage by her crazy fiancé and have Tanya get shot before watching the guy off himself."

"You and Milo had your own trauma. *You* don't have nightmares."

"I did for the first week or so," I admitted. "I still dread the possibility of a trial. Maybe our perp won't be judged sane enough to be tried. It'll take two more months before he's evaluated at Northern State Hospital. Giving all those depositions was bad enough."

Vida stood up. "But you've come through it. As for Tricia, she may be manipulating Milo. She can't accept the idea he's marrying again, especially since her second husband betrayed her and they're divorcing. So foolish to think he wouldn't philander after cheating with her while they were both still married to other people. Which reminds me, I must work on my advice column. I still can't believe Pastor Purebeck ran off with Daisy McFee. What will become of us Presbyterians?" Straightening her hat, she walked away in her splay-footed manner.

I decided to delay answering Mavis's letter. My sole reporter, Mitch Laskey, entered my office and put some hard copy on my desk.

"Here's the last of my RestHaven series," he said, placing a foot on the chair Vida had vacated. "I finally got some straight answers from Dr. Woo, the chief of staff. ReHaven is the corporation out of New York and Rest-Haven is for smaller facilities, like here. Have you taken a tour?"

I shook my head. "Is the grand opening still firm for Saturday?"

He nodded. "Converting the former Bronsky villa took longer than they figured. Ed and Shirley weren't big on upkeep even before they blew all of his inheritance on fancy furniture and expensive cars."

" 'All for show, not much for go,' as Vida would say. The architect, Scott Melville, is very competent. He worked on a RestHaven project when he lived in California."

"So Scott told me," Mitch said. "The facility's already at seventy percent capacity. They can take ninety patients — forty in rehab, a dozen post-ops in the adjacent unit, and twenty-two in what they call the emotional restoration ward." His lanky frame slumped a bit.

I knew what he was thinking. After his son, Troy, had failed in his second escape from the Monroe Correctional Facility just before Christmas, Mitch's wife, Brenda, suffered a breakdown. She'd spent time in the psych ward at Seattle's Harborview Hospital. Instead of bringing her back to Alpine, he felt it might be better for her to stay with their daughter, Miriam, in Pittsburgh. The Laskeys were newcomers to Alpine, having moved from Royal Oak, Michigan, in September. While he hadn't said so, I wondered if Mitch thought Brenda might benefit from a stint at RestHaven.

"I may go on the formal tour," I said. "You'll take pictures?"

"Sure. What else have I got to do?" he asked wryly.

"Thanks." I smiled, but I, too, had bad memories of ReHaven. I'd first heard of it when Tom Cavanaugh's wife had been shipped off to their Bay Area facility. I'd finally stopped grieving for Tom, but oc-

16

casionally something came back to hit me like a nagging pain from an old injury.

Mitch had started out of my cramped office, but stopped short to turn around. "Jack Blackwell's still raising hell with the sheriff."

"Now what?" I asked in exasperation. "Why doesn't that jackass stick to running his mill? It's the only one left in town."

"He came in this morning just before I got there to check the log," Mitch said, leaning one hand against the door frame. "His latest alleged brush with death was brake tampering on his SUV. Cal Vickers is checking it out at his Chevron station."

"Did Jack get into it with Milo?"

Mitch shook his head. "Dodge wasn't there. He had to take his daughter to the ER."

"What?" I shrieked. "Is she sick?"

Mitch looked pained. "Dodge caught her downing a bunch of tranquilizers."

"Oh, crap!" I cried, falling back in my chair.

"I guess she's okay, but he wanted to make sure," Mitch said.

"Right." I realized my reporter looked puzzled. His absence from Alpine seemed to have left him out of the loop when it came to my relationship with Milo. This didn't seem like the right time to enlighten

17

Mitch. "There are so many people with emotional problems," I said. "Your wife has had her share and that's hard on you. Maybe we should all be in RestHaven's psych unit."

Mitch hung his head. "Maybe so." He shrugged and walked away.

I was considering going to the hospital to check on Tanya when the phone rang. It was the city librarian, Edna Mae Dalrymple. "Emma, dear," she twittered in her chickadee-like voice, "I must congratulate you on standing up to Dixie Ridley last Thursday about the attempt to suppress *Tom Sawyer* from the high school curriculum. I meant to call you sooner, but I've been so busy. Did you write that editorial about it?"

"I did, but naming no names," I said. "You'll see it when the paper comes out today. I reminded readers that Samuel Clemens was related to Carl Clemans, despite the difference in the spelling of their last names."

"Oh, excellent! No one in Alpine will dare criticize the original mill owner or his kin. He's a legend here for being fair and generous. Dixie, as a football coach's wife, should be the last one to quibble. You should hear how some of those players talk

18

on the sidelines!"

"Shocking, I'm sure," I said, wanting to get off the phone.

"If you think that's shocking," Edna Mae rattled on, though she'd lowered her voice, "have you heard about the pornography that was found in two of the basketball players' lockers?"

"No. When did that happen?"

"Over the weekend when they played Granite Falls. Oh, dear — I shouldn't tell tales."

I made a note. "I don't suppose you know any specifics?"

"I wouldn't want to know," Edna Mae asserted.

"Of course not," I said. "Thanks for the heads-up, though."

"You're not putting it in the paper, are you?"

I hedged my bets. "The paper's printed. Got to go. Thanks again."

I put on my jacket and grabbed my purse, but stopped at Mitch's desk to relay Edna Mae's porn rumor. "Check with Principal Freeman. He'll probably stonewall you, but you can deal with that. Keep track of Blackwell's latest attention-getting stunt. I've got to run an errand."

Vida was on the phone, looking vexed. She

stared at me as I rushed past her. Behind the reception desk, Amanda Hanson's eyes widened. "What's wrong?" she asked, her pert face alarmed.

"Family emergency," I said, half stumbling out the front door.

The rain was a mere drizzle, so I walked the two blocks uphill to the hospital. My response to Amanda had come unbidden. Tanya wasn't family — not yet. But she would be when Milo and I got married. *If* we ever got married, I thought dismally. The new year had not treated us kindly. Not only had we narrowly escaped death, but trying to blow up a county sheriff and a newspaper publisher made regional news. We'd been pestered by the media, which had asked for everything from personal interviews to the possibility of a made-for-TV movie. Neither of us wanted our private lives invaded. We'd hunkered down in my snug little log cabin as much as our jobs would allow. Between KSKY's Spencer Fleetwood and my own media contacts, we'd discouraged most of the snoops without Milo resorting to the strong-arm tactics he swore he'd use if needed. I'd cringed at the thought of the sheriff decking a big-shot Seattle TV reporter or one of my former *Oregonian* colleagues.

Mavis hadn't a clue about Skykomish County's sheriff, I thought as I waited for a Public Utility District truck to go by at Pine Street. Behind that often laconic exterior, a volcanic personality lurked in his imposing six-foot-five-inch frame. My only regret was that it had taken me fifteen years to realize how much I loved him. Mavis was right on one count — I'd been bat-blind when it came to men. Milo had finally woken me up, though I was no Sleeping Beauty and he wasn't Prince Charming. The words "Milo" and "charm" in the same sentence would have to include "not even close."

I was panting with exertion by the time I reached the hospital. Jenny Bjornson sat behind the front desk. She and I had a bit of a history, but her father worked for Milo part-time as a handyman.

"Ms. Lord!" she cried. "Are you here about the sheriff's daughter?"

Unable to catch my breath, I nodded and leaned on the desk.

"She's still in the ER," Jenny said, apparently not holding a grudge. "They got here about an hour ago."

I took a deep breath. "Where's the sheriff?"

Jenny made a face. "I'm not sure. I haven't seen him."

Milo couldn't be in the ER. Maybe he was outside smoking.

"Which doctor is on duty?" I asked. We only had two in Alpine.

"Dr. Sung," Jenny replied. "He pulled night duty and was just leaving when the sheriff arrived. I think Doc Dewey is over at the clinic."

"I'll check in at the ER nurses' station," I said.

I'd gone into the corridor when I saw Milo exit the pharmacy.

"Emma!" he exclaimed, sounding relieved.

I ran toward him and fell into his arms. "What's happening?"

He didn't answer right away, but held me tight. I could feel his heartbeat close to my ear. "She'll be fine, the dumb shit."

I craned my neck to look up at him. "Where can we talk?"

"Maybe we could find an empty bed."

I giggled, but Milo had already let go of me. "Let's try the waiting room. It's quiet around here. It may be empty."

The sheriff was right. We sat down on a well-worn faux leather settee. "Screw it," he said, taking out a pack of cigarettes. "Want one?"

"Yes, but there's no ashtray."

"Use the rug. It's beat up, like everything

else in SkyCo. The hospital's as desperate for money as my operation is." He lit the cigarettes and handed one to me. "Tanya seemed better, except for the nightmares. I was leaving for work and didn't know she was in the can. When I opened the door, she was shoving pills in her mouth. I grabbed her, saw she had more in her hand, and tried to shake out the ones in her mouth. The bottle was empty. I didn't know she was taking the stuff."

"What did you do then?" I asked as he took a drag on his cigarette.

"I hustled her into the SUV and hauled her ass over here. She was loopy and couldn't make sense. I knew about the Valium but not the Celexa. The pharmacist here says it's for depression." He sighed. "She'll be okay, but Sung's keeping her overnight. Can I come home?"

I saw the wistful look in his hazel eyes. "Oh, please do," I said, leaning against him. "I've missed you so much, it hurts."

He put his arm around me and kissed my forehead. "Tell me about it. When you stop by the office, I want to grab you and . . . damn it, Emma, this is a hell of a start to our life together. We're starting it apart."

"Except for having you and Tanya to dinner, I've hardly seen you." I ran my finger down his cheek. "Did something set Tanya off?"

He shrugged. "She saw an old pal last night, Kristy Olsen. She seemed okay when she got back, but we didn't talk much."

"Have you told Tricia?"

Milo winced. "No. Mulehide will say it's my fault. If a cloud of locusts invaded, my ex would blame me for that, too."

"Can I do anything?"

Milo looked as if I'd missed "c-a-t" in a spelling bee. "Are you nuts?"

"I mean other than that. What do you want for dinner?"

"I've been eating pretty well. Tanya's a better cook than her mother. Is crab in now?"

"I'll check." I took a last drag on my cigarette just as Milo finished his. "I'll dump the butts. I haven't smoked since you were living with me."

The sheriff stood up. "I don't smoke much around Tanya. She disapproves. She'd rather do heavy-duty drugs."

I was also on my feet. "What are you going to do now?"

"Check to see if they found a room for Tanya. Then I'll head to the office. I'd kiss you, but I might not be able to stop. I'll wait until tonight."

I smiled a bit weakly. "That's fine. See you then."

Milo mussed my hair. "Go away. I have to stay focused on Tanya."

I was still smiling as I headed for the women's restroom. And realized I hadn't smiled much at all in the last two weeks.

Vida was agog. "My nephew Billy told me Tanya overdosed."

I plopped into her visitor's chair. My ad manager, Leo Walsh, looked up but kept quiet. "You were on the phone when I left," I said. "Why didn't you grill Mitch? He told me what happened."

Vida frowned. "My phone kept ringing. I've no idea why my fellow Presbyterians think I can resolve our problems. That's for the elders. Mitch left before I could ask him. I had to call Billy on a family matter."

My evil self hoped that Roger had been arrested — again. But I shoved the thought aside and related what I knew about Tanya to Vida, Leo, and Kip, my back-shop tech wizard. I suspected that Amanda, our replacement for the dithering Ginny Erlandson, was practically falling out of the receptionist's chair to eavesdrop.

"Kids," Leo remarked. "They never stop needing parents, do they?"

Vida shot him a sharp glance. "Are you reconsidering your retirement and a move to California?"

Leo shrank back in his chair as if he expected Vida to pounce on him. "Hey, Duchess," he said, using the nickname she claimed to hate, "I don't know if Liza wants me back in the fold. She's leaning that way since she dumped the guy who filled in for me while I stepped out of the house for the past sixteen years."

Vida stiffened in her chair. "Another divorce?"

Leo sighed. "I didn't know until I went down to Santa Maria on Thanksgiving that they were never married. After we divorced years ago, she told me they'd tied the knot. But Liza's a good Catholic girl and she wanted to keep up appearances of a legal union."

"Oh, how ridiculous!" Vida exclaimed. "Some Catholics," she went on, darting a look at me, "don't care what people think."

The conversation was going downhill fast. I stood up, shrugging out of my jacket. "Did Bill mention Blackwell's latest allegations?"

"No," Vida admitted. "But if someone wants to kill him, it's Patti Marsh. I can't believe they parted after so many years of . . . doing whatever they did together.

There must be another woman. Jack was her meal ticket. They're no spring chickens. Milo probably hopes someone will shoot Blackwell. They've never gotten along."

"That's Jack's fault," I said, edging toward my office. "Back when the sheriff was elected, Jack ran against Milo because he didn't like the way the murder investigation of Patti's former son-in-law was being handled. He got his rear end kicked at the ballot box."

"It goes further than that," Vida declared. "Those two have gone head-to-head since Milo got back from Vietnam."

I stopped backpedaling. "How so?"

Vida lifted her chin. "If Milo hasn't told you, it's not my place to talk about it. You know I don't gossip."

And beavers don't build dams on Goblin Creek, I thought. Vida's attitude on this gloomy Wednesday was beginning to annoy me. All I needed was Amanda rushing off to throw up — again. Now that she was past the first trimester of pregnancy, I hoped that problem would go away.

"Maybe," Kip said, finally breaking his silence, "Blackwell thinks Ed's after him. Didn't he want to get appointed to Alfred Cobb's county commissioner's post instead of Jack?"

27

Vida waved a hand in disgust. "Oh, there was never any chance Ed would get that job. I thought they'd let Alfred's son stay on. He'd been doing most of his father's work after Alfred became gaga. I suppose Myron didn't want the responsibility. He's in his seventies, you know."

Leo grinned. "Ed's too lazy to go after anything but McDonald's takeout. I shouldn't bad-mouth him. He makes me look good."

"You are good," I said. "Ed was bad. The first couple of years I thought we'd go broke. We still can, in this current toxic economy." On that dismal note, I retreated to my office.

By noon I'd set up appointments with RestHaven's chief of staff, Dr. Woo, and short-term care's Jennifer Hood. I could've let Mitch handle the interviews, but I felt I needed to show my face. I'd already confirmed dates with the rehab unit's Iain Farrell and Rosalie Reed, who was in charge of psych patients. Our special edition was shaping up.

I asked Vida if she wanted to eat at the Venison Inn, but she was skipping lunch. "Buck gave me a lovely box of Russell Stover chocolates for Valentine's Day," she explained, referring to her longtime companion, who had recently moved from Startup to a condo at Pines Villa. "I can't resist them, which means I have to watch what I eat for a while."

I accepted the excuse, though Vida's weight never seemed to vary no matter what she ate. My Valentine's Day had been passed alone, though Milo did call to tell me Tanya had plugged up the kitchen sink.

Having been rejected by Vida, I realized that I should go home and change. My caramel slacks and crimson sweater weren't appropriate for Delia Rafferty's funeral. I could forage for food in my fridge.

While I ate a ham sandwich, I started a letter to Mavis on my laptop. "Glad you liked the vase," I typed. "Sorry about Ray. Hope His Royal Grumpiness is improving." I stopped to munch on a carrot stick and think of a tactful way to tell Mavis she was off base. But my mind was blank. After three false starts, I headed to the funeral. Scandinavians and other northern Europeans have historically dominated Skykomish County, so there'd be a big turnout. The Lutherans also ran the retirement and nursing home in the same block between Cedar and Cascade Streets. Seating would be at a premium. Vida would no doubt manage to get up front, but if the service ran long, I

29

preferred to make a quick escape and go back to the office.

My concession to funeral attire was forest-green slacks and a matching sweater. My new Donna Karan winter jacket was black, and Francine Wells of Francine's Fine Apparel had told me it was a real steal at her post-holiday sale. Noting that the price was still three hundred bucks, I asked her if I could steal it. She said no, but she said it nicely.

Parking was already scarce, though I found a spot not far from the lot's entrance. It was still raining, the clouds so low that I couldn't see more than fifty feet up the side of Mount Baldy. Avoiding the puddles that had accumulated, I entered the church, which was already two-thirds full. I couldn't spot Vida, so I sat in the third row from the back.

That was a mistake. I hadn't taken into account the Wailers' arrival five minutes later. They sat down in the last row almost directly behind me. The trio of black-clad women never missed a funeral — unless it was at St. Mildred's or Trinity Episcopal. In acts of Christian charity for the sake of their mourners, Father Dennis Kelly and the Very Reverend Regis Bartleby had banned the Wailers. They wailed, keened, groaned, and moaned at what apparently constituted the saddest moments of any service. Most Alpiners were able to ignore them. I didn't know how to do that, still finding them disruptive.

But I was stuck. At least I'd managed to edge over to the far end of the pew. Meanwhile, I focused on the Rafferty family members who obviously weren't going to sit in the more private mourning area. I'd come mainly for Delia's daughter, Beth, who was the daytime SkyCo 911 operator. When Beth's brother, Tim, had been killed, we'd formed a tentative friendship. Beth was accompanied by a man I didn't recognize, but I assumed he was Keith Jacobson, the recently hired Nyquist Construction foreman. I'd heard they'd been dating since November. I was glad for Beth. An early marriage had ended badly. She needed someone in her life after losing her brother and now her mother.

Tim's widow, Tiffany, was another matter. She'd been pregnant at the time and so self-absorbed with her unborn child that I'd lost sympathy for her. She walked down the aisle between her parents, Wayne and Cookie Eriks. Cookie was rather vapid. Wayne wasn't one of my favorite people. He'd made a pass at me once and had problems with the word "no." Milo had fingered him as the prime suspect in his son-in-law's murder, but I'd never gotten the sheriff to admit if he'd collared Wayne on the basis of evidence — and there was some — or because the lecher had hit on me.

I was so fixated on Wayne that at first I didn't notice the tall, saturnine man who was following the Eriks family. It was Jack Blackwell, who sat down with the rest of Delia's kinfolk. I was puzzled, unaware of a connection between Black Jack and the Rafferty or Eriks clan.

My rubbernecking allowed me to catch Vida moving into the second row. I hadn't seen her come in. Maybe she'd entered through a rear door — or had descended from the ceiling like a prophet in the Bible.

Pastor Nielsen conducted a dignified service. I drifted, only being jerked back into attention when the Wailers wailed or otherwise made some ungodly noise. Near what I hoped was the ceremony's conclusion, I noticed Milo standing across the way at the back. I decided that was my cue for making an exit.

The sheriff noticed my departure. By the time I got out into the vestibule, he was waiting for me. He didn't look happy.

"What's wrong?" I asked, craning my neck

to stare up at him. The more-than-a-foot difference in height between us always made me feel as if he were looming over me.

He glanced around to make sure nobody was lurking in the alcoves or on the stairway. "Mulehide. She's driving up here later this afternoon. Did you buy the crab already?"

"No," I said. "I haven't had time. Can you come later?"

His big hands clutched at his regulation hat as if he wanted to rip it to shreds. "No. She's staying at the house. Linda Grant hasn't got any heat. Her furnace went out last night."

Linda was the high school P.E. teacher and an old chum of Tricia's. The last time Milo's ex had come to town, she'd spent the night with Linda. "Oh, damn! Can't you . . ." I stopped. "No, you can't leave her there by herself. She's probably worried sick."

Milo looked as disappointed as I felt. "Maybe she'll take Tanya back to Bellevue. If I walked out on Mulehide, it would only give her an excuse to make me miserable. She already figures I'm responsible for every one of our kids' problems, including chicken pox. Hell, I was lucky to see them once a month after she took off. I'll never know what godawful bullshit she told them about me and why she left. . . ." He winced as the Wailers let out an earsplitting cry like a dying elephant. "Jesus," he said under his breath, "can't I arrest those old bats for breaking an anti-noise statute?"

"Do we have one? Do you want them wailing away in the jail?"

"God, no. I'd ship them to Everett."

We turned as Al Driggers, the funeral director, opened the double doors. I could hear the organ playing. Apparently the funeral was over.

"Hello, Sheriff. Hello, Emma," Al said in his suitably mournful voice. "You can go downstairs to the reception hall now."

"I stopped in for Beth," Milo said. "I have to get back to work."

I told Al I had to do the same. Milo steered me outside. "I'm blocking the exit, so I'd better go." He gave me a quick squeeze. "Later."

I watched him head for the Yukon SUV. I headed for my Honda. I knew life wasn't fair, but that didn't make me feel better. I'd never met Tricia. I trusted Milo, but the idea of him spending the night under the same roof with his ex irked me. My perverse nature goading me, I purposely stepped in a big puddle. Now I could bitch about ruining my good black shoes along with everything else that had gone wrong lately.

Amanda greeted me with a friendly smile. "I didn't think you'd get back so soon. Mayor Baugh wants to meet with you Friday morning."

"Why doesn't the old coot just wander in the way he always does?"

"He said this was official business." Amanda shrugged. "Don't ask me. He sounded very formal. He forgot to use his Louisiana accent. Is he really from down there in the Bayou?"

"Yes," I said, wiggling my toes inside my damp shoes. "The Baughs moved here thirty years ago. Their son married a girl whose family owned a dairy farm by Monroe. The senior Baughs moved nearby, but later, he and Irene split up. The farm was sold and his son's family moved to Edmonds. After Fuzzy and Irene reconciled, they came here and he ended up as mayor."

"He must be eighty. Does he *do* anything as mayor?"

"It's mostly ceremonial." I removed my jacket. "He does have a rare brainstorm. Eleven is okay. If he's too windy, I'll say I have a lunch date."

"Will do," Amanda said, making a note. "How was the funeral?"

"Fine, except for the Wailers. And before

35

you ask, I still haven't heard from Ginny. I sense she isn't coming back. With three kids, she's got her hands full. Maybe she should stay home and play mommy. I'm just glad you were freed up from your holiday duty at the post office."

"So am I," Amanda said. "With Roy still recovering from going off his rocker over his missing mama, it was more chaotic than usual. I hear he's doing better. Doc Dewey prescribed some meds that work for him."

The saga of Roy's mother, Myrtle Everson, had gone on for sixteen years after she disappeared without a trace. Every time anybody found some bones, Roy and the rest of the family would get them tested to see if they belonged to Myrtle. I had my own theory about what had happened to her, but there'd been no opportunity to prove or disprove it. Roy's obsession with Mama had landed him in the hospital after Christmas.

"Maybe," I said, "when you have your baby in July, Ginny can fill in for you. Unless you think you'll want to be a stay-at-home mom, too."

Amanda turned serious. "Walt and I've talked about that. Over the years when I worked part-time, I'd get antsy." She offered me a quirky smile. "But a baby takes up a lot of time and I hope I've changed for the better. You know my pathetic history." The smile broadened. "I can't believe I actually considered taking up with Jack Blackwell back then."

I'd forgotten about their near fling. "Funny you should mention him," I said. "He was at the funeral with Beth and the Eriks gang."

Amanda looked sly. "I hear he's been seeing Tiffany since he broke up with Patti Marsh. Can you believe it? He must be almost sixty!"

"True," I said. "But Tiffany's not as young as she looks. I figure her for mid-thirties. That's still a huge age difference. But Tiff may be looking for a sugar daddy. She didn't do very well as a wife."

Amanda turned somber. "I didn't do so well for a while, either."

I smiled. "You rectified that situation. Skip the regrets."

Her own smile came more slowly. "The baby did that." She paused, and her smile grew brighter. "There wouldn't be a baby on the way if Walt and I hadn't decided to grow up before we had kids. Playing the blame game on each other for not having a child almost ruined our marriage."

I nodded. "That's what grown-ups do —

37

they move on. Then you got lucky — and pregnant."

I left Amanda with a smile on her face. For the next half hour I went over the backgrounds of RestHaven's staff. Shortly before three, Mitch asked if I'd checked his latest installment on the new facility. I told him I had, and only some minor tweaking had been necessary.

"Good," he said. "But I'd like to know how Fleetwood scoops us on some of the RestHaven news. I had the radio on when I went to the ranger station to get the trail openings schedule. KSKY's on-air guy said Dr. Woo eventually plans to add another unit for Alzheimer patients. How do we keep getting beat on that stuff?"

This was at least the fifth time Spence had broken a RestHaven item first. "I've no idea. Verify it and we'll put it on the website."

"I did," Mitch replied. "Kip's putting it up now. But damn, it's annoying. There's a leak somewhere. Have you asked Spence about it?"

"No. He wouldn't tell me. We share some ad revenue, but not news sources." Seeing Vida stomping through the newsroom, I gestured at Mitch. "Stand back. Our House & Home editor looks fit to spit."

38

"I cannot believe what ninnies those Eriks people are!" she exclaimed, almost elbowing Mitch out of the way. "Dot Parker told me Tiffany's moving in with Jack Blackwell! Doesn't that beat all?"

"Amanda said —" I began, but Vida hadn't run out of steam.

"She's going to be his housekeeper and is quitting at the Grocery Basket," Vida continued. "Dot and Durwood are beside themselves."

The Parkers were Tiffany's grandparents. Cookie Eriks was their younger daughter. Her older sister, known as La-La, lived in Bremerton. Scandal had never tainted the Parker name except for Durwood's record as the worst driver in SkyCo. His reputation as the longtime owner of the local pharmacy was unsullied.

Mitch looked skeptical. "Isn't Blackwell older than I am?"

Vida removed her swing coat as if she were a champion boxer about to take on a contender. "He is. It almost makes me feel sorry for Patti Marsh, but her vices are too numerous." Her gray eyes turned to me. "You say Amanda knew about this outrage? Why didn't she tell *me*?"

"Because," I said, trying to sound reasonable, "she probably didn't think it was suitable for your 'Scene Around Town' gossip snippets."

"It's not, but Amanda should have mentioned it anyway."

"I only found out when I got back from the funeral," I said.

"Dot confirms it," Vida declared. "I wouldn't blame the Parkers for trying to kill him. Maybe Milo should let Durwood renew his license."

Mitch's phone was ringing. "Excuse me, Vida. I'd better answer that. Detroit was never like this." His long stride took him to his desk before the call trunked back to Amanda.

The afternoon passed quickly. I didn't answer Mavis's letter, but I had an insight. Vida's weekly radio program, *Vida's Cupboard,* was the jewel in KSKY's crown. The chatty fifteen-minute show featured Alpiners' hobbies, travels, and other homely subjects. SkyCo listeners stayed glued to the radio. It was all Alpine, all the time. Thus she was Spence's star performer, with advertisers begging to buy commercials in her time slot.

"I've got a question," I said, sitting in Vida's visitor's chair. "Have you noticed that Spence is getting the jump on us with Rest-Haven?"

She frowned. "Not really. But I rarely handle straight news. Perhaps Spencer's been keeping closer tabs on what's happening there."

Mitch looked up from his keyboard. "Fleetwood couldn't ferret out any more items than I do unless he checked himself in to the facility."

Vida refused to look chastened. "Spencer only covers major stories for his news broadcasts. Perhaps he's able to dig deeper than we can."

"Whoa," Leo said, entering the newsroom. "Are we damning the competition? I just got a co-op deal with KSKY for two more businesses."

"Hooray for you," I said. "It's the news side we're discussing. Spence seems to get a lot more out of RestHaven than we do."

Leo removed his rumpled raincoat and hung it on his chair. "Maybe that's because he's doing a live broadcast at Saturday's open house. He's hosting the chief of staff after your show, Duchess. You're the lead-in. Doesn't that make you feel grand?"

"Well . . ." Vida's effort to look modest failed. "I'm sure Dr. Woo will keep listeners tuned in. My nephew Ross Blatt says he's very intelligent."

Ross was one of Vida's many relatives, the

41

son of Wingfield Blatt and his wife whose
name was May or June or April. Wingy and
Pick-Your-Month had died by the time I arrived in Alpine.

"Say," I said to Vida, "Ross has been working at RestHaven. How come he hasn't
given you any tips about what's going on
there?"

Vida scowled. "Ross's company, Alpine
Service & Repair, is a subcontractor. If Ross
heard anything, don't you think I'd know
about it?"

"Yes." I stood up. "I guess we're stuck
with Spence beating us."

"It's galling to get scooped," Mitch said.

"I do hate not knowing things," Vida declared.

Leo chuckled. "It's not as if RestHaven
will make big headlines."

"True," I admitted.

Before our next deadline, we'd discover I
was wrong — dead wrong.

Two

I spent the evening alone, without even a phone call from Milo. I was only vaguely miffed, knowing that he was coping with both Tanya and Tricia. But I missed him. We'd had less than three weeks living together in my little log cabin, and half the time we'd been so worn out from our own ordeal that by evening we were dead tired.

Milo hadn't had time to assemble the new king-sized bed I'd bought during the January sale from Lloyd Campbell's store. It had been delivered the day before Tanya arrived at his house in the Icicle Creek development. The standard-sized bed I'd bought thirty years ago in Portland wasn't big enough to accommodate the sheriff. Even when we were a couple almost ten years ago, Milo didn't stay over that often and neither of us ever complained. But now it was different. He'd be living here all of the time — if he could ever lose his ex and their daughter.

What was almost as frustrating for the sheriff was that he hadn't been able to go fishing. Unlike Tricia, who'd balked at his need for solitude to slough off the rigors of his job, I understood. Fishing is part sport and part spiritual experience. Milo had recently told me he often used the time for introspection — something I thought he rarely did. But there were depths to him that I'd never plumbed. The truth was I'd never wanted to, for fear that maybe there weren't any. Or that if there were, I'd realize how much I'd always loved him and give up the dream that had been Tom Cavanaugh and the enigma that had been Rolf Fisher. Emma Lord, Love Dunce — I'd spent thirty years perfecting the role.

It was still raining Thursday morning. The dark clouds hung over Alpine almost to the tree line at the rear of my house. As a native Pacific Northwesterner, I didn't mind. Gray, not green, should be Washington's official color, at least in the western half of the state.

As I drove down the hill to Front Street, I glanced toward the sheriff's office. There was no sign of Milo's Yukon. Maybe he'd stopped at the hospital to see Tanya.

Amanda had the bakery run that morning. When I arrived she was setting out sugar doughnuts, maple bars, and cinnamon twists. After greeting her, I poured a mug of coffee and grabbed a doughnut. Vida and Leo were both on the phone, Kip apparently was in the back shop, and Mitch arrived just as I started to head for my office.

"Hey, boss," Mitch called to me, almost on my heels by the time I reached my desk, "you free for lunch today?"

"Yes," I said, wishing I sounded more enthusiastic. I hadn't given up hope that Milo might be free during the noon hour.

My reporter tapped his fingers on the door frame. "I've got some things I'd like to discuss with you. Not related to work."

"Okay," I said. "Unless things get hectic, that's fine."

Mitch nodded and went to his desk.

What to do with Brenda? I thought, sitting down. So many people had mental problems. Was the atmosphere full of emotional-disturbance germs? I'd spent thirty years waiting for Tom's wife, Sandra, to drive him to divorce or run off with somebody else. She'd once done the latter, but her affair with a much younger man had ended abruptly. Eventually she had died from an overdose of her funny-bunny meds. Tom was finally free to make me his wife, but

instead of marrying him, I ended up burying him. Now it was Tanya, and in between,
Roy Everson with his Mama fixation and
Mitch's wife, Brenda. I'd never really gotten
to know her. Though I blamed myself for
lack of trying, she hadn't seemed very
social. Given her recent breakdown, I
wondered if she'd brought her mental
problems with her from Royal Oak.

Mitch left at eight-thirty to check the
sheriff's log. I had a ten-thirty interview
with Rosalie Reed, so I went over my notes.
Dr. Reed was forty-nine, a native of San
Rafael, and had gotten her doctorate of
psychology from UCLA. Married, one son.
She'd moved to the Seattle area in 1997
and set up practice on the Eastside with offices in Bellevue. The glossy photo showed
a serious, patrician woman who exuded
strength and purpose. She was no beauty,
but she had a kind of mystique that I figured
men would find attractive. Maybe if I could
get her to smile, she'd turn radiant. I
resolved not to resort to a pratfall — being
basically clumsy, I might do that without
trying.

Mitch returned just as Amanda was delivering the mail. "Not much in the log today,"
he said, poking his head into my office.
"Nobody's taken a shot or tried to run

46

down Blackwell in the last twenty-four hours, but Cal Vickers thought the brakes in Jack's car were iffy."

I didn't give a hoot about Blackwell's brakes. "Was the sheriff in?"

"He got there just as I was leaving," Mitch said. "He looked grim. Given that he ignored me, I didn't ask about his daughter."

My watch said it was nine-thirty, giving me time enough to visit the sheriff's office for a firsthand report. "The deputies didn't say anything?"

"Nothing. You know how they close ranks, especially if it's anything about their boss."

"Right." I smiled faintly at Mitch before he returned to his desk. Milo's attitude about the job had not changed after we became engaged. In fact, we'd agreed that neither of us could bend, even after we got married. The often adversarial but necessary conflict between law enforcement and the press remained in place.

Five minutes later, I greeted Lori Cobb at the reception desk. My first question was a personal one for Lori. "How's your grandma doing now that Grandpa Cobb's been dead for almost two months?"

Lori's plain face drooped. "She's dating."

I gaped. Mrs. Cobb was almost ninety. "Ah . . . who's the lucky guy?"

"Chester Treadwell from Gold Bar. They met at senior bingo night in Sultan. He's not much older than my dad."

"My," I said. "May-December romances are in vogue around here."

Lori's eyes widened. "You mean Jack Blackwell and Tiffany Eriks? I mean, Tiffany *Rafferty*. I only heard about that last night. He escorted her at Mrs. Rafferty's funeral. Yuck!" She sighed. "I think Chester is after Grandma's money. Grandpa had a nice little nest egg."

"Well," I began, not sure what to say, "if it's a comfort to her, maybe it's nice for them to . . . play bingo."

"Maybe." Lori didn't look convinced. "It's good that you and Sheriff Dodge are close in age. You seem like a *normal* couple."

The other half of the normal couple stormed out of his office. "Got to go to the courthouse, Lori. It may take a while." He practically knocked me out of the way coming through the swinging gate in the curving reception counter. "Later, Emma," he muttered, and went out through the double doors.

"Now what?" I said under my breath. "Is it about Tanya?"

"I've no idea," Lori said. "He's not in a very good mood today."

"No kidding," I said as Jack Mullins strolled out from the jail area.

"Hey," Jack said, his impish expression in place, "I hear your love nest's empty lately. When do you expect the big bird to land?"

"Shut up," I snapped. "Do you want Dodge to deck you again?"

Jack involuntarily rubbed his chin. "I only stepped over the line with the boss that one time. I thought I was being funny. Don't worry, I've never said anything else about you two that was remotely — what did old Father Fitz call it when he was pastor at Saint Mildred's — 'suggestive'?"

Lori, who wasn't Catholic, looked puzzled. "Suggestive of what?"

"Good question," Jack said. "It's an old-fashioned RC word for anything to do with sex. You know — like saying 'underpants' or 'bosom.' "

Lori shook her head. "And I thought Grandpa and Grandma's Baptist church was strange."

Dwight Gould came through the door, looking like Dwight always did — sour. "It's only ten o'clock and I've already cited five people for speeding. One of 'em right on Front Street. Those other idiots out on Highway 2 don't know how to drive in the rain, especially Californians. Why do those

49

people come up here to cause trouble?"

"Zip it," Jack said cheerfully. "It's money for SkyCo. God knows we need it. It's a wonder we've got streets for people to drive on."

"Damned budget," Dwight muttered, moving behind the counter on his way to the coffee urn. "I haven't had a raise in three years."

On that glum note, I decided to leave before Dwight turned his ire on me. He seemed to have trouble deciding if I was the best thing that had ever happened to Milo or the worst. Maybe I should ask him to write a letter to Mavis explaining how herculean the sheriff appeared to his staff.

Out on the sidewalk, I was tempted to walk to the courthouse to see if I could find Milo. But that was a bad idea. Would I have done that if we weren't engaged? Maybe. I was never good about boundaries. Breaking them is part of a journalist's job. But I refrained.

All was well at the office. I went back to my Honda and drove toward River Road, site of the former Casa de Bronska. Turning off Front Street, I had to stop at Railroad Avenue for an eastbound Burlington Northern Santa Fe freight lumbering through town. After the barrier lifted, I was across the tracks on River Road, past Milo's house in the Icicle Creek development, over the Icicle Creek bridge, beyond the golf course, and finally turning onto the drive leading to RestHaven. Gone were Ed's gilded lions, which had always looked more like Bert Lahr in *The Wizard of Oz* than the kings of an African jungle. Gone, too, was much of the so-called Italian rose garden, which had succumbed to lack of care. The only recognizable thing about the Bronskys' ill-advised attempt at grandeur was the building's basic exterior. And even that was mercifully changed, the pink stucco having been replaced with a dull but less garish pale green.

Despite the wait for the BNSF train, I was three minutes early. The young woman at the desk in what Ed had called "the Atican" informed me there'd be a short wait, as Dr. Reed was still with a patient. I took a seat in a comfortable armchair, admiring the changes that local architect Scott Melville had made in converting the ostentatious home into a usable yet attractive facility. The atrium had never lived up to its name, only going up a single floor, but the open area that had been the living and dining rooms along with a den was now a functional reception area with offices leading at angles from the front desk. Nor was there a single Burger Barn wrapper, empty Fritos bag, or Twinkies box in sight.

At 10:35, I was ushered into Rosalie Reed's office.

"So sorry about the late start," Dr. Reed said, holding out her hand. "We're still rushing to get ready for the grand opening. Please sit down. I'm afraid I can only give you about twenty minutes. Dr. Woo has called a staff meeting for eleven."

"That should be fine," I said, seating myself in an armchair covered in serviceable but handsome blue fabric. Pen poised, I opened my notebook. Unlike Vida, I couldn't rely on a prodigious memory, nor did I trust tape recorders. "You had a practice for many years in Bellevue," I began. "Why did you take a job here, in a more remote part of the region?"

Dr. Reed smiled, though her sharp dark eyes didn't seem to get the message. "I wanted a new challenge, I'd known Dr. Woo as a colleague in the Los Angeles area, and I'm a firm believer in change. It helps us grow."

"Very sound," I murmured, scribbling as fast as I could. "I understand you have a son. Did he move to Alpine, too?"

"No," she replied. "He started his first year this fall at UCLA. He wants to specialize in genetics. And," she went on, "my husband is retired. He had his own practice for many years." She patted her smooth, dark hair in what struck me as a congratulatory gesture.

My next queries focused on what I knew would produce psychobabble responses about services, philosophies, and patient protocol. But I had to ask, if only to show I'd done my homework. Most of the *Advocate*'s subscribers would have been more interested in personal information, such as favorite TV shows, eccentric hobbies, or what kind of toothpaste Rosalie Reed preferred.

She cut me off at precisely 10:54. "I do hope to see you Saturday," she said, walking me to the door. "We understand there will be a large turnout. Oh!" She suddenly looked chagrined, though for some peculiar reason, I didn't find the expression genuine. "We've been remiss in finalizing the program. Will first thing tomorrow work?"

"Is the advance copy incorrect?" I asked. "That's what we ran in Wednesday's paper."

"Just a tweak or two. You have the proper stock to print it on?"

"Kip — my back-shop genius — said it arrived Tuesday afternoon."

"Excellent." She proffered her hand again.

"I hope this is the first of many pleasant meetings between us."

I concurred. But walking back through the open reception area, I had my doubts. Maybe my unease was partially caused by the sight of Wayne Eriks emerging from a PUD truck near the entrance.

"Well, well," he said with his gap-toothed grin, "if it isn't the sheriff's lady. Guess I was slow figuring out why Dodge tried to nail me for Tim's murder. I didn't know until lately that you two were a hot item."

Had it been just about anybody else, I would've said that I hadn't known it, either. But Wayne's remark annoyed me. "We're engaged."

"That's nice," he said. "From all I hear, it's about time he made an honest woman of you. But you weren't that from the start, were you?"

He was referring to my arrival with a grown son and no husband, which had fueled gossip. Not only did I have money to buy the *Advocate,* but I drove a Jaguar. The assumption was that I'd had a wealthy keeper. The truth was that my former fiancé, Don, had put me on his Boeing life insurance policy and forgotten to take me off after we broke up. When he died unexpectedly of a heart attack at forty-five, I'd come into enough money to buy both the newspaper and the secondhand car.

"Funny you should mention that," I said, wishing that the burly jerk wasn't blocking me on the path to my Honda, "now that your daughter is moving in with Jack Blackwell. Don't you find that ironic?"

"Ironic?" Wayne wrinkled his snub nose as if he didn't know the meaning of the word. "No. She's going to work for Blackwell. It beats standing all day at the Grocery Basket ringing up bags of canned goods and half racks of beer."

"I'm sure she'll be off her feet at Blackwell's." I paused, seeing another figure approaching from the other side of the building. If memory served from looking at staff photos, it was Iain Farrell, the head of the rehab unit. "You know why Dodge considered you the prime suspect in Tim's homicide. If nothing else, you impeded justice by lying —" I stopped, seeing that Farrell had passed the entrance and was about to join us.

Wayne's back was turned to the newcomer, but noting my gaze move beyond him, he glanced over his shoulder. "You're still a prick-tease and Dodge is a son of a bitch," he muttered before greeting Farrell.

"More problems?" Farrell asked, gesturing at the PUD truck.

"Nothing serious," Wayne replied. "The biggest problem is that the wiring and its connections had to be redone. For some damned reason, Bronsky hired from outside instead of using Alpine Service & Repair."

Farrell's lean face was thoughtful — or maybe he always took his time answering questions. "Good. So no holdups with our opening?"

"Not as far as I see," Wayne said. "I'm just checking a few things. I'd better get busy." He walked away, leaving me alone with Farrell.

I hastily introduced myself. "I won't keep you. I know there's a staff meeting about to start."

Again there was a pause. "Yes. A pleasure." He moved to the entrance but didn't seem to be in a hurry.

A pleasure? Attending the meeting? Shaking my hand? Having Wayne on the job? I wondered how the afternoon's interview with Farrell would go. At best, slowly . . . at worst, I couldn't guess.

Predictably, lunch with Mitch at the Venison Inn turned out to be exactly what I'd expected. He was in a quandary about Brenda. Her emotional state was worse than I'd feared.

As my reporter unburdened himself at obvious personal cost, he began by telling me that his wife's problems hadn't been triggered solely by Troy's most recent escape from prison. Her psyche had always been fragile, though it began to worsen after empty-nest syndrome set in.

"Brenda is first and foremost a mother," he explained after our salads had been delivered by Nicole, one of Vida's many relatives. "Not to say she hasn't been a good wife. She has. But Brenda worked on her weaving at home while our kids were growing up. Our older two stayed close by and graduated from Wayne State. Jacob accepted an offer from Kimberly-Clark in Wisconsin and married a girl from Green Bay. They live in Appleton. After Miriam graduated, she went to work for a Pittsburgh landscaping firm." He paused as Nicole brought our entrees.

"It sounds as if Jacob and Miriam are fairly close in age," I said.

Mitch nodded. "Two years. There was a gap of five years before we had Troy. He was Brenda's baby. In fact," he continued, with a rueful expression, "Brenda insisted on calling him Troy rather than an Old Testament Jewish name. It seemed as if she stamped him as her own from the day he was born." He stopped to take a bite of his pastrami on rye sandwich. "You know the rest of it," he continued. "Dropping out of school, following a girl to Spokane, getting dumped, and then into drugs. In the meantime, Brenda wasn't just frantic, she made herself sick. That's when I decided to move here so we could be close to Troy. I thought it would save her sanity. It didn't."

I swallowed some of my shrimp salad sandwich. "Can you attach a name to whatever is wrong with her?"

"Clinical depression was the original diagnosis when we were in Detroit. Once she got here, she seemed better. Then Troy made his second escape, and that really threw her. At this point I don't know what a professional would call it. The last few weeks before Troy broke out, she didn't want to leave the house. I can't keep her with Miriam. Our daughter has a job and can't play round-the-clock nursemaid. I can't, either. I may put her in RestHaven and hope for the best. From what I've seen of the place, it's first-rate. Right now I feel as if I've abandoned her."

"You've done the best you can," I said, "but I understand. Are you covered for that sort of thing through SkyCo?"

Mitch looked at me curiously. "You're the

one who had me sign up for it. Don't you know what the coverage is?"

I was embarrassed to admit that I didn't. "I'm not very good at reading fine print. It's not something I've ever had to check on."

"Then I guess we both should do that." Mitch stared at the rest of his sandwich as if it were poisoned.

"I'm sorry," I said lamely. I liked Mitch, but he had a habit of putting me in the wrong, and this wasn't the first time. "When you run a small newspaper, there are a lot of things you have to put on hold. I try to keep focused on the tasks at hand. This may not be Detroit or the *Free Press,* but these days I'm lucky to keep the paper going."

"Then let's do it as soon as we finish here."

"How about now?" I said, pushing my plate away.

"Fine." He appeared to be reaching for his wallet.

"I'll pick up the tab. Let's go."

Mitch didn't argue. Nicole quickly added up our bill. I handed her twenty-five dollars, telling her to keep the change. We walked the half block in a torrential downpour. The clouds hovering over the rooftops had turned an ominous black. We arrived semi-soaked to find an empty office. I got out the SkyCo health care binder and placed it on Mitch's desk. "You want to look or should I?"

A bit sheepishly, Mitch said he'd do it. I went into my office and called Ellen Nordby, the hospital's benefits maven. Not surprisingly, she was out to lunch. While hearing the rain pelt our tin roof, I went over Dr. Farrell's background. I realized he hadn't recognized my name or remembered our two o'clock interview. It was now almost one. On the off chance that Milo might be in his office, I dialed his number.

"Not here," Sam Heppner said, sounding as close as he got to glee.

"Is he still at the courthouse?"

"No."

"When do you expect him?"

"Can't say."

I slammed down the phone. When it came to choosing between Sam and Dwight as the most misogynistic deputy, it was a dead heat.

Mitch appeared in the doorway, looking gloomy. "It doesn't sound as if mental health is covered unless it's accident-related."

I refrained from suggesting that maybe he could run over Brenda with his car. "Has she ever suffered any sort of head trauma?"

"Not that I recall. In over thirty years of marriage there might've been an incident I missed or forgot."

"Maybe she had a head injury when you weren't home. You could ask her and quiz your kids to see if they remember anything like that."

"I suppose." He put the binder on my desk and walked away just as lightning flashed.

A boom of thunder soon followed. Such storms weren't infrequent in our high-elevation aerie. They could occur any time of year. In summer, there was often no rain, just spidery lightning over the mountains and thunder rolling down the Valley of the Sky. An awesome sight, though in dry weather I worried about forest fires.

Amanda was back at her post. Leo and Vida arrived a minute later. The lights flickered several times. I heard Vida complain because she'd forgotten her rain bonnet and her maroon pillbox was soaked. A few minutes later, Kip appeared to tell me we'd lost our online connection.

"Just hope nothing big happens until it's restored," he said.

"With any luck," I responded, "lightning will hit KSKY's antenna."

61

Vida had overheard. "That's unkind. My program is on tonight."

"Sorry. I'm still miffed about Spence scooping us."

I'd barely spoken when our lights dimmed. My first reaction was to check to see if the phones worked. Mine didn't, but I had my cell.

"A pole must've been hit," Leo said, raising his voice to be heard over the thunder. "At least it's not dark enough to need candles."

"Coleman lanterns," Vida said. "That's what they used in the old days in Alpine until the houses got electricity."

Another five minutes passed before the storm moved on. I asked Mitch to check on the extent of damage. Heading to my office, I heard sirens, no surprise in severe weather. The storm passed just after one-thirty. Through the window above Vida's desk I could see that the rain had dwindled. There were no visible lights across the street. Before I got to my desk, my cell rang.

"Emma," Milo said, "Wayne Eriks is dead."

"What?" I shrieked.

"He either fell off a pole or got fried by a hot wire. Maybe both." Milo hung up.

THREE

My staff was mildly stunned by the news of Wayne Eriks's death.

"He always was the careless type," Vida asserted.

"I don't think I know him," Mitch murmured.

"The Widow Rafferty's dad, right?" Leo said.

"Dumb stunt if he was on a pole in this weather," Kip remarked.

"That creep hit on me once," Amanda declared.

"A bad habit of his," I noted — and wished I'd kept my mouth shut.

Most of all, I wished I knew where the accident had happened. Milo hadn't given any details. "Those sirens," I said. "They probably were for Wayne. Did it sound as if they were headed to RestHaven?"

"Possibly," Vida replied. "They were going east."

It was a quarter to two. "I'm heading up there to interview Dr. Farrell. Maybe I'll go now, just in case that's where it happened. Wayne was working on some glitch when I was there before noon."

Vida nodded. "I must call Dot Parker. She was never fond of her son-in-law, but she'll feel sorry for Cookie. The Erikses have had more than their share of problems. First their son, Ringo, died in a rafting accident, then Tiffany's husband, Tim, was murdered, and now Wayne is dead. Don't forget his brother Mel's sister-in-law, Crystal. She came to a dreadful end. They do seem hexed."

"Hexed?" Mitch echoed. "They sound doomed."

I wondered if Mitch was thinking that maybe his own problems weren't as horrific by comparison. But I didn't take time to carry on a conversation, especially if it involved Crystal Bird, my onetime nemesis. I was too curious about where and how Wayne had died. Telling Kip to stand by in case our power was restored, I headed out into what had subsided to our normal February rain.

No freight trains held me up, but there were big puddles of water on Front Street and River Road. I was forced to drive slowly, and once I passed the golf course, I could see an ambulance blocking the entrance to RestHaven's sloping driveway. I pulled onto the verge, trying to spot Milo's Yukon. Just as I was about to get out of my car the fire engine pulled out. It was only then that I spotted the sheriff standing by the medic van and talking to Del Amundson, one of the drivers.

As I trudged to where they were talking, I saw Sam Heppner and the only female deputy, Doe Jamison, getting into a cruiser. This was the first time I'd assumed my editor's role — except for our own frightening story — since Milo and I became engaged. To my surprise, I felt awkward.

Sam and Doe took off just as I reached Milo and the medic. "Hi, Emma," the sheriff said. "Your power's back on?"

I shook my head. "Not yet."

His hazel eyes turned wary. "How'd you know where Eriks was?"

"I'm here to interview Dr. Farrell," I said, my awkwardness overcome by annoyance. "Besides, the last time I saw Wayne Eriks he was here at RestHaven."

Milo nodded vaguely. "It probably was an accident with a hot wire. The dumb shit had taken his gloves off. Doc Dewey can do his thing now." He gestured over his shoulder

65

at the river, which was running high and off-color. "Weird. Almost the same spot where Ursula O'Toole Randall was found facedown in the Sky."

I thought back to the long-ago incident that had occurred while Milo and I had been a couple the first time around. I wondered if the site was jinxed. "That's it?" I said, nodding at Del, who'd given the sheriff a semi-salute before heading to the medic van.

"What did you expect? Somebody shot him and he fell off the pole? The ambulance is heading out," Milo continued as the vehicle descended the driveway. "Eriks is on the way to the morgue. You want pictures?"

Del had pulled out and was making a U-turn on River Road. Milo and I both stepped out of the way. "I didn't bring a camera."

"Good thing. You take lousy pictures."

I waited until the van had passed us. "You're in a lousy mood."

Milo grabbed my arm. "Buy those crabs. Goddamn it, Emma, I could cart you off now if I didn't have to fill out a bunch of paperwork."

I stared up at him. "You're free of Tricia and Tanya?"

"You bet." He grinned and squeezed my

arm. "Now beat it, before I ruin our staid new public image."

"Okay," I said meekly. "What if they don't have crab?"

The sheriff had let go of my arm and started to turn toward his SUV. "I don't give a shit. I'll eat sawdust if that's all you've got."

Smiling, I went back to my Honda, but waited for Milo to drive away first. He waved as he passed by. I was still smiling as I got out of the car and headed for the entrance. But my smile faded when I went inside. A half-dozen somber people were gathered in the atrium, including the receptionist. She saw me and hurried to indicate Dr. Farrell's office, directly opposite Dr. Reed's.

"He's waiting for you," she said in a hushed tone.

Apparently I was two minutes late. Iain Farrell looked somber as he greeted me and stayed put in his gray leather chair.

"The driveway was blocked," I said.

"Yes." He scowled at a yellow legal pad. "Editor and publisher, *Alpine Advocate.* Emma Lord." He paused, gray eyes still fixed on his notes. "You have ten minutes. We've called a special grief encounter."

I already felt like an idiot, so I might as

well sound like one. "Because of the accident?"

Farrell finally looked at me. "Word gets out. Patients don't need exterior stimuli. We have to deal with it at once to minimize trauma."

I decided not to comment. "Why did you come to RestHaven?" I asked, figuring I'd better make the most of my ten minutes.

"I didn't. They came to me."

"Because of your reputation?" I asked, wondering exactly what the hell his reputation was. The bio I'd received was brief.

"I assume so."

"You'd had a practice in Milwaukee and you taught at Marquette. Will you do any teaching here?"

He frowned, heavy dark eyebrows coming together. "At a community college? Hardly."

"You're a Chicago area native. Why did you come to Alpine?"

"Money."

"You mean a large pay raise?"

He shook his head. For the first time I noticed a small bald patch in his graying black hair. "Cost of living."

I knew he was single and that no children had been mentioned. "Are you looking for property?"

Farrell drew back in his chair as if the

68

question offended him. "Do you sell real estate on the side, Ms. Lord?"

My perverse side rebelled. "Are you interested in buying some?"

"No."

"Too bad. I know of a nice rambler that's coming up for sale in the Icicle Creek development," I said, referring to Milo's plan to sell his house. "Maybe two of them. The accident victim's widow may want to sell if she doesn't want to live there alone. Or maybe she could rent you a room. She'll probably need the money."

The gray eyes narrowed at me. "You can't possibly be serious."

"Oh, but I am," I said, standing up. "One final question — what kind of toothpaste do you use?"

Farrell didn't answer right away. I didn't think he would. By the time he uttered the single word "Crest," I was halfway out the door.

The power was on by the time I got back to the office. In fact, it might've gone on while I was en route to RestHaven. Certainly there'd been no sign of outage or even dimmed lights at the facility.

"Whoa," Leo said as I stomped into the newsroom, "you're pissed."

69

"I am," I admitted. "I'm off to a crappy start with the RestHaven people. What's worse is that when I drove away, Fleetwood was just arriving. Let's check the hour turn at three to see if he beats us again."

"RestHaven does advertise with KSKY — and us," Leo pointed out.

"I know, I know," I said, taking off my jacket. "I managed to blow it with Farrell, but the whole setup bothers me."

Leo chuckled. "Maybe Ed's aura lingers."

"There's not much of that left. They've done a good job of erasing the Bronsky imprint." I sank into Leo's visitor's chair. "I'm going to pass the other interviews to Mitch. Where is he?"

"Doing the story on Blue Sky Dairy's new equipment," Leo said after lighting a cigarette. "Give him the job. He needs to stay busy."

Vida entered from the back shop. "Well now! Was Wayne drunk?"

"I doubt it," I said. "If he was a serious boozer, Milo would know, living just a few doors away."

Vida had her hands on her hips. "Then what happened?"

I made a face. "You think the sheriff would tell me this early in an investigation? We're engaged — we don't have a pact to

70

administer truth serum to each other."

"Can't he bend a bit now that you're going to be man and wife?"

"I give you two words — Milo Dodge. Think again."

Vida sighed. "You're right. Maybe my nephew Billy could be coaxed with some ice cream."

Leo looked puzzled. "Isn't Billy like thirty-five?"

Vida shot my ad manager a haughty look. "He still likes ice cream. Besides, he and his fiancée broke up on New Year's Eve. Just as well. I preferred that he not take on a woman who already has a child."

"You could've taken the child *and* Billy for ice cream," Leo said in a serious tone.

"Hush, Leo," Vida said, with less than her usual severity. "The outage was limited to the commercial area. Walt Hanson told Amanda they never lost power out at the fish hatchery — or at the college."

I stood up. "Did Kip put the bare facts about Wayne online?"

"Yes," Vida replied. "I was offering family background. As you recall, Emma, you once had a notion that Mel and Wayne were cousins. You know better by now. Oh!" She clapped a hand to her cheek. "Mitch is at Blue Sky Dairy. I wonder if Mel knows what happened to his brother?"

"He does if Mitch told him," I said. "Were they close?"

"Well . . ." Vida tapped one foot. "Not very, but I don't think there was any animosity between them."

Leo grinned. "No typical Alpine a-feudin' and a-fightin'?"

"Really, Leo," Vida said in reproach, "you make us sound like hillbillies. At least we don't go around constantly suing each other the way people do in Southern California."

I left them to their argument, a sport they both seemed to enjoy. When the news came on at three, Spence's only reference to Rest-Haven was that they hadn't lost power. The hospital had gone dark, but they had a backup generator. He also aired a brief bit on Wayne's demise.

Mitch returned just after the broadcast. Mel had already heard from Cookie Eriks. His wife, April, had gone to comfort her sister-in-law. Mitch said Mel seemed more angry than upset. "He thought his brother may've done something stupid."

"It's possible," I allowed. "But it's dangerous work, especially in bad weather. He shouldn't have been working outside in the first place."

"Don't say that to the county commissioners," Mitch warned. "Want to bet Cookie doesn't sue?"

"She has no spunk. And bear in mind that her daughter may be sleeping with one of said county commissioners."

"That's . . . incredible." Mitch shook his head.

I not only gave him the other two interviews, but asked if he'd check with the sheriff for any late developments regarding Wayne's death. Mitch gave me a curious look but didn't ask any questions. I still sensed that he hadn't quite figured out yet what was going on between his boss and SkyCo's sheriff.

Which, of course, was what was uppermost in my mind. I was beginning to feel that Milo and I were ill-starred lovers. Since I first realized how much I loved him back in late November, we had now gone through two long separations. If the Eriks family was hexed, maybe we were, too.

There was no further news from headquarters, so I left at five to head for the Grocery Basket. Luckily, they had fresh Dungeness crab in the seafood case, though I winced at the price: $22.99 a pound. Darryl, the seafood manager, asked if I wanted smelling salts.

Two crabs and ninety dollars later, I had

dinner for the sheriff and a rising sense of anticipation in my breast. All I had to do was make a salad, put the French garlic bread in the oven, and unwrap the crabs, which Darryl had cracked and cleaned for me.

Milo showed up at 5:40, still in uniform. "Got anything on the stove?" he asked.

"No. I only have to turn on —"

That was as far as I got. With words, anyway. Obviously, *we* didn't need to be turned on. Forty-five minutes later, I rolled over onto Milo's bare chest and kissed the small scar above his right eye.

"Oh, God, I can't believe you're here!" I pressed my face against his and clung to him as if my life depended on it.

"That makes two of us," he said, one big hand caressing my back. "I had one hell of a time getting rid of Tricia and Tanya."

I raised my head and rolled over slightly. "How did you do it?"

"By beating Tricia at her own game. I started by saying that maybe I shouldn't have spent the money to send her and Tanya to Hawaii. Seeing all those happy couples on the beach might've caused a setback for Tanya. Maybe it was my fault for not thinking it through."

"Devious," I murmured, unaccustomed to

Milo playing games. "It was her idea."

"You don't know Tricia," Milo said after kissing the top of my head. "She's never been wrong in her life. Her latest crazy idea was to put Tanya in RestHaven. I told her that was really smart. Then I mentioned that the shrink Tanya had been seeing in Bellevue couldn't be much good or she wouldn't have tried to kill herself. I knew damned well that Tricia had handpicked the guy. Of course she started defending Strudelblob or whatever his name is, and she decided he was still the one to save Tanya. They took off after Sung signed the release papers."

I grinned at Milo. "You don't feel kind of guilty?"

"For what? I didn't do anything to create this whole mess. Last night Tricia and I searched her room to see if Tanya had any more pills. She didn't. In fact, there were no pills at all. The Celexa came from a bottle that had been for a med prescribed by the Bellevue shrink. Tricia knew it'd just been refilled, so Tanya must've gotten the Valium somewhere else. Maybe it backfired on her or she took both."

"But," I said, "shouldn't she be closely supervised? Do you trust Tricia to do that?"

"I talked to Bran today. My son's got more sense than Tricia and Tanya put together, though where he got it from, I'll never know."

I poked the sheriff in the chest. "How about from you, big guy? Even Vida admits you're the only Dodge who has good sense."

Milo made a face. "Maybe. Don't get me wrong — I'm not sure I was totally fair with Tricia, but she was the one who walked. Or ran, given that she was so hot for Jake the Snake. Too bad she couldn't see that while snakes might shed their skin, they don't change their habits."

"You did well with the situation. I'm unused to you being crafty."

I felt him shrug. "I have to go that route with perps sometimes. Make them feel we're wrong for busting them in the first place."

I rolled over onto my back. "Hungry?"

"Not anymore," Milo said, running his hand from my thigh to my chin. "But I wouldn't mind eating some dinner. Maybe I'll try putting the new bed together later on. Should we store your old one at my place, or are you still thinking about putting it in Adam's old room?"

"I don't know," I hedged, reluctantly getting out of bed and wondering where my clothes had ended up between the front door and the bedroom. "The twin in that bedroom is small, my son is not, but that room's crowded. Adam has most of his worldly goods stored in there. He has no extra space in his village rectory."

"Maybe I can get together with Scott Melville over the weekend about putting on the addition," Milo said. He yawned and stretched before getting to his feet. "And don't argue. We can afford it."

"I can't," I said. "Those crabs will keep me broke until I pay myself out of what's left for my staff at the end of the month."

"Damn it, Emma, don't worry about it. I'm going to sell my house."

"That may not happen right away. Besides, you told me you had to do some basic maintenance. And cleanup," I added archly as I put on my good bathrobe. Even Milo had finally despaired over the ratty blue one I'd worn for most of my years in Alpine. Maybe that was because one of the sleeves fell off.

"Tricia thought the house looked pretty good, considering," Milo said, now out of bed and getting dressed.

"No thanks to you," I shot back. "You turned me into a household drudge while I was in your so-called protective custody. The only thing I refused to do was wash your damned windows."

"Hey, I fed you," he said, taking out a

plaid shirt from the closet where he'd already stashed some of his clothes.

"I cooked," I reminded him, seeing the clock on my bedside table. "Oh! It's almost seven! I'll make drinks while you turn on Vida's show."

I'd poured Milo's Scotch and was reaching for my Canadian Club when the sheriff ambled out to the living room and turned on the radio. Spence's recorded intro was just concluding. Vida began with an apology.

"Dear friends and neighbors, I know some of you expected me to host my nephew, Ross Blatt, the owner of Alpine Appliance & Repair, but alas, poor Ross came down with the flu this afternoon. Instead, I have another nephew, Ross's brother, Ronnie Blatt, one of our fine volunteer firefighters when he's not working his UPS job. Tell me, Ronnie, what's the most unusual parcel you've ever delivered on your route?"

"A baby," Ronnie said. "A ten-pound, two-ounce boy to the Vanderburts on Second Hill."

"Good God," Milo muttered. "That was five years ago."

"Seven," I said, sitting on the sofa across from where Milo had parked himself in the easy chair. "They moved not long after that."

"It must be fascinating," Vida went on, "to bring other bundles of joy to our listeners. Do tell us some of your other happy memories."

"Well . . ." Ronnie paused. "Grace Grundle's always excited when I deliver new cat toys for her menagerie. Averill Fairbanks was pretty pumped when I brought his new UFO-sighting glasses last month, though he complained about the cloudy weather. Oh, Coach Ridley was relieved when the new Bucker basketball uniforms arrived before the season started. Only problem was they were for girls, so he had to send them back. The high school doesn't have a girls' team except for P.E."

"More's the pity," Vida said. "I heard the boys' team did get theirs."

I saw Milo holding his head and knew what was coming next.

"Right," Ronnie replied, "but they were for fifth and sixth graders. Coach is still waiting."

"A manufacturer's problem," Vida said. "Not buying locally, but that can't always be helped. We have so many fine merchants in Alpine, and we'll now let them tell you about their latest outstanding products."

"Holy crap," Milo said, shaking his head, "this is the worst bullshit Vida's put on in months. Why doesn't she ask Ron about his volunteer firefighting? He's been doing that for longer than he's worked for UPS."

"You're right. But if Ross cancelled, Vida didn't have much notice."

Milo took a quick swig of his drink before getting a pack of Marlboro Lights out of his shirt pocket. "You want one?"

"Please. You're a bad influence, Dodge."

"Come and get it. You can sit on my lap. That'll make the rest of the show more tolerable."

I obliged the sheriff, though I left my drink on the end table. The second half of *Cupboard* was no better than the first — except for Ronnie's final response to Vida's query about how much he liked his job.

"It's fine," he said. "Good benefits, nice people, decent hours. But I'd really like to be a full-time firefighter. The county has only two regulars because they can't afford to pay for more help. That's a shame, and not just for me personally."

"That's a . . . remarkable statement," Vida said, uncharacteristically taken aback. "Thank you, Ronnie. You've delivered food for thought." She signed off, followed by the sound of the cupboard door closing.

"Good for Ronnie," Milo said, squeezing my waist. "Doc Dewey and I get tired of being the only ones who bitch about lack of funds. Frankly, it's galling to see all that money being poured into RestHaven. Sure, they're spreading it around now in the remodeling part, but except for a couple of dozen jobs, the staff's made up of outsiders."

"Maybe Dr. Woo can inform us of other ways they'll benefit Alpine," I suggested. "He's up next."

"Screw Woo," Milo said. "You know it'll be a bunch of bullshit. Let's eat. I just figured out that I'm starving."

I scooted off his lap. I'd turned on the oven when the show had started. "I'll put the bread in. Can you wait fifteen minutes?"

Milo had gotten out of the easy chair to shut off the radio. "Why can't we start in on the crab —" He stopped. "What the hell? That Bree Whatzername announced ten uninterrupted minutes of Golden Oldies."

"Bree Kendall," I said, referring to Spence's part-time DJ. "Woo must've cancelled."

Milo turned the radio off. "I don't like that."

"I thought you didn't want to listen to him."

"I don't. But why is he cancelling? Has he got the flu? Or . . ."

The sheriff never liked to speculate, which I realized was what he was doing before he caught himself. Downing the rest of his drink, he handed me the glass. "Just a short shot. I'm calling Doc."

To my annoyance — even if I understood the reason — Milo went out into the carport to make his call. *Boundaries, Emma,* I lectured myself. *You have his heart and his body, but you don't have his badge and his job.* I started putting the crab and the salad on the kitchen table.

When Milo came back inside, he didn't look pleased. "That flu thing's no joke. Doc's up to his ears. Why the hell can't those high-roller doctors up at RestHaven pitch in?"

"Woo and Farrell are the only M.D.'s," I said, sitting down.

Milo ripped a crab claw into pieces. "What about the shrinks? Psychiatrists have medical degrees."

"True. And Jennifer Hood is an R.N. with a master's. It'd be a goodwill gesture on their part to volunteer when things get rough."

"They already are," Milo said. "Doc and Sung have been trying to get somebody up here for a year. Nobody wants to be a G.P. The money's not there. Gerry and Elvis can't pay big salaries. I can't, either. I could use two more deputies. The county's grown since the college opened. Not a lot, but enough to stretch services across the board."

"Hey," I said, kicking him gently under the table, "nobody knows that better than I do. Don't you ever read my editorials?"

Milo feigned indignation. "Sure. Usually. Sometimes." He nodded toward the stove. "Smoke's coming out of your oven. Again."

"The bread!" I cried, jumping up.

"Is it toast yet?" Milo asked over his shoulder.

"No. The bread's fine. It's just some . . . grease."

"Emma." The hazel eyes conveyed a reprimand.

"Okay, so I haven't turned on the oven since you were here. My appetite's been off." I switched subjects. "Why did you go to the courthouse today? Or is it some SkyCo state secret?"

Milo looked pained. "It won't be in a day or so. Holly Gross is getting out of jail."

I gasped, almost choking on a radish from the salad. "No!"

"Yes." He turned in his chair. "Where's

the potato salad? You usually have that with crab."

"I'm weaning you away from grease since your gallbladder surgery. It helps keep off the ten pounds you lost after the Bellevue siege."

"You think I'm fat?"

"No. It hardly showed, but it's better for you to stay leaner. Now tell me about Holly before I take away your melted butter for the crab."

"You lost weight, too," Milo said. "You'll get so skinny that I'll have to shake the sheets to find you."

"I only lost six pounds. Come on, Dodge, let's hear it."

He chewed on some bread before answering. "She filed an appeal. That is, her attorney did. Our new judge, Diane Proxmire, is allowing her to post bond until the appeal can be heard, which can take at least two years. I met with Proxmire and Rosemary Bourgette today. As the prosecuting attorney, Rosie will make the announcement tomorrow or Monday. I hoped you wouldn't ask." He took another big bite of bread.

"Vida will pitch a five-star fit," I said — and caught my breath. "Or does she already know?"

"Who always knows everything?" Milo

said glumly. "When Roger was involved in that trailer park mess, Vida was a witness — a muddled one — to Holly shooting another customer. Second-degree manslaughter may not hold up on appeal if a jury decides it was self-defense."

I was still shocked. "Holly could get her kids back, including the one she had by Roger. No wonder Vida's been testy lately. Roger's parents have taken in that baby as their own."

"Let's hope they haven't bonded with . . . what's the kid's name?"

"When Vida mentions him — and she rarely does, being embarrassed — she calls him Diddy. I think he must be going on two."

" 'Duddy' would fit Roger's kid better," Milo remarked.

I cleaned out another crab leg and went back in time to October, when Roger had been busted for some DUIs. His relationship with the town hooker had resulted in Vida finally admitting her grandson wasn't the paragon of virtue that she'd claimed. The kid had been a spoiled brat from the time I met him, when he was nine. Milo had gone easy on Roger after he gave valuable information about a drug-running operation. Holly had played a minor role with the local dealer and had killed him while they were holding Vida hostage. The chaos and cramped quarters inside Holly's trailer had hampered even Vida's remarkable powers of observation. She'd also lost one of her favorite hats in the melee.

"What about the drug trafficking?" I asked, suddenly realizing that Milo had eaten practically an entire crab by himself.

"Secondary to the man-two charge. The operation was shut down after Holly shot the main man." He started in on the other crab. "We can still act on it, but Rosie advised holding off. Holly's role was minor."

"Vida hasn't said a word. Maybe she's hoping it won't happen."

"Could be." Milo paused in the act of grabbing a third piece of bread. "Oh — I almost forgot. I picked up something at the courthouse. It's in my jacket. Let me get it before it slips my mind again."

He went into the living room. I used his absence to snatch up the last claw. "Here," he said, returning with a single sheet of paper and handing it to me. "Knowing you, I figured you'd want to read this before you do anything about it." He ruffled my hair before he sat down again.

My jaw dropped. "It's a m-m-marriage license th-th-thing!"

"Right." Milo scratched at the graying sandy hair behind his ear. "You want a ring, too?"

I was stupefied. "You kn-kn-know it's going to t-t-take a long time to get the allumnut," I gasped. "I mean an—"

Milo reached across the table and wiped my chin with his napkin. "Stop. You've got butter on your face." He swabbed my cheek, too. "Yeah, I know that, but we should get a justice of the peace to marry us first. I'd like to call you Mrs. Dodge. While Mulehide was here I kept thinking how she trashed that title and it made me want to puke. Besides, it'll put an end to some of her weird ideas."

I'd regained my equilibrium. "What weird ideas?"

He leaned back in the chair. "She's been jabbering about how great it was to have me around while Tanya was recovering, how it was like being a family, and maybe after all this time we . . . you get the picture."

"You never told me that."

"I didn't want to think about it. She and Jake the Snake are kaput. He's got somebody else, maybe whoever he was banging when Mulehide filed for divorce last fall. She started in on me again last night. She knows about us — her chums here keep her informed — but she doesn't believe it's serious. It wasn't on our first go-around, as you may recall."

"I know." I smiled feebly. "I was an idiot when I dumped you."

Milo waved a big hand. "No, the timing was wrong. As long as Cavanaugh was still around, you wouldn't have married anybody. It galled the hell out of me, but you're a stubborn little twit and I couldn't do a damned thing about it."

I looked again at the application. "There's a waiting period, right?"

"Three days. Hey, I'm not rushing you. But sometimes you have a hell of a time making up your mind. Relax. I'm not going anywhere unless it's to Sekiu with Doc Dewey for some Chinook fishing next week."

I was finally able to smile. "I guess that's not a honeymoon trip."

"Hell, no." Milo went back to decimating more crab. "You'd get seasick. Or so you've said."

"It's true. I did that when I had to take the ferry across the Columbia River."

"You want an engagement ring?" he asked again.

"I gave the one I got from Don back to him thirty years ago. A wedding band's fine.

What about you?"

He shook his head. "I never wore one the first time. I was afraid a ring might get in the way if I had to use my sidearm."

I nodded. "Are you sure it won't bother you if I keep my maiden name for the newspaper?"

"Hell, no. It's better that way. Mrs. Dodge calling Mr. Dodge an idiot in one of her editorials would be even weirder than Ms. Lord doing it. Never mind that everybody knows us. We have to separate our jobs —"

Milo's cell phone rang. He stood up, glanced at the caller ID, and went into the carport. Assuming the sheriff had finished eating — and wanting to save some crab for sandwiches — I began clearing the table.

"Dare I ask who that was?" I ventured when he came back inside.

"Doc." Milo frowned as I loaded the dishwasher. "We're done?"

"Yes. Did Doc say anything of interest?"

He sighed. "It's official. Eriks died from electrocution. Doc thought so, but he wanted to make sure there weren't other injuries."

I stared at Milo. "No chance he fell off the pole?"

"No." He fingered his chin. "That's why Doc looked for other signs of trauma. Nothing. Now I'm wondering if it was an accident."

"You mean . . . ?"

"You got it." He grimaced. "Murder."

FOUR

Amid a lot of thumping, thudding, and cussing, the sheriff took down the double bed. I kept out of his way. It was only after he'd finished putting up the new one that I realized the sheets I'd ordered hadn't yet been delivered.

"What do you mean, we don't have sheets?" he bellowed. "You've had three weeks to get the frigging things. Is Adam sending them by dog sled from Alaska?"

"Maybe I should've checked with Ronnie Blatt," I said humbly. "I placed the order online from Penney's at the end of January."

"What year?" Milo grumbled, kicking at a screwdriver on the floor. "Damn it, I should've followed my instincts and gone back to the office."

"To do what?" I inquired, still docile.

He took out a blue-and-white handkerchief and wiped sweat from his forehead. "I had Sam and Doe collect Wayne's gear from the site. I wanted Todd Wilson from the PUD to check for tampering or other safety flaws. It looked fine to me, but I wanted to be sure. Now I have to figure out how Eriks could have gotten fried."

"How long had he been dead?" I asked, sounding less meek. "You never told me who found him."

"Marlowe Whipp, coming back from the end of his River Road mail route. Marlowe practically needed an ambulance ride, too. He swore he blacked out for a minute."

"He often does that on his route," I remarked. "No doubt that's why he drops so much mail along the way. What time was that?"

"Around one-thirty," Milo replied. "Eriks hadn't been dead for more than a few minutes. He was still warm when we got there. Nobody else has come forward to say they saw anything, but the weather was bad. That's probably why Eriks wasn't up on the pole. But it doesn't explain why his body was on the ground and not inside the van. His PUD jacket wasn't on quite right, either. Maybe he got hit while he was putting it on or taking it off. There's something not quite right about any of this."

"That does make electrocution suspicious," I murmured. "Did you say he wasn't wearing gloves?"

The sheriff looked pained. "Right. Eriks was the kind of macho guy who might not always wear them. I suppose there could be hot wires in the van. I'll ask the PUD about that. It could've been lightning. It'd help if a witness turned up. But once you get past Ed's old villa, there aren't a lot of houses. Those big Bonneville cross-state power lines go right through there, and somehow they discourage home owners."

"The river narrows about fifty yards from there, too," I recalled. "Flooding's another problem."

"True." Milo stuffed the handkerchief back in his pocket. "You didn't put Doc's report online, did you?"

"No. I wasn't sure what to say at this point. You hadn't made a formal statement, and Doc's conclusion is . . . awkward."

"Good," Milo said, giving my rear a squeeze. "Want to try this thing out? You didn't make dessert. I'll settle for seeing if the springs work."

I hesitated, but saw the gleam in his hazel eyes. Didn't the man ever get tired? But that too-long enforced separation made me forget that I'd been shortchanged in the sleep department without Milo lying beside

93

me. "Why not?" I said, grabbing his shirt-front. "But we'll have to fake it with the short sheets."

"Fake it, hell." He unzipped my bathrobe. "With you it's the real thing. Took long enough, though."

"But worth it," I sighed as we fell onto the bed. And forgot about putting on the sheets.

Morning has never been a good time for either of us. We both tend not to talk much and move like automatons. Milo left ten minutes before I did. I arrived at the *Advocate* under still cloudy but rainless skies, finding only Amanda and Kip on the premises. Leo had the bakery run, and Mitch showed up as I was stalling in the newsroom waiting for Vida. I wondered if she'd mention Holly's release from jail or wait until Rosemary Bourgette made the official announcement.

"I hope," I said to Mitch, "you have better luck with the RestHaven people than I did. In fact, I really messed up with Farrell."

"Woo and Hood, right?" Mitch remarked, standing by the coffee urn as if he could will it to finish perking. "How come Woo didn't follow Vida's show last night?"

"I meant to call Vida," I said, "but I

got . . . distracted. By the way, the autopsy report's in on Eriks. Dodge should have something to say about it. There'll also be an announcement from the prosecutor's office on another matter, but I'll handle it. I don't want to overload you."

Mitch's lean face was tired. "That's okay. Work distracts my mind."

"Yes," I murmured, "I've had times like that, too."

The coffee was done. I let Mitch fill his mug first. Leo showed up just as I was heading for my office. "Where's the Duchess?" he asked, noting Vida's empty chair. "She's never late. Flu?"

"Amanda didn't say she called in sick," I said.

Leo shrugged. "Maybe she knows her show last night was a dud." He began to place bear claws, three kinds of doughnuts, and poppy seed muffins on the tray. "I agree with Ronnie's closing statement, though."

Mitch frowned. "Is money really that tight around here?"

"We've been stalled for years," I said. "The voters keep turning down every ballot measure for improvements, including school levies. They're just too damned thrifty."

Vida made her entrance. "Emma! Language, please!"

"Good morning to you, too," I retorted. "We have muffins. They're not fattening."

"I've already breakfasted," she said, removing her tweed winter coat before adjusting the *chapeau du jour,* which was a remarkably ugly taupe-and-red striped fedora. Apparently not in a chatty mood, she sat down and began going through her in-basket. The rest of us drifted to our respective desks and got to work, too. I remembered Mayor Baugh was coming at eleven and wondered why. Fuzzy rarely had anything newsworthy to say, though he could run on about trivialities.

When Mitch returned from his morning rounds, he had the sheriff's statement. Wayne's death was being investigated as a possible accident. Milo was hedging his bets. I called him after ten to ask if he knew if Rosemary Bourgette was announcing Holly's imminent release.

"I haven't talked to her yet," he said. "I had Todd Wilson in here looking at Eriks's safety equipment. It all looked fine to him. He doubted there were any live wires in the van. His guess is lightning."

"Nothing from you about" — I lowered my voice — "foul play?"

"I don't have proof it wasn't a freak thing. I may send the body to Snohomish County

96

to let their fancy equipment have a go. I hate doing it on a weekend. They'll have a dozen stiffs piled up. We'll be last in line."

"Poor you," I said, meaning it.

"I'm used to it." He hung up on me. Some things never changed.

I'd just put the phone down when Vida came into my office, looking like a dill pickle. "Well!" she huffed. "The least you could do is let me announce your engagement if you're planning to get married so soon."

I gaped at her but hastily recovered. Of course Vida would hear about Milo picking up the marriage license application. The county auditor was another relative, her late husband's niece, Eleanor Runkel Jessup. "We're not," I said.

She sat down, still sour. "Why did Milo request the application?"

I sighed. "He happened to be in the courthouse and . . ." I paused, wondering if Vida's tardiness had been caused by a visit to Rosemary Bourgette. "I guess he thought I should know what one looks like. As you may recall, I've never been married before."

"Then you have no immediate plans?"

I shook my head, and felt like saying that we didn't even have sheets. "If we do, I'll let you know. I'd want you to be a witness."

Vida's face softened. "Would you? That's very . . . flattering. But isn't it time to at least put the engagement in the paper?"

"Let me check with Milo," I said. "You know we didn't want it made public those first few weeks after we'd attracted so much attention by almost getting killed. We were going nuts coping with so much at once."

"True. But let me know," she said, standing up. "It would be lovely to have a photo of you two for my page this week."

"Hey," I said, "how come Dr. Woo wasn't on after your show?"

"Oh!" Vida adjusted her glasses. "Spencer told me he felt it would be inappropriate with someone dying so close to the facility. He didn't want Wayne's death to detract from the grand opening."

I was puzzled. "That doesn't make sense. Wayne's still dead."

Vida shrugged her broad shoulders. "I gather it was more of an internal thing. Something about disturbing patients and staff. A distraction, perhaps. You know the Chinese are very superstitious."

"Dr. Woo was born in San Francisco," I pointed out.

"Oh? Well . . . family traditions, you know. Very strong among the Chinese. Very admirable, in my opinion."

98

I merely smiled — and called Milo again as soon as she left.

"What now?" he barked.

I relayed Vida's request, including the picture idea.

"I thought she'd already put it in the paper," Milo said.

"No. I told her to wait. Damn it, don't you ever *read* the *Advocate*?"

"Yeah, sure, but you know how busy I've been. Sometimes I only get a chance to skim it."

I gritted my teeth to keep the argument from escalating. "Just answer the question, Sheriff."

"Hell," he said, "she can run the announcement, but forget about the photo. That means spending a couple of hours and big bucks at Buddy Bayard's studio. Do you really want to do that right now?"

"No, but if I didn't mention it to you, Vida would pitch a fit."

"She would. Hey, Scott Melville's due in about five minutes to talk about the addition to the house. We're going to add another bathroom."

"What?" I shrieked. "This isn't the Taj Mahal, you dolt!"

"Stop fussing. Got to check my notes for Melville." He hung up.

I knew that Vida and Leo had heard me, but I didn't care. I held my head and wondered how in hell we were going to pay for a larger bedroom, a workshop, and now a second bathroom.

A few minutes later Leo strolled in. "Ahem. Trouble in paradise?"

I looked up from the mail Amanda had dropped off. "The sheriff's turning the once-small attached workshop into a palace."

Leo chuckled. "Hey, as a veteran of the child support wars, I can testify that even my income rose perceptibly when our kids hit eighteen. Milo isn't making starvation wages. His kids have been off the dole for years. Don't you know his annual salary? It's a matter of public record."

"I *don't* know," I admitted. "I've never checked."

Leo's weathered face fell. "You're kidding!"

"No. My reporters have always handled budgets. I never look at what other people earn. I got into that habit on the *Oregonian*. It always infuriated me when I saw some worthless civil servant who was being charged with embezzlement and was already making at least four times what I earned as a journalist. It's a crime that newspaper people don't get paid enough. Teachers are in the same boat. You know all that. It's so unfair."

"It's also useless to stew about it," Leo said, leaning on the back of one of my visitor's chairs. "But if you asked your future husband, I'll bet he'd tell you *he* makes at least three times what you do."

I stared at my ad manager. "He does? You don't know that."

"Actually, I do. I checked it out last fall for our Labor Day special."

"Keep it to yourself. I don't want to know."

Leo guffawed. "Emma, you must be the only woman in the world who doesn't want to know what her other half earns. You're unreal."

"I don't care," I said stubbornly. "If Milo tells me, that's fine. If he doesn't, that's fine, too. I'm not marrying him for his money."

"Gosh," Leo said in mock disappointment, "and I thought that's why you never let me make a serious pass at you. I'm one of the few men around here whose salary you do know because you're paying it."

"And it's not enough," I said, and meant it.

Leo straightened up and grinned. "I'll survive. As for Dodge, if it's not his money, then it must be love. I never thought it'd happen."

I smiled wanly. "Neither did I."

Mayor Fuzzy Baugh arrived at exactly eleven. I hadn't seen him up close for some time and noticed he looked older, even a bit haggard. His dyed red hair had lost any luster it once had. The sparkle in his green eyes had dimmed. In fact, his eyes looked a trifle murky.

"Emma darlin'," he said, the Louisiana accent in place before kissing my hand. "Love becomes you."

"Thank you. To what do I owe this pleasure?" I asked.

He gestured at the door. "May I?"

"Close the door? Yes, go ahead."

After ensuring our privacy, Fuzzy sat down and grew serious. "You recall that last month I attended the annual state conference of mayors for towns with under ten thousand people."

I nodded. "We did an article on it." It was a rather informal affair, more cronyism than politics. There was, however, some beneficial exchange of ideas along with the backslapping.

"A fine article it was, sugar. But," he went on, "one thing that rankled was our homicide rate. Now, I know some of the people who met their Maker before their time weren't residents of this fine town or county. That brings up how we count heads. We've got just under four thousand folks within what we unofficially call the city limits and almost as many in the county. You know Alpine has never been incorporated." He paused, apparently waiting for me to say something.

"The commissioners rule," I said, unsure of what I should say.

The mayor nodded. "I won't criticize those men who've given us long years of service, but Alf Cobb is dead, and Engebretsen and Hollenberg are even older than I am." He uttered a self-deprecating chuckle. "Maybe we should rethink our government. This isn't for publication, but Irene feels it's time for me to take it easy, travel some, go back to the bayou and put our feet in that fertile black Delta soil. Isn't your brother there now?"

"Yes, in Mississippi."

"Then he'd understand. We don't need a mayor and three commissioners. We're strapped for funds. What this county and town need is a professional *manager*. We'd save salaries and election costs."

I was stunned at Fuzzy's perspicacity. It

was possibly the best idea the mayor had ever had. "It makes sense," I said. "It should've been done years ago, back when the timber industry tanked in the eighties."

Fuzzy shrugged. "Change isn't easy here. Out of the mainstream." He narrowed his eyes slightly. "That's where you come in. You have great power here. You should exert it more often." He smiled, and I caught a hint of his former sparkle. "You also have a personal stake in this. Think what it would do for your much-respected future mate."

"Does Milo know about this?"

Fuzzy shook his head. "Nobody knows except you and Irene. If you need facts and figures about places where this has been done, I can get them to you. Bainbridge Island is one example, though they incorporated only the island itself, but it's a mighty big chunk of property."

"Can I tell Milo about it?"

The mayor scratched at his temple. "I'd rather meet with him and the commissioners first. I wanted to secure your support now. You're as smart as you are comely, darlin', and I value your powers of persuasion."

"You overestimate my influence," I said frankly. "When was the last time I used my so-called clout to get a levy or a bond issue passed?"

"This is different. We're talking saving money, not spending it."

"But it's still a huge change. Our residents balk at change."

"That," Fuzzy said, standing up, though not as easily as he once did, "is why I'm counting on you to change their minds before we change our government."

Naturally, Vida wanted to know why Fuzzy and I had held a private meeting. For once I kept my counsel. She was annoyed, but I tried to soothe her by telling her to write up the engagement announcement. The vetoed photo, however, set her off again. "What's wrong with you two? You're both rather nice-looking. Milo's aged well. He looks better now than when he was young. You've held up nicely, too."

"Thanks, Vida, but I think most people know what we look like. As I recall, when you thought Milo and I were acting like lovesick teenagers in public, you were quick to point out that we had very high profiles."

"All the more reason for readers to want to see what you look like when you're not groping each other in the middle of Front Street."

"We never —" Mercifully, her phone rang. I fled to the front office to see if Amanda had made out the mid-month paychecks.

She had just finished. "Did I gather," she said, looking somewhat embarrassed, "that Wayne Eriks tried to come on to you, too?"

I sighed. "Yes, about a year and a half ago. He didn't get very far. How about you?"

Amanda made a face. "It was just before I started working here last fall. He was doing something with the transformer box on a pole across the street. I'd been watching *Oprah* and the TV went out, so I saw the truck and went outside to ask if he'd screwed up the reception. I'd seen him around before but never really talked to him. He said he didn't think so, but maybe he should check his computer in the truck. He went inside the van, then asked me to come take a look — he couldn't tell which cable went to which house. I started to get in and realized we don't have cable, we've got a dish like everybody else around here. He grabbed me, saying I was the only dish he cared about. It started to get ugly — he was a strong guy — until Marlowe Whipp pulled up in his mail truck. I ran like a deer. Marlowe thought I was chasing him to get our mail." She laughed. "It was all so dumb, and I almost reported Eriks to the PUD, but then I remembered his son-in-law's murder and thought maybe it'd unhinged him."

"That dish bit was the same line he pulled on me," I said. "I suppose it worked in bars and restaurants, too."

Amanda shrugged. "I'm sorry he's dead, but there was something creepy about him — the van, too. At least it *felt* creepy. Maybe I'm nuts."

"I wonder," I said, "if Wayne used the van with women who were more willing. I lucked out — it happened to me on a Saturday in my office, right after Tim was killed. That seemed crass."

Amanda frowned. "Makes you wonder about Tiff, doesn't it? Why would she want to move in with Jack Blackwell? In fact, why would Jack want a toddler in his house? Or is she leaving the child with her mother? Maybe Cookie would like the company now that Wayne's dead."

"I don't know what's going on or even when the funeral will be." I nodded in Vida's direction. "But we'll be brought up to speed as soon as the real source of news puts her ear to the ground."

"Oh, yes," Amanda agreed. "How does she do it?"

"Sources, most of whom are related to her in oh-so-many ways," I replied, seeing Spencer Fleetwood in the doorway. "Mr. Radio,"

I said in greeting, but he put a finger to his lips and motioned for me to join him. After exchanging puzzled looks with Amanda, I stepped to the threshold. "Are you the new James Bond?"

"No," Spence said, keeping his mellifluous voice down. "Is Vida around? I don't want her to see me."

"She was on the phone. What's going on?"

"I'll tell you over lunch at the ski lodge coffee shop. Can you meet me there in fifteen minutes?"

I checked my watch. It was a quarter to twelve. "Okay. Why didn't you just call?"

He gestured at the Bank of Alpine across the street. "I had to make a deposit, so it was easier to come in person. I didn't see Vida's Buick. I thought she was out."

"She's not, but she got here late and probably lost her regular spot." A few passersby were beginning to stare at this improbable site for a meeting of the media. "See you there." I closed the door and wondered what was on Spence's sometimes devious mind.

Just before noon I pulled into the ski lodge parking lot. Mr. Radio's Beamer was already there. The sun was trying to peek out as I walked to the entrance. Maybe spring wasn't as far away as I'd thought, or else we were getting our annual midwinter dose of unseasonably warm weather. That meant a sudden spurt in local growth, only to be followed by a killing frost and more snow. It could also cause avalanches if the white stuff melted too quickly. Ironically, we'd had more snow in November and December than in January. The Stevens Pass ski area had been shut down due to the lack of good powder.

Spence was waiting for me in the lobby. "Let's skip the coffee shop," he said, a hand at my elbow. "Too many eavesdroppers. The bar in the restaurant won't be as busy."

One of the usual blond waitresses appeared to take our orders as soon as we sat down in the shadow of Odin, Frigg, Loki, and other deities who evoked Nordic traditions. Given that we were in the bar, we both ordered screwdrivers. It seemed wrong not to have a drink. But then it was rare for Mr. Radio and Ms. Print Media to eat meals together.

"You're not glowing like a bride-to-be," he said, looking down his hawk-like nose at me. "Have you broken off with the bellicose sheriff?"

"He's not bellicose," I declared. "It's your fault he broke your nose. You took a cheap shot at both of us. How is your nose, by the way?"

He smiled wryly, running a finger from brow to lip. "Not quite like the original, but close. I thought Dodge could take some light-hearted male joshing. I misgauged his feelings. So you're still a couple?"

"Yes. Skip the history. Why are we here and why is it secret?"

Spence kept quiet while Birgitta or Brittany or Beelzebubba was setting our drinks in front of us. Ski lodge manager Henry Bardeen had a penchant for hiring blondes whose names began with a B.

Spence raised his glass. "To the happy couple, then," he said.

"Thanks." I clicked glasses with him. "Well?"

He sighed. "Vida's show last night was a bomb. Last week's wasn't much better. Deputy Mayor Richie Magruder's composting lecture didn't light up the airwaves last week. I don't expect all of her programs to be as electric as some she's had recently, with her family airing their trauma over the trailer park tragedy or the Petersen banking heir brothers savaging each other, but dull does not become Mrs. Runkel."

I nodded. "Vida's been off her feed lately." I had no intention of telling Spence what I suspected might be the cause.

He frowned. "Buck has finally moved to

Alpine, so I assume that's not the problem. That leaves Roger as the likely suspect."

"Roger is always a likely suspect," I agreed.

"I thought he was going back to college or joining the military," Spence said after a pause. "Do you know if he's doing either one?"

I shook my head. "She hasn't talked about him much lately." That was true — and, in its way, revealing.

"The kid's too dumb to be a con artist," Spence said. "You may recall she's had him on her show more than once. He'll never make it to a degree, even at a community college."

"You're probably right." I watched Spence light one of his exotic black cigarettes. Like the sheriff, he seemed indifferent to the smoking ban in the bar. Unlike the sheriff, he'd brought along a pocket ashtray. Milo used whatever was handy, including the floor. "Are you going to discuss the lack of content in her recent shows?"

Spence grimaced. "I'd rather not. I'll wait to see what she's got in mind for next week. How come she didn't ask you and the sheriff to be on *Cupboard*? That would've been a natural and a real grabber."

"She did. We refused. You know we were

trying to avoid publicity."

Spence grinned. "I'd never consider either of you shrinking violets."

"We try to guard our private life," I said primly.

He laughed, a cultivated yet somehow pleasant sound. "Please. You were the talk of the town back in December."

"Stop." I shot him a warning look. "You know damned well we didn't do anything except kiss on a street corner." Before Spence could offer a rebuttal, I went on the offensive. "What I'd like to know is how you get so much news out of RestHaven. I'm pissed. What's your pipeline?"

He feigned innocence. "Maybe I'm just good at newsgathering."

"No. You've always claimed to be more of a DJ than a newscaster. I know your early history around here, but not what came after that. You originally told me you were from Boston. That was a lie."

Our waitress returned. We hadn't looked at a menu. I ordered clam chowder and a spinach salad. Spence said he'd have the same.

"It wasn't a lie," he said after the blonde left us. "I did come here from Boston. I lived and worked there at WZLX for over ten years."

"That's quite a change," I said. "Why should I believe you?"

Spence looked pained. His eyes moved to the waterfall and trees etched on the mirror behind the bar. "I met a Radcliffe lit prof. We fell in love and lived together for eight years. She drowned off Nantucket on a faculty outing. It damned near killed me. Boston was the only real home I ever had. I couldn't stay without her." He leaned forward. "Satisfied?"

"Yes."

"Do you believe me?"

I nodded. His eyes spoke the truth. "I don't know what to say."

"Then don't. You know what it's like to lose someone you love. It all came back to me when Cavanaugh was killed."

I recalled Spence's kindness. He'd told me Tom was dead. Milo had already taken off to catch the killer. "You were . . . very compassionate."

Spence sat back in his chair. "We won't talk about it again."

We didn't — then. But sooner, rather than later, we would have to.

FIVE

The rest of lunch passed without discussing topics that incited either of us. Spence and I could agree on many things, including the growing tendency of reporters and writers to make the story about *them,* rather than the event. Ego was not a quality that good journalists displayed in their work. We parted amicably just before one. I had not learned how he kept beating us with Rest-Haven news. He, of course, did not know about Mayor Baugh's big idea. I figured we were even.

The newsroom was empty when I returned. Amanda informed me that Vida had gone to see the Parkers during her lunch hour and might be late getting back. She had made them "a lovely casserole" the previous night to offer as comfort food. Having been forced to eat Vida's casseroles, I hoped that Durwood, as the retired local pharmacist, kept an antidote on hand.

Leo was out hustling ads and Mitch was stopping by the sheriff's office before his interview with Dr. Woo. I hadn't had a chance to ask how the morning session with Jennifer Hood had gone, but I assumed that if there had been a problem, my reporter would have told me.

Vida returned at one-thirty. "Needless to say," she said, standing in my doorway and shedding her coat, "Dot and Durwood aren't deeply mourning their son-in-law. They don't know when the funeral will be, though. Is Milo really sending the body to Everett for a full autopsy?"

"That's what Mitch intended to find out," I said.

"Certainly it has to be a freak accident," she remarked.

I shrugged. "Don't look at me. How's Cookie?"

"Her sister-in-law spent the night with her." Vida sighed. "Cookie wanted Tiffany to come back home, at least through the weekend, but she wouldn't leave Blackwell. It's as if — Dot told me — he's cast a spell over her. I suppose that 'spell' is spelled with a dollar sign."

"Tiffany's nice-looking, but she's no knockout," I said. "She's got a toddler in tow. I wonder how Jack likes that."

"He never had children by his wives or girlfriends. Maybe he actually likes children. Did anyone try to kill him today?"

"No, not that I know of. Is Cookie in deep mourning?"

"More like a state of shock," Vida replied. "If she doesn't want to be alone, she could stay with Dot and Durwood. They have plenty of space. You've been to Wayne and Cookie's house. What's it like?"

"The same as the other tract homes in the development. It's fairly well maintained. The only one that looks different is Scott and Beverly Melville's house after he redesigned it and they renovated several years ago. They needed more room for their growing family."

A raised voice in the front office captured our attention. "My goodness!" Vida exclaimed. "Is someone angry with Amanda?"

"Let's find out," I said, getting out of my chair.

Vida beat me out of the newsroom. From behind her formidable figure, I could see Patti Marsh leaning over the counter, shrieking at our office manager.

"You, of all people, know what Jack's like! You tried to take him away from me!"

Amanda was obviously trying to remain calm. "I never did any such thing. At most, it was a mild flirtation. Jack isn't my type. He's *old.*"

Patti swung around to glare at Vida and me. "If it isn't Mrs. Busybody and Ms. Lord of the Newspaper. I want to make a statement."

I managed to maneuver around Vida. "What kind of statement?" I asked before Vida could erupt with indignation.

Patti put her fists on her hips. "That I'm not trying to kill Jack. I deny anything that anybody's said otherwise. How's that?"

"Who," I asked reasonably, "accused you of attempts on his life?"

Patti swung an arm so wildly that she nearly hit me. "Everybody!"

"This is ridiculous," Vida muttered, and stomped back to her desk.

"I'd have to find out who's making these accusations before I could let you deny them in print," I explained, not with any hope that Patti would understand. I was still trying to figure out if she was sober. "You might have grounds to sue for slander."

"I don't want to sue anybody," Patti retorted. "I just want people to know it's not me who's trying to kill him."

"Have you been questioned by the sheriff?" I asked.

Patti threw back her head and guffawed.

"Hell, no! He's too busy banging you these days to care about me."

My temper was rising just as Leo came through the door. "Well," he said, and stopped, apparently at an uncharacteristic loss for words. "Hi, Patti. You want to buy an ad?"

It was the wrong thing to say.

"Yes!" She whirled on him. "You're my kind of guy, Walsh. I'll take out an ad. I'll even pay for it. Ms. Snooty and Ms. Snob don't believe me."

The phone rang, allowing Amanda to temporarily withdraw from the fray. I decided I should, too. If anybody could handle Patti, it was Leo. I backpedaled into the newsroom and all but ran to my cubbyhole. As I went by Vida's desk, I heard her murmur the word "ninny." I assumed she meant Patti and not me.

A sudden calm ensued. I peeked into the newsroom but saw only Vida, who was talking on the phone. Leo must have removed Patti from the premises. Ten minutes later Amanda came to the door and confirmed my assumption.

"Is Patti nuts?" she asked.

"Not really. As you know, she and Jack have been together for years. He's often strayed, but always comes back to her. This live-in setup with Tiffany is different. I see why Tiff wants a sugar daddy. She's unmotivated and self-centered. But why him and why now? Surely she realizes her mother needs her. Cookie's always spoiled her."

Amanda shrugged. "Her mother's not a man."

"True," I allowed, "but after Tiff and Tim got married, she didn't seem interested in being a wife. It was all about her and the baby."

Amanda looked as stumped as I was. But she smiled. "I don't want to be like that. Guess I'll go home and pamper Walt to pieces tonight."

"Good plan," I said.

Leo came back shortly after two while I was getting a coffee refill. "Well?" I said, seeing Vida give him her gimlet eye.

"I bought Patti a drink at the V.I.," Leo said. "I should've guessed she'd be all over me. Somehow I managed to escape with my virtue intact. But I calmed her down. She's just pissed off at being dumped by Jack for a younger woman."

"Language, Leo," Vida said. "Do you believe her about Jack?"

Leo sat down at his desk. "Yeah, I think so. It'd take some effort. Brake tampering doesn't strike me as Patti's forte. Neither does taking a shot at him while he was at the mill's holding pond. I can see her trying to run him down, except he couldn't ID the car or the driver. Sure, it was dark, but he'd recognize her Jetta in a thick fog."

Vida nodded. "You be careful, Leo. Patti might be seeking comfort. You have a family in California to consider these days."

Leo laughed. "At least they seem more like family lately. But don't worry — I'm not ready yet to defect from the *Advocate.*"

Vida nodded in approval. "You've adjusted quite well to Alpine. I've been surprised by that, since you're a California native."

Leo made no comment. It was just as well. It was never a good idea to get her started on why Alpine was Eden. I'd had my own problems acclimating, but after fifteen years I was starting to fit in. Of course, I'd never be fully accepted. It didn't work that way in small towns.

Mitch had good news from RestHaven. He'd gotten a nice interview from Jennifer Hood, and Dr. Woo was a fine source of the facility's philosophy. His news from the sheriff's office was less heartening.

"Dodge shipped Eriks to Everett this afternoon," Mitch said. "The sheriff wasn't in when I stopped by earlier, but he was in his office when I showed up after I got back from RestHaven. Did you know there's a danger of flooding in the rivers around here?"

I fought an urge to cuss Milo aloud. "It's the burst of warm weather. Have Kip put both items online and check to see if sandbags are at the ready."

As Mitch went off to the back shop, I all but had to put my hands behind my back to keep from calling the sheriff and giving him hell. Being engaged made no difference when it came to Milo — or his staff — recognizing what was news. Granted, we'd agreed to keep our personal feelings separated from our professional dealings. But even before we'd ever slept together, neither he nor his employees seemed able to tell a news item from a hat rack.

I'd written my interviews with Reed and Farrell as best I could, given the little amount of information I'd gleaned from them. We'd have to run bigger mug shots to take up space in the special edition.

By five o'clock I was tired and ready to head for the Grocery Basket to pick up something for dinner. Leo, Vida, and Kip had already left. The last thing I needed was Jack Blackwell charging through the newsroom just as I turned off my monitor.

"What the hell are you doing?" Jack

demanded, leaning on my desk and glaring at me with narrowed dark eyes. "Has Patti been here bad-mouthing me and telling tales?"

"One question at a time," I said, forcing myself to stay calm. "Patti was here briefly. She didn't bad-mouth you."

Jack looked as if smoke should be coming out of his nostrils. His saturnine features may have seduced a lot of women, but I was immune. "Bull," he snarled, standing up and folding his arms across his chest. "Why else would she come here? You're not exactly best pals."

I hesitated, wondering if I would violate confidentiality. I wasn't going public with Patti's outburst, so I opted for candor. "She wants everyone to know she's not making the alleged attempts on your life."

Jack scowled. "I never thought she was. She'd hire somebody to do that." He paused for a second. "What do you mean, 'alleged'?"

"It's a newspaper term for something that's not yet proven."

Jack waved a hand in protest. "Hell, that dumb bastard of a sheriff couldn't prove it was February! How he's kept his job all these years beats the crap out of me. He must be paying somebody off."

"If that were true," I said through taut lips, "then you would know. He's responsible only to the county commissioners, and you are one."

"That doesn't mean those other two goofy old farts would tell me."

"May I quote you?"

For a moment I thought he might vault across the desk and slug me. But except for turning red, Jack stayed put. "You wouldn't dare."

"Don't push me, Blackwell."

He took a deep breath. "You're right. Dodge hasn't done squat to investigate my complaints. Sure, I can't stand the S.O.B. and the feeling is mutual, but can't he do his damned job?"

It occurred to me that Jack — even more so than the oblivious Mitch — wasn't aware of my relationship with the sheriff. It was no surprise, given his self-absorption with all things Blackwell.

"He had Cal check your brakes. Were you notified of the results?"

"Cal." Jack looked disgusted. "He's in Dodge's pocket. Vickers told me it was an amateur job and they wouldn't have failed completely."

"He ought to know," I said. "Count your blessings. There were no witnesses to whoever tried to run you down in the country club parking lot that night, and the bullet was never found."

"The damned bullet went into the holding pond," Jack retorted. "As for whoever tried to hit me, I had a rip in my slacks to prove it."

"Torn pants won't ID anybody. Sorry, Jack, I may not be a cop, but I know that without solid evidence, the sheriff's hands are tied."

"Bullshit." A sneer formed on his thin lips, making him look as if he should be twirling a long, dark mustache. "Dodge has you fooled, too."

I shrugged. "I think he does a good job. You're still mad because you ran against him and lost your ass at the ballot box."

"To hell with you," he said, turning on his heel to bolt out of my office. I heard Mitch say something to Jack, but there was no response. Putting on my jacket and grabbing my purse, I went into the newsroom.

"What's with him?" Mitch asked. "I only interviewed Jack once, when the mill was testing new uses for sawdust. He seemed okay then."

"As long as Blackwell sticks to business, he's fine. Otherwise he's a jerk. What do you make of the so-called attempts on his life?"

Mitch turned thoughtful. "Didn't he can your neighbor recently?"

"Doyle Nelson, the tree poacher? Yes, not long before the incident with the maples in November. But he and his eldest son are in jail. The two younger kids are in juvenile detention awaiting sentencing for setting fire to my carport. I've no idea where the wife — Laverne — is. Their house is vacant. Maybe she's with her relatives in Index. Vida would know."

My reporter looked vague. "I missed all of that. I didn't get back to Alpine until things quieted down. It sounds as if you had a rough time."

I tried not to look taken aback. Granted, Mitch's main concerns at the time had been his wife and their son. He'd spent most of his career on the *Detroit Free-Press* in a city where crime was more rampant and the coverage of violence was a daily ritual. A small town must seem tame to him. He'd been in Alpine for less than six months. It had taken me close to a year just to get all of the town's major players sorted out. And I still could get lost in the money branches on Vida's family tree.

"It was upsetting," I allowed, having no

desire to recount the horrendous experience. If Mitch really gave a rat's ass, he could read about it in back issues of the *Advocate.*

"Anyway," he went on, "I'd guess that whoever is harassing Blackwell could be a disgruntled employee. Your Nelson neighbor can't be the only one he's ever canned."

"True," I said, though I was unable to recall any other recent firings. "I'll see you tomorrow at RestHaven."

"Hey," he called after me. "I'm afraid I spoiled our lunch today. Any chance you'd let me buy dinner for you?"

Controlling my emotions was beginning to strain what little patience I had left. "Thanks, but I can't tonight. Some other time, okay?"

Mitch looked faintly wounded but forced a smile. "Sure. Next week, maybe."

It was after five-thirty when I got to the Grocery Basket. I hoped Milo wasn't home yet or he'd wonder what was taking me so long. Darryl called to me from the seafood section. Wild sockeye salmon filets had just come in that afternoon. I bought sixteen dollars' worth and a boysenberry pie, allowing me to go through the express lane.

My luck ran out. Ginny Erlandson was arriving as I was leaving.

"Oh, Emma," she said, assuming her most doleful expression, "are you still mad at me?"

"I was never mad at you," I responded. "I don't blame you for wanting to stay home with your kids. I was in a bind when you dithered about whether or not you'd return after your maternity leave was over. How's the family?"

"Good." Ginny paused. Nothing was ever completely good with Ginny and Rick. "Well . . . the older boys had the flu earlier this week. I had to take Bando to Donna's day care for three days. Now he has sniffles. Rick still thinks things are unsettled at the bank. He's sure Andy Cederberg is only the temporary president until an outsider is found to fill the job. That Petersen family ruined everything with so many of them dying."

"That'll spoil things," I said, leaning into the door.

"Oh — I just picked up the Valentine pictures of the boys from Buddy Bayard's studio. Want to see them?"

"Ah . . ."

Ginny rummaged in her purse. "Oh, drat! I left them in the car. I got rattled after telling Donna I'd be late collecting Bando. She was stuck anyway because Tiffany hadn't picked up Ashley yet."

"Your sister-in-law has the Rafferty kid?"

Ginny nodded. "Only temporarily until Cookie can manage. Probably after Wayne's funeral."

"I don't get it. Why can't Tiff take care of Ashley?" I nodded toward the checkout stands. "She quit her job here. This was her shift. Is she that upset about her father's death?"

"Maybe." Ginny lifted a shoulder and let it fall. "I went to school with Tiff, but I never really got to know her. She was more into boys than books."

"Or the other way around with her and the boys," I murmured.

"What?"

"Never mind." Ginny was smart, but innuendo was lost on her. "Have a good weekend," I said, and finally got through the door.

Milo wasn't yet home, so I turned on the oven before taking my jacket off. Ten minutes later, as I put the potatoes in to bake, the sheriff arrived, looking disgruntled.

"Do you know your backyard is solid rock?" he asked, shrugging out of his regulation jacket.

"It *is* built on a mountainside," I said. "Don't I get a kiss hello?"

128

"Huh?" He was taking a sheaf of papers out of an inside pocket in the jacket. "Oh. Sure." He leaned down and brushed my lips with a halfhearted kiss. "Melville says that's a problem."

"For him? For us? For . . . hey, Scott knows what the terrain is like around here. Is he trying to jack up the price?"

"Hell, no." Milo reached for the Scotch. "We aren't putting in a basement, for God's sake, but he has to sink some pilings into the ground. We do have earthquakes, in case you left your brain at the office."

"Listen, you big jerk," I said, shaking a cooking fork at him, "I don't need more guff today. I couldn't escape the office until after I had to face off with Jack Blackwell."

"Jesus." Milo finished pouring himself a drink. "Spare me anything about that asshole. I just want to crash. When's dinner?"

"In about an hour. And where's *my* drink?"

The sheriff gazed around the kitchen. "Damned if I know. Where'd you put it?"

"I never got a chance to make it!" I yelled. "I just got home a few minutes before you did! Maybe I'd like to crash, too!"

Milo winced. "God, Emma, knock it off." He took a deep breath. "Fine. I'll make your drink, too." He opened the cupboard and

129

got out the Canadian Club.

I kept my back turned on him as I poured water into a kettle for the fresh Brussels sprouts. A moment later I felt his arm encircle my neck. "Still mad?" he asked, resting his chin on top of my head.

I leaned against him. "Yes. No. Have I ever stayed mad at you for more than about five minutes?"

"Not that I remember." His hand strayed to my breasts. "Do you know how weird it is to come home and be able to act like a jackass?"

I laughed. "I can guess. You do a really good job of it. I could've sworn you'd had practice."

"Nope. Never had a chance to say much with Mulehide, even in our earlier years, before she declared war. It was always about her and the problems she'd had with the kids or the house or whatever the hell kind of bug she had up her ass."

"You need to vent. So do I. But watch where those hands of yours are going or we'll starve to death."

"Oh. Right." He let go of me. "Did the sheets come?"

"I forgot to look. Ronnie usually leaves parcels in the carport. See if there's anything out there."

Sure enough, Milo came back inside with a big package from UPS. "This looks like them. Want me to open it?"

"Go ahead. We can put them on after dinner."

The sheriff went into the living room. I heard him utter a sigh as he sat down in the easy chair. I smiled as I put the sprouts in the kettle. Despite the hectic day, I couldn't remember when I'd been so happy. There had been only brief and infrequent intervals of joy with Tom. I'd had fun with Rolf, but looking back, I'd never had the kind of deep feelings for him that led to happiness. The closest I'd come to contentment had been with Milo the first time around. And then I'd sabotaged even that. I wasn't accustomed to being happy. I shook my head in wonder. How could I have been so foolish all those years when the source of my new state of mind had literally been looming over me for fifteen years? Maybe I was as crazy as any patient at RestHaven.

"What did Blackwell want?" Milo asked when I sat down on the sofa. "He didn't give you a bad time, did he?"

I shook my head. "He was too busy giving *you* a bad time."

"That's not news." Milo lit a cigarette. "Let me guess. He griped because I haven't caught whoever's trying to kill him."

"Right. Patti had already stopped in to let us know it isn't her."

The sheriff passed a hand over his forehead. "Jesus. You got a double dose. I wish they'd get back together. It makes life more peaceful for the rest of us."

"Seriously," I said, "do you have any suspects?"

He paused to sip his drink. "Blackwell's pissed off quite a few people around here, but offhand, I can't think of anybody who'd want to kill him. He's got the only mill in town and that's a big deal. He employs seventy, eighty people. No safety violations, damned few complaints about working conditions. If he wasn't such a horse's ass, I'd like him. What I don't like — besides the personal stuff between us — is his power play with the county commissioners. The way I see it, he's biding his time until Hollenberg and Engebretsen retire or keel over. Then he'll find replacements to go along with him and run the county his way. He might do a good job, but I'll bet his first move would be to can me."

I stared at Milo. "No. He couldn't do that, could he?"

"Sure. Oh, he'd have to find a reason, even a trumped-up one — but the commissioners are my bosses. Still, that's down the road."

I flinched inwardly, wishing I hadn't tacitly promised Fuzzy Baugh that I wouldn't confide in Milo about the mayor's proposed change in government. "The commissioners may be abolished," I blurted out.

Milo looked justifiably puzzled. "What are you talking about?"

"Fuzzy Baugh has a plan," I said, and revealed what the mayor had told me. As was his way, the sheriff didn't interrupt.

"Jeez, Emma, that's a shocker. I didn't think Fuzzy could come up with something like that. It makes a lot of sense."

"I broke my word, but I know you won't tell anyone."

"I sure as hell won't." He shook his head, apparently still stunned. "I hope Blackwell doesn't get wind of this."

"Nobody knows but us — and Irene Baugh."

Milo grinned. "What do you bet it was Irene's idea?"

"I never thought of that. You're right — she's always been as good a politician as Fuzzy. Maybe smarter, too."

"So's a two-by-four."

I got up to put the salmon in the oven. "You never told me who you thought was threatening Blackwell."

Milo followed me out to the kitchen in search of a refill for his drink. "I wonder if he's doing it himself. But why?"

Six

I slept in the next morning. When I woke up around nine-thirty, I didn't see any sign of Milo, but the Yukon was in the driveway blocking my Honda. So was a third vehicle, a silver SUV that looked familiar, but I couldn't place it. After showering and getting dressed, I went into the carport, where the sheriff was talking to Scott Melville.

"Hey," Milo called to me, "Scott's got an idea on how to enlarge the carport and find some easier ground for the addition."

"Hi, Scott. I haven't had coffee. Come in and I'll find my brain."

Both men followed me into the kitchen. There were two used mugs on the counter. There wasn't much coffee left, but I poured enough for myself and told the Pig Pair they'd have to wait for a new pot to perk.

"The plan," Scott began, "was to add on out back. But now I think it would be better to extend the east side of the house in order to balance off the west-side carport extension. The ground's softer on the sides, too."

"But," I said in dismay, "we want to keep the cabin's look intact."

"We will," Scott said with his easy, still-boyish smile. "Instead of making the addition a mere frame, it'll match the rest of the dwelling."

I took another swig of coffee. "Won't that cost more?"

Milo was rinsing out the mugs he and Scott had used. "We'll do it right. When was the last time you did maintenance around here? You're supposed to clean and recaulk the logs every so often. I offered to do it a couple of years ago and you turned me down."

"I didn't want to bother you," I said.

The sheriff sat down. "It's a wonder the place doesn't fall apart."

"It's got a stone foundation," I snapped. "The logs look fine to me."

"They look like crap," Milo said, glancing at Scott. "You saw them."

Scott's expression was apologetic. "You're overdue for caulking and staining, but that can be done with the rest of the job. Arnie Nyquist can give you a quote when I finalize my own plans."

Milo's hazel eyes sparked. "No, he can't. I won't let that bastard near here. Hire somebody else — from out of town, if necessary."

For years, Arnie and the sheriff had gone head-to-head over various issues, including a remodel of Milo's office. Arnie — whose nickname was "Tinker Toy" — had savaged the sheriff at every opportunity. The Nyquist males tended to be arrogant. And Milo was stubborn. He had never forgiven Arnie. Maybe I'd acquired a small-town mentality, too. I couldn't stand him, either.

But I had a more valid reason. "Years ago, Arnie built thirty houses in Ptarmigan Tract. Three fell down and many of the others had problems. That's when he began focusing on commercial properties."

Scott nodded. "That's okay. I've worked with other contractors. Nyquist made a mint off of RestHaven, so he's not hurting."

The coffee was ready. Milo did the honors and sat down again. "Better explain how this side addition will work," he said to Scott. "Emma doesn't want to screw with the bathroom if we can help it."

"No problem," Scott said. "The new bathroom will be next to the present one with a wall between them. Access will be via Milo's work area and the spare bedroom,

137

which we'll extend, as it's quite small."

"But," I protested, "that means removing all the logs on the side of the house instead of just some at the back."

Scott nodded. "As long as they're still in good shape, we can use those and add a few more."

"How much is this going to cost?" I asked in a weak voice.

"Emma," Milo intervened, "Scott hasn't added up all the numbers. We just came up with the plan this morning."

"But —"

He put a finger to my lips. "Stop fussing. You're driving me nuts."

I failed to bite his finger as he withdrew it. "I'll shut up. I haven't eaten. I'll go out and graze in the yard. I doubt we can afford food."

"Before you do that," Milo said, "sign off on the release for Scott to put the quote together. You own this place, including the grazing land."

I took a pen from Scott and scribbled my name. Milo set his mug aside. "I have to head for the office, Scott. Two of my deputies are working security for the RestHaven opening, so I have to hold down the fort at headquarters. If I can get away, maybe I'll see you at the facility."

The men shook hands. I'd turned away from the fridge to glare at the sheriff. "Hey, big guy, you didn't tell me you had to work today."

"I didn't?" Milo looked faintly sheepish. "Well — now you know. Got to change into my uniform." He left the kitchen.

"I'd better go," Scott said, getting up. "My SUV's blocking Dodge's Yukon." He paused at the kitchen door. "He's right, Emma. You won't go broke. I did his headquarters remodel and he was satisfied with the final cost. I've gotten to know him as a neighbor. I still remember how kind you both were to us when Bev's brother was killed." He smiled. "That was ten years ago. We thought you made a good couple even then."

"You did? I mean, we weren't. A couple." I needed food to clear my fuzzy brain. "We started going together later, but . . ." My voice trailed off.

Scott laughed. "Don't try to explain. You and Dodge have always provided a lot of buzz. It livens up the community. Coming from L.A., Bev and I prefer it to gang warfare and other unsavory aspects of city life. The grapevine is local entertainment. Now that you're engaged, people may lose interest. Maybe the RestHaven newcomers will provide some gossip."

"You expect them to do that?"

Scott shrugged. "They've already had a dead body virtually in their front yard. It's a start." He suddenly broke into a trot. "Here comes Dodge. I'd better move my SUV."

The sheriff waved at Scott but kept heading for the carport. "Don't I get a kiss goodbye?" he asked, approaching the carport steps.

"Honestly, Milo," I said in exasperation, "you're too used to living alone. You should tell me what your plans are before you spring them on me. I didn't know you had to work today."

"I forgot." He looked a trifle abject.

"It does take getting used to, doesn't it?" I said softly.

"Yeah." He lifted me off the top step and kissed me. "But I like it."

I had not forgotten that Milo's birthday was coming up the first of March. We had never given each other presents, not even when we'd been a couple a decade earlier. Maybe that was because he never remembered my November birthday. I had often treated him to drinks or dinner over the years, and if I did remind him about my birthday, it was only after the fact, and then he'd apologize — and forget again.

But this year I was going to buy him a present. The sheriff's wardrobe needed refurbishing. A new men's shop had opened recently in a vacant space next to Francine's Fine Apparel. It was owned by Francine's husband, Warren — a couple with a track record as rocky as our own. After the Wells remarried, he'd worked at Harvey's Hardware. It was assumed that when Harvey Adcock retired, Warren would take over the store. But over time, the college had created a need for a better selection of men's clothing than Alpine Inner & Outerwear could provide.

I was finishing breakfast when the phone rang. I hurried into the living room before it trunked over to voicemail.

"Where were you?" my brother asked in his crackling voice. "Not at St. Mildred's helping Father Den with his Lenten soup kitchen, I gather?"

"You know Father Den doesn't have a soup kitchen," I said. "The Lutherans do because there are so many of them. God prevent the Presbyterians from having one. Vida might donate a casserole."

"Stop! As you may recall, Adam and I were forced to eat one of those things. I didn't know you could bake Elmer's Glue."

"It was that good? I'm shocked. Where

are you?"

"Still in Biloxi, helping the local Redemptorist with his flock. I'm moving on at the end of the month. The Home Missions finally caught up with me, and I'm needed in El Paso to help with the influx from Mexico."

"That's a long way from here," I said.

Ben chuckled. "You and Dodge don't need me to chaperone. Any chance you're going to make it legal? I'd think he'd want to, being an officer of the law."

"Um . . . he would. I mean, he does. We've talked about it."

Ben sighed audibly. "Damn, the Lord family curse of not being able to make up your mind. Don't say it. I suffer from the same disease. That's why I'm glad I have a job where I have to take orders, holy and otherwise. Just do it. By the way, Dodge should be getting a bunch of forms soon from the Archdiocese. He'll pitch a five-star fit, but try to keep him from throwing something — like you — through your picture window."

"He hates paperwork."

"He'll really hate this. It involves having his ex fill out a bunch of stuff, too. Have you ever met her?"

"No."

Ben paused. "Maybe you should."

"No."

"Sluggly," my brother said, reverting to his childhood nickname for me, "swallow your pride. You're the other woman. Show — what's her name besides Mulehide?"

"Tricia."

"Show Tricia that you're a good person. Fake it, if you have to. Let her see you realize why her marriage to Dodge failed without making her look like a villainess. Play on her sympathy, do what it takes, but win her over or there won't be an annulment until you're too old to care."

"Oh, Ben, I . . . I'm not sure Milo wants me to meet her."

"You're not playing by his rules, you're playing by the Church's. Here comes my fellow priest. Got to save souls or something. Peace."

A face-off with Tricia daunted me, if only because she'd speak ill of Milo. I'd get upset — and defensive. I couldn't think about it. I preferred taking the woman's way out. I'd go shopping instead.

Wardrobe by Wells was the name of Warren's shop. I recognized one of the college profs I knew only by sight and, of all people, Iain Farrell, who was apparently having trouble choosing between a dozen subdued ties. I avoided him by hiding behind the sport coat sale rack. Unfortunately, none of the items was large enough to fit Milo.

Farrell made his choice and his exit. Warren spotted me and came out from behind the counter. "Hi, Emma," he said, sounding surprised to see me. "Are you sure you're in the right Wells emporium?"

"Your wife already fleeced me," I said, and told him what I wanted.

Warren frowned. "I only have a couple of longs in his size. Not many locals are as tall or broad-shouldered as Milo. You'd never believe he used to be a skinny, gawky kid."

"No, I wouldn't," I said. Warren and the sheriff had gone to school together. "I do know he's put on a few pounds since I met him."

"He needed to fill out," Warren said, displaying a black sport coat from the non-sale rack. "Here's a Hugo Boss. Or were you thinking a brighter color?"

"I doubt Milo would go beyond black, brown, or navy."

Warren's eyes slid to the college prof, who was holding a couple of dress shirts. "Hang on, Emma. Let me take care of Bo Vardi. Check out that navy Versace — it'd fit Dodge."

I looked at the price tag on the Hugo Boss first — and almost *had* a fit. It was six hundred dollars. Milo would kick my butt if I spent that much. I never told him what I spent on my clothes. I would, if he'd ask — but he didn't. I had a professional image to maintain. All Milo had to do was stand around in his uniform and look formidable. It worked for him, but it wouldn't do the same for me.

". . . turned me down," the prof was saying to Warren. "Odd duck, which was why I thought he'd be an interesting guest lecturer."

I remembered that Mitch had interviewed Vardi during the fall quarter. He was new to the college, teaching science, though his true love was genetics. Assuming Vardi referred to Iain Farrell, I sidled up to him.

"Excuse me," I said, putting on my friendliest face and introducing myself, "I've been hoping to meet you. My reporter, Mitch Laskey, wrote a story about you last November."

Vardi smiled, showing brilliant teeth in a darkly handsome face. "Yes, a very flattering article. He made me sound intelligent."

I smiled back. "Being a journalist, I'm a professional snoop. Did I hear you say Dr. Farrell refused an invitation to speak to your students?"

Vardi's limpid dark eyes grew wary. "Is this for publication?"

I shook my head. "I'm curious. I've already had a run-in with him. I wondered if it was just me or if he's unwilling to participate in the community. That seems unwise for a newcomer."

Vardi sighed. "Maybe I caught him at a bad time. It was early Thursday afternoon and he sounded rushed. They must be swamped at RestHaven, getting ready for the big event later today."

"Are you attending?"

Vardi frowned. "I should. I'm still a newbie in town, but it's my wife's birthday." He gestured at the shirts that Warren had rung up. "We're going to Le Gourmand for dinner tonight, but first, we promised our kids to take them to Old Mill Park so they can play on the Big Toy — if it doesn't rain. At least the river hasn't risen too much. That's a relief."

"So far so good," I said, and wished the Vardis a happy evening.

"Have you decided?" Warren asked.

"Milo would arrest me for being extravagant if I spent too much. Any chance of getting something in for him that isn't as pricey?"

He checked his computer. "Would three hundred break the bank?"

"What bank?"

"How much is he worth?"

I stared at Warren. "Oh, hell, go ahead. He never spends any money on himself unless it's fishing gear."

"He's got a fine-looking new SUV," Warren remarked with a smile.

"The county helps pay for that," I said. "Milo uses it as his official vehicle. And the Nordby brothers gave him a good deal."

"I'll see what I can do. By the way, he has a fine-looking lady, too."

"Stick it, Doubles," I said, using his old nickname. But I laughed.

RestHaven's grand opening started at one-thirty. I purposely arrived late, hoping to miss any speeches or other mind-numbing formalities. When I reached the former Bronsky ballroom, which had more often been a makeshift bowling alley, a speaker was going to the rostrum. It was Jack Blackwell. Luckily, Milo was nowhere in sight.

Jack began with thanks to all of the movers and shakers on the stage behind him, including Dr. Woo and his department heads. What followed was a mention of their careers and expertise, plus a lot of other sucking up. I drifted and was only roused by a comment from behind me.

"Twaddle," said Vida, not quite under her breath. "Really," she went on as she barged her way over next to me, "Jack fits in as a county commissioner. He's as much of a blowhard as the rest of them."

A couple of people I didn't recognize frowned at my House & Home editor. She ignored them. "Patti never pressed charges when he beat her. She's a bigger fool than he is."

Jack was winding down. I looked for Mitch and spotted him off to the side up front. I hoped he was taking notes or taping the speech. On the other side of the stage Fleetwood was doing his remote broadcast. Applause broke out as Jack finally finished and introduced Dr. Woo. The chief of staff was a spare-looking man in his late forties whose face crinkled nicely when he smiled.

"Thank you all for coming," he said in a deep voice that belied his slight physique. "We hope you enjoy the tour of our facilities. I wish to introduce your guide, who knows this beautiful building better than anyone. Here is one of Alpine's favorite sons — Mr. Ed Bronsky."

"Oh, good grief!" Vida exclaimed, drawing more stares. "Was he listed in the program?"

"No," I said. "Apparently they couldn't fit him in."

"Literally," Vida said, alluding to Ed's girth. "Oh! He's *speaking!*"

I'd missed Ed's opening, but caught him in mid-sentence: ". . . tell you about every nook and cranny of the way it was and how it is now with these great RestHaven people. At the tour's end, I'll be selling souvenirs from our time at Casa de Bronska. I know all of you swell folks will want mementos of this occasion, and I'll be happy to . . ."

"Ninny!" Vida cried, the pigeon on her sailor hat looking as if it wanted to fly out of the building. "The least he could do is mention the volunteers who are offering their time and talent to RestHaven."

We moved aside for the line that was forming. "Volunteers?"

Vida beamed. "Yes. Roger, for one. He's not ready to return to academic life and he has no interest in joining the military. Instead, he's helping here at RestHaven. Isn't that generous of him?"

I felt like saying that it beat having him sit on his fat butt at Mugs Ahoy and downing schooners every night. "Is he here?" It was the only non-derisive thing I could say about the lazy wretch.

"I believe he's in the medical rehab section," Vida said. "That's where Ainsley Sigurdson works as an aide."

I backed up even further as the audience became bottlenecked at the exits. Maybe Ed had gotten stuck in one of the doors. "Ainsley?"

"Roger's sweetheart. Such a sweet blond girl. Her father works for the state wildlife department. Her mother — a distant Gustavson relation — teaches at the grade school. Ainsley joined Roger when he led the young people on the search for that recluse over a year ago."

I recalled the buxom blonde, who, along with Roger and some other kids, had stopped their search in my yard to drink beer and smoke a joint. But it was Vida's cavalier reference to "that recluse" that rankled. "You mean Craig Laurentis," I snapped. "You've seen his *Sky Autumn* in my living room. He's very talented, if wary of people."

"What?" Vida was lost in thought, her thumb and forefinger on her chin. "Oh — of course. Have you news of him since he was shot last fall?"

"No," I admitted, "but I haven't been to Donna Wickstrom's art gallery recently. I've been busy."

"True," Vida allowed. "Here comes Dr. Woo. Have you met him?"

"Not yet," I said.

"I'll introduce you. Yoo-hoo, Dr. Woo!" Vida sounded like an owl.

Dr. Woo detoured around a couple of people who were still in the auditorium. "Mrs. Runkel! How nice to see you so soon after our meeting at Parker's Pharmacy this morning. I'm glad you could join us."

"I wouldn't dream of missing it," Vida said with her cheesiest smile. "You must meet Emma Lord from the newspaper."

Dr. Woo's expression altered slightly. "Of course. Weren't we originally scheduled to meet earlier?"

"Yes," I said, shaking hands. "I had to turn the interview over to Mitch Laskey at the last minute."

Dr. Woo nodded. "Mr. Laskey did a fine job." He looked at Vida. "It must be hectic running a newspaper, even in a small town, Mrs. Runkel."

"We're online," Vida said, "so we must keep up to the minute."

For the umpteenth time, I endured an outsider's assumption that Vida was the boss. It was natural, given her long tenure and take-charge air, which extended not just

151

to the *Advocate* but to all of Alpine. I was seeking a tactful way to correct Dr. Woo's impression when I spotted Milo leaning in the doorway.

"Excuse me," I said. "I must talk to the sheriff."

I virtually shoved Milo back into the corridor. "Lucky you," I murmured. "You missed Blackwell's speech and Ed's tour guide spiel."

"Good. Let's get out of here." The sheriff grabbed my arm and led me down the hall. "Where's an empty office?"

"Milo! We can't —"

"We aren't. I guess the offices are in the atrium." He grimaced. "Nobody's around. I got the autopsy report. Eriks wasn't fried by lightning, which is a DC current. It was an AC charge, jabbed in his chest near his heart."

" 'Jabbed'?" I echoed, not sure of what Milo meant.

He took off his hat and rubbed his head. "It's crazy. Whatever electrocuted him left a definite pattern on his skin, but the M.E. said the burn marks on Eriks's clothes didn't match the ones on his body. That sounds like somebody killed him. Damned weird, isn't it?"

"That," I gasped, "is shocking!"

Milo's expression was wry. "I realize you couldn't stand the guy, but did you have to say that?"

"Oh!" I put a hand over my mouth.

He chuckled. "I know you weren't trying to be funny. Or were you?"

"No! It's gruesome. Who'd do that even to a jackass like Wayne? It had to be premeditated, right?"

Milo grimaced. "You know I won't speculate."

"I wish you talked in your sleep."

"*You* do."

I was aghast. "What do I say?"

"Just half-assed stuff that doesn't make sense. Kind of like you do when you're awake."

"Milo!" I made as if to punch him, but he held up a big hand.

"That's 'Sheriff' to you, Ms. Lord. Here comes Bronsky and his flock of curiosity seekers. If you want my official statement, check in later. I won't give it to Fleetwood first." He turned around and loped away.

I had no choice but to follow him, though he'd disappeared by the time I made up my mind. I managed to reach the atrium, where Vida was talking to a pretty, fortyish auburn-haired woman I recognized as Jennifer Hood, R.N., head of the medical short-term rehab unit.

"Emma, dear," Vida said loudly, "come meet Ms. Hood. She was so disappointed that you had to cancel your interview with her."

Jennifer didn't look disappointed when she smiled and shook my hand. "Mr. Laskey was an excellent substitute. I see he's taking pictures today. Which of you is writing the main story?"

"I am. As the *Advocate*'s editor and publisher," I added, "I feel obligated to cover such a big event."

"That's very good of you," Jennifer said. "We're excited about being part of the town. Such a big turnout! I know we're going to enjoy getting acquainted with everyone in this community."

"My, yes!" Vida enthused. "Alpiners are such down-to-earth folks. We're all so . . ." She stopped, her gray eyes veering off to her left. "There's my dear grandson, Roger, one of your fine volunteers. I'll introduce you." She rushed off after Roger, who had the bovine Ainsley in tow.

Short of faking an aneurysm, I would do anything to avoid an encounter with Roger. "I have to head back to the office," I said to Jennifer. "Perhaps we can get together sometime soon."

"I'm going outside," she said. "It's nice this afternoon and I'd like some fresh air. Medical rehab's in a separate building with a connecting corridor," she continued, moving quickly to the entrance, "but I find mountain air invigorating."

I glanced over my shoulder. Vida seemed to be having difficulty talking Roger into meeting Jennifer. Maybe he already had, which was why she was making a quick exit. Once we were under the porte cochere, I cast tact aside. "Have you already met Mrs. Runkel's grandson?"

Jennifer looked uncomfortable. "I'm sure he's a fine young man, but he seems a bit slow at catching on. Does he have ADD?"

"Roger is many things," I said, "but give him some time. He has trouble staying focused. Mrs. Runkel thinks the world of him."

Jennifer nodded. "He volunteered, and that's an encouraging sign." She sighed. "I was raised in a small town not unlike Alpine — Dunsmuir, near Mount Shasta. Maybe you know it — you go through it on I-5."

"I do. I always thought it was quite charming."

Jennifer nodded. "Yes. It was once a thriving railroad hub. But it got stuck in a time warp eighty years ago. That wasn't all bad. Dunsmuir was made a California historical town. A lot of tourists still visit, and like Alpine, there are plenty of outdoor activities. But social life is limited."

"You mean when it comes to eligible men?"

"Or the wrong kind," she said grimly. "It was weird when that poor workman died next to this property. Medical rehab is closer to the road and it was raining hard, so I didn't see him, but I noticed smoke by the van. I thought it was odd, but figured the wet weather would douse whatever was burning. Do you know if that had anything to do with the accident?"

The word "fried" came back to haunt me. But I had no idea if the smoke might have come from Wayne or something else. "No," I said. "How soon was that before you heard the sirens?"

Jennifer considered. "Five minutes at least."

"The sheriff will make a formal announcement later this afternoon. You might want to check our website."

"I will." She smiled. "I must dash. Our first two patients are arriving soon. Keep in touch, Ms. Lord."

"Make that Emma," I called after her.

I heard a familiar laugh not far behind me. "Wooing sources, I see," Spencer Fleetwood said. "Jealous?"

I turned around to face Mr. Radio. "Then you admit you have a special contact here?"

Spence shook his head. "I thought we dropped that subject."

"You brought it up."

"Alas, I did." He sighed. "If anybody should be jealous, it ought to be me. I'm not sleeping with the sheriff."

"You know damned well that Milo never tells me anything until he's ready to go public. He never has and he never will."

"The man has incredible willpower, I'll give him that."

"The man is a stubborn — if disciplined — mule."

"Not quite the word I'd have chosen." Spence pointed down to the road. "Obviously, Dodge suspects the possibility of foul play. Have you spoken yet with the Widow Eriks?"

"No. Have you?"

He shook his head. "I tried to this morning, but her sister-in-law — April, isn't it? — wouldn't let me in. Cookie must be overcome with grief."

"Maybe she's just overcome. Wayne wasn't an ideal husband."

Spence grinned. "I forgot — Dodge arrested him for grabbing some part of you that belonged to Dodge."

"Milo arrested Wayne because he had sufficient evidence. In case you forgot, Wayne lied in his original statement concerning Tim's death. He also had a credible motive to kill his son-in-law."

"The tale was much juicier on the grapevine."

"We're old news now," I said. "Come on, you must have *some* ideas about who might want Wayne dead."

Spence wore his most serious expression, which was fairly convincing. "An irate husband or boyfriend is my guess, the same motive that caused your favorite bear to resent Eriks. But names?" He shook his head. "I'm not in the gossip loop. Have you asked Vida?"

"No. Right now I'm disgusted with her for acting as if Roger were still her little darling. Didn't she learn her lesson?"

Spence steered me out of the way to allow some visitors to make their exit. "She wants to see this volunteer stunt of his as positive. She can't let go until he lands in prison for twenty years. Her priority is keeping him close, which wouldn't happen if he joined the military or went away to college. My latest nightmare is that she'll invite him to be on her show to talk about his altruistic volunteer duties at RestHaven."

"You're right," I agreed. "I wish she'd listened to Buck."

"Speaking of listening, I've got to head for the studio," Spence said. "Have you ever tried withholding your charms to see if that'll make Dodge open up about his investigations?"

"No."

Spence stared at me, grinned, and shook his head. "God, Emma, you are one strange woman." He sauntered off to his BMW.

I waited until he drove away before going to my car. Driving down to River Road, I had a whim to pull onto the verge where Wayne's body had been found. The Sky was running high, but not yet near flood stage. Clouds flirted with the sun as they lowered over Mount Baldy. Depending on the temperature, I didn't know if that was good or bad.

I parked twenty yards away from the pole where Wayne had been working. I knew Milo and his deputies had scoured the area, but my curiosity was piqued by Jennifer's remark about something burning near the van. There was no sign of ash. The rain would have erased any traces. I moved to the drop-off between the verge and the riverbank, treading carefully in case the ground was undermined. The water ran fast and off-color, coursing past a half-dozen houses at the base of First Hill. Windy Mountain was now obscured at the three-thousand-foot level. We'd have more rain before sunset. Why, I asked myself, would someone try to burn anything during a downpour? Why not throw it in the river? Because, I realized, there were snags, branches, even trees where items could get hung up no matter how swift the current. I looked around the near bank, where exposed roots stuck out like grasping fingers. A candy wrapper dangled from one, a scrap of newsprint from another. I moved back to the pole, where I saw a white rag hanging on a branch above the river. The cloth was wet, perhaps from the rain. There was no path nearby, and I doubted that I could reach it. I wondered if I should mention it to Milo. He'd probably scoff. I went back to my car.

As I started down River Road, I recalled Spence's comment about calling on Cookie Eriks. April had probably rebuffed him because he'd gone there as a newshound. I, however, had a personal relationship with the widow. After the loss of her son-in-law,

I'd offered comfort. Following Wayne's arrest, I'd consoled Cookie — and managed to scoop Spence in the process. I decided to see if I could one-up him again.

I turned into the Icicle Creek development, driving by Milo's split-level and the Melvilles' remodeled house, both of which were almost adjacent to the golf course. The Erikses lived several doors north, closer to the railroad tracks, where property was cheaper.

Maybe it was just the circumstances, but the house's exterior looked bleaker than I remembered it. The cream-colored paint was faded and chipped in places, the chimney was missing a couple of bricks, the small front lawn was patchy, and the roof — which had needed replacing on my last visit — was still deteriorating. I put on my most sympathetic face before I rang the doorbell.

April Eriks came to the door after, I assumed, she'd peered through the peephole. "Emma," she said with a wary look in her big brown eyes, "are you here to interview Cookie?"

"No," I replied. "I wanted to offer my condolences. Cookie has been through some awful things the past couple of years. I understand how she must feel. A lot of us have had some bad luck."

Flipping her prematurely gray hair over one ear, April stepped aside to let me pass into the small foyer. "Isn't that the truth? You certainly had a scare a few weeks ago. Cookie's baking scones. Let me see how soon they'll be done. I'll put on the tea-kettle."

Indicating I should sit in a rocking chair by the empty fireplace, April went out to the kitchen. The interior looked as well maintained as I remembered it. Basically, the house was similar to Milo's, if somewhat smaller. There was no TV in sight, so I guessed there was a family room, probably downstairs.

April and Cookie entered the living room together. Though not related by blood, both were slim, almost wraith-like women. Given that the Eriks brothers were burly, I figured they shared a penchant for waifs. I stood up to hug Cookie, something I rarely do with people I know only slightly, but I had devious motives. Journalists are born with them.

"So kind of you to stop by," Cookie said, sitting on the leather sofa as April excused herself. "How are you? I haven't seen you since the explosion at your house. You're looking very well."

"I am," I said, surprised at Cookie's concern, though I couldn't say the same for her. Not only was she haggard, but she appeared older since our last meeting. Yet it was her manner that had changed most. During the crisis following Tim's death, Cookie had seemed unhinged. I'd compared her spates of jerky speech and mannerisms to a wind-up toy. Maybe she'd been on drugs — or she was on them now. Losing a husband must be harder than losing a son-in-law. "I'm glad April's here," I said.

Cookie smiled. "We've always been more like sisters than sisters-in-law. Like the rest of us, she's had her own trials."

"You seem to be coping," I remarked.

Cookie shrugged. "What can I do? Wayne shouldn't have been working in that storm. He always said weather never stopped him."

I heard a teakettle whistle in the distance. Cookie got up. "I must check my scones. I'll make some tea, too."

Just as she went out to the kitchen, Tiffany wandered into the room carrying a small child. "Oh, hi," she said vaguely. "Ashley just woke up. You want to hold her while I get some juice?"

I could hardly refuse. "Will I scare her?"

Tiffany shrugged. "She doesn't mind strangers. We're taking off soon anyway." She handed over Ashley before exiting the living room.

Ashley stuck a finger in her mouth and regarded me with big blue eyes. Sure enough, she didn't seem to care that I was a mere visitor. At a little over a year, she was a cute, plump little creature, more intrigued with looking over my shoulder out the window than with me.

Tiffany returned, glass in hand, but didn't offer to retrieve Ashley. "How come you're here?" she asked, slouching in an armchair and flipping limp strands of blond hair over her shoulder. In her faded jeans and shabby bouclé sweater, she didn't look like a kept woman.

"I wanted to tell your mom how sorry I am about your dad," I said.

"Oh. Right. Mom's okay. Aunt April's solid."

"And you?" I asked as Ashley turned to look at Tiffany.

"Me?" The query seemed to surprise her. "I'm fine." She glanced at a wall clock set in a metal frame of grape clusters and leaves. "Gee, it's after three. I should get going." Tiffany drank some juice, set the glass down, and got up. "I'll change Ashley first."

I handed over the child and watched them disappear into the hallway. The doorbell rang. April rushed out of the kitchen to answer it. I heard her faintly from the entryway, but the moment the second voice spoke, I held my head.

"Come into the living room," April said. "Emma's here, Sheriff."

"So she is," Milo said, looking as if he'd like to stuff me up the chimney. "Hello, Emma."

"Hi," I said with a fixed smile as he loomed over me.

"I'll tell Cookie you're here," April said, scurrying to the kitchen.

"Beat it," Milo murmured to me. "I'm delivering the bad news."

"But —"

Milo grabbed my arm and hauled me to my feet. "I mean it. This is official — and ugly — business. Go home, clean the damned oven."

I left the sheriff to make excuses for my hasty exit, but I only drove as far as the development entrance. If Milo's announcement was official, I wanted to hear it before Fleetwood did. Ten minutes later, it started to rain and I was still waiting. Milo didn't like tea and I'd never seen him eat a scone. What was worse, I realized I was hungry. I'd skipped lunch because of my late breakfast. I wondered what the RestHaven staff had served at the reception following Ed's tour. Visions of salmon sandwiches were dancing in my head when I saw the Yukon coming toward me. In a fit of pique, I turned the ignition key and blocked the sheriff's exit.

"God damn it, Emma," Milo roared as he got out of the SUV, "why'd you pull a stupid stunt like that?"

I'd rolled down my window. "Because I want to know what you told Cookie and I want to hear it before Spence does. Well?"

The sheriff heaved an exasperated sigh. "Follow me to my office. No — *lead* me there, you ornery little pain in the ass."

I smiled sweetly. "Okay." After giving my future husband an obscene gesture, I rolled up the window and pulled back onto the Icicle Creek Road. I was sorely tempted to take Milo's reserved parking place just to see how he'd react. But this was business, both mine and his, so I parked two spaces down, next to Jack Mullins's pickup.

"Mullins is back from security duty at RestHaven," Milo said as I joined him on the sidewalk. "He better not be screwing off."

Jack looked up from whatever he was doing at the reception counter. "Hey, it's my favorite pair of —"

"Shut the hell up, Mullins," Milo growled.

"Are you AWOL or are they finished with the big bash at RestHaven?"

"Just got here," Jack replied, patting down his red hair, which had a tendency to stick up in various places. "All's quiet on the nut shop front."

"Where's Doe?" the sheriff asked.

"She was officially off duty," Jack said. "I'm about to go on patrol."

"No, you're not," Milo countered. "Heppner's on patrol. You're staying here so I can go home after I put together the statement about Eriks. Ms. Lord and Fleetwood have a need to know." He turned to me. "Stay here until I'm finished."

"Gee," I said, "guess you don't need anybody with writing skills to help you . . . Sheriff."

"No, I don't." He headed for his office and slammed the door.

"Is he always so nice to you?" Jack asked with a mischievous grin.

"Pretty much," I said. "On the job, anyway. We agreed to keep our personal and professional lives separate."

"Hunh. Nina and I did the same thing, except in our case, she agreed to keep our personal lives separate."

"Jack, don't talk about Nina like that. You know you're nuts about her. I've seen you

167

hold hands in church."

The deputy's eyes twinkled. "That's to keep her from stealing my wallet. Say," he said, lowering his voice, "what are the odds you can get the boss man to go to church with you? I haven't seen him there yet."

"About as good as the chances of the Mariners winning the World Series. The sheriff is not a churchgoing kind of guy."

"I know, but . . ." Jack shrugged. "Seriously, he's marrying into a family with two priests. Don't you think that makes a difference?"

"Not to Dodge. They're just a couple of guys who have a different job than he does."

Jack's puckish grin returned. "He'll have to go inside a church if he gets his marriage annulled. The real question is, how are you going to get him to wear a suit?"

I laughed. "That thought *has* occurred to me. In fact, this morning I went to look for —" I stopped as Milo reappeared.

"Come and get it," he said, motioning to me.

I sat down in a visitor's chair while he remained standing in front of his SkyCo wall map. To my critical eye, the statement looked fine. The bottom line was that Eriks had died from a lethal 110-volt charge to the chest and that his death was under investigation.

"You don't mention ruling out an accident or foul play," I said. "Is that because you and Colin Knapp can't be sure?"

"That's right," Milo replied, turning around. "Those burn holes in his clothes not being a match makes me suspicious — Knapp, too — but there's always the possibility of something weird in terms of the entry from a hot wire. And where did anybody get one in the first place?"

"The truck?"

"That's the most likely. But why would a live hot wire be there in the first place?" Milo took out a pack of cigarettes. "You want one?"

I shook my head. "I'm on the job. I want to avoid temptation."

He ruffled my hair. "Me too. Go away so I can give Fleetwood the news. You'll put it online, right?"

"I'll have Kip do it," I said. "I'll call from home."

"See you there," he said after lighting the cigarette and picking up the phone. "I wouldn't mind a steak for dinner."

I'd gotten up and was in the doorway. "I'm working. Go shoot a cow." I made my exit.

If the sheriff wanted steak, I'd go to the

Grocery Basket before I went to my little log house, which was inexorably being turned into a stately mansion. I called Kip from my car and read Milo's statement to him. He was bewildered. "Weird," he said. "Did Eriks fall on a hot wire?"

"It's possible," I hedged. "That's why Milo's investigating."

"He doesn't mention an accident," Kip pointed out.

"That's because he isn't sure."

"Wow. If it's not, then it's really grim."

"That's why Milo's cautious. Can you put it on the site now?"

"Sure," Kip said. "Is it raining where you are? It just started here, so Chili's letting me stop doing yard cleanup. It'll spoil the Erikses' barbecue, though. Isn't it a little early in the season for that?"

Raindrops were falling on my windshield, a half mile from Ptarmigan Tract, where Mel and April Eriks also lived. "April's not home," I said. "She's staying with Cookie. Why is Mel barbecuing? That's odd."

"Maybe their kids are here for Wayne's funeral. They both work in Seattle. Heck, I don't know. I can't see over the fence. It could've been a brush fire. I didn't think of doing that with the dead stuff I hauled out of the yard. Now it's raining."

"Enjoy your leisure," I said before disconnecting.

Driving up Alpine Way, I wondered what Mel was really doing outside. Small fires seemed to be a leitmotif in connection with the Eriks family. My musings were diverted by the store's reader board, where a Help Wanted sign was posted. The O'Tooles had to replace Tiffany. After picking up two T-bones, I saw Betsy facing out deli shelves.

"Looking for a second job?" she asked with a smile.

"I should, given our remodeling project. Any applicants yet?"

"Two," she replied. "College students, no experience. Not that Tiff was the sharpest cutter on the cheese wheel."

"Were you surprised when she quit?"

"Yes." Betsy rubbed Lubriderm on her hands. "No notice, either. Jake and I were irate, but what could we do? I wrote a check for the money she'd earned this month and that was that."

I shrugged. "She got a free ride and a man to lean on."

Betsy stepped aside to let an elderly couple pass. "Oh? I wonder."

"What do you mean?"

Betsy made a face. "She seemed scared, which was odd. When Jake or I had to chew her out, which we sometimes did, she'd get sullen. This was different, but I don't know why."

I didn't, either. But, as with all bad things, we'd find out.

SEVEN

Milo wasn't home by four, so I reread Mavis's letter, trying to figure out how to tell her she was wrong about my marriage plans. Maybe I should call her. I was still mulling when I heard the sheriff arrive, cussing his head off.

"Now what?" I asked from the kitchen doorway as he came inside.

"You put the garbage can lid on half-assed and raccoons got in it. There was stuff all over the place. Didn't you see it when you came in?"

"No. I was carrying the groceries. This morning I was rushed when I took out the garbage. Guess what — you could do that instead of me."

"I do," Milo said, brushing raindrops off of his jacket. "The can under the sink wasn't full last night."

"It was this morning."

Fuming, I started for the carport, but

173

Milo stopped me. "I cleaned up the mess. The solution for foraging wildlife is to enclose the garage. I don't know why you didn't do that when you moved in."

"Because there wasn't even a carport then and I couldn't afford a full garage. That's why, you big jackass."

Milo took off his jacket. "It's the best way to go now. With our weather, it's the only way. It's a damned nuisance when one of our cars is blocking the other one. As long as we extend the addition, an enclosed double garage will balance off the whole thing."

I put my hands over my ears and screamed. Milo walked past me into the living room. I followed him with fire in my eyes. "Why not add a couple of stories? Maybe an elevator? A rec room with a movie theatre . . ."

The sheriff hung up his hat and jacket on a peg by the front door. He put a big hand over my mouth and his other arm went around my waist. "Why don't you shut the hell up? Don't you want to do this thing right? Just nod, and then I'll let you jabber."

I refused to budge. Milo simply stood there and waited. Finally I leaned my head against his chest, forcing him to take away his hand. "How much will this cost?" I asked weakly, though I didn't want to know.

"With the garage, about a hundred and twenty grand."

My head jerked up. "You're serious?"

"It's an estimate, but close. Melville stopped by headquarters on his way back from RestHaven. I asked him about the garage then."

"Where do we get that kind of money until you sell your house?"

Milo lifted my chin with his free hand. "Emma, I've got that much saved up. More, if you want to know. I don't throw my money around. I started investing what I'd been shelling out to my kids a long time ago. If I can't spend it on us, what's the point?"

"Oh, Milo . . ." I buried my face against his chest.

"Hey," he said, chuckling softly, "did you really think I'd go into debt over this? I know you don't have a lot of your own money. I never intended for you to be out a dime on this addition. I've always felt more at home here than I ever did at my place after Mulehide and the kids walked out. But the only way this can be *our* house and not just yours is for me to put money into it. That's only fair, right?"

I nodded and finally looked up. "You really are wonderful."

"I guess so." He kissed my forehead. "I wouldn't have finally snagged you if I wasn't. Hey — are you purring?"

"I think so," I said, and giggled. "I really am fourteen."

He let me go but swatted my behind. "We're maturing, though. You might be up to sixteen, even seventeen. Hell, I might hit twenty by March. I'll change. You can make me a drink as the first thank-you."

"Dare I ask what the second one is?"

Milo's eyes sparked. "You know damned well what it is. But we'll save that for later."

I'd just finished pouring our drinks when the phone rang, and I had to hurry out to the living room again. Snatching up the receiver, I heard Vida assault my ears.

"Wherever did you disappear to this afternoon? You and Jennifer left like thieves in the night. I so wanted her to meet Roger."

"She had to go to the rehab medical unit," I said. "Patients were due to arrive. Didn't Roger tell you he'd already met her?"

"He had? Well, no, he didn't. He was so caught up in explaining his new duties. He wants to make Grams proud of him."

I was glad that Vida couldn't see my

176

expression. "I hope he can do that," I said a bit stiltedly.

"He will," Vida declared. "He's so eager to do his best. Which is more than I can say for Ed. He made less than twenty dollars from his so-called memorabilia. He had to lower prices to get that. Can you imagine anyone who'd want napkin rings engraved with Mr. Pig?"

"He did sell his self-published life story to Japanese TV."

"As a cartoon. Did anyone in this country see it? For that matter, did anyone in Japan see it? I heard it was cancelled after a few episodes. Surprising in a way, for people who sleep in bureau drawers."

"They're a sort of pullout bed for travelers."

"Very odd," Vida said as Milo went through the living room into the kitchen. "They're short, so I suppose they'd fit into drawers."

"They're not as short as they used to be," I said. "Besides, they —"

"Oh," Vida interrupted, apparently not in the mood to listen to reason, "I must give Cupcake a bath. He's quite fractious today, hopping about in his cage and not singing."

"A dirty canary is a temperamental bird," I said as Milo returned to the living room and put my drink on the end table. " 'Bye."

Milo sat down and picked up the *Seattle Times* from the magazine rack next to the easy chair. "Spring training's started. Is there any hope for the Mariners?" He didn't wait for an answer. "Why do I ask? The front-office dumbasses will trade anyone who's decent. Damn. I'd like to see a couple of games, but they'll want an arm and a leg for a decent seat."

"You've got lots of money," I said cheerfully.

Milo glowered at me. "Watching a bunch of bums who make a hundred times as much as I do and don't work half as hard is why I have money saved up. Parking costs too much. The concessions cost too much. Screw 'em. We'll catch the games on TV."

"Gee, you sound like a husband."

He shrugged, and all but the top of his head disappeared behind the sports section. I got up to go out to the kitchen, but detoured to the easy chair and kissed the top of Milo's head. "Guess what? I like it."

He uttered a short laugh. "Good thing. According to the first Mrs. Dodge, I flunked the job."

The phone rang again before I could reach the kitchen. But I realized it was Milo's phone, so I kept going. Dinner was simple

— baked potatoes, fresh broccoli, and the T-bones. Or so I thought, until I realized I still hadn't cleaned the oven. I was scrubbing it with a Brillo pad and Comet when I caught some of what Milo was saying.

"Didn't the damned fools lock their doors? With a herd of people going through the place? . . . Right, they think they're safe here in the woods. . . ." He lowered his voice again, but my curiosity was piqued. I hurriedly cleared away the worst of the grease and went into the living room just as Milo put his cell back in his shirt pocket.

"What's wrong?" I asked.

Milo lit a cigarette before he responded. "Dr. Woo called Dwight — he'd just come on duty at five — to say somebody ransacked his patient records. I thought they kept those on a computer these days, but Dwight told me they hadn't had a chance to do that since the new system was installed. Anyway, Woo reported a burglary and wants to see me ASAP."

"Are you going to headquarters now?"

Milo fingered his chin. "Oh — I should, I suppose."

I sat on the arm of Milo's chair. "I'll hold dinner. It shouldn't take long, right?" *I can finish cleaning the oven,* I thought.

"I hope not. You're not mad?" He looked

faintly surprised.

"Why would I be? When have I ever been mad at you for doing your job? You're a news source, big guy. I need to fill space."

Milo grinned. "I asked because *you* don't sound like a *wife.*"

"Maybe," I said, "it's because I've never been one."

By the time I'd finished cleaning the oven and started the potatoes, my curiosity kicked back into gear. Why would anyone want to look at Woo's files? As far as I knew, all the patients had been transferred from outside of the area. It didn't make much sense.

Milo returned shortly after six-thirty. I put his steak in the skillet and started water to boil so I could steam the broccoli. "Well?" I said as he poured us each half a drink.

"Those damned fools, Woo included, pawed through the files to see if any were missing. They don't lock their offices because they want, and I quote, 'patients to have a sense of freedom and access.' That means any nut job who can tell a patient file from a banana peel can swipe the staff's wallets. Maybe the inmates *are* running the asylum."

"Did you go to RestHaven?"

"Hell, no. Woo came down to headquarters. Dwight went to the scene of the screwup. He did his job, but I doubt we'll get much."

I took my drink from Milo. "Was anything missing?"

Milo leaned against the opposite counter. "Not that they could tell. If they wanted patient information, Woo's printer has a copier, so they wouldn't have to take anything out of the office. But that woman doc— Reed? — told Dwight he didn't understand. They all felt violated. I didn't want to know how Dwight handled that remark."

I laughed. "I don't, either. Deputy Gould isn't the soul of tact. How could they be sure it wasn't one of their own looking for something?"

"All the big guns swore they didn't go near Woo's office. That doesn't cover the rest of the staff, though. Maybe I can nail Roger."

I turned Milo's steak and put mine in the skillet. "He doesn't have that much imagination — or curiosity. Did you soothe Dr. Woo?"

Milo shrugged. "I told him never to mess with what he called a crime scene. Reporting a burglary when nothing's been taken

181

isn't smart, either. You can't even call it a break-in if the door's not locked. Sure, we'll check for prints, but we won't find much after they rummaged through everything but the ceiling. The fingerprint lab in Marysville might be worth a shot, but I hate to bother them." He paused. "Unless this was a cover-up for somebody who's up to something."

I looked at the sheriff with an expression of mock surprise. "Gosh — are you speculating? Are you using imagination? I'm stunned."

Milo grimaced. "Damn. Living with you has a bad effect on me. Pretend I never said what I just said."

"How about *good* effects? It works both ways. I cleaned the oven."

In the morning, the river was too high and off-color for Milo to go fishing. I left him reading the *Times* while I headed to Mass shortly before ten. It was the second Sunday in Lent. Father Dennis Kelly's homily was on St. Matthew's gospel of Jesus's Transfiguration. As usual, it was very well-organized and slightly soporific. Den was a much better administrator than he was a speaker, tending to sound as if he were lecturing a class. It was understandable, given that he had taught in a seminary for several years before coming to St. Mildred's.

Francine and Warren Wells were the first parishioners to accost me outside. "I can get that Hugo Boss in navy," Warren said. "Don't you think the color would suit Milo better? In a black sport coat he'd look as if he was about to gun down somebody in the middle of Front Street."

I started to tell Warren that I really didn't want to spend that much money, but in a sudden fit of perverse pique over Milo's reticence about his investments, I said yes.

Francine's eyes bulged. "My God, you're going to spend . . . I mean, it's for his birthday, right?"

"Yes," I said. "I want to spoil him."

"I guess spring is in the air," Francine said with a bemused expression. "Tiffany Rafferty came in yesterday with a wad of cash and bought a boatload of Tory Burch separates and Hanky Panky lingerie. Patti Marsh never had that kind of money to toss around when Blackwell was keeping her in a style to which she never became accustomed."

I glimpsed Betsy and Jake O'Toole talking to Father Den. "Really?" I said, recalling Betsy's remark about Tiffany looking frightened. "Of course Patti's never been a fashion maven."

"Neither is Tiff," Francine said. "The collection is very trendy, but she put together some ghastly combinations. And frankly, she hasn't lost all the weight she gained with the baby. I don't think she works out."

"She sure doesn't work," I said.

"Define work," Francine retorted. "Got to run. We haven't had breakfast yet. Oh — spoil yourself! I've got some new Max Mara items coming in this week."

"Right," I mumbled, already feeling guilty about the Hugo Boss sport coat. Milo would pitch a fit if he knew what it cost. Worse yet, I wasn't sure I had room on my credit card to pay for it.

Caught up in my cash flow crisis, I didn't see Ed Bronsky coming. "Hey, hey, hey," Ed greeted me, looking unusually cheerful. "Guess what? I talked Fuzzy Baugh into letting me set up a booth to sell my memorabilia at the Summer Solstice Festival. Terrific, huh? I didn't get a chance to show the tour folks the bigger stuff I had in Cal Vickers's pickup. Anything you and Milo need? I've still got those Louie Kens chairs."

"Those . . ." I stopped, realizing that Ed meant the spindly reproductions of a Louis Quinze dining room set. The chairs probably had never been used, given the girths of the Bronsky brood. It was no wonder that

184

Ed had gone broke after bumbling away his inheritance. "I doubt those would work for Milo," I said. "He's kind of a big guy."

"You're right," Ed said, frowning. "Not his style, maybe. Well, you'll see all of it at the Solstice shindig. I may loan some things for the parade, like the Venus de Milo statue for the Miss Alpine float. Hey," he said, beaming, "that's good. Maybe Milo would like the Milo statue."

"It's actually pronounced MEE-lo, not MY-lo," I said gently. "I don't think the sheriff is into large garden statuary, either."

"You sure that's how to say it? It's spelled like Dodge's first name."

Luckily, Shirley was calling to her husband as she waited with the rest of the Bronsky brood by the SUV they'd gotten after they traded in their last Mercedes. I wished Ed a pleasant day and practically ran to my Honda. It had started to rain again by the time I got home. To my surprise, the Yukon wasn't in sight. Milo had moved it onto the verge so I could get out of the carport. Maybe he'd gone to headquarters. I hurried inside to check my phone messages, since I always turn off my cell in church.

There was no call, but I found a note by the phone on the end table in the living room. "Emma," Milo had written in his big

185

but legible handwriting, "Mulehide called — Tanya's a mess — won't go back to the shrink — I'll try to be home for dinner."

I uttered a frustrated sigh. I should have known that we hadn't yet heard the last of the Tanya crisis. The rest of the day suddenly stretched out before me long and lonely. Not that we'd made any plans. We'd had so little time to ourselves that just being together was enough.

I wasn't in the mood to call Mavis or answer her letter. Instead I opened my laptop and decided to look at bathroom fixtures online. I was dismayed by the cost for the addition, but I wasn't going to buy a Louis Quinze chamber pot from Ed, even if he had one.

I was dizzy from staring at plumbing fixtures when the phone rang half an hour later. I hoped it was Milo, but Vida's number came up on the caller ID. "I hate to say this," she began, "but these interim ministers simply don't compare with Pastor Purebeck when it comes to sermons. For all his foolishness in running off with Daisy McFee — who, I might add, had lived in Alpine for less than two years — no wonder they moved to Mukilteo! But he knew how to preach. These fill-ins are quite young and they talk more Bible interpretation instead of sin. With Pastor Purebeck, you knew what sins were being committed and sometimes by whom if you were alert to what was going on. And poor Selena hasn't been able to show her face at church since her husband left town."

"That's a shame," I said after Vida ran out of breath. "I forget — are their children still in town?" Frankly, I wasn't sure they had children.

"You mean their daughter and her family? No. Martha married an engineer who works in one of those dreadful emirates. Something to do with oil, I believe. Imagine bringing up two children in a place like that! All that sand! How do you keep your house clean? If they *have* houses."

I gathered Vida had never seen pictures of some of the emirates. Except maybe for the beaches. "Selena must have family somewhere."

"She's from South Dakota," Vida said. "Most of her relatives are still there. Goodness, people live in such peculiar places. Black Hills, indeed. I can't imagine Selena moving there after so long in Alpine. Speaking of relatives, I saw my niece Marje at church. Do you remember Clarence Munn?"

I thought for a moment. "I don't think I do."

"Clarence owned one of the smaller mills Jack Blackwell bought out several years ago. The Munns moved away a year later, to Anacortes, I think. His wife died just before Thanksgiving. His niece is Julie Canby, who's working full-time at the hospital. Oh, you know that. I had it on my page right after New Year's. Julie had Clarence put in RestHaven. Marje found that out from Doc Dewey. Clarence's mind hasn't been quite right for some time and he couldn't live alone anymore."

I barely recalled Vida's short piece, having being too overwhelmed with my own problems at the time. "That's kind of Julie. Is she paying for Clarence's care?"

"I don't know, but Jack paid him a goodly sum for the mill. Clarence is a skinflint, which is probably why the Munns had no children. They can be an expense. I must run. It's Ted's birthday. I'm helping with the party. I offered to bake a cake, but Amy said she'd do it."

"Very kind of your daughter," I remarked, wondering if Vida had actually baked a cake in the last twenty years. I hoped not. "Have fun."

"I will. Roger is bringing Ainsley. Young

love is so sweet!"

On that note, Vida signed off. I wondered if this would be the last family gathering that included Diddy at Amy and Ted Hibbert's house in The Pines. Tomorrow Rosemary Bourgette would probably make her announcement about Holly Gross being out on bond and possibly taking back her children. I realized that Vida had seemed more like herself the past few days. Or maybe she was whistling in the dark.

But as the days ahead would prove, so were the rest of us.

EIGHT

Milo called around five to tell me he'd be home between six and six-thirty, depending on traffic. The message was terse. Not surprisingly, he sounded like he was in a bad mood.

I'd spent the rest of the afternoon figuring out what to feed the sheriff and decided to dig out my chicken lasagna recipe. I hadn't made it for so long that I'd forgotten it required three ingredients I didn't have. After a quick trip to the Grocery Basket, I put the recipe together, made a green salad, and buttered some French bread to heat later. I didn't put the lasagna in to bake until six. By six-thirty, Milo still wasn't home, so I turned the heat down. Sunday cross-state traffic over the pass was always heavy, both ways. I paced the living room, with a glance every few minutes to see if the Yukon was pulling into the driveway.

Ten minutes later the sheriff finally arrived. I met him at the door. His kiss was perfunctory. He headed straight for the kitchen and the Scotch without saying as much as hello. But he did make a drink for me while I impatiently waited for him to speak.

"Here," he said gruffly, handing me my glass.

"Thanks." I kept silent while he settled into the easy chair and lit a cigarette.

"Why in hell did I ever marry Mulehide?" he asked, staring not at me but at the beamed ceiling.

I didn't say a word.

Milo finally looked at me. "I swear to God she's never going to stop trying to make my life miserable. She insisted I meet her for lunch at a restaurant near Bellevue Square. 'So we can talk privately,' " he said in his grating imitation of his ex's voice. "Michelle — sorry, she prefers Mike, being a lesbian, after all — came up from Portland and is at the house. Tanya was supposed to go back to Bellevue in a couple of days, but she didn't want to leave Alpine. That's why she tried to commit suicide. She hates every-thing about Bellevue and the Eastside since Buster shot her and offed himself." He paused to sip his drink.

"Is that true?" I asked.

"Yes." His hazel eyes were hard, the same look he gave mulish suspects.

"So why not move? She's in her thirties, a college grad — she could go anywhere."

"Tanya only feels safe in Alpine. With me."

"Oh, shit!" I cried.

Milo showed the first glint of humor since he'd arrived. "You got it."

I held my head. "What happened next?"

He heaved a big sigh. "I tried to level with Mulehide, but she kept interrupting me. She insisted she didn't believe we were getting married and said I was mad — I sure as hell was — and I'd make a scene in this very chic bistro, where she'd spotted a couple of friends. I told her in that case, we'd better take a boat out in the middle of Lake Washington — or head to the house. Then I asked for the check, paid the bill, and left."

"You went to the house, I assume?"

Milo nodded. "All that back-door stuff pissed me off. Tanya was due to go back to her job at Seahawk headquarters March first, but she's not ready. I suggested since she wasn't able to strike out on her own, why didn't she stay with Mike for a while in Portland? Mike said her partner was living with her. I didn't know she had a partner." He paused again to run a hand through his hair. "I asked about the shrink she'd been seeing and why she seemed turned off by him. Tanya danced around that one, saying it was more about just being in Bellevue."

I held up a hand. "Help me out here. How much of this is Mulehide trying to manipulate both of you?"

"I don't know. Sure, I realize Tanya appreciated having me with her for the three weeks after she got shot. She seemed to enjoy being up here with me, too, even though I wasn't around during most workdays. I never knew how much of a father figure Jake the Snake was to her. He liked to *act* as if he was Good Old Dad in Residence, but I always felt it was more for my benefit than because he really gave a rat's ass. After he ran out on his first wife, he hardly ever saw his own two kids when they moved to the Tri-Cities. I've talked to Bran about him, and he said Jake was okay — for a stepdad."

"Where was Bran today?"

"He and Solange — the girlfriend — went to some artsy deal in Seattle. Solange may have a weird name, but I kind of like her. She seems to have her feet on the ground."

"How did everything wind up?"

"Inconclusive. I finally was able to make my point about us, I think. At least with

Tanya and Mike. And I showed them the application for the marriage license. I took it along with me as backup."

I glanced at the end table, where I'd last seen it. "I knew something was missing when I saw your note, but I was too upset about what you wrote to figure out what it was. Did that convince your daughters?"

"Maybe. It didn't faze Mulehide, though."

"Ben insists I have to meet her."

Milo leaned back and looked up at the ceiling again. "Good God."

"I'd rather not, but Ben has a point. He thinks maybe I can convince her I'm a decent person. We need her help with the annulment. Of course, my brother doesn't know what Mulehide's like."

"I didn't, either, when I married her." He finished his drink. "She always was headstrong, but she was nice about it. Then gradually she changed. Hell, I know a lot of it was my fault — the job, the calls in the middle of the night, the cancelled vacations, the whole nine yards. She had too much responsibility on the home front. Somehow it gave her a sense of superiority over me. That's when she started ragging on me, even in front of the kids. Then I'd go fishing and she'd really get pissed off." He passed a hand across his forehead. "Sometimes it

194

seems like a hundred years ago. Other times, like now, it seems like yesterday."

I got off the sofa. "I made lasagna," I said, leaning against his chair and putting my hand on his shoulder. "It won't taste like it came from a chic bistro in Bellevue, but I think you'll like it. Let's eat."

Milo lifted my hand and kissed it. "Where were you in 1972 when I met Mulehide?"

My smile felt ironic. "On the Mississippi Delta with Ben, bearing my illegitimate son. Where were *you* nine months before that happened?"

The first call I received Monday morning was from Rosemary Bourgette, asking me to come to the courthouse. I knew the reason from the tone of her voice. Luckily, Vida was on the phone when I went through the newsroom. I told Amanda where I was heading but asked her not to let Vida know. Our office manager instinctively understood.

The courthouse — which is also city hall — is a block beyond the sheriff's headquarters on the opposite side of the street. The original had been a small wooden two-story building on the same site but was moved in 1933 to a vacant lot on the corner of Front Street and Alpine Way. The Great Depression had caused construction to grind to a series of halts. Completion of the new building with its brick facade and dome hadn't taken place until 1939. Seventy-five years later, the courthouse was still the most imposing edifice in town, though the harsh winters had dulled the red bricks to a dun brown and earthquakes had shaken the dome, so it listed slightly to the west.

Rosemary's office was on the second floor. I smiled, nodded, and greeted a half-dozen people who were gathered in the rotunda. At least that's what Fuzzy Baugh called it, though technically the building itself is not round. His point of reference was the old Louisiana State Capitol in Baton Rouge, with its neo-Gothic architecture and many turrets. The mayor was practically beside himself with joy when I told him that Ben and I had visited the historic edifice while I was staying on the Delta. I didn't tell him that we thought the revivalist architecture was right up there with Mad Ludwig's Castle in Bavaria.

Rosemary's office is larger than mine, but the furnishings date back over half a century. I sat down in a wooden chair that Clarence Darrow might have offered his clients. She didn't bother with chitchat.

"Holly gets out today," she said, her pretty

face disgusted. "Is it my fault for not presenting a solid case against her?"

Her tone seemed rhetorical, so I didn't answer directly. "Milo knew from the start she could plead self-defense."

Rosemary flipped a strand of dark brown hair behind one ear. "I know Vida will be upset, but if only she'd made a better witness . . . Yes, I understand the situation inside that trailer was chaotic. Esther Brant's a tiger. I wish she hadn't taken on Holly's case pro bono, but she's well-known for siding with poor — and stupid — women. A real crusader when she's not hauling in big bucks with her Everett practice. Esther's the only person I know who could rattle Vida."

"She was confused," I said. "She told me right after it happened that she couldn't be sure what actually went on in just a few seconds."

Rosemary nodded. "Even Vida can be traumatized, especially when she'd just realized Roger was no angel. Holly will try to get her kids back. The two older ones are in Sultan in foster care." She pushed a sheet of paper across her desk. "This is my formal statement."

"Do you want editorial comment?"

Rosemary smiled, erasing her uncharacteristic gloom. "Only if you see something egregious. I have to stick to the basic legalities while making it understandable to the public."

I scanned the three grafs and made two minor suggestions, which she accepted. "Is this your version of a press conference?"

"Right. I know the paper won't come out until Wednesday, but I have to do it now or I'll be in dereliction of my duties. As a favor to a fellow Catholic, I won't alert Spencer Fleetwood until this afternoon. I held back until today because I didn't want to ruin Vida's weekend."

"That's kind of you," I said. "When will Holly show up in town?"

"Maybe tomorrow." She glanced at her daily planner. "Today is her official release date, but there's a lot of paperwork involved at her end. I understand the trailer's vacant, though I don't know if she's paid the monthly fees since she went to jail in Everett."

"That wouldn't stop her if nobody else is using it," I said.

"Probably not," Rosemary agreed, "but to get her children back, Holly will have to prove she has a stable home situation. That could take some time unless she's already made arrangements."

I nodded as I stood up. "Now I get to be

the bearer of bad news. Maybe I'll take Vida to lunch." As soon as the words were out of my mouth, I realized that was a bad idea. A public venue was no place to discuss such a volatile matter. "No — I've got leftover lasagna at home. I always make too much, even for the sheriff."

Rosemary had also gotten to her feet. "Speaking of Dodge, what's going on with Eriks's death?"

"You may think this sounds crazy, but I don't know."

Rosemary smiled halfheartedly. "Cookie Eriks is my next appointment. She wants to have the funeral on Wednesday."

"She needs a lawyer to help her make the arrangements?"

"No." She grimaced. "It's a different matter. I can't say, of course."

"Just like Milo," I murmured, and took my leave.

It had started to rain again when I met Mitch coming out of the sheriff's headquarters. "Dodge is in a bad mood," he said. "Sam Heppner thinks it's because he's frustrated over the PUD guy's death."

"He probably is," I responded, wondering if Mitch would ever figure out the relationship between Milo and me. "No leads, no witnesses?"

"Heppner says nobody's come forward as a witness," Mitch replied as we ducked around rain dripping from the canopy over the entrance to Parker's Pharmacy. "If they have any leads, they aren't telling. They're going to interview RestHaven staff and residents in the area today."

"Not many home owners have a good view of the accident site. Anything of interest in the log?" I asked, passing the hobby shop.

"A couple of accidents on Highway 2, three DUIs, one possible break-in, a prowler on First Hill." He shrugged. "The usual."

"Where was the alleged break-in?"

"I'm not sure. I only have the address on River Road," he said as we entered the *Advocate.*

I figured that was RestHaven, but kept mum — for now.

Vida looked up when we came into the newsroom. "Well! Early coffee klatch for you two?"

"We met by chance," I said with a smile. "Where's Leo?"

"Off to check the special edition ads," Vida replied, standing up. "He got four-color inserts from the Grocery Basket and

Safeway."

"Great," I enthused, realizing that Vida was following me into my office. "I guess Leo was right to do the Spring Fling section last week and hold off the RestHaven edition until it officially opened. We might make some real money this week."

"Very nice," Vida said through lips that barely moved. She leaned on my desk. "Well?"

I know when to surrender. Not only does Vida have eyes in the back of her head, but she seems to possess X-ray vision. I hauled my handbag onto the desk and took out Rosemary's statement. "See for yourself."

We both sat down. She adjusted her glasses before removing the single sheet of paper from the manila envelope. Without any expression, she quickly read the three paragraphs before wordlessly handing the statement back to me.

"I'm sorry, Vida," I said. "So is Rosemary."

She still didn't say anything for a long, uncomfortable moment. And when she did, I wished she hadn't. "Rosemary, Milo, the new judge, and everybody else should be ashamed of themselves. They are all incompetent fools. I shall never speak to any of them again."

Stunned, I forced myself to keep from lashing out at her. "Fine." I turned away, poised at the keyboard of my computer.

Vida hesitated briefly, stood up, and made her majestic way out of my office. I sat frozen in place, trying to calm down. Had it not been for Roger, this whole mess would never have occurred. Yes, there would have been the inevitable falling-out among thieves, but Vida wouldn't have been there when it happened. If the stupid kid hadn't gotten involved with Holly and knocked her up, there wouldn't be an innocent child caught in a trap between mother and father. And Vida wouldn't have had her heart broken. I might have wept if the whole situation hadn't made me so angry. There would be no warmed-over lasagna for lunch at my house. In fact, if Vida kept to her word about not speaking to Milo, she might never cross the threshold of my little log cabin again.

I took a deep breath and went to work.

The frost between Vida and me didn't melt during the rest of the morning. But I was busy. Leo sensed that something was amiss. He came into my cubbyhole shortly before eleven-thirty.

"What's going on, babe?" he inquired,

keeping his voice down.

"Want to go to lunch at the diner?" I asked.

"Sure. It'll be a lot better than being in the morgue that used to be the newsroom. Even Mitch is noticing that Vida's really off her feed. Kip and Amanda sense it, too. I've been hiding out in the back shop."

I shook my head. "We'll talk at lunch, okay?"

Leo nodded. "Meet you outside at a quarter to twelve."

Ten minutes later Kip appeared in my doorway, his face flushed. "You talked to Dodge in the last hour or so?"

"No. Why?"

Kip brushed back his wavy red hair. "I had the radio on in the back shop. Fleetwood broke in with a special bulletin about a witness in the Eriks death."

My mouth fell open. "No! Who is it?"

"Unidentified. That's why I wondered if Dodge knows. Do they listen to KSKY at headquarters?"

"Not if they want to keep their jobs," I snapped. "You know there's no love lost between Dodge and Spence."

Kip grinned. "I kind of like the way the sheriff rearranged Fleetwood's nose." He sobered quickly. "Where do you suppose he got wind of this witness?"

I already had my hand on the phone. "I'll ask Milo if he knows about it. Thanks, Kip."

He leaned further into the doorway, gesturing discreetly at Vida. "What's going on with Mrs. R.?"

I pointed to the manila envelope. "Sneak in here after I go to lunch and see for yourself. I haven't written it up yet, but you'll be putting it online this afternoon. As for the paper, we'll . . ." I stopped. I didn't want to run Rosemary's statement on the front page. Maybe I could slip it in at the bottom of page four. "I'll keep you posted," I said lamely.

I dialed Milo's number as soon as Kip left. "He's not here," Sam Heppner said, always glad to give me negative news. Or no news at all. "I don't suppose there's anything I can do for you."

"Yes, there is. Who's Fleetwood's eyewitness to Wayne's demise?"

Silence. "I have to check with the boss before I can release that information," Sam finally said in his most formal tones.

"Thanks, Sam. You're a sweetie." I banged down the phone. The doofus was clueless. Milo probably was, too. I fought off the temptation to call Spence and harangue him. But that would only make him happy.

I wasn't happy, especially after looking into the newsroom, where Vida sat staring at a news release. I hadn't seen anything that sour since I left a quart of milk in the back of my fridge for six weeks the previous summer.

Vida had already left by the time Leo and I rendezvoused to head over to the Heartbreak Hotel off of Alpine Way. Two of Rosemary's brothers had founded the fifties-style diner some seven years ago. It seemed like an appropriate place to deliver their sister's bad news.

We took Leo's aging Toyota to the restaurant. During the short drive, I filled him in with the brief version of Holly's release. He took the news with a sad shake of his head. "Damn that useless Roger."

Arriving just a few minutes before noon, we beat the rush. Terri Bourgette, another of Rosemary's siblings, greeted us with her usual cheerful countenance. I told her we wanted to talk business, so we'd appreciate being seated away from anyone who might want to eavesdrop.

"I'll put you across from an older couple who are driving through to Seattle from Ohio," she said. "Ever hear of Fostoria?"

"Only in dinnerware," I replied.

Terri laughed obligingly. "I saw you in

church yesterday," she said as we settled into a booth that featured glossy photos of Buddy Holly, Elvis Presley, and Jerry Lee Lewis. "I heard Sheriff Dodge asked Dad to work on your log cabin. He's never done one of those before."

That was news to me. "I'm sure he'll do a good job," I said.

"I'd better scoot," Terri said. "They're lining up. Joshua will be your server. He's new." She dashed away.

"Nice girl," Leo said. "I'm glad she didn't ask why I wasn't at Mass."

"Well? Why weren't you? It's Lent."

"I've backslid since my burst of piety at Christmas in Santa Maria," Leo said sheepishly. "Don't worry. I'll be back for Easter."

I let the subject drop. We studied the menus, making up our minds just before Joshua arrived to take our orders. I chose the Love Me Tender Steak Sandwich; Leo went for the Blue Monday Special, which was chicken-fried steak. The freckle-faced Joshua poured coffee for each of us and went off to put in our requests.

"So what's the cause of the Duchess's high dudgeon?"

"Milo and Rosemary are now personae non gratae to her," I said, still smarting from her tirade. "Oh, and Judge Proxmire."

"Damn," Leo said under his breath. "Deep down, she must know she's got this whole thing backwards. I wonder how Buck will react."

I hadn't considered how he'd deal with her hostile attitude. "Buck does exert some influence over her. But she revolted against his suggestion that Roger join the military to get his head straight. She also didn't do anything about his backup plan for the kid to go back to college."

Leo shook his head. "From what I can tell, Roger can't handle that. He's not very smart and lazy as hell. I don't see how long he can last volunteering at RestHaven. That's just an excuse not to get a real job."

"And to hang out with the amply endowed Ainsley," I added.

Leo's brown eyes twinkled. "Hey, maybe he'll knock her up. The Duchess would probably be proud of him."

"That's another thing — she seems to have forgotten what a jerk he really is. What more of a wake-up call does she need?"

Leo's leathery face turned somber. "Let's hope we never find out."

The conversation turned to ad revenue. We were up 8 percent over the past year. I grudgingly credited the co-op ventures with

Spence for much of the gain, though the arrival of RestHaven had helped, too. Just as Joshua brought our bill, the Ohio couple left. A few minutes later, when Leo and I were about to exit our booth, Cookie and April Eriks were shown to the empty table. They didn't notice us until we stood up.

Leo greeted them first, though he knew the women only slightly. He offered condolences to Cookie, who looked appropriately saddened.

"It'll be an adjustment," she said, after saying hello to me, "but April and Mel are such a huge help. I don't know what I'd do without them." She reached over to pat her sister-in-law's hand.

"Family," I said, hoping to sound sincere, "is always the best comfort. Is it true that you plan to hold the funeral on Wednesday?"

"Just a graveside service," Cookie replied. "Wayne wasn't religious and Tiffany hates funerals. I had to practically drag her to Mrs. Rafferty's service last week. We're going to see Al Driggers after lunch to make the arrangements. I wonder if we should put the notice in the paper." She glanced at April as if she expected an answer.

But her sister-in-law looked at me. "Is it necessary?"

"It's expected," I said. "Everyone knew

208

Wayne, if only because of his job. Besides, he's a longtime resident."

Cookie turned thoughtful. "I'll think about it. Nice to see you."

Leo and I knew we'd been dismissed. "Jesus," Leo said when we were walking to his car, "Cookie's not exactly the grieving widow, is she?"

"That was my impression when I saw her. She acted very different when Tim died. She seems relieved. Maybe Wayne abused her."

Leo waited until we got in the car before responding. "I gather he played around — or tried to. That doesn't mean he beat up on Cookie."

"It doesn't mean he didn't. I wish I knew why Tiff moved out."

"Blackwell wouldn't have to try hard to seduce her." He paused, having trouble setting his windshield wipers on high. The rain had turned into a downpour. "He's rich. Did anybody try to kill him today?"

"Nothing in the log," I said. "Milo won't make the complaints official until he has proof that Blackwell isn't inventing the so-called threats."

Leo concentrated on getting onto Alpine Way in the poor visibility. "You sure Dodge isn't taking Jack seriously because he hates his guts?"

"Yes," I said. "Milo is fair, even when he deals with jackasses."

"I'll take your word for it," Leo said, pulling out of the parking lot.

"You don't sound convinced."

Leo slowed to make a left onto Front Street, giving way to a Blue Sky Dairy truck. "You know my opinion of the sheriff has always been blighted by my infatuation with you," he said. "Okay, so it was more like lust. I still think you're a doll, but my renewed relationship with my ex, Liza, and your obvious passion for Dodge has changed my attitude. I've grudgingly come to respect him. He's smarter than I thought. Hell, if he could win you, he must be a damned genius. But he's a stubborn S.O.B. I don't think he forgives and forgets. Wasn't one of his deputies dumped by a wife who ran off with Blackwell?"

"Yes, Dwight Gould," I said as we drove past the sheriff's headquarters. "Kay married Jack, but it didn't last long. She left town."

Leo was temporarily distracted trying to cross traffic to park in front of the *Advocate.* "This morning I went to see the woman who handles P.R. and marketing for Rest-Haven to finalize their special-section ads. She lived here years ago and was married to a couple of jerks." Leo pulled into his parking space without getting us killed. He switched off the ignition and looked at me. "Her name is Kay Burns. Ring any bells?"

NINE

I was stunned. Kay Barton Gould Blackwell Arthur Burns had left Alpine before I arrived. I had known she was the cause of Dwight Gould's antipathy toward women, but I wouldn't have recognized her if she fell through the roof and landed on my desk. Mitch, who had probably been in contact with her, might be unaware that she was a former Alpine resident. Even if she'd mentioned it to him, he wouldn't be able to place her.

"That is too weird," I said after a long pause. "She must be in her late fifties. Did she say where she'd worked before?"

"Yes," Leo replied with a wry expression. "She and the late Mr. Burns had their own P.R. agency in Tacoma for fifteen years. He keeled over of a heart attack last summer. Kay didn't want to run the business alone, and her only kid and his family live over the pass in Leavenworth. She jumped at the chance to take a job in Alpine. Nice-looking woman. I would've guessed her closer to fifty than sixty."

"Wait until Vida hears this," I said, starting to get out of the car.

"Vida's not speaking to you. Or is she?"

"I'm not sure. I'll have to find out." I exited the Toyota.

Vida wasn't back from lunch. I could temporarily avoid an awkward scene if she still was, as she'd put it, "on the peck." I grabbed Rosemary's statement and found Kip in the back shop.

"I gather you saw this already," I said. "You might as well put it online now, before Spence broadcasts it on the two o'clock hour turn."

"This sucks," Kip declared, holding the paper as if it might be toxic. "I don't blame Vida for being upset, but what's with the deep freeze?"

"She's hating the world," I replied. "Mainly me, because I'm engaged to Milo and I'm friends with Rosemary and her family."

Kip shook his head. "That's not fair to any of you guys."

"I know, but Vida isn't willing to blame Roger — or herself. I understand, though it still upsets me. She's usually so clear-headed."

Kip smiled ruefully. "She isn't speaking to me, either."

I threw up my hands. "Oh, great! She's *really* mad at the whole world."

"Hey, she'll get over it. Vida *not* talking can't last long."

I smiled back at Kip. "True. She has to or she can't do her job. And that matters to her almost as much as Roger does."

Back in my office, I pondered calling Milo to ask about Dwight's ex being back in town. But Dwight might be within earshot. I'd save it for when we got home. I wondered if there were any new developments in the investigation of Wayne's death. As ridiculous as it seemed, I couldn't get over being self-conscious about checking in with the sheriff now that we were engaged. In the past, I'd have marched to his office and done my journalist's in-your-face act. But though we weren't married yet, I felt like a nagging wife instead of a news-hungry editor. *Oh, hell,* I thought, *do your damned job, Ms. Lord. The sheriff is doing his.*

At least Sam Heppner didn't answer the phone. The receptionist, Lori Cobb, took the call in her pleasant manner, saying that the boss was on the phone, but would I mind waiting? I said I wouldn't — and sat for almost five minutes until Milo came on the line.

"I missed lunch," he said. "What's for dinner?"

"I don't know," I shot back. "Ask the cook when she gets home from *work*. If you missed lunch, might it be because you were investigating a possible homicide?"

"It might," he said without inflection.

"Well? Have you got any *news*?"

"Nope. Early days, as we say in law enforcement. Go away, Emma."

"Come on, big guy, throw me a crumb."

I heard him sigh. "Don't use this. Marlowe Whipp stopped in today when he brought the mail. He remembered that when he began his River Road route, he'd seen Fleetwood's BMW parked near Wayne's PUD van. He didn't see Spence or Eriks. The car was gone when he finished the route and found Wayne's body, but he spotted Blackwell's Range Rover going away from Rest-Haven. Work all that out." Milo hung up.

I glanced into the newsroom. Mitch and Leo were both at their desks, but there was still no sign of Vida. Maybe she was at Ted and Amy's house, consoling them over the probable loss of Diddy. I didn't blame her. But she was my sounding board when it came to tricky stories. Never mind that it was assigned to Mitch. He wouldn't know Marlowe Whipp from Philip Marlowe. Well, maybe he would, but I doubted he'd want to ponder why Spence's BMW or Jack's Rover had been seen near the PUD van. That was Vida's forte.

Five minutes later the phone rang. "Okay," Milo said, "I'll throw you a real bone. Or was it a crumb?"

"Never mind. Just give."

"I missed lunch because Roy Everson came in just as I was leaving. He seems recovered from his Christmas breakdown over his mama's bones. Talk about a good news–bad news scenario."

"And?" I prodded.

"He wants us back on the case. Believe it or not, his goofy wife, Bebe, found some bones in their yard when she was digging up the ground to plant some damned thing. Dahlias, maybe?"

"It's early for that, but never mind. Bebe was digging in the rain? That's a little weird even for her."

"It was yesterday when it wasn't raining," Milo said. "Even Roy has enough sense to not show up on a Sunday when we're short-staffed. As usual, he wants the bones sent to SnoCo to see if they're Mama's."

"How close was Bebe to the dump site

where I thought Myrtle might be found?"

"Not that close," Milo said. "From Roy's description, fifty, sixty feet. We'll see what the Everett lab rats come up with. My guess is dog. But I wanted to give you a heads-up."

"Thanks," I said. "I appreciate it. Hey, does Spence really have an eyewitness to Eriks's murder?"

"Showmanship. Turns out it was Durwood Parker bicycling into the gatepost at Rest-Haven. Poor Durwood — he doesn't ride a bike any better than he drove a car. Maybe he needs new glasses."

"I hope you told Spence to keep his mouth shut."

"I told him I'd shut it for him if he didn't. How about pork chops?"

I hung up on him.

I spent the next half hour working on my editorial, trying to figure out a way to get the ball rolling on Mayor Baugh's reorganization plan. Until he made his idea public, I had to tiptoe around possible solutions. Over the years I'd written tons of editorials about budget cutbacks, insufficient school funding, and all the needed improvements that were shelved due to lack of money as well as public support.

I decided to use RestHaven's opening as the hook for the editorial. A new enterprise in town, new people, new ideas, but old problems, such as decaying streets, threats to cut school classes, shortages of law enforcement and medical personnel. Not inspired and certainly not new, but it was a start. I suggested we needed to change our approach to problem solving so that the town and the county could meet the demands of the twenty-first century. I hoped Fuzzy would be pleased.

By three o'clock Vida still wasn't back. I went out to the front office to ask Amanda if she'd called.

"No," Amanda said, looking worried. "When she left before noon, she didn't say anything about her plans. Kip told me about Holly's release. No wonder Vida's upset. Mrs. Parker's been trying to call her. She sounds stressed, too. Why would she be concerned about Holly?"

"Did Dot say it was about Holly?" I asked.

Amanda shook her head. "I just assumed that must be it. She was really anxious to talk to Vida. I asked if she'd tried to call her cell, but Mrs. Parker had already done that. No answer."

I wasn't really worried, but I was disturbed. I couldn't remember when Vida had been derelict in her work duties. The only recent occasion when she'd had to go home early had occurred back in December when she'd had a mild meltdown — over Roger, of course. He seemed to be the only thing that could unhinge my otherwise indomitable House & Home editor. The obvious next step was to call her daughter Amy. I suspected Vida was at the Hibberts' house in The Pines. But given her current chilly attitude, I refused to do that. If she wasn't back before five, I'd swing by the Hibberts' to see if her Buick was there.

Mitch came to see me around three-thirty. "I'm stalled on the Eriks story," he said, draping his lanky frame over the back of a visitor's chair. "I checked a few minutes ago with Heppner, but he told me there were no new developments." My reporter laughed wryly. "What makes Heppner and that other deputy, Gould, such a pair of hard-asses?"

I shrugged. "Heppner's always been that way. I don't know much about him except that he doesn't like women. And before you ask, no, I don't think he's gay. As for Dwight, he got burned by his first and only wife. By the way," I went on, wanting to see how tuned in Mitch was to small-town life, "have you met Kay Burns at RestHaven?"

"Sure," Mitch replied. "She's been my

main contact. Nice woman. Seems to know what she's doing." He suddenly grinned. "I think she's got a thing for Fleetwood. I figured that out when I went up to Rest-Haven this afternoon to run some copy by her for accuracy. I'll bet she's the leak who's given Fleetwood the news before we get it."

I wasn't amused. "That's unfair. You may be right about her being interested in Spence. She's a widow and he has a certain unctuous charm. Is there any tactful way you could bring up the sub with her?"

" 'Tactful'? No. I'll just ask her outright. I left tact behind me when I started working for the *Detroit Free Press.*"

I told Mitch to go ahead. If he was right, Kay was playing favorites. Having lived here, she should know better.

The rest of the afternoon seemed to drag, though I kept busy with proofing the copy Mitch and Vida had already handed in. Kip and I had made decisions about photos, carefully choosing which ones to use in the RestHaven section. The best was an outdoor scene in what had been the Bronskys' so-called Italian rose garden, which had usually been decorated with empty pizza boxes. The area had become overgrown after the family was forced to move out, but the Rest-Haven staff had hired Mountain View Gardens to spruce it up. We selected a nice shot Mitch had taken of a dozen visitors, including a couple of children, strolling by the fish pond, which was now mercifully free of empty soda cans.

Just after four, Milo called to say he and Doe Jamison had queried the RestHaven staff. "The lunch hour was over, nobody had gone out during the storm, and most of the employees hadn't seen anything and could account for their whereabouts at the time Eriks got himself fried."

I pounced on the key word the sheriff had uttered. "Most?"

"An orderly, an L.P.N., and Dr. Reed were vague. The first two maybe went out to smoke, judging from the tobacco stains on their fingers."

"Nice detective work, Sheriff."

"Shut up. I noticed a pack of Winstons in the orderly's jacket. Dr. Reed claimed she was lost in thought. I wanted to ask where Thought was located, but I kept my mouth shut."

"You? The soul of tact?"

"I don't need witnesses with 'liar' stamped on their foreheads. Maybe she went out for a smoke, too."

"You know she didn't."

"Never mind what I know or don't know.

Farrell was kind of iffy, but he said he could produce a witness for his time, though he had to consider patient privacy. Woo's solid. He was on the phone to the parent company in New York. Phone records to verify it. Hood was back and forth but used the covered walkway and was with a volunteer. No, not Roger. It was Mary Lou Hinshaw Blatt, Vida's sister-in-law."

"I gather you're not done with the Rest-Haven crew yet?"

"Not quite. Talking to patients is tricky. Woo's damned protective, especially of the ones in the psych unit. They might not make sense anyway."

"Some of them might," I said. "But I understand Woo's concern."

"Good for you. You can't use any of this, can you?"

"No. But I appreciate the heads-up."

"That's for the pork chops. Get me two." He rang off.

But by five, Vida was still AWOL. I drove through The Pines, but her car wasn't in sight. Maybe she'd been there and gone home. Feeling helpless and still angry, I headed for the Grocery Basket.

To my surprise, I ran into Mel Eriks in the meat department. He, too, was looking at pork chops. I first offered him my condolences. A burly man like his brother, he shrugged his broad shoulders. "That's a damned dangerous job. Wayne liked to take chances now and then. Maybe it was bound to happen. Do you remember the time he was working with the Bonneville crew and they almost went over that two-thousand-foot drop by the cross-state power lines near RestHaven?"

I recalled the near tragedy that had occurred in the dead of night six years earlier. "That was a close one," I said. "I saw your wife with Cookie today at the diner. She seems to be holding up fairly well. Maybe it hasn't really hit her yet."

Mel's gaze switched to the pork chops. "Yeah, I'm thinking of calling her 'Tough Cookie' from now on. But maybe she'll fall apart later on, especially with Tiff moving out."

I gestured at the two packages of chops he was putting in his basket. "Are you grilling again tonight?"

"What?" Mel looked puzzled.

"Oh," I said, faintly embarrassed. "Kip MacDuff thought you were barbecuing the other day."

Mel's laugh seemed forced. "No, I was burning some old trash. A little early spring cleaning. I'm taking the chops to Cookie's for the three of us. I'll be glad when April gets home. I forgot what being a bachelor is like." His smile became genuine. "Nice to see you, Emma."

I chose three thick chops, wondering why Mel seemed evasive. Maybe it was my imagination. One loaf of bread, a dozen eggs, and a head of cauliflower later, I was at the checkout stand and then out the door.

Just before I turned off Alpine Way onto Fir, I saw Vida's Buick pulling into the parking area at the Pines Villa condos, where Buck Bardeen lived. I breathed a sigh of relief, knowing she was safe. But I hoped that her longtime companion would pound some sense into her head. He might be the only person who could.

Milo still wasn't home when I arrived a little after five-thirty. I changed clothes before I started cutting up the cauliflower and peeling potatoes. I planned to broil the chops, so I'd wait for the sheriff to arrive before I started them.

Just as I was getting out glasses for our preprandial cocktails, he stalked through the kitchen door at ten to six. "I had to suspend Gould today," he announced before he'd taken off his regulation hat. "The stupid S.O.B. lipped off to me."

Ignoring the raindrops on his jacket, I

moved closer and put my hands on his shoulders. "What happened?"

Milo took off his hat, tossing it onto the counter before wrapping his arms around me. "Amy Hibbert phoned to see if any of us had seen Vida. She'd tried to call her mother at work, but Amanda told her Vida hadn't been in the office since before noon. Amy hadn't heard from her all day and wanted one of the deputies to go look for her. Dwight told Amy to stick it. Then Bill Blatt went after Dwight and they got into it. I broke it up before either of them landed a punch, but it wasn't pretty. Bill was only trying to defend his aunt. Then Dwight said a couple of things I didn't want to hear about women in general, so I did what I had to. I won't stand for insubordination or that kind of lip."

"Oh, Milo," I said, heedless of the dampness that was permeating my UDUB sweatshirt, "what a mess!"

"Yeah." He sounded tired. "Hey — you're getting wet." He brushed my forehead with a kiss and let go of me. "I'll change while you make the drinks. Stiff drinks. I'm guessing you didn't have a good day, either."

"You got that right," I called after him.

Five minutes later, I was on the sofa with my Canadian Club. The sheriff's Scotch was next to the easy chair. He ambled into the living room, pausing to muss my hair. "Damn, what would I do if I didn't have you to come home to?"

I smiled as he loomed over me. "You're tough. You survived."

He sat down in the easy chair. "I wonder how I did it. What in hell is going on with Vida? Bill's clueless. Is it Rosemary's statement?"

"Yes," I said, and then explained Vida's reaction.

I expected the sheriff to blow his stack, but he merely shook his head. "It just shows how messed up she is when it comes to that damned Roger. What are you going to do about it?"

I told him that I'd seen her car going into Pines Villa and figured she was consulting Buck. "Maybe he can help."

"Don't count on it," Milo said, after tossing a cigarette and his lighter my way. "She can't stay mad at you. You'd have to fire her."

"I don't want her staying mad at *you* — or Rosemary."

Milo shrugged. "I don't give a shit. Rosie probably doesn't, either."

"Well, I do. I won't stand for her attitude toward three innocent people, including

Judge Proxmire, especially when one of them is you."

"She'll get over it. She won't quit. Vida thinks she *is* the *Advocate.*"

"Don't I know it," I said bitterly. "And in a way, she is."

"Forget it for now. There's nothing you can do until she thinks straight." He grinned. "You could suspend her, like I did with Gould."

"Oh!" I exclaimed. "Did you know Kay is back in town?"

Milo frowned. "You mean Dwight's ex or his sister, Kay? The sister never left."

"The ex," I said. "Mitch told me she's RestHaven's P.R. person."

Milo leaned his back in the chair. "God! That'd explain why Gould's been such an asshole lately. I wonder if he's seen her around town. Maybe I should take Blackwell seriously."

I stared at the sheriff. "You mean Kay might try to kill him?"

"No, but she might want to scare him. She went after him with a meat fork when he dumped her. Then she left town."

"Mitch took a liking to her," I said.

"Mitch would. He's a contrary kind of guy. At least he shows some respect when he sees me at headquarters," Milo added, referring to the tension that had surfaced between the two men when Mitch's son escaped from prison.

"I don't think he knows we're engaged."

"So? I wasn't going to ask him to be my best man."

"Who will you ask?"

"Doc Dewey. I feel closer to him than I do to my snooty brother. I haven't seen Clint in ten years. He likes it in Dallas. Good place for him. I'd like to see him in a cowboy hat. If he wore boots, he might be as tall as I am. He never forgave me for turning out to be taller than he is."

"Are you still going fishing with Doc later this week?"

Milo grimaced. "We can't. Gerry and I are both on overload. He usually is, and now with Dwight off for two days, I'm short-handed. Besides, we both forgot they had the annual salmon derby at Sekiu this past weekend. The strait's probably fished out."

"Maybe the river will drop and you can go steelheading," I said, getting up to check on the pork chops.

"Not if it keeps raining like this," Milo said, following me into the kitchen. "We'll be lucky if we aren't on flood watch again. The only thing that'll prevent that is the lack of a decent snowpack so far."

I turned the chops over and closed the oven. "Six minutes," I said.

"Need a short shot?"

"Why not? Anything new from Tricia?"

"No," he replied, pouring a half inch of Canadian into my glass. "Mulehide likes to leave me hanging. She keeps hoping I'll get an ulcer."

We went back into the living room and resumed our places. "I don't mean to be a pain," I began, "but . . . oh, never mind."

"Don't pull that crap," Milo said. "The answer is no."

"Am I that obvious?"

"After fifteen years? Yeah, you are. And you're about as subtle as a sawdust grinder."

"Okay, so subtlety isn't my strong suit and my feminine wiles never worked on you. I know . . ."

Milo held up a big hand. "You don't have any feminine wiles. That's one of the things I like about you. What you see is what you get. And I got it. Took me long enough, though. Tell me what's buzzing around in your brain. Something's driving you nuts."

Damn the man, I thought, *he knows me too well. Why can't I be at least a little mysterious?* "It's Cookie. She isn't acting the way I'd expect of a recent widow. I remember what a mess she was when her son-in-law,

229

Tim, died. You probably do, too. What did you make of her attitude?"

Milo took a sip from his drink and a puff from his cigarette. "I know what you mean. I figured maybe she hasn't taken it in yet. Doe talked to some of the neighbors, who thought she and Wayne fought quite a bit. At least he yelled at her loud enough so the Dugans and the Lundquists on each side could hear him. But Cookie'd already lost a son, a son-in-law, and now her husband. Maybe she's numb."

"I keep forgetting the son drowned in a rafting accident."

"It happened over on the Snake River not long before you arrived. They called the kid Ringo. I guess Cookie was a big Beatles fan. That wasn't his real name — I think it was Robert or Richard. He was nineteen."

"I remember hearing about it. He wasn't alone, was he?"

"There were three of them from here. The other two survived." Milo paused to scratch behind his ear. "Damn. I can't remember the one kid's name. The family left town not long after that. But the third one was Travis Nyquist, Arnie's son."

"Oh." I avoided Milo's gaze. "Travis moved away after Bridget left him. Then he got in trouble with his role in that investment scam."

"He plea-bargained his way out of that," Milo said. "Travis still visits Arnie and Louise. I ran into him last month at Harvey's Hardware. He's still a jackass. You're thinking he pushed Ringo off the raft."

I sighed and resumed eye contact. "It could have been the third kid who did it," I said with a straight face.

"Get up, Nancy Drew. I'm hungry, and I want to rescue those chops before the oven catches fire. Again."

I rose from the sofa. "I told you I cleaned it. Didn't you notice?"

Milo grabbed my backside as he followed me out to the kitchen. "No, but I knew something was missing. Like smoke and flames."

Our dinner conversation turned to the remodeling project. I had to admit that Milo seemed to know what he was doing — or at least he knew what Scott Melville was doing. It wasn't until we were snuggling on the sofa at halftime of a college basketball game that I asked Milo how Wayne could die from a live wire through his chest.

"Jesus, Emma," he said, exasperated, "can you focus on what we're doing here instead of worrying about Eriks?"

"I *was* focusing." I removed my arm from

231

around his neck and poked him in his chest. "If I had a live wire, I could jab it into you right now. But how would I keep from electrocuting myself?"

Milo slowly shook his head. "Why don't you try it and find out?"

"I will if you don't answer the question."

He sighed but kept his arms around me. "The person would have to wear gloves. But he *could* have fallen on a hot wire. That's why the M.E. and I are being cagey until we get more evidence."

"If the burn marks on Wayne didn't match those on his clothes, he must've taken them off. What if he was with a woman?"

Milo stared at me for a long moment without blinking. It was a tactic he used when questioning suspects — and had done it to me on one disturbing occasion. "Yes," he finally said, "that's possible. Maybe he was trying to make love to her and got mad when she asked if he'd like her better if she had purple hair. Then she got pissed off, put on his safety gloves, grabbed a hot oven coil, and ran him through. About now, I can believe that scenario." Abruptly he pulled me closer. "Shut up, you little twerp, and pay attention to what *we're* doing."

"Okay," I said in a sort of squeak. We both stopped talking.

But that didn't mean I'd forgotten my weird theory. The problem was that I didn't have Vida as a sounding board. When I arrived at work, Amanda informed me she'd called to ask for a personal day off.

"A family matter," Amanda said, rolling her eyes. "Do you suppose Holly has shown up to collect her kid?"

I leaned on the counter. "That's my guess." I shook my head in dismay. "It's deadline day. I don't know if Vida's finished all of her page or started 'Scene Around Town' for the gossip tidbits. I should call a staff meeting. In fact, I'll do it as soon as . . . who has the bakery run?"

"Mitch," Amanda replied.

"Tell Kip." I glanced in the newsroom and saw Leo sitting down at his desk. "As soon as Mitch gets here, we'll start. You too, Amanda. Okay?"

I greeted my ad manager before going through the items Vida had on her desk. "This," I declared, "has never happened before. Vida's taken time off, but she's never left us hanging."

"At least I can smoke in peace," he said, lighting a cigarette.

"So can I." I reached out to Leo. "Give me one of those things."

Leo complied. "Dodge is a bad influence on you."

"Would you believe neither of us smoked for several years?"

"I never tried quitting. My major achievement was cutting back on the booze. Liza thinks you're a saint to see me through that sad chapter."

"Gee, that's good of her. I mean it. Milo's ex thinks I'm a she-wolf."

"You're more of a fox," Leo said as Mitch came through the door, followed by Amanda and Kip. "Looks like the meeting's about to start."

"Not until we fuel ourselves," I said, going over to help Mitch lay out the Upper Crust pastries. I grabbed the first sugar doughnut out of my reporter's hand.

"No Vida?" he asked, glancing at her empty chair.

"Personal day off," I said, pouring out my coffee. "That's all we know." I sat down at the missing person's desk and kept quiet until my staff had gotten their own goodies and filled their coffee mugs.

"I found two of Vida's 'Scene' items," I said when everyone was seated. "Mimi Barton carrying forsythia into St. Mildred's rectory and Harvey Adcock washing his hardware display windows, egging vandalism courtesy of teenagers, as noted in last week's police log. Who's got something?"

"Who's Mimi Barton?" Mitch asked.

"Father Kelly's secretary," I said, recalling that she was also Kay Burns's sister. I'd forgotten the family connection. "Come on, guys, think."

Kip winced. "Chili took our dog to the vet Friday. Dr. Medved said the Dithers sisters put down one of their horses. Is that too grim?"

"Yes," I said. "It's a wonder they didn't send us an obit. I'll hear all about it at the next bridge club meeting."

Leo grimaced. "Can we stand an Ed Bronsky sighting? I saw him driving Cal Vickers's pickup full of villa items from RestHaven Saturday."

"Let's not," I said. "Got anything else?"

Leo grimaced. "How about giving that out-of-town guy a boost for taking out the ad about buying sports memorabilia? I had to bury the ad a bit because of all the RestHaven-related stuff."

"That's fine," I said, making a note. "Mitch, you got anything from the open house?"

"The kids in that garden photo? Just after

235

I took it, they went wading in the fish pond. Sorry — I don't know their names."

"That's okay," I said, making another note. "Probably just as well *not* to ID them. Their parents might get upset."

Amanda raised her hand. "I hate to tell on Walt, but he tripped over a hose at the hatchery Friday and almost fell in one of the ponds."

I considered the item. "Two pond incidents? Why not?"

"Thanks," Amanda said, smiling. "Walt has a sense of humor."

"What about you, boss lady?" Leo asked with a playful grin.

"I'll think of something. When I do, that's all we need. Amanda, could you go through Vida's in-box and mail to make sure we aren't missing any late-breaking news? I'm thinking engagements. It's only been a week since Valentine's Day."

"Sure," Amanda said, apparently glad to vary her daily routine.

"Dismissed," I said. "And thanks. This feels so weird without Vida. I'll peruse her advice column letters."

I found the copy she'd turned in. There were three letters, always anonymous per Vida's instructions, even though she usually knew the writer's identity. Two were about

St. Valentine's Day disappointments. The third was from an irate First Hill resident whose neighbors owned a dog that barked all day. Vida had given sensible advice to all of them. I wished she could write to herself and ask for help.

A few minutes later, Amanda brought me two unopened letters she'd found in Vida's in-box. Both were postmarked from last Thursday, indicating that Vida had already been too distracted by the possible loss of Diddy to open all of her mail. The first was from a teenager whose mother criticized her wardrobe as "too revealing." The girl tried to explain that she wore the same kind of clothes her friends did and that they weren't hassled by their parents. Vida could answer that in short order. The second letter, signed "Disturbed Wife," concerned her mate's reading of "provocative" men's magazines, which made her feel "inadequate." "I am a willing partner, but I'm afraid I'll lose my husband to even more depraved and stimulating reading material. I am not fat, being five foot three and weighing a hundred and eighteen pounds." It might be true, but Vida could also handle that one with dispatch. Unfortunately, neither letter would make it into this week's edition.

The teen's clothing problem inspired a

"Scene" item. I typed up the sightings of Professor Bo Vardi and Dr. Iain Farrell making purchases at Warren Wells's store. I sensed Farrell wouldn't like the mention, but he had to get used to small-town ways. If he complained, I'd tell him it fit in with the RestHaven edition.

Finally I turned to my editorial. Deciding that it was ready to go public, I zapped it to Kip just as Mitch poked his head in.

"Nothing new on Eriks," he said. "I asked Jack Mullins for a quote from Dodge, but he was on the phone. Should I wait for him to call me?"

"Wait," I said. "If the sheriff doesn't call you, call him. Don't let him off the hook." I made a face as I had a sudden thought. "Mrs. Eriks wants to have the service tomorrow. I'll ask Al Driggers at the funeral home if it's set. I just realized I don't have an obit from Vida on Eriks. Damn. I'll see if I can get some information from Al. If so, could you write it up?"

"Sure. I gather he didn't lead a hugely eventful life?"

"Not that I know of. The only unusual thing is how he died."

"That's the real story," Mitch remarked before heading to his desk.

Al's wife, Janet, answered the phone. "Yes,

I'm doing the dead thing today," she said in her husky voice. "Burying people is better business this time of year than sending them off on vacation at Sky Travel. How's cohabitation with the sheriff going? You sure you're not bored and would like Al and me to join you for a foursome?"

I was used to Janet's bawdy tongue. "We're planning our addition."

"Dodge knocked you up? I thought you were past that!"

"I am," I said wearily. "I'm talking about my house. Hey, I'm up against deadline. Has the date been set for Wayne Eriks's funeral?"

"No funeral," Janet replied, sounding unnaturally glum. "Private graveside service Thursday. Talk about cheap!"

"Cookie told me, but I thought maybe Al could twist her arm."

"Cookie!" Janet cried in disgust. "When did that meek little twit get a spine? Think she's got a guy on the side?"

"Which side? Get real. Did Cookie provide obit information?"

"He was born, he lived, and he died. Oh, he screwed. Tiff and poor Ringo. Good-looking until he smacked into some boulders. Closed casket."

"That's it? I mean about Wayne?"

"He's being cremated. In his case, we call it refried."

"Stop, please. You're —"

"Killing me?" Janet said. "Sorry about that, but we could use the money. Wait — don't die. You've got a lot to *screw* for — I mean *live* for."

"Good-bye, Janet." I went to the newsroom and asked Mitch to call Cookie about Wayne's obit. My phone rang as I got back to my desk.

"Hold the Eriks announcement," Janet said. "Dodge just called. He's not releasing the body."

"What?" I practically shrieked. "Are you serious?"

"When was I ever not?" Janet asked in mock indignation. "Don't you two ever stop doing it long enough to actually *talk*?"

"He'd better talk now," I said grimly. "Did he give you a reason?"

"No. Someday *you're* going to talk about what it's like in the sack with that guy. I have to wonder how he —"

"Shut up," I snapped. "I have to call Milo. I've got work to do."

"You call that work with Dodge? If I were you —"

I hung up and dialed the sheriff. Lori said her boss was on the phone. I realized Mitch

240

should stay with the Eriks story. But he, too, was on the phone. It sounded as if he was talking to Cookie. Amanda brought my mail and Vida's. I was getting more coffee when Mitch hung up.

"The widow does natter," he said, looking a little dazed. "We don't run baby pictures of the deceased, do we?"

"Only if it's for Ed Bronsky. It'd be the only way we'd get one of him weighing under a hundred —" I stopped as Milo entered the newsroom.

"You wanted to see me?" he asked gruffly.

"Yes, but you should really talk to —"

"Stop." He paused to pour coffee and grab a maple bar before stalking into my office. I shrugged at Mitch and followed the sheriff.

Milo sat down. "Close the door."

I obeyed and took my place behind the desk. "What's wrong?"

"No wonder we couldn't figure out how Eriks was electrocuted. He wasn't. What do you make of that, my little smart-assed newspaper sleuth?"

TEN

"I've no idea," I said, stupefied by the sheriff's bombshell.

"You mean . . . what *do* you mean?"

Milo finished chewing a chunk of maple bar. "I admit I was stumped about how it could happen. So was the M.E., Colin Knapp. I had the body shipped back to the hospital morgue, but I literally couldn't let it go. You may not believe this, but I paid attention to what you said last night. The stiff's already headed to Everett for a second opinion. Knapp's good, but he's fairly new, at least to doing autopsies in a county as big as SnoCo. This time he'll bring in the veterans, like Neal Doak."

I was confused. "You don't mean he could've died of natural causes and . . ." I shook my head. "I don't get it."

The sheriff grimaced. "Maybe he was run through after he was dead. We still don't know why he died. This time we'd better

242

find out."

I shivered. "That's creepy."

"You bet." Milo paused to finish the maple bar. "Keep this to yourself. That's why I bypassed Mitch. Your star reporter can think we're having a lovers' quarrel or some damned thing."

"He doesn't even know we're a couple."

Milo glanced over his shoulder. "The door's closed. Want to open it so he can figure it out?"

I giggled. "No. We're working, remember?"

"Right." The sheriff unfolded himself from the chair. "Got to go. How come you look so cute? The last I saw of you, you were staggering around the kitchen trying to find the coffeemaker and cussing a lot."

"It *was* morning. Go away, Sheriff."

He picked up the mug and opened the door. "Where's Vida?"

"She took the day off. Personal reasons."

"Christ," Milo said under his breath. "See you around, Emma."

Watching him amble out through the newsroom with a curt nod for Mitch, I couldn't resist smiling. But my reporter blotted out that brief bright spot when he came into my office two minutes later, demanding to know if I was usurping his story. "Hey," he said, leaning on my desk, "I thought I was handling news from the sheriff. If you want to take over, tell me. I don't like being kept in the dark."

"I don't like being bullied," I shot back. "Vida's diva act is bad enough. The Eriks story is still yours. There are other issues involving the sheriff's department. If you read my editorial, you'll find out."

Mitch slumped into a visitor's chair. "Sorry," he said wearily. "I'm not functioning at full speed mentally. It's bad enough having a son in prison, but it's worse with my wife clear across the country."

"It must be hell," I said with genuine sympathy. "Anything new?"

"I talked to Miriam last night. Brenda was asleep. It was after ten in Pittsburgh. She won't leave the condo. I guess the only thing I can do is bring her back here and send her to RestHaven. But I can't do that until our daughter can fly out here with her. Or I go get her. I don't know if they'll take Brenda or what it'll cost. I should ask Farrell."

"Do you think that once she's here in Alpine Brenda would be able to stay at home?"

Mitch looked bleak. "Maybe. Miriam's working, of course, but she has an elderly neighbor keeping tabs on Brenda during the day."

"You might be able to make the same kind of arrangement here," I said. "There are quite a few widows and other women who would be willing to do that, if only to relieve boredom or loneliness." Cookie Eriks came to mind, but I'd hold that thought for now.

Mitch smiled wanly and stood up. "Thanks, Emma. You're a good person. By the way, when I checked the log earlier, I gathered that one of the deputies had been suspended. Do we run that kind of thing?"

"No. That's an internal matter. It'd be a bad idea to broadcast that the sheriff was shorthanded. It might give would-be crooks ideas."

"In Detroit, they had plenty of their own. Do you know who it is?"

"Dodge didn't mention it to me this morning," I hedged.

"I just wondered. He strikes me as a hard guy to work for. He's pretty damned prickly and he's got a temper."

"He wasn't always like that," I said candidly. "He was more laid-back and quiet. He was always stubborn, though."

Mitch shrugged. "Maybe I'm wrong. You've known him longer than I have. I didn't like his attitude when Troy escaped

245

from Monroe. He seemed insensitive to our request to keep our son here at the hospital when he got pneumonia instead of shipping him back to prison."

"That wasn't his decision," I said. "He had to defer to the state."

Mitch looked incredulous. "Cops bend rules. They did it all the time in Detroit."

My face tightened. "This isn't Detroit. It's Alpine. And Dodge goes by the book. He always has."

Mitch shrugged. "Okay, you have a point. But I don't like his book much. How long has he been sheriff?"

"Twenty years? It used to be an elected position."

"Maybe we should do that again. Why was the process changed?"

"It doesn't make sense. Several counties appoint their sheriffs. I wrote editorials about it. Campaigning for a law enforcement official is a waste of time — and money. It interferes with the sheriff's duties. Police chiefs don't run for office. I don't think judges should be elected, either."

"Well . . ." Mitch ran a hand through his thick gray hair. "Maybe it's time to investigate Dodge's operation. How long has it been since anyone looked into how things work on his watch? Twenty years is a long time for a guy to run his own show without some serious scrutiny."

I was just a breath or two away from telling Mitch to stick it. But I held back. "Until something comes along that raises our hackles, let's not ask for trouble. I understand your feelings about how your son was dealt with. But it would never have happened if Troy hadn't escaped from prison twice *and* then caught pneumonia. He wouldn't have been behind bars if he hadn't been dealing drugs."

"That's a low blow," Mitch said softly, but with fervor. "I'd better go back to work."

He strode off to his desk. I held my head, thinking that the last thing Milo or I needed was a reporter on a vendetta. Reminding myself that I had a paper to put out, I too went back to work.

It was almost noon when Ross Blatt of Alpine Service & Repair came to see me. He was looking for his aunt Vida.

"If," he said after I informed him she'd taken the day off, "she's not here, where is she? I was supposed to check her furnace. I planned to do it last week, but I got the flu. She told me she'd leave the key under the mat, but it isn't there and her car's gone. Was she going out of town?"

"Not that I know of," I replied. "Did you

call her?"

Ross settled his stocky body into a chair. "I tried her home and her cell phone. She didn't answer. That's why I figured she'd be here."

"Did you call your cousin Amy?"

"She didn't answer, either." His bushy graying eyebrows almost met in a frown. "Maybe they went somewhere together."

I had a sudden thought. "Have you talked to Buck Bardeen?"

The query seemed to catch Ross by surprise. "No. That might be worth a try." He grinned. "Somehow I can never quite take in that Aunt Vida has a boyfriend. I've met him a few times, but I always think of her as . . . sort of old-fashioned. I mean . . ." His broad face reddened slightly.

"I know what you mean," I said, to save Ross embarrassment. "But believe it or not, your aunt's human."

He chuckled. "Yeah, sure. Sometimes the rest of the family forgets that. Thanks," he added, getting up. "I'll call the colonel right away."

I was tempted to ask Ross to let me know if he found out where Vida was, but I didn't want to sound like a snoopy boss. Instead I changed the subject. "Is your part of the work done now at RestHaven?"

"It is, unless something breaks. Hey, do you remember Clarence Munn, the guy who owned Bucker Logging?"

"I recall the name," I said. "In fact, your aunt mentioned him just recently. She told me he's at RestHaven."

Ross nodded. "I had a long talk with him last week. He's got that problem where he forgets what happened five minutes ago, but boy, has he got a memory that goes way back. I told him he should write a book about the gyppo loggers he bought his timber from. That kind of logging is almost gone around here. He's got stories to tell if you're interested."

"I might be," I said. "I'll make a note."

Ross thanked me for my time and left as my phone rang.

"Are you free for lunch?" Rosemary Bourgette asked.

"Yes. Do you want to join me?"

"Is the ski lodge coffee shop okay?"

"Sure." My watch showed a quarter to noon. "I can leave now."

"Meet you there," she said, and rang off.

Rosemary had just pulled into the parking lot when I arrived. We exchanged chitchat until we were seated in the busy coffee shop.

"Good," she said after the hostess left us. "I don't recognize anybody who might overhear us. They're hosting a gardening conference."

"Yes, Vida wrote it up. Is she the subject of our get-together?"

"Wait until we order," Rosemary said as the typical blond ski lodge waitress came toward us. Rosemary opted for the Caesar with extra anchovies. I decided to have the same.

"Holly has landed," Rosemary announced after the waitress left. "She has an older sister in Centralia who's offered to take on her and the kids. Esther Brant helped Holly make the arrangements."

"And it's been approved?" I asked in surprise.

Rosemary nodded. "The sister's name is Dawn Harrison. Married, two kids of her own older than Holly's brood. Unlike Holly, Dawn has apparently led a blameless life. I think she's very brave. Or crazy."

"Is Holly in town?"

"Supposedly. Esther notified me Holly was on her way and asked me to make sure the child's transition goes smoothly. That's the problem. I can't reach Amy Hibbert, and Amanda said Vida wasn't at work today. She's not home, either. Do you know where she is?"

I sighed. "No. Did you call her son-in-law,

Ted, at the state highway department?"

"Yes, but he's in Olympia at a meeting. Roger's not at RestHaven. Being a volunteer, he isn't accountable for his time."

"He's not accountable for much," I murmured, feeling a sense of unease come over me. "Maybe Vida and Amy have gone to visit someone and took Diddy with them. Does Diddy have a real name?"

Rosemary looked askance. "It's Leonardo. Holly must be a DiCaprio fan. I think she saw *Gangs of New York* once too often."

Our salads arrived along with a basket of warm rolls. I speared an anchovy before speaking again. "Is it your duty to oversee that Holly gets her child back? Doesn't Roger have rights as a father?"

Rosemary looked exasperated. "No, it's not my duty, and yes, Roger has rights, if he can prove he's the dad. Has he taken a paternity test?"

"I don't know," I said, adding dressing to my salad. "It might be the one test Roger could pass. How come you're stuck with the job?"

"Esther Brant's a control freak. She likes to remind us little people how much clout she has. An officer of the court should do this, but we don't have enough staff. When there's a custody battle, we turn it over to the state. I'm hoping it won't come to that. This could get ugly, though."

I paused before taking a bite of roll. "What do you mean?"

Rosemary leaned forward and lowered her voice. "You know that Holly Gross is a piece of work. More to the point, if the Hibberts and Vida are trying to keep her from getting her hands on Diddy — especially if Roger has no proof that he's the father — they could be subject to criminal charges. You wouldn't want to see Vida in jail, would you?"

Driving back to the *Advocate* office, I wondered what next could happen to my staff. I had visions of Amanda giving premature birth in the office, Kip becoming so absorbed in his high-tech world that he became catatonic, and Leo draining a fifth of Scotch before my very eyes.

But all seemed calm when I returned. Both men were sane and sober, while Amanda was quite chipper and still pregnant. I did ask if there was any word from Vida. There wasn't, but Amanda told me that Mitch had gone to see Dr. Farrell at RestHaven. "He's so gloomy," she said. "It's his wife, isn't it? I heard him on the phone when I put a couple of engagement announcements on your desk. They were in Vida's mail."

I made short work of the engagements, which involved two couples I'd never heard of, though both would-be grooms attended Skykomish Community College. My phone rang just after I sent them to Kip.

"Why," my own fiancé groaned, "didn't I become a game warden like I wanted to do as a kid?"

"I never knew you had a yen for that," I said. "Are you considering a midlife career change?"

"I'm too damned old. Laskey's not in, so I'll give you the latest pain in the ass. Jack Blackwell just reported Tiffany Eriks Rafferty as missing. She's been gone since Sunday."

I was nonplussed. "Where's her kid?"

"Not with Jack or Cookie, so I guess the kid's with her. She took all her clothes and some of the kid's stuff, along with Jack's Range Rover. Cookie's hysterical. I can't get a coherent sentence out of her."

"Good grief! Is Jack upset or mad?"

"Except for threatening to run me out of town if I don't find her by sunset, he's being his usual asshole self. Do you want to send Mitch to get the APB or should I have Lori drop it off?"

I paused. "I'll send Mitch, but I warn you, he's not in a good mood."

"Who is?" On that sour note, the sheriff rang off.

For the next hour I scrambled around, checking with Kip to make sure we had Vida's page ready, taking a last look at my editorial, and proofing the cut lines in the special section. I finally read the brief Lord-Dodge engagement announcement. It was the last of four, which perhaps was due to Vida's current opinion of Milo and me. At least she didn't refer to us as ninnies.

By three, Mitch had handed in the rest of his items, including Tiffany's APB and Wayne's obit. "I didn't know he had a son who died."

"The Eriks family has had their share of tragedies. Most people do before it's time to write their obits."

Mitch looked chastened. "He must've been young. How did he die?"

"A rafting accident on the Snake River. He was with two other teens who survived."

"Not foul play?"

The question surprised me, even if I'd thought of it myself. "I guess not. I didn't know about it until after I moved here."

Mitch shook his head. "I covered boating accidents not only on the lakes, but on the

Detroit River. It's actually a strait. For years it was so polluted that you expected to see almost anything floating in it, including a body. A few were dead before they hit the water. Talk about filth."

The reference to filth reminded me of the follow-up on Edna Mae's rumor. "Did you ask Karl Freeman about porn at the high school?"

Mitch looked pained. "He fobbed me off, saying it was a matter of student privacy. Given that the majority of kids aren't yet eighteen, he couldn't discuss it."

"So there *is* a problem," I said.

"That's my guess. Have you got any spies on the faculty?"

I shook my head. "I play bridge with Molly Freeman, Coach Ridley's wife, Dixie, and Linda Grant, but they've never joined my fan club."

"When do you play bridge again?"

"Not for a couple of weeks." An idea landed on my brain. "I have one ally in the group, Janet Driggers. Maybe I'll get her to broach the subject. She's a gamer with a bawdy mouth."

Mitch nodded once and made his exit.

Shortly after four I called Vida, but she didn't pick up. I dialed Amy's number next — with the same futile result. I was about to bite the bullet and call Buck when I heard raised voices in the front office. I went through the empty newsroom to find Holly Gross shaking her fist at Amanda. To my office manager's credit, she didn't flinch. "Go ahead," Amanda said. "I'm not lying. Ask the boss."

Holly whirled around so fast that she knocked a paper cup off the counter. Luckily, it was empty. "You better come clean, Emma Lord. If you don't, there'll be all hell to pay for everybody who works here!"

I studied Holly with an appraising eye. If she'd acquired any prison pallor while being locked up, it didn't show under the heavy layer of makeup. As I recalled, her skin was naturally pale. The dishwater-blond hair trailed over her narrow shoulders, and her pewter-gray eyes seemed sharper than when I'd seen her in October at the Icicle Creek Tavern.

"What do you want?" I asked calmly.

"That old bat of a Runkel woman. Where is she?"

"I don't know," I said. "I just tried to call her, but she isn't home."

"Bullshit," Holly snapped. "If *you* don't know, who does?"

"Good question," I said, still calm. "Why don't you call her daughter, Amy Hibbert?"

"I've already been there," Holly replied, losing a bit of steam. "Nobody's home. I can't get Rog, either."

I'd never heard anyone call Roger "Rog" before. At first I thought she said "Raj" and was referring to somebody from India. "He might be working at RestHaven," I suggested.

Holly scowled. "What's RestHaven?"

"The rehab facility on River Road. Don't you remember that they were remodeling the Bronsky place before you went . . . out of town?"

"Who gives a shit?" Holly retorted. "I want my Dippy."

" 'Dippy'?" I echoed. "I thought his name was Diddy."

"It's Dippy, for Leonardo DiCaprio. Get it?"

I shrugged. "I guess you'll have to wait until the Hibberts or Mrs. Runkel gets home."

Holly fumbled with the long silver chain that dangled over her tight black V-neck top. "They won't get away with it," she finally said. "I'm going to see the sheriff."

Before I could say anything, she hurtled through the door.

"Wow," Amanda murmured, "am I glad Walt and I didn't do something rash and take in one of her kids."

I picked up the paper cup and tossed it in the wastebasket. "I'd better warn Milo," I said, heading back to my office.

The sheriff answered on the second ring. "What's for dinner?" he asked, obviously having seen my number on the caller ID.

"Never mind. Holly Gross is on her way to see you. She can't find any of the Runkel gang."

"Shit!" Milo was silent for so long that I wondered if he'd gotten up and made for the rear exit. "Okay," he finally said in a tired voice. "I take it you don't know where Vida is?"

"She's not answering either of her phones. No response at the Hibberts' house. Ted's in Olympia. Holly came here and pitched a five-star fit."

"I'll let Doe handle it. She's good at that sort of thing. She can play good cop and bad cop all at once when she's dealing with women." He paused. "How about fried chicken? You haven't made that for a while."

"How about you picking some up at the Grocery Basket's deli? I've got a paper to put out." For once I hung up on the sheriff.

I followed through on my call to Buck Bardeen. "Well," he said, chuckling, "if you're asking about Vida's whereabouts, I can't tell you."

"Can't or won't?"

He chuckled again, a deep, rich sound. "Now Emma, do you expect me to keep track of Vida's every move? She's always on the go. I can't keep up with her sometimes. I suppose that's part of her many charms."

I wasn't in the mood to contemplate any of Vida's charms, but I suspected that the colonel was stonewalling me. "Okay, I guess I'll just have to wait for her to show up." I also figured that Buck either didn't know her whereabouts or, being an honorable military man, didn't want to know. "Thanks, Buck," I said, and rang off.

It was going on five. I went into the back shop to check on Kip's progress. So far everything was going smoothly.

"Are we expecting late-breaking news?" he asked.

"I don't think so. Did you put Tiffany's APB on our website?"

Kip nodded. "That's really weird. If she's taken off, she'll miss her dad's burial service. I mean, she showed up at old Mrs. Rafferty's funeral but won't be here for her own father's?"

I hadn't thought about that. "Maybe she'll be back by then. Tiffany's in your peer group. Do you know of any close friends

259

she might be staying with?"

"She was a year ahead of me in high school," Kip replied, looking thoughtful. "I can't think of anybody. She was the kind of girl who was always with a group of kids. You know — at school, the mall, wherever. The only guy she went steady with was Tim, and that was after graduation. Wouldn't her mom know?"

"Milo says Cookie's reverted to type and is a mess." I shrugged. "It's not up to us to find her. We've got enough trouble tracking down Vida."

I started to head out of the back shop, but Kip stopped me by asking what had caused the ruckus in the front office. I explained it was Holly Gross, trying to find Vida or any of the Hibberts.

Kip frowned. "I guess Holly was born to make trouble."

I nodded. "She already has." I didn't need to add that I suspected there was more on the way.

ELEVEN

Shortly after five, Kip and I were the only ones left in the office. He was still in the back shop, where he'd spend the evening finishing his part of the job. Unless he ran into problems or there was late-breaking news, my on-site responsibilities were complete. But I would stay by the phone until he put the paper to bed around eleven.

I was gathering up my belongings when Jennifer Hood stepped into the newsroom. "Ms. Lord?" she called, seeing me standing by my desk. "Have you got a minute?"

"Sure," I said. "Come in. And please call me Emma."

She gave me a tentative smile as I offered her a visitor's chair. "I'm not sure I should be doing this," she said. "I feel awkward, but I need your advice. I know we just met, but you seem very levelheaded."

"Thanks," I said, trying not to hide my surprise. "What's wrong?"

Jennifer brushed at her curly auburn hair. "I had the radio on when I left work just now. The news on the local station mentioned that a woman from Alpine was reported missing. Tiffany something. I didn't catch the full name. Do you know about this?"

I nodded. "Yes. She's the daughter of the PUD man who was killed near RestHaven last week."

Jennifer gasped. "No! Really?"

"I'm afraid so." Briefly I explained Tiffany's background, including Tim Rafferty's tragic death. I kept my tone neutral, the same way I reported straight news in the *Advocate.*

"That poor woman must be half crazed," Jennifer said. "No wonder she came to Rest-Haven this afternoon."

I couldn't conceal my shock. "You mean she asked for help?"

"I don't know," Jennifer admitted. "She went to see Kay Burns. I assumed at the time that she had some sort of P.R. business. But I saw her go into Kay's office and overheard just enough before the door was closed to know who she was. Of course she fit the description on the news except for the hair color, and Kay called her by name."

My brain was going around in circles. Kay,

who had been married to Jack Blackwell. Tiffany, who had moved in with him. Was that all they had in common? I certainly didn't know. And why wasn't Tiffany spotted in town? "What color was Tiffany's hair?" I asked.

"Black."

"Tiffany's fair-haired," I said. "She must be wearing a wig, or perhaps she dyed her hair. You have to report this to the sheriff. Shall I call for you?"

Jennifer seemed conflicted, fingering the edge of my desk as if she were playing the piano. "Will it get her in trouble?"

"She may be in trouble already." I picked up the phone. "I have to do this, but if you want to remain anonymous, that's fine."

"Maybe I shouldn't give my name," she said. "It *is* a new job. I don't want to jeopardize my position."

To my relief, Milo answered. "Don't nag," he barked. "I'm going to the damned deli as soon as I finish up here."

"Never mind that," I said, hoping Jennifer couldn't hear him. "I've got a Tiffany sighting from this afternoon at RestHaven."

"No shit. This better not be Averill Fairbanks seeing her land a spaceship in the Italian garden. Is that where Ed ate spaghetti?"

263

"No, *Sheriff*," I said, hoping he'd catch on that I wasn't free to tell him to shut the hell up.

"Where and when?" Milo asked, now very much the lawman.

I scribbled "What time?" on a piece of paper and pushed it at my visitor, then said into the phone, "In one of the RestHaven offices."

Jennifer wrote down "3:15." I scrawled another note: "ID Kay?"

I gave Milo the time, but Jennifer was shaking her head. The sheriff didn't like vague answers. "Whose office?" he asked sharply.

"I can't say," I said.

"You will," Milo said, sounding more like his old laconic self. "I gather the person who reported this is with you now."

"Yes."

"Have you got a gun to your head?"

"No, of course not."

"I'll grill you at home. If I don't see you in half an hour, I'll put out an APB on *you*." He hung up on me. Again.

Jennifer looked sheepish. "I'm sorry. But I hope you understand the position I'm in."

"Journalists are used to this sort of thing — 'an anonymous source.' It's a start. I

don't suppose you saw a Rover parked outside?"

"I didn't go outside. It was raining, so I
took the covered walkway between the
buildings. Even if I had gone the other way,
I might not have noticed it. At the time, the
incident didn't seem important."

"Of course. I really appreciate your coming forward. But I have to ask, why me? You
could've gone straight to the sheriff."

Jennifer shook her head. "I don't know
the sheriff, but I know you. Being from
Dunsmuir, I'm familiar with small towns.
You have to feel your way when it comes to
trusting people. I instinctively felt you could
be discreet. Small-town newspaper editors
have to be, don't they?"

"Yes, they do," I said as we both stood up.
"Though I assure you, Sheriff Dodge is very
trustworthy."

She smiled. "He wouldn't be picking up
dinner if he wasn't."

I laughed. "He's also kind of loud."

Her smile faded. "All the same, I hope
you can keep me out of this."

"Don't worry," I said as we walked out of
my office together. I wasn't about to make a
promise I couldn't keep.

Milo arrived home fifteen minutes later than

he'd indicated on the phone. "Your ice is probably melting," I said, nodding at the fridge.

He wrapped an arm around my neck and kissed me. "I got waylaid by Jake O'Toole at the Grocery Basket. He's filing a complaint tomorrow about shoplifters. There's an epidemic, according to him. Not kids, he figures. The big-ticket item is wine."

"Why not kids, if they're broke and under age?"

"Because the thieves only steal the good stuff. Kids don't know the difference. Where do you want me to put the fried chicken?"

"Leave it on the counter. Go change. I'll rescue your drink. I'm making potato salad because you wanted it the other night."

"Good," he said, swatting my rear before leaving the kitchen.

Ten minutes later he returned as I was setting the oven to heat the chicken. It took me another five minutes before I finished explaining about Dwight and Jack's ex-wife, Jennifer, and Tiffany. By that time we'd migrated to our usual places in the living room, drinks in hand.

"If I'd known about Kay," Milo said, looking faintly remorseful, "I wouldn't have been so rough on Gould. Nobody knows better than I do what a pain an ex can be.

Still, that's no excuse for his going after Bill Blatt. Damn, I wish people could leave their private lives at home."

"I could say the same about Mitch. But we all do. You were a real beast after we broke up. So was I. It's a wonder my staff didn't mutiny."

Milo looked surprised. "You were? I didn't think you cared."

"I didn't think so, either," I admitted ruefully. "But obviously I did. That's how I ended up on sleeping pills and Paxil."

Milo grinned at me. "God, Emma, didn't that tell you something?"

"No. I was still in my 'dopey phase,' as you call it. I blamed it on menopause, and maybe it was, but I couldn't get along without you."

"Same here. I tried to avoid you, but with our jobs being so close, it was tough. Maybe you should've worn a disguise." Milo sipped his drink. "Why's Tiff skulking around in a black wig? Why was she seeing Kay? They have one thing in common — Blackwell. If Kay's P.R., she knew he was speaking at the opening."

I nodded. "But nobody else has seen Tiffany?"

"No. It doesn't mean they haven't or that she didn't leave town for a day or two. This

Jennifer didn't say Tiff had the kid with her, right?"

"I imagine she'd have mentioned it."

"I guess I'll have to tell Blackwell," Milo said. "I don't like doing that. If he can find Tiff, he might beat the crap out of her. He used to do that with Patti Marsh. Not that she ever had the guts to file a complaint."

"I saw the bruises. She always lied about how she got them."

"Classic case of abuse. I wonder if Patti's seen Tiffany."

"I don't get it," I said. "Tiffany moved in with Jack a week ago. How did she get disillusioned so fast? He gave her money to buy clothes from Francine Wells. It makes no sense."

"Maybe," Milo suggested, "he didn't give her the money. She might have swiped it from him. That could've started a row and she walked."

I nodded halfheartedly. "Tiff's not the quick-thinking type. You figure she's making the rounds of Blackwell's ex-squeezes?"

"Could be." Milo drummed his fingers on the arm of the easy chair. "I'll talk to Patti tomorrow. She's a lousy liar."

"Good idea," I said, standing up. "Maybe by that time my usual font of all knowledge will be back to work."

"Vida can't stay away forever. Rosemary's pissed," Milo said, following me into the kitchen to top off our drinks. "She figures the Hibberts are pulling a fast one."

"I hope not, but I'm worried," I said, putting the chicken into the oven before turning to Milo. "Should I report the Tiffany sighting in the paper? I don't want to set off Blackwell if they've had a big fight."

Milo gave me a wry look. "You're asking *me* for newspaper advice?"

I put my hands on his shoulders. "Maybe I do sound like a wife."

He leaned down to kiss me. "I like that. I won't tell you what to do, but as a husband, I'd say news of the sighting could cause big trouble."

"You're right," I said — and kissed him back.

There were no back-shop crises or urgent calls for the sheriff that evening. "Why," I said to Milo after we were in bed and he'd turned off the light, "do I feel this is like the lull before the storm?"

"Are you looking for a crisis?" he asked, holding me close. "Don't."

"I know what you're thinking," I said. "We both know it's coming. We just don't know from which direction."

I felt him sigh. "Right. It's built into our jobs." He rested his chin on the top of my head. "I wonder when I'll get a second opinion on the Eriks autopsy. It could take days. By the way, the bones Bebe Everson found belonged to a gopher."

"Poor Roy. What do they expect to find with Eriks?"

"If I knew, why would I need a second opinion?"

"Maybe you don't." I turned just enough to try to look at him. "You could be holding out on me, big guy."

Milo didn't say anything. I shut up and went to sleep in the sanctuary of his arms.

To my relief, Vida was at her desk when I arrived the next morning. She looked tired, an unusual state for her. But she greeted me in a pleasant fashion. "You managed without me," she said. "I'll do the advice letters first. Did I miss anything vital?"

"You did," I said, pouring a mug of coffee. Amanda hadn't yet arrived from the bakery run. "Or have you already heard about Tiff?"

"Kip informed me," Vida said, fiddling with the silk roses of her felt sailor hat. "I'm not surprised."

I felt smug. "But Kip doesn't know Tiff

showed up at RestHaven.”

Vida’s gray eyes widened behind her big glasses. “Well now! As a patient or seeking a job?”

“I don’t know,” I said. “I thought Roger might have seen her there.”

“Roger took the day off. He felt a cold coming on.” She paused as Mitch made his entrance, mumbling a subdued greeting to both of us.

Vida shot me a curious glance. I shrugged. “Is there anything else I should know?” she asked, fists on hips.

“Oh — Kay Barton Burns is doing P.R. at RestHaven.”

It was rare that I could surprise Vida. “No!” She fingered her chin and scowled. “My, my — she’s been gone for twenty-five years. Why would she come back to Alpine after so long? It’s very smart of her — she *is* a native. The tug of her hometown must’ve done it. Of course Roger wouldn’t realize who she is. He was just a wee lad when she left.”

In my opinion the chunky Roger had never been wee, except in the brains department. I turned to Mitch, who was sitting down at his desk with his own coffee mug. “Fill Vida in on Kay Burns. I’ve never met her.”

Mitch didn't look happy about the request, but he got up and went over to Vida's desk while I headed into my cubbyhole. Maybe, I hoped, things were returning to some state of normality.

Less than an hour later, after Mitch had returned from checking the sheriff's log, the storm Milo and I had predicted hit.

"All hell broke out," my reporter announced, slumping into one of my visitor's chairs. "I'd just gotten there when Jack Blackwell came roaring in about his missing girlfriend. She'd been spotted at the ski lodge last night by somebody who went to high school with her. Blackwell and Dodge almost got into it right behind the reception counter."

"Oh, no!" I gasped. "Is . . . are they okay?"

Mitch nodded. "Mullins and Heppner got between them. They managed to haul Blackwell outside. Dodge was pissed because he wanted Blackwell to slug him so he could arrest the guy for assaulting an officer of the law. Didn't I tell you the sheriff's a prickly guy?"

"I don't blame him," I declared. "Dodge didn't cause Tiffany to run off. Jack probably slugged *her.* Beating up women is a habit of his."

"That's what the sheriff said, and that's

what really set Blackwell off. He told Dodge he wasn't one to talk about guys who shacked up with women who weren't their wives. That really riled Dodge. I'll bet Blackwell reports this to the other county commissioners."

I didn't know what to say. Luckily, Leo appeared in the doorway, apparently having overheard part of Mitch's account.

"A dust-up at the sheriff's?" my ad manager remarked with a puckish expression. "Laskey, it's time for you to choose sides in this town. Stick with the good guys — Dodge is one of them. Sure, Blackwell employs a lot of people and he runs a decent operation. But his private life's a mess. Trust me, when he leaves his mill, Jack's a jackass."

Mitch shrugged. "I've talked to him a few times. He seems okay. He doesn't look half as intimidating as Dodge."

"That's because Blackwell's shorter," Leo said. "Emma's known Dodge longer than I have." He looked at me. "Has he ever scared you?"

"Aggravated, yes. Scared, never."

Leo held up his hands. "See? Vida will say the same thing."

"Nobody scares her. Okay," Mitch said resignedly, standing up. "But it seems this could be the kind of thing we're waiting for."

"Uh . . . ," I began, but Leo interrupted.

"Waiting for what?" he asked, looking at Mitch and then at me.

Mitch cleared his throat. "Emma and I were discussing an investigation of how Dodge runs law enforcement. He's been on the job for twenty years — too damned long without some transparency."

Leo flung an arm around Mitch's shoulders. "We need to have lunch. It's Wednesday, a day of semi-rest. Why don't we . . ."

I didn't hear the rest of what my ad manager was saying as he led my reporter back into the newsroom. *Thank God for Leo,* I thought. *What will I do without him if he retires and goes back to his family in California?*

But I didn't have to think about that. What I did have to do was wait a decent interval before I went to see the sheriff. Meanwhile, I pondered why Tiffany had been at the ski lodge. On a whim, I called the manager, Henry Bardeen, who was also Buck's younger brother.

"My daughter saw her," Henry said. "Heather was a year ahead of Tiffany in school. She didn't recognize Tiff at first because her hair was dark, but when Heather heard she was missing, she realized it was her."

"Who told Jack Blackwell she'd been seen?"

"Not Heather," he replied. "The only one she told was her pal Chaz Phipps. Chaz works for Blackwell, so I suppose she told Jack."

"Was Tiff just passing through?"

"Heather saw her in the lobby talking to a man she didn't recognize. Maybe a guest from the gardening group or a dinner patron. Oh — here's Bill Blatt. I bet he'll ask the same questions you did."

I rang off, wondering about the stranger. Henry and Heather knew all the locals, except maybe not the entire RestHaven staff. Visitors kept the ski lodge in business. It was futile to dwell on an unknown patron.

A few minutes after nine-thirty I headed out into the morning drizzle toward the sheriff's office. Just as I was passing Parker's Pharmacy, Donna Wickstrom crossed Front Street and stopped to wave at me.

"Guess what?" she said excitedly. "I finally heard from Craig Laurentis. He's got a new painting. I won't get it at the gallery for another week or so, but I thought you'd like to know he's okay."

Relief swept over me. There had been no word of our reclusive artist since his release from the hospital in early December after being shot by someone who thought he might be a homicide witness. "That's great," I said. "I've been worried. Why aren't you at your day care?"

Donna smiled. "It's tax time, so I made your truant receptionist, Ginny, sub for me. Owning two businesses makes filing complicated. Steve surrenders and tells me to farm it out to a tax expert. I hand all the financial stuff to my brother, Rick, at the bank, and my sister-in-law fills in for me at the day care. We like to keep everything in the family."

"Sensible." I realized a puddle was forming underfoot. The potholes were another reminder of SkyCo's lack of funds for basic maintenance. "It's raining harder," I said. "I'd better let you get on with your errands. Let me know when Craig's painting arrives."

Donna promised she would and hurried on her way. I moved quickly along the half block to the sheriff's office. Milo's Yukon was in its usual spot, so I figured he was in. Bracing myself for the usual glower from Heppner and the familiar leer from Mullins, I made my entrance.

"Wow!" Jack exclaimed. "I'll bet you're worried that your favorite stud might be in a bad mood. Are you armed?"

"Watch your mouth, Jack," I retorted. "I'm not armed, but I'm dangerous. His door's closed. Is he beating up an innocent bystander?"

Jack laughed, but Sam scowled. "You better not pester him with some dumb questions about your remodeling. Save that for after hours."

"Don't I always?" I retorted. "Stick it, Sam. *I'm* not in a good mood."

Sam's scowl turned into a full glower. "I don't take orders from anybody except Dodge. You forgot who's boss here?"

I glared right back. "Have I ever?"

Lori Cobb's arrival broke the tension. "I've got coffee," she announced. "Hi, Emma. We ran out this morning. Dwight was supposed to buy some, but he's . . . not here."

"So that's what's wrong with everybody," I said, turning to Sam. "You take it with sugar, right? It might improve your disposition." I opened the swinging half door in the counter and marched to Milo's office. My knock elicited a barked response that sounded like "Yeah?" but could have been a growl from the resident bear.

"Hi," I said, entering the sheriff's lair and closing the door. "I heard about your confrontation. Didn't you drink enough coffee at home?"

"A gallon wouldn't be enough to keep me from wanting to kick Blackwell's ass all the way to Wenatchee."

I'd sat down in my usual place on the other side of the desk. "He's not originally from here, is he?"

"He's a California native, but came here from Oregon — Albany, I think." Milo gazed at the ceiling. "That was almost thirty years ago. He had mills in Oregon and Idaho. The old Wellington & Scenic Mill was up for grabs. Two brothers from Darrington owned it, but they were in their eighties back then. The place needed updating, logging was in its decline, and Jack was willing to put money into it. Not long after that, he bought out Clarence Munn's Bucker Logging operation and managed the two mills. Everybody thought he was a hero. Marius called him the town's savior."

I smiled. "From what I've heard about Marius Vandeventer, he called anybody who spent more than a grand around here a savior."

"Oh, yeah," Milo agreed. "Marius was a booster. We were surprised when he moved away after he sold the paper. I don't think Vida's forgiven Marius for what she called his 'defection.' Is he still alive?"

"I'm not sure," I said. "Vida always heard from him at Christmas, but she hasn't mentioned him lately. The Vandeventers retired to the desert. I only met him twice, and he left town before I arrived. Vida broke me in. And you're the one who told me he'd been trying to sell the paper for a couple of years. That's when I discovered I'd paid too much for it. I wanted to kick myself."

"Sounds like Marius." Milo leaned back in his chair, hands behind his head. "Funny thing about you, little Emma. You make me feel better even when I'm not feeling you."

"Oh, Milo . . ." I almost simpered.

"Let's change the subject before I . . . Skip it," he said, sitting up. "Why are you here?"

"Mitch's report unsettled me. I was worried about you."

Milo looked askance, but proffered a cigarette. "Is the coffee on?"

I accepted the cigarette and leaned over so that Milo could light it for me. "Lori just came back. No word from SnoCo's lab junkies?"

The sheriff shook his head. "I don't expect to hear yet."

"No more Tiffany sightings?"

"No. Bill phoned from the ski lodge. Tiff wasn't staying there. She had dinner with some guy nobody recognized. No kid with her."

We were both silent for a few moments. "I can't think of anybody from out of town that Tiffany would know. She hardly ever left Alpine."

Milo's shrugged. "So where's the kid?"

"You mean Ashley Rafferty?"

"Ashley?" Milo shrugged. "Yeah, that kid." He was staring off into space. "Go away, Emma. I'm trying to think."

I started to stand up, but hesitated. "About what?"

He still didn't look at me. "I'll let you know when I figure it out."

I left Milo to his thoughts. After I stopped at the bank to make a payment on my Visa card, Amanda greeted me with news of a visitor waiting in my office. "She says you'll be surprised to see her."

I thought of Mavis. "Is she about my age or maybe a bit older?"

"Yes," Amanda said. "She got here just a few minutes ago. I gave her coffee. She mentioned having had quite a long drive."

Leo was the only staffer at his desk and he was on the phone. But as I went through the newsroom, I saw the back of the woman sitting in one of my visitor's chairs and realized it wasn't Mavis. In fact, I didn't recognize the dark blond middle-aged woman when she turned around.

"Emma Lord," she said, remaining seated. "You look befuddled. I think I've caught you off guard."

Somehow I managed to sit down without falling over my own feet. "You did," I said. "Have we met? I'm not very good at remembering faces."

"No." My guest's faintly ruddy face looked smug. "I thought you might have seen pictures. I'm Tricia, the first Mrs. Dodge."

TWELVE

"Oh." I couldn't keep from slumping in my chair. "I'm sorry. I mean, I've never seen a photo of you."

"Milo probably burned the ones I left behind." Tricia licked rose-colored lips. "I would've thought you'd be curious enough to check out our wedding picture in the newspaper."

I shook my head. "No. I believed Milo when he said you used to be married. I *have* met your children a few times over the years."

Tricia nodded. I wondered if she was enjoying her advantage over me. I still felt knocked for a loop as I tried to see what this plump, blue-eyed, tinted-haired woman might have looked like thirty years ago. Her features were good, if somewhat coarsened by age. She was probably a few inches taller than my five-four, but most people are. I couldn't judge much about the rest of her, which was covered by a Burberry raincoat. Aware that I was trembling, I kept my hands in my lap.

"I didn't mean to upset you," she said, looking pained. "I came here as one mother calling on another mother for help."

"For Tanya?" I said, beginning to get a grip on my nerves.

She nodded again. "I'm at my wits' end. She refuses to stay in Bellevue. Short of crawling back into my womb, Tanya insists she feels safe only here in Alpine, where she grew up. And with her father, who, I will admit, was a pillar during her recovery from the gunshot wound."

"Milo is a very strong person," I said. "He was extremely disturbed when she took those pills. Frustrated, too."

"I was shocked. At first her spirits seemed improved in Hawaii." Tricia licked her lips again. "We were there almost a week, but by the fourth day Tanya didn't want to go to the beach. So many of the young men reminded her of Bruce."

I'd never heard her late fiancé's real name. Milo only called him Buster. "That would be upsetting," I conceded, trying to recall if the men in Rome had evoked Tom's image when I went there with Ben to recover my own equilibrium. But I had not needed —

or wanted — any look-alikes to bring back my fiancé's image. It was always with me, like a bad habit.

"It got worse when we came home," Tricia went on. She shook her head. "Never mind the details. I'm here to ask you to be understanding about my — our — daughter. She needs her father now more than she needs me. Milo wasn't with us when Bruce shot Tanya and then killed himself. I was." She shuddered. "It was beyond horrible."

I fought the memory of Tom falling dead at my feet. Maybe Tricia had forgotten — or never knew — what I'd been through. That didn't matter. "I do sympathize," I said.

Tricia smiled, though I didn't sense much warmth. Maybe she didn't have any to give. "I must go. Milo wasn't in when we stopped at his office. I left Tanya with Aunt Thelma and Uncle Elmer at the retirement home. Perhaps we'll meet again."

I recalled Ben urging me to make an ally of Tricia. Maybe this was a start. "I hope so," I said, standing up. "Will you be in town long?"

"No," she said, also on her feet. "I'll go back as soon as I get Tanya settled. I have an appointment tomorrow morning in Bellevue. By the way, do you have a key to

Milo's house?"

"No. I never had one."

"Oh." Tricia looked mildly surprised. "Then I'll wait until he gets back from wherever he is. Typical — so often he wasn't around when I needed him." She shrugged and walked out through the newsroom.

Leo appeared as soon as Tricia left the premises. "Was that Holly's lawyer from Everett, by any chance?"

"That," I said wearily, "was the first Mrs. Dodge."

"No shit!" Leo exclaimed, sitting down. "Did she harangue you?"

"She wanted my help with Tanya. I actually felt sorry for her." I bit my lower lip. "Or maybe she's trying to guilt-trip me."

He offered me a cigarette and I took it. "What are you supposed to do? Adopt her?"

"Be sympathetic. I can do that, but it plays havoc with our private life. Milo can't babysit Tanya. He doesn't even know she's back in town."

"Maybe he knew they were coming and fled the scene."

"Milo wouldn't do that."

"Vida will be sorry she missed Tricia. Or did she like her?"

"No. Tricia was from Sultan. That's where they got married. Vida never got over the affront to Alpine. Where *is* Vida, by the way?"

"Still off on her appointed rounds," Leo said, after a glance into the newsroom. "She was going to see Dot Parker. Vida thought maybe Tiffany left her kid with Grandma and Grandpa."

"Good guess. Nothing about a Holly Gross encounter?"

"Not a peep." Leo stood up. "I'm taking Mitch to lunch to try to get his head straight about Dodge. Do you want me to mention your not-so-professional involvement with the sheriff?"

I grimaced. "No. I'll do it myself. I'm waiting for the right moment."

"Fine. Hey, babe, Tanya can't hang around with Dodge forever. She's, what? In her thirties? She'll settle down and want a life of her own. Right now, maybe she's just a pawn in some game of Tricia's."

"I hope it's not a game," I said. "The timing stinks."

"I don't mean to be nosy," he said, flicking off his cigarette ash, "but you two never lived together when you were dating before?"

"No. He wanted a more permanent arrangement. I didn't." I gave Leo a sheepish look. "I was still clinging to the Tom Cavanaugh dream."

"Well . . ." Leo's expression was wry. "Tom was as screwed up as the rest of us. It was just less obvious. Ever think what might've happened if Dodge had to arrest him and turn him over to the feds for running guns to the wild Irishmen?"

I extinguished my cigarette. "Yes. It took me a couple of years before I could think about Tom technically being a criminal."

"Tom didn't see it that way. He thought he was being noble."

"I know. But the government wouldn't have agreed. I wondered if, after he was killed, his role would've been made public."

"No point in doing that." Leo took a last puff on his cigarette. "Too much paperwork involved."

"I'm glad for Adam's sake. He was fond of his father, but he saw Tom through realistic eyes. In fact, Adam knew him better than I did."

"Maybe he heard Tom in confession."

I stared at Leo. "I never thought of that."

"Well!" The single word shot out of the newsroom as Vida practically flew across the floor. "If that doesn't beat all! I just ran into Tricia Dodge! I mean, Tricia . . . what *is* her last name now?"

"It's still Sellers," I said, catching my

breath. "Her second divorce won't be final until this summer."

"Really," Vida said, straightening her rose-covered hat, "she hasn't improved with time. I saw her last fall when she met with Milo to discuss Tanya's wedding to that idiot who killed himself. Tricia's aged since then. Living in Bellevue will do that to you. So crowded, so busy. A close friend of Amy's lives in Kirkland. She looks ten years older than my daughter."

"All this fresh mountain air," Leo remarked before sauntering back to his desk. "Good for the complexion."

Vida frowned at me. "Is Leo being sarcastic?"

"Of course not," I said. "Well? Does Dot Parker have Tiffany's daughter in her care?"

"No." Vida leaned both hands on my desk. "She claims to know nothing about Tiffany or her child." She paused, scrutinizing me. "You look a bit peaked." She wagged a finger at me. "Tricia was here!"

"Yes."

Vida pursed her lips. "It's almost eleven. We shall take an early lunch. I must hear all about it. The Venison Inn, of course."

"Fine. A quarter to twelve?"

Vida nodded. "Now I must finish those letters. Such silly problems people have nowadays! Whatever happened to straying husbands and lazy adolescents? Now it's Twitter and tweeting and Facebook dilemmas." She made her indignant exit.

I picked up the phone and called Milo. Maybe he was back from wherever he'd been when Tricia had first called on him.

"Dodge went to Everett just after you left," Lori said. "He's seeing their lab people. Shall I have him call you when he gets back?"

I hesitated. "Did he have another visitor earlier?" I suddenly remembered that Lori had met Tricia when she'd come to Alpine in October. "I mean his ex-wife," I added hastily.

"Yes, she just missed him. She seems kind of nice, doesn't she?"

"She does. Thanks, Lori."

Our next visitor arrived ten minutes later. Postmaster Roy Everson showed up in the newsroom, seemingly restored to sanity if not to reason. Vida was his victim, which was fine with me.

"Really," she was saying to Roy as I darted to the restroom, "you must accept the lab tests. Your mother in no way resembled a gopher. . . ."

Maybe if I hid in the restroom or the back shop, Roy would be gone when I finally

289

emerged. If all else failed, I could sneak out the back way. But when I peeked into the hall between the newsroom and the front office, I saw Spencer Fleetwood come through the front door.

"Emma," he called, "is Vida here?"

I gestured at the newsroom. Spence nodded and disappeared.

Roy Everson was leaving when I emerged from the restroom. Spence was talking to Vida. Scooting into my cubbyhole, I closed the door and called Ben.

"I'm standing outside of Jefferson Davis's home," Ben said in his crackling voice. "It's called Beauvoir, and in all the years I spent on the Delta, I've never seen it. It's really not that much of a house. Nothing like Bronsky's villa. Are you and Dodge married yet?"

"No," I said, and spilled out my conversation with Tricia.

"Think how grateful Milo's ex will be if you lavish kindness on Tanya," Ben said when I finished. "Unless she's playing a double game."

"I wonder," I admitted. "Is she pissed because her ex is happy and she's not? I do feel sorry for Tanya. She's still a mess and probably does feel safe with her father. I've always felt safe with Milo, more than I ever did with anybody except our parents."

"That doesn't speak well for me."

"You're hardly ever around, you jerk. But Tanya can't live with us. It'd be too crowded while we're doing the remodel."

"She can't stay at Dodge's house alone?"

"She tried to kill herself rather than leave him. That's a bad sign."

"Attention getter, maybe. I thought she worked for the Mariners."

"It's the Seahawks."

"Working for either of those teams might bring on deep depression. Anybody tried to jump off the roof of Safeco or Qwest Fields?"

"You have to buy a ticket to do that. There's a waiting list for distraught fans. I suppose she's still on leave. It's not as if there are a lot of jobs around here for somebody with a college degree."

"Dodge bitches he's shorthanded. Why not put her to work?"

That wasn't Ben's dumbest idea. "She still has to live someplace."

"Work it out. I've got a dozen people to herd back to the mission church outside of Pascagoula. Some of them don't have homes, either."

Ben did have a way of putting things in perspective.

By the time I'd finished a phone call from Fuzzy Baugh thanking me for my "discreet yet provocative" editorial about changing public opinion, Vida was ready for lunch. "We'll find a cozy booth to chat," she said, leading the way into a mere drizzle. "I was peckish the other day — so much to do in the house and garden this time of year."

I didn't believe her, but murmured agreement as we covered the short distance to the Venison Inn. Vida's idea of a cozy booth was a street view so she could watch the passing parade. We'd arrived early enough that the restaurant was only a quarter full. Predictably, her opening query was about Tricia.

"So sad," she declared when I finished my recital. "She was quite good-looking when she married Milo. Leggy, with a decent figure and nice skin. But living in suburbs like Bellevue, you can't walk anywhere — you must drive. And all those traffic fumes — that would ruin anyone's looks. Not to mention your disposition. No wonder Tricia's marriages failed."

"She was still in Alpine when she left Milo," I pointed out.

"But she never belonged here, being from Sultan. It's not the same. Oh!" Vida leaned to her right. "Here comes my niece Nicole.

How nice."

"Hi, Aunt Vida," Nicole said, beaming. "I haven't seen you lately." She realized I was also present. "Hi, Ms. Lord. Have you two decided?"

Vida grimaced. "We haven't seen the menu. What's the special?"

"Pork sandwich with mashed potatoes, gravy, and herb stuffing." Nicole's dark eyes twinkled. "Not exactly seasonable, but it's hearty."

"Hearty . . ." Vida mulled briefly. "Yes, I skimped on breakfast. Now I can do the same with dinner. Does it come with a salad?"

"It can," Nicole said.

"Fine, dear. That's what I'll have. Oh — a glass of ice water, please."

"Got it." Nicole turned to me. "The same?"

"No. I'll have the clam chowder, a small salad with Roquefort dressing, and a Pepsi."

Nicole departed. "Such a nice girl," Vida murmured. "She's taking morning classes at the college. She wants to be a journalist, like her aunt. Isn't that flattering?"

"With Carla the Typo Queen as her advisor?" I said, referring to my former reporter.

"Of course," Vida said. "Carla *is* the student newspaper advisor."

"True." I recalled the last edition I'd seen with a headline I wanted to forget: "Coach Loses Balls in Gym Food." It had taken three paragraphs to explain that there had been a leak in the sports complex's pipes. I changed the subject. "What did you do yesterday?"

"Amy and I drove up to Bellingham to visit Meg. We hadn't seen her since Christmas. She's suffering from empty-nest syndrome with their children temporarily off on their own. Charles is so busy with his city job in human resources. Too many evening meetings."

"Has Meg ever worked?"

"Off and on," Vida said, "but she volunteers quite a bit."

Nicole delivered our beverages. "Mr. Walsh and Mr. Laskey just came in," she said. "Are they joining you?"

"No," I said a bit too quickly. "I mean, they're discussing business."

She looked down the aisle. "I guess they're discussing it in the bar. There they go."

"It's quieter in there," I murmured.

"What's that all about?" Vida asked after Nicole went on her way.

I didn't answer directly. "Are you still mad at Milo?"

Vida frowned. "What has that got to do

with Mitch and Leo?"

"Mitch doesn't like Milo. It goes back to when Troy escaped."

"Oh, yes. The pneumonia episode. Very unreasonable of Mitch. Of course you'd expect that from someone who lived in Detroit."

"You didn't answer the question," I said.

"What question? Oh — here comes Nicole." Vida paused as her niece delivered our orders. "My, that looks lovely, dear. But they skimped a bit on the gravy, don't you think? Of course I am trying to lose a few pounds. My Valentine chocolates were just too tempting."

Nicole smiled conspiratorially. "From the colonel?"

"Well, yes. He's a very thoughtful gentleman. Is there some extra dressing for the salad?"

"I'll get more, and extra gravy, too," Nicole replied. "Be right back."

"Such a sweet girl," Vida said. "Is there any news about Wayne's death? There was no funeral date given in the obit. Who wrote it?"

"Mitch, via Cookie," I said. "We were pushed for time. Milo asked SnoCo for a second autopsy. The services are private and graveside."

Vida looked askance. "That's very peculiar. Why?"

"Why what?"

"You know private services are rare in Alpine," Vida declared. "In our close-knit community, grief should be shared. What's wrong with Cookie? Did she finally collapse?"

"Yes, but she made the decision before Tiffany disappeared."

Vida munched on salad. "Billy went to the ski lodge after Tiffany had been seen there."

Nicole showed up with two small boats — one of gravy, the other of ranch salad dressing. "Is that okay?" she asked.

Vida studied the items. "Yes, quite ample. Thank you." As Nicole departed, her aunt slathered her plate with most of the gravy. "Tiffany's antics have upset the Parkers. I never understood why Cookie is so spineless. Her older sister is the opposite. Cookie was the baby. Maybe they spoiled . . ." Vida stopped, staring at her plate. "Oh, I see — there's more stuffing between the pork layers. I wondered."

I sensed that what she really saw was an image of Roger. "I wish you weren't mad at Milo," I said after tasting my chowder and finding it a bit watery. "You make it very awkward for me."

"Why? You weren't part of how he handled the trailer park case."

"Milo did what he had to do. If he hadn't considered your feelings, he might not have let Roger off so easily. Your grandson could be in jail."

Vida glared at me. "Nonsense! Roger had valuable knowledge about the drug ring. In a way, it's almost as if he'd been working under cover."

I know when to hold and when to fold. Vida might believe Roger *had* been working under cover. But the only cover he'd been under was on Holly Gross's bed. "Want to do a piece on Clarence Munn?"

I seemed to have surprised Vida. She relaxed and speared a slice of pork before answering. "I plan to visit him, even if he's a bit gaga."

"He recalls the past clearly. You know the history — and Clarence."

"Yes." Vida briefly stared into space. "He and Marius were close. Clarence was young enough to be his son, but the Vandeventers were childless. I suppose Clarence was like a son to him."

"Is Marius still alive?"

Vida shook her head. "He died in March of '01. He was in his nineties. His wife had passed away the previous year."

We were back on safe ground. Talking about the former *Advocate* owner couldn't cause any friction between us.

As it turned out, the ground beneath us was already shaking.

THIRTEEN

Vida and I returned from lunch ahead of Leo and Mitch.

"I do hope those two aren't drinking their lunch," Vida said, removing her hat and scrutinizing the damp roses. "You never can tell with someone like Leo, who's had a problem with alcohol. For all we know, Mitch is a secret drinker. They're the worst."

"Leo's attempting to straighten Mitch out on how small towns operate," I said, flipping through the not-so-urgent phone messages Amanda had left for me. "Mitch is still adapting."

"It's a pity Brenda couldn't have managed to do that. Imagine being in Pittsburgh with all those steel mills."

"I don't think they have them anymore," I said, and retreated into my office, wondering if Milo had gotten back from Everett. I'd been at my desk for only five minutes when Vida rushed into my office.

"My niece Marje called to tell me Patti Marsh is in the ER. She claims to have fallen down her front steps. I don't believe it. Do you?"

"I don't know what to believe," I admitted. "It seems that half the town is accident-prone lately. You think Patti was shoved by Blackwell?"

Vida sank into a visitor's chair, removed her glasses, and began rubbing her eyes in that gesture of frustration that made me wince. "Ooooh . . . I'd say so," she said, at last mercifully folding her hands, "but Jack's been on his best behavior since being named a county commissioner."

"You believe the so-called attempts on his life are real?"

Vida put her glasses back on. "I don't know. You must admit that Milo will doubt his word."

"Neither Jack nor Milo has any proof."

"Is Milo waiting to find Jack's corpse on his doorstep?"

I thought that would probably suit the sheriff just fine, but ignored the remark. "How badly was Patti hurt?"

"I don't know yet. Doc was having X-rays taken. She might've broken some ribs. Marje will let me know."

"Maybe Patti was drunk," I said. "She

likes her liquor. Speaking of which, here come Leo and Mitch. They look sober to me."

"You can't tell by looking," Vida murmured. "I'll see for myself."

I watched Vida approach Leo, who was going to his desk. Mitch had already sat down. My phone rang, distracting me from whatever was about to happen in the newsroom.

At first I couldn't hear the caller except that it was a female voice. "I'm sorry," I said, "can you speak up? We may have a poor connection."

A pause followed. If I hadn't heard voices in the background, I would've thought the person had hung up.

"It's me," Lori Cobb said, still hushed but audible. "Mrs. Sellers is here. She tried to take Tanya to Sheriff Dodge's house, but she doesn't have a key. Could Mrs. Sellers drop Tanya off at your house? She has to get back to Bellevue."

I hesitated. "No," I finally said. "I can't take the responsibility. Mrs. Sellers and her daughter have friends here. Why can't Tanya stay with one of them until the sheriff gets back from Everett?"

"I guess I'll ask her. Sorry to bother you." Lori hung up.

I felt like an evil stepmother — a role it seemed like I was assuming. I hardly knew Tanya. When I'd hosted her for dinner, she'd been pleasant, if quiet. It was the first time I'd seen her in years. But my real concern was that I didn't want Tanya alone at my house. If anything happened, I'd be responsible, and I couldn't leave work to hold her hand. Surely Tricia could leave Tanya with a friend or wait to go back to Bellevue.

Leo and Mitch passed muster. Vida finished her advice letters and announced she'd call on Clarence Munn while she had some spare time. Still feeling guilty about Tanya, I called Lori to ask if Milo had returned.

"No," she virtually whispered. "Mrs. Sellers asked Bill Blatt for a master key to get into the house, but Bill couldn't do that without the boss's permission. They're going to try getting in through a window."

"Oh, swell," I groaned. "Let me know when the sheriff gets back."

Lori promised she would and rang off. Maybe it wasn't the last thing I needed, but it was the next thing that happened when Holly Gross stormed into the newsroom. She went straight to Leo, maybe because he'd shown her kindness earlier. If I'd had any sense, I would have closed the door and pretended I didn't know what was happening. But instead I ventured into the newsroom.

"Come on, Walsh, you know frigging well where that old hag is," Holly screeched. "I can tell when a guy's lying to me. I'll find her if I have to tear this town apart!"

Leo offered Holly a cigarette. She hesitated, but finally snatched the whole pack from him. "Well?" she said. "Gimme a light."

He leaned across his desk and lighted the cigarette. "I told you, she's on an assignment. Why do you want to see Mrs. Runkel?"

Holly exhaled. "You know damned well why I want to see her." She swerved around to look at me. "So do you." She darted a glance at Mitch for good measure. "You all do. I want my kid."

"I've never seen your kid," I said. "Why don't you ask Roger?"

Holly deliberately blew smoke in my direction. "Because I can't find the fat bastard, that's why. I'll bet he's left town and taken Dippy with him. I went to the sheriff's office yesterday and warned that squaw who works for him that if they didn't find Dippy for me, I'd raise hell."

303

"What squaw?" I asked.

Holly shot me a disgusted look. "The Indian who works for Dodge. Or does he call *you* his squaw?"

"Doe Jamison is part Muckleshoot. She's not anybody's squaw, she's a deputy, and you better show her some respect. She's your best ally right now. Leave Mrs. Runkel alone. You should be dealing with Roger. Unless," I added, "you're not sure if he *is* Dippy's father."

"Hey!" Holly yelled before taking the cigarette out of her mouth. It fell to the floor and bounced off one of her faux leather cowboy boots. "Watch it! You're the one who's shacked up with the sheriff!"

Leo stood up. I glimpsed Mitch out of the corner of my eye. He looked puzzled. I started to speak, but my ad manager beat me to it. "Take it easy, Holly. You're all worked up. Come on, I'll walk you to the sheriff's office so you can talk to Deputy Jamison. You need to sort through this in a way that doesn't involve pissing off a lot of blameless people. Unless," he added, pausing as he started to put his jacket on, "you'd rather just raise hell and never see your kid again."

As was her way, Holly lost steam in the face of rational behavior. "Okay, Walsh," she said, retrieving the cigarette before it burned a hole in the floor. "I almost forgot you're one of the good guys. There are damned few around here. Let's hit it."

Mitch and I watched as they exited the newsroom. I didn't hear anything out of Amanda and guessed she'd retreated to the back shop with Kip. My reporter spoke first. "Is she nuts or just messed up?"

I sat down by Mitch's desk. "Both. Leo's right. We don't know anything about Holly's kid. Roger's the only one who can sort this out."

"I've never met him," Mitch said. "I remember the trailer park mess, though. Roger was lucky to get off so cheap. Troy didn't."

"The situations were different. Roger provided solid information about the drug dealers and the trucker connection. From what you told me, Troy was operating on his own."

Mitch nodded faintly. "Holly shouldn't spread rumors about you and Dodge. That's bad for your reputation. I saw way too much of that hand-in-glove back-door stuff between the press and law enforcement in Detroit. I never went for that. It violated my ethics."

Mitch had a copy of the *Advocate* on his

desk. I picked it up and turned to page three. "Read this," I said, pointing to the engagements.

"Good God!" Mitch stared at me. "Why didn't you say so?"

I made a helpless gesture. "Milo and I've been close since I moved here. He wanted to marry me ten years ago. I said no because of Tom Cavanaugh. You know that sad story. Except for a fling with Rolf Fisher from the AP, there never has been any other man in my life except Milo. We've always loved each other. I was just slow figuring it all out."

Mitch hung his head. "You must hate me."

"No. I did wonder why you never realized we were a couple. We got engaged just after Christmas, while you were gone. I had Vida hold back the announcement until all the snoops stopped pestering us. Milo and I both needed time to recover."

Mitch was staring into space. "I should've guessed. No wonder Leo told me I should pull back on investigating Dodge. I thought maybe he and the sheriff were fishing buddies or something."

"Leo doesn't fish," I said. "In fact, it took him a long time to realize that Milo is very good at what he does. The sheriff prefers that people don't notice how he works. He's very closemouthed when he's investigating a homicide case. I had to learn that the hard way, too."

Amanda appeared in the doorway. "Thank goodness Holly is gone. Did you throw her out?"

"Leo escorted her," I said.

"Dodge is on hold for you," she informed me.

"Okay," I told her, then patted Mitch's shoulder. "Don't be upset. I'm glad you finally know I *am* shacked up with the sheriff." I hurried to my phone.

"Where the hell were you?" Milo asked. "In the can?"

"Never mind. Has Holly arrived?"

"Yeah, with Leo. I'm barricaded in my office. Never mind that. Doe can handle it. I got the autopsy report. It's what I thought. Pay attention and write this down. It's s-u-x-a-m-e-t-h-o-n-i-u-m. Call it 'sux' for short. It's a relatively new poison that can be missed if you're not looking for it."

"Wayne was poisoned?"

"You got it. Keep it to yourself for now. The full report won't be in until tomorrow. I'm telling you because if I don't spell it a few times, I won't be able to say it out loud. Besides, you're cuter than Fleetwood."

"How in the world did you get on to that?"

"Because the electrocution thing didn't

make sense. You know I don't like things that don't fit. I'd seen something on TV about this stuff and it made me wonder. It's administered where it can't be noticed — like a mole. Eriks had one on his left shoulder. Now think about that and come up with one of your weird ideas about whodunit."

"What's going on with Tanya?"

I heard Milo sigh. "I don't know what the hell to do, but I've got to do it now. I can't abandon her. We'll talk later." He hung up.

I couldn't pass the poisoning news on to Mitch until it was official. I hoped that would be by the time he checked the Thursday log. I asked him to call the clinic to see if Patti Marsh had been hospitalized.

"Who exactly is she?" my reporter asked.

I sighed. "Blackwell's longtime squeeze. I suspect he beat her up just for the hell of it. Tiffany's not around to take his abuse. If, in fact, he doled some out to her just to show he isn't playing favorites."

Mitch frowned. "You don't like Blackwell, either, do you?"

"No, and it's not because of Milo. I've always been wary of that guy. He may run a respectable mill, but he's way too oily for my taste."

"Okay." Mitch shrugged. "I'll withhold

judgment for now."

"That's fine. But check on Patti. She's kind of pathetic."

Half an hour later, Vida returned from RestHaven with Rosalie Reed in tow. "Dr. Reed and I have had a most pleasant visit," she said as the two women stood in my office. "She's on her way to a dental appointment with Dr. Starr and thought she'd come by to say hello."

I was on guard. The visit struck me as suspect. But I offered Dr. Reed a chair. Vida beamed at us before heading to her desk.

Rosalie seemed composed, but her eyes darted this way and that before she spoke. "I hope I'm not intruding. Mrs. Runkel was so kind to offer to let me see how a small-town newspaper operates. I'm still adapting to life away from an urban environment. She insisted that Wednesdays are a down-time after your weekly publication."

"Kip MacDuff, my back-shop manager, can give you the tour," I said. I couldn't remember anyone except the sixth-grade class from Alpine Elementary coming to see what went on at the *Advocate.* Most of them had been bored and fidgety, except for a couple of boys who asked how Kip had gotten an autographed baseball from Ken Griffey Jr. "Was somebody in your family involved in newspaper work?"

"My uncle was a reporter for the *Spokesman-Review,*" Rosalie replied. "He covered business and agriculture in the Spokane area."

"Oh. The Inland Empire beat," I noted.

"A very important beat on that side of the mountains," Rosalie said. "It must be exciting . . . no, that's a regrettable word." She grimaced. "I should say a break in routine to have a puzzling death to write about. I haven't had time to see today's edition, but I had to answer some questions the sheriff posed. Fascinating, in a way."

"The questions? Or the answers?"

She laughed — sort of. "It was like a film or TV. 'Where were you . . . ?' 'Droll' describes it better. Not that I let any amusement show. The sheriff seems rather stern. I thought it prudent not to be flippant."

I nodded. "Dodge goes by the book."

"Yes. I found him rather interesting. Very macho, if you like that type. But not the sort of macho who flaunts it. Then again, it's hard to categorize people at a first meeting."

I was wondering where this conversation was going. It had certainly strayed from putting out a weekly newspaper. "I'm sure you answered his questions satisfactorily," I said.

She shrugged. "Frankly, I couldn't account for my time to the minute. There was the storm, a first for me in the mountains. I've lived in the Seattle area long enough to experience bad weather, but one feels more insulated in an urban setting. There's something raw about storms in primitive surroundings. Our psych ward patients became quite agitated. Oh!" She suddenly clapped a hand to her cheek. "I just realized where I was — with a patient who was disoriented by the thunder. It reminded him of combat in the first Gulf War. How could I forget that? Should I tell the sheriff? I can't reveal the patient's name, but . . . Dodge, isn't it?" She saw me nod. "He wouldn't need to know that, would he?"

"I can't speak for the sheriff, but if you had to identify the person, the sheriff wouldn't have Spencer Fleetwood broadcast it over KSKY."

Rosalie's pale face turned slightly pink. "No, of course not. That is, the sheriff wouldn't do that." She glanced at her watch. "Goodness, it's going on three. I don't want to be late for my dental appointment. Then I have to make rounds. How late is the sheriff's office open?"

"Dodge is usually there until at least five," I said.

Rosalie stood up. "I can't believe how the afternoon has flown. Thanks so much for your time. I must take the tour another day. We should have dinner together soon."

I murmured an appropriate response but didn't get up. Rosalie Reed might be a fine psychiatrist, but she was a lousy actress. Her role as a forgetful shrink hadn't played well with me. It was the first thing I said when Vida entered my office a few minutes after my visitor had left.

"I wondered," Vida said, sitting down. "She accosted me as I was getting out of my car. It was as if she'd been lurking by the cleaners. She knew I'd been to see Clarence Munn."

"How was Clarence?" I asked.

Vida frowned. "He rambled. Oh, he talked about his mill, but he mentioned so much else. Logging was still the mainstay in SkyCo then. I was in my teens when Clarence came here. He was young, mid-twenties, but his father owned a mill near Forks on the Olympic Peninsula and one by Port Townsend. Clarence wanted to strike out on his own. It was right after World War Two and Clarence had just gotten out of the Coast Guard." She paused. "Dear me, I'm rattling along, just like Clarence."

"That's okay," I said. "Even after all these

312

years, I don't know as much as I should about Alpine's history."

"I wasn't born until just after Carl Clemans closed the original mill," Vida continued. "Mr. Clemans was an exemplary owner. He ran his business like a gentleman. But some of the owners who followed him in later years were of another sort. So were many of the loggers and mill workers. The Great Depression, you know. Men desperate for work, and not always able to bring their families with them — if they had families. I was a child in those days, but I heard some wild and woolly tales."

I could imagine a pint-sized version of Vida, a cowgirl hat or a sombrero on her head, listening at keyholes and outside open windows, soaking up every bit of information that came her way. It was more than likely that she retained all of it to the present day. "I assume you're referring to liquor and women and maybe other vices?"

Vida grimaced. "Yes. The worst, however, were the accidents. There was carelessness and a lack of safety precautions. The workers were often risk takers, but the timber industry has always attracted the bold and the reckless. That's what Clarence alluded to. Even after the war, some of the vices remained — not in the town, but around the edges."

"Would this have been while Eeeny Moroni was sheriff?"

"Eeeny — the old fool — wasn't sheriff until the fifties, though he'd worked as a deputy after he got out of the army. He erased some of the corruption, which was how he kept getting reelected for thirty-odd years. But according to Clarence, Eeeny turned a blind eye to some illicit doings and was on the take. Has Milo mentioned anything like that to you?"

"Never," I replied. "Up until Eeeny got into trouble a year or so after I came to town, Milo always had nothing but respect for his predecessor."

Vida nodded. "I was never taken with Eeeny — he was so full of himself — but I didn't think he was a crook. Clarence feels otherwise. He insists Eeeny took money to ignore a brothel on First Hill. Neeny Doukas, Eeeny's close friend, was involved, too. There may've been gambling at the old Alpine Hotel, and not everything that went on at the ski lodge was above reproach. That would've been after my father-in-law passed away, of course. Rufus Runkel wouldn't have put up with such shenanigans. He virtually saved the town by promoting the new skiing fad early on."

"How was all this resolved? I've never heard anything about it."

"The curtailment of logging put an end to it. I suppose that's why Milo never knew about it. He didn't start at the sheriff's office until after he returned from Vietnam and finished his criminal justice degree."

I leaned back in my chair. "Somehow it seems so long ago. Is there any point in dredging up all this for an article?"

Vida's gray eyes sparked as she stared at me. "If what Clarence has told me is true, the answer is yes. Oh, Eeeny died in prison several years ago, and Neeny is in a nursing home. But it's the third person who was involved that the public needs to know about." She took a deep breath. "You haven't asked the obvious question, Emma."

I stared right back, puzzled. "Which is?"

"Why didn't the press expose this corruption?" She sat up straight again. "The answer is because the person running the whole sorry show was Marius Vandeventer."

I gaped at Vida. "Marius was a crook?"

She nodded. "He was if I can believe Clarence. I never guessed, not even when I worked for him. That's why I wonder if Clarence is fanciful. But he insisted it's true. He is, after all, a fellow Presbyterian."

"No wonder Marius was anxious to get

out of town," I murmured. "Oddly enough, Milo and I were just talking about my predecessor. But I still have to ask what good it would do. Marius is dead, too."

"You'd prefer that Clarence tell his story to someone else? He and Marius were very close, almost like father and son."

"I have to think on it," I said. "There are descendants to consider, and one of them is a lawyer — Simon Doukas. I don't want to get sued, especially by that guy. He was the first one in town to call me a whore."

"Hypocrite," Vida murmured. "Wasn't he having an affair with Heather Bardeen at the time?"

"Yes. She's young enough to be his daughter. At least Heather finally settled into married life."

"Losing her mother so young sent Heather briefly off the rails," Vida remarked absently. "Buck is very fond of his niece." She stood up. "I assume I didn't miss anything here while I was at RestHaven."

"Well . . ." There was no point in evasion. Bill Blatt would tell his aunt about Holly Gross's demands. "We had a visitor. Holly came back looking for you. Leo took her to talk to Doe Jamison."

Vida's eyes were liked gooseberries behind her big glasses. "And?"

I shrugged. "I don't know anything else. We suggested Holly talk to Roger. Maybe that's what she's doing now."

"No, she isn't," Vida declared. "Roger is in Bellingham with Meg. He's rethinking the resumption of his college education and wanted to spend some time on the Western Washington University campus. His old chum Davin Rhodes is still there, finishing his degree."

"That's . . . good," I said.

"Yes. He's still considering a career in theater."

Of the absurd, I thought. But I smiled as Vida returned to the newsroom. Roger, I assumed, was probably sacked out at Meg's house — with Diddy or Dippy or whatever the poor tyke was called.

Leo didn't return until after four. Vida grilled him about Holly's visit to the sheriff's office, but Leo insisted he'd left immediately. I felt his flight was the better part of valor. I did wonder if Roger had taken a paternity test. I also wondered if he cared enough to bother.

Mitch had gotten word of Patti Marsh's condition. She had two broken ribs, a sprained ankle, and multiple bruises. Vida was miffed. "What's wrong with Marje Blatt? She usually keeps her aunt informed.

Did Patti accuse Jack of beating her?"

"No mention of anybody," Mitch said. "Patti stuck to her story."

"She might be telling the truth," I said. "The sprained ankle could indicate she fell. Had she been drinking?"

Mitch looked taken aback. "I didn't ask. That seems like an intrusive question. I thought you wanted to know about her injuries."

"I did, but —"

Vida interrupted me. "See here, Mitch, this isn't Detroit — thank goodness. This is Alpine, and we take an interest in each other. Some might call it being nosy, but that's not so. There are people we may not like or admire, but we are interested in their well-being. Have you no curiosity about your fellow human beings?"

"Only as background for a story," Mitch replied. "Otherwise, it's irrelevant. And nosy."

Vida rose from her chair, her eyes impaling Mitch across the room. "You've been here a very short time. You don't understand small-town ways. Cities are anonymous and impersonal. My own daughter Beth admits that after almost twenty years in Tacoma she doesn't know half the people on her block. What does that say about a sense of community? I may despise Patti's lifestyle, but if she sought my help, I'd be willing to offer it. And I'd be able to help her because I know her."

Mitch finally managed to avert his gaze. "Fine. I'm a city guy. The private lives of people I covered wouldn't be just a drawback — I'd lose objectivity. Besides, city dwellers are jammed into their neighborhoods, crowded on their streets. They need their privacy. I'm trying to adapt, but I'll be damned if I'll pry into somebody's personal life unless it's pertinent to the story I'm covering. Patti's not a story, she's an accident victim."

Vida sat down. "You're entitled to your opinion. But mind your language." She turned to her keyboard and began typing at warp speed.

The workday finally ran down. I headed to the Grocery Basket. This week's ad featured lamb chops on sale at seven bucks a pound. I mulled whether Milo would want two or three. He always griped that they were too small. Wincing, I asked for four. At least they were thick. I was in the produce section checking out early asparagus when a dark-haired woman I didn't recognize called my name from two bins away.

"You don't know me," she said, smiling.

"Betsy O'Toole told me where to find you. I'm Kay Burns." She offered her hand. "I wanted to thank you for the fine job you people did on the RestHaven edition."

"You're in P.R.," I said, returning her firm grip. "Mitch Laskey told me he'd been working with you. I hope all of you are pleased."

"I haven't had a chance to talk with everybody, but I'm sure they are," Kay said. "May I ask you a personal question?"

"Go ahead. If I won't answer it, don't be offended."

She smiled again. "I understand. I noticed in the paper that you're engaged to the sheriff. Congratulations."

"Thank you," I said, wondering how personal this was going to get.

"You may not know I was married briefly to Dwight Gould," Kay said, her smile disappearing. "That was before you lived here. Anyway, I felt it would be wrong to move here and not get in touch with him. I called the sheriff's office today, but the receptionist said Dwight wasn't in and she wasn't sure when he'd be back. I tried to reach him at home — he still lives out on Burl Creek Road in the house where we lived together — but he didn't answer. Then I phoned his sister, Kay — or Kiki, as she's called — but she . . . well, she doesn't like me." Kay paused and pursed her lips. "She wouldn't tell me anything. Is Dwight ill?"

I wouldn't reveal Dwight's suspension, so I hedged. "He's fine as far as I know. He may have gone fishing."

Kay looked faintly incredulous. "In this weather? I'm a native. I know when the river's too high and off-color. Not even Dwight would do that." She paused again, this time to let a young couple with two children get by us. "This may sound silly, but I'm worried about him. Could you ask the sheriff if he's all right?"

"Sure," I said, "but I've seen Dwight recently and he seemed fine."

Kay nodded once. "Good. But I'm still concerned. People can have health problems that aren't caused by disease."

"You mean . . . an accident?"

She avoided my gaze. "Maybe. I should finish my shopping. It was nice meeting you." She pushed her grocery cart back toward the tomatoes.

I got home at five-thirty. It was going on six when the phone rang.

"I'm stuck," Milo said, sounding unhappy. "I couldn't talk Tanya out of staying here at the house, and Mulehide just took off."

I didn't respond right away. "Why don't

you bring her here? If you can spare a lamb chop, I can feed her. You both have to eat."

It was his turn not to say anything for a moment. "I'll see if she can cope with that, okay? I'll call you back."

I stood by the sink, hanging my head and silently cussing. I really didn't blame Tanya. But I'd waited my entire adult life to be happy with a man I loved, and now it seemed there was one damned obstacle after another. Yes, I'd fouled up my relationship with Milo for years, but at least I'd finally come to my senses. I knew life wasn't fair, but I felt hexed. I was fifty-two years old. Maybe this was payback for my delusions about Tom and my folly with Rolf. I thought about what Ben would tell me. He'd say it served me right — but I still didn't deserve it. Life is random, not dictated by God.

It was ten minutes before Milo called back. "She'll come. I had to coax her out of the bathroom. At least she didn't have any pills."

"Good," I said, awash with relief. It was a small victory and eased the lingering guilt I felt for not letting Tanya take refuge at my own house. "I hope she likes asparagus."

"See you in a bit. Tanya has to get herself together."

"That's fine. I haven't started dinner." I

had a sudden thought. "Milo — why don't you put the house up for sale now?"

There was a brief silence at the other end. "It needs work. But that's not your weirdest idea. A For Sale sign in the front yard might be motivation." He hung up.

It was going on seven before the sheriff and his daughter arrived. I'd put the potatoes on the stove to boil and had the lamb chops ready to go under the broiler in the oven. I'd steam the asparagus, which would take only a few minutes. I knew Tanya preferred wine, so I got out an unopened bottle of Merlot that I had on hand for my bridge club.

I stood at the front window watching Tanya come out from around the Yukon's passenger side. She was wearing a brown hooded car coat and had her head down to avoid the heavy rain. She walked slowly, carefully, as if she thought the ground might swallow her. Milo had loped on ahead, but stopped to go back and take her arm. He looked more like a son helping his mother than a father guiding his daughter. Tanya seemed to have deteriorated since I'd seen her less than three weeks ago.

I met them at the door. Up close, she appeared more like herself. She was almost pretty, a tall, more angular version of how her mother might have looked as a young woman. Except for the sandy hair, she bore no resemblance to her father. Of the three children, only Brandon took after Milo. He wasn't as tall or as broad as Milo, and though he had hazel eyes, they didn't have the intensity of his father's. The sheriff's gaze revealed his every emotion — unless he didn't want a witness or suspect to know what he was thinking. Even I couldn't read him then.

Milo leaned down and brushed my lips with a quick kiss. "Tanya says she isn't hungry. I told her you could change her mind."

"I'll try," I said, smiling. "Here, Tanya, I'll help with your coat."

Tanya mutely submitted to my assistance. Milo took the coat and hung it next to his. "Lamb chops, right?" he said, to break the silence.

"Yes." I turned to Tanya. "Do you like Merlot?"

She nodded — and finally spoke. "I do. Thanks."

"Good," I said. "Come out to the kitchen and let your dad collapse. He's had a busy day with his trip over to Everett."

"Is that where he went?" she asked, trailing me like a lost waif.

"He had to get an autopsy report on Wayne Eriks. Do you know the family? Their daughter, Tiffany, is about your age."

"Tiffany Eriks." Tanya studied the wine bottle. "Yes, I think she was in the class ahead of me. She had a brother who was a little older."

"He was killed in a rafting accident. Maybe that happened after you moved to Bellevue."

Tanya looked mildly surprised. "I guess so. I don't remember it."

I got out a wine goblet and two cocktail glasses. "The corkscrew's in that drawer to your right. You want to do the honors?"

"Okay." She opened the drawer but seemed to have trouble finding the corkscrew. Not that I blamed her. As Milo often pointed out, I'm not organized. I rarely use the corkscrew except when I host bridge club.

"It's in there somewhere," I said.

Tanya found the damned thing just as I finished pouring her father's Scotch. To my relief, she deftly removed the cork and managed to pour the wine without spilling it — something I might not have achieved. I made my own drink and lifted my glass to her. "To better days. For all of us. I'm glad you're here, Tanya." To my astonishment, I

325

meant it.

"Thanks," she said as we clicked glasses. For a second our eyes met. A glint of tears shone in hers. I put my arm around her. Tanya leaned against me, then pulled away with what seemed like reluctance.

We moved out to the living room. Milo was in the easy chair, looking as if he'd been about to nod off. "The barmaids," he said, stretching his long arms. "Want me to build a fire?"

"Sure," I said, indicating that Tanya should sit on the sofa. I handed him his drink. I realized I hadn't turned on the broiler or the stove, but it'd take that long for Milo to get the fire going and finish his drink. I sat next to Tanya in my usual spot. "Hey," I said to Milo's back as he stuffed newspaper into the grate, "any word from Dwight?"

"No," he said. "I don't think he misses me."

"Kay's trying to find him."

The sheriff turned to look at me over his shoulder. "The hell she is," he said. "How do you know that?"

I explained about meeting her at the Grocery Basket. "She's worried about him."

Milo finished adding kindling and a couple of cedar logs before setting off the newspaper. "After twenty-five years?" he said, standing up.

"I remember Dwight," Tanya said. "Doesn't he look like a frog?"

"He's no prince," her father said, sitting down. "Why the hell is Kay worried? Something's up."

I shrugged. "I don't know, but she really seemed concerned."

Milo fingered his long chin. "Money? Didn't you say she's got a P.R. job at Rest-Haven? They must pay well."

"It was like she thought something had happened to him," I said.

The sheriff shook his head. "Nothing ever happens to Dwight. He likes it that way."

"Maybe," I suggested, "she's heard about the threats to Blackwell's life and thinks Dwight's finally getting even."

Milo scowled at me. "You're in fantasyland."

I didn't argue. Instead, I went out to the kitchen to start the chops and the potatoes. I overheard Milo ask Tanya if she was going to look for a job in Alpine. I couldn't hear her answer, but by the time I returned to the living room, her father was suggesting she check out the community college. "It's the state, so they may have some money to spare," he said.

She shook her head. "I had enough of college life. I wouldn't want to deal with students."

"I suppose you could start doing stuff around the house," Milo said after a pause. "I'm putting it up for sale soon."

"Dad!" Tanya cried. "You can't do that! It's home."

The sheriff scowled. "Not for me. It hasn't been your home since 1985. I have to unload the place to help pay for the remodel here. Don't get excited. The market's slow right now due to the recession. It could take months. You and Bran and Mike still have stuff downstairs."

Tanya looked puzzled. "You mean from when we lived here?"

Milo nodded. "Mostly toys and games, but I never threw that stuff out. I thought for a while you guys might still want it when you came here to visit." He sounded slightly wistful.

"I guess we outgrew it," Tanya murmured.

"Donate it to the Salvation Army," Milo said. "They've got a bin in the Safeway parking lot."

"Maybe I'll look. I can't push myself," Tanya continued after a generous sip of wine. "My psychiatrist told me it takes years to get over the kind of thing I've been through." She finally looked at me. "Did

Dad tell you I have post-traumatic stress disorder?"

I caught Milo's uneasy expression. If he'd mentioned PTSD to me, I'd forgotten it in the muddle that had been my own life in recent weeks. "That's difficult to deal with," I said. "I assume your psychiatrist has given you good advice about how to cope with it so you can move on."

"He's not a specialist in PTSD," Tanya replied. "He gave me a referral to someone on the Eastside, but by the time Mom and I got back from Hawaii, the doctor had moved out of the area. That's just as well. I wanted to move out of the area, too."

Milo had taken a puff on his cigarette and exhaled. "I thought you told me that part of the treatment was to slowly relive the cause."

"That's true," Tanya agreed, looking at her father before turning back to me. "It's cognitive behavioral therapy, but it has to be taken very gradually and very slowly. I'm not ready yet to do that. I'm still dealing with the part that requires identifying the stress points of the trauma itself to figure out exactly which thoughts are genuine and which might be distorted or irrational." She glanced back at Milo. "I thought you understood that."

"Sorry, honey," he said, putting out his cigarette. "You know I'm not up on all that shrink stuff."

His daughter shifted uneasily on the sofa. "It's not 'stuff,' Dad. It's therapy. What would help is if you and Mom would sit in on the sessions when I finally find someone who can treat me."

Milo took a deep drink of Scotch. "Unless they've got somebody at RestHaven, you won't find anybody around here. Hell, most law enforcements have their own shrinks. SkyCo can't afford that. In fact, we've never had one in the whole county until now."

"That's okay. I'm not ready to deal with anything more than sorting through my memories and thoughts. That could take months."

I didn't dare look at the sheriff. Instead, I stood up and announced I had to check on dinner. I caught most of their conversation, which somehow had switched to his other children. Brandon and Solange had been living together for a year and were considering marriage. Michelle's partner was a surgical nurse at the Shriners Hospital for Children in Portland. I'd done a series on the facility for *The Oregonian* some twenty years earlier. A flood of memories overcame me as I mashed the potatoes. I wondered how I'd managed all those years, trying to juggle my job with single parenthood. Maybe I'd never had time to think about it, but it hadn't been easy. The only other thing I heard Tanya say was that she wished her father wouldn't smoke.

We got through dinner without any more references to Tanya's emotional problems except for her telling us she was now on Prozac and that it would take some time before she could tell if it was helping her. Dessert was chocolate chip ice cream. We lingered briefly at the table before Milo announced a little after eight that they'd better head to his house. I noticed he didn't say "home."

Tanya thanked me and said she hoped she would see me again. Milo gave me another quick kiss. I couldn't look him in the eye. I knew I'd see the reflection of my own dejected state. And then they were gone, their figures blurred by the rain. Tom's two orphaned children had wanted no part of me. Tanya had a mother, so she didn't need me, either. And I had no magical powers as a fairy godmother. The only way I could make myself useful was to clean up the kitchen and try to stop feeling more sorry for myself than I did for Tanya.

FOURTEEN

I wanted to talk to Ben, but it was after ten on the Delta. Probably too late, if my brother had gotten up to say Mass. I considered phoning Vida, but she would pontificate at length about Tanya's lack of spunk, which would be worthless. And annoying.

I thought of calling Adam, but the connection was always so uncertain in his remote Alaskan village. I could email him — it was only six in St. Mary's Igloo. But typing my woes had no appeal. It'd sound like one of the letters Vida received for her advice column.

By nine o'clock I'd tried to distract myself by cleaning out Adam's closet. I was debating about giving away the snorkeling gear Adam had used in Hawaii when my doorbell sounded. Feeling uneasy, I asked my caller's identity.

"Your archrival," Spencer Fleetwood said in his mellow voice. "Is the coast clear for our weekly rendezvous?"

"You jackass," I said, opening the door. "You must've noticed that the sheriff's Yukon wasn't parked outside."

"I certainly did," he said, brushing rain off his latest top-of-the-line all-weather jacket. "I wouldn't admit to him that I'm escaping the clutches of a would-be seductress."

"It's not me," I said. "Who are you talking about?"

"May I?" he asked, indicating the easy chair after removing the jacket and hanging it on the peg that Milo usually used.

I almost said no, but relented. "Go ahead. But that chair — like its owner — belongs to Dodge."

"You needn't remind me," Spence said, sitting down. "I don't suppose you'd care to offer me an adult beverage?"

"Why not? I could use one myself. What'll it be?"

"A simple brew. Dark ale, if you have it."

"I've got Henry Weinhard. Stay put. I assume you want a glass."

"Please. I guess Dodge to be a bottle man. Do you find me effete?"

"You're a lot of things, but not that," I said over my shoulder as I entered the kitchen.

It didn't take long to pour my Canadian whiskey into a clean glass and add a couple of ice cubes. I opened the Henry's but would let Spence pour it himself. I never could get the head right on beer.

"Thank you," Spence said, his dark eyes twinkling. "It's a pity you aren't the one who's trying to seduce me. But then you never did."

"Gosh, I can't think why not," I said, sitting down on the sofa. "Maybe it's because you always annoy me so much."

"I thought you thrived on antagonism." He carefully poured out his beer and, of course, achieved the perfect amount of foam. "Well? Where's your famous curiosity? And by the way, may I remark that you look like you've been through the mill, as Vida would say? Don't tell me you and the beastly sheriff had a spat."

"We did not," I declared. "So who's the temptress?"

Spence looked genuinely put off. "Kay Burns, RestHaven's P.R. person. An attractive woman of a certain age, but I'm immune. I believe she has a history, though I didn't care to ask her about it. I figured that if anyone knew about her, it'd be you."

"Vida knows more than I do — as usual."

"Yes, but I wasn't driving by her house on

my way home."

"I'll give you the short version. I never met Kay until this evening."

"Maybe I should've gone to Vida's," Spence murmured into his glass. "Ms. Burns's history must go back a long way."

"It does," I said, and proceeded to fill in Spence. "By any chance, did she ask you about husband number one, Dwight Gould?"

"I'm still reeling from the information that Gould was ever anybody's husband," Spence said. "It's bad enough that she was married to Blackwell. He's the one she dwelled on, seeming very curious about what he's up to these days."

"Maybe that's because Tiffany paid Kay a call at RestHaven."

Spence looked startled. "I thought Tiffany was missing."

"She is. That's what makes it interesting."

He ran a finger down his hawk-like nose. "This becomes very complicated. Maybe Kay wasn't lusting after my body."

"I already heard you two were an item."

"You did?" He grimaced. "When?"

"A few days ago. I was told Kay thought you were a real stud. Maybe I misheard and it was a real dud."

Spence ignored my jab, which was fine. I

felt a touch of remorse. He had been a comfort during the Bellevue hostage crisis and had kept me from going crazy. "Payback," he'd called it, as I'd been there for him during a family crisis of his own. If we weren't exactly friends, we were at least companions-in-arms.

"I think," he said at last, "that Kay suspects Blackwell may have killed Wayne Eriks. Or so I gathered when she wasn't rubbing my leg with hers and allowing her breasts to brush against my arm."

"Wow. Where were you? Guzzling beer at the Icicle Creek Tavern?"

"No, I was having dinner at the Venison Inn in the bar, being alone and wanting to stay that way. She joined me. Uninvited."

"What makes you think she's fingering Blackwell for Eriks's death?"

"Tiffany, of course. Wayne wasn't happy when his daughter moved in with Jack. Then daughter runs away. Maybe Wayne threatened Blackwell first. Who knows? Tiffany didn't take off until after her father was dead."

The scenario was credible. "If Milo had any evidence against Blackwell, he'd haul him in. No love lost there, either. But I'll be honest — the sheriff hasn't mentioned Jack as a suspect."

"Knowing Dodge, that means he has no evidence."

"True," I admitted.

"You don't seem evasive," Spence said after lighting one of his expensive black cigarettes. "Thus I gather that even in the throes of passion, Dodge doesn't reveal how his mind is working about a case."

"His mind is otherwise occupied," I said.

"I'm sure it is." Spence gazed at the ceiling. "The method of murder — if it was murder — doesn't make a lot of sense."

"I know," I said, but I wouldn't reveal that Milo had discovered otherwise. I refused to get scooped in my own living room. Mr. Radio and I would have to wait for the formal announcement. But of course Spence didn't know that was going to happen.

"Where *is* the sheriff?" Spence asked. "Or dare I inquire?"

"Coping with his daughter Tanya." That was no secret on the grapevine. "She says she has PTSD."

"Good Lord," Spence said. "And you don't after what you and Dodge went through?"

"Guess not," I said, "unless it's contagious."

"You're both made of sterner stuff."

"So are you."

Spence smiled. His expression seemed genuine. "I hope so. I wasn't in very good shape at the time, though."

"But you got through it."

"I did. You helped." He took a deep drink from his glass. "Kay's version about who killed Eriks — assuming he was murdered — has merit."

"Blackwell's an easy villain," I said. "You were at RestHaven about the time Wayne died. Did you see anything?"

If the veiled query about his presence near the murder scene jarred Spence, he did a good job of concealing it. "I was checking the sound setup for the remote broadcast. When I left, Eriks must've still been there. I saw his PUD van. It was raining like hell and I didn't linger." He grimaced. "Damn, if my timing had been better, I might've been an eyewitness. Wouldn't you have been green with envy?"

"I'd have hoped you'd been struck by lightning," I said. "Then I could've gotten a double scoop."

"You are crass," Spence declared. "I like it. It makes me feel better about myself." He finished his beer and put out his cigarette. "As enchanting as I always find your company, I must go. I shall remain on guard against any further attempts on my virtue by Ms. Burns. Frankly, her taste in men is otherwise deplorable."

I'd stood up, too. "Maybe the other husbands weren't as awful."

Spence put on his all-weather jacket. "I hope so. You look frazzled," he said seriously. "Are you having doubts about Dodge?"

My head jerked up. "No!"

Spence grinned. "I guess that answers the question. Therefore, I must conjecture that he's not worrying you, but the daughter's worrying him. Has she returned to Dad's nest for the duration?"

"Go away, Spence."

"Okay." He opened the door. "God, I'm glad I never had children." He exited into the rain, which had made small rivulets in my driveway. I was almost sorry to see him go. If nothing else, despite being a phony most of the time, he was basically real. That might not make sense to anybody else, but it did to me. Maybe it was because we were both in the same business, earning a living off other people's miseries. It made our own seem more bearable.

I went to bed around eleven, but I couldn't sleep. I stopped glancing at the digital clock shortly before one. I must've drifted off not long after that, given that I was awakened by the alarm at 6:45, the time that Milo got up on workdays while I lingered in bed, waiting for him to get out of the bathroom.

I went through my routine like a zombie. Never alert until after I reached the office, it took me twice as long to do even the simplest of tasks. In the shower, I'd turned on the cold water and forgotten to turn on the hot tap. That should have woken me up, but it only made me mad. I got a piece of bread stuck in the toaster and had to upend the blasted thing to get it out. By the time I went to my car, I wondered if I could drive without running over somebody. At least the rain had stopped, though the gray clouds matched my mood.

"Good morning," Amanda said in her chipper voice when I somehow arrived at the *Advocate* without a mishap. "Or maybe it's not," she amended, seeing my sour face.

"It's not," I said, trying to smile. "But I'll live."

Leo apparently had gotten to work just ahead of me. He was taking off his jacket when I entered the newsroom. "Hey, babe, what's wrong?"

"Everything," I said, but paused at his desk. "Tanya's back at Milo's house, so he's not at mine. Maybe I'm a selfish, horrible person."

He lit a cigarette and offered me one. I took it, not seeing any sign of Vida. "No, you're not," Leo said. "You're frustrated. Does Dodge feel guilty about this? I mean," he went on, "I did. Not lately, but my kids were still in their teens when Liza tossed me out. They had problems at school, did minor drugs, shoplifted, got in with bad company. I was here, not there. They never went to jail or went nuts. But I blamed myself."

"You never told me about any of that."

Leo shrugged. "Neither did Liza until after the fact. I still felt guilty. Turns out she did, too."

Mitch entered and stopped short before actually stepping into the newsroom. "Hi," he said. "What's up?"

I shook my head. "You don't want to know. Boss brings family troubles to work." I glanced at Vida's vacant chair. "It's contagious."

Mitch proceeded to his desk and nodded. "I know. I've got a case of it, too. I have to leave early tomorrow to catch a flight to Pittsburgh. I'm bringing Brenda home with me. I should be back at work Monday."

My reporter's problems distracted me from my own. "I hope that turns out well for both of you," I said. "When do you leave?"

"The flight's at five, so I'll have to get out of here around one," he replied. "I should have everything wrapped up by then."

"That's fine. Really, I wish you good luck."

"Thanks, Emma." His own smile was as feeble as my own.

Leo went over to get his coffee. "Vida has the bakery run. I hope she's still on the job. Hey, babe — meant to tell you your editorial was good. It should hit home with some of the people around here."

I'd forgotten all about my first attempt at putting Fuzzy's plan in motion. "Thanks. I'm thinking of a series. Maybe find some ways to reorganize how the town and the county operate. If anybody's got an idea, let me know. We need to change how we raise funds. I imagine the storm caused some damage." I looked at Mitch. "You're doing a follow-up?"

He nodded. "I can wind that up today. The heavy rain last night may've caused more problems. I'll check after I see the sheriff's log."

He'd barely finished speaking when Vida burst onto the premises. I hurriedly put out my cigarette. Luckily, she didn't notice, being absorbed in the presentation of the bakery box she was carrying. "The Upper Crust's ad had some new items, Leo. You should've told us in advance."

Leo looked puckish. "Why? You don't read the paper, Duchess?"

"Fie on you, Leo," she said, opening the box. " 'Advance' means before publication, you ninny. I have croissants with cream cheese filling, red velvet cupcakes, filled florentines — though I'm not sure what they're filled with — and a selection of petit fours."

"Hey," Leo said, "you must've blown up the monthly bakery fund."

Vida shook her head, which was adorned by a green hat with a long pheasant feather that looked as if Robin Hood should be wearing it. "My treat for missing an entire day."

Mitch and Leo began to plunder the baked goods. I let them go at it while I went to my office. A few minutes later I plucked up a cream cheese croissant. It was delicious.

Mitch hadn't returned by nine-thirty, so I couldn't ask him if the sheriff was at work. Just before ten Milo appeared. He greeted Vida perfunctorily, got some coffee and a cupcake, and came into my office. He closed the door. I could imagine Vida seething in the newsroom.

"I had to bring Tanya to work with me."

"How come?"

He'd taken a bite of cupcake and waited to swallow it. "This is breakfast, by the way. Tanya was too nervous to stay alone. She'd had the nightmares again. When she was up here before, she stopped having them after about three days. It was a long night and a short sleep."

"Poor you. Poor Tanya."

Milo lifted one broad shoulder. "Maybe she'll stop doing it after another night or so. I called Doc this morning and she's going to see him at eleven. Tanya likes Doc. She can do that on her own. I don't know if he can help, but I want his opinion. Hell, he's known her since the day she was born. He delivered her, one of his first babies." He polished off the cupcake and gave me a close look. "Are you okay?"

"Just worried." I reached out to touch his hand. "I feel worthless. Is there anything I can do to help?"

"Yeah," he said, a faint spark in his eyes, "but not here. This place is small and so cluttered we'd probably have to ask Vida to untangle us."

I laughed — which felt good. "You can't bring Tanya with you every day. She stayed alone before."

Milo nodded. "That's what I'm hoping for. But she can't just sit on her ass. There's plenty for her to do around the house. The first time, she mostly watched TV all day."

"Hey," I said, feeling almost human, "Mitch is going back to collect Brenda tomorrow. Maybe she and Tanya can watch each other. He's already said he can't leave her alone."

"Shit." Milo shook his head. "What's wrong with all these people? It's getting to the point that Crazy Eights Neffel seems normal. I hardly noticed on my way here that he was wearing an Uncle Sam outfit and saluting the Sears catalog office."

"Maybe that's where he got the Uncle Sam outfit."

Milo grinned and squeezed my hand. "God, Emma, what would I do without you? I feel better already. Will you marry me?"

"I already told you I would. Did you forget?"

"No." He turned serious, but he kept hold of my hand. "I mean right away. If we file the application today, we can get married Monday or Tuesday. At least that'll keep Mulehide from insisting we're not serious."

"Tuesday's pub day," I said.

"So? It'll only take about ten minutes."

I hesitated. "Sure. We could honeymoon in the back shop."

"That sounds about right. I'm glad you're not very romantic."

"Neither are you, big guy. Romance is highly overrated, as I found out to my sorrow."

He let go of my hand and got to his feet. "May I kiss the bride?"

I giggled. "Yes." I got to my feet and fell into his arms. He kissed me, a long, lingering kiss that made me feel a little weak in the knees.

"Wow," he said softly, finally letting me go and picking up his hat. "I'm coming home tonight if I have to get Crazy Eights to sit with Tanya."

"Play it by ear," I urged him.

He opened the door. "I'll get somebody to give me a break for a couple of hours. See you later, Emma."

He grabbed another cupcake, nodded to Vida, and departed. I was about to see if there were any croissants left, but Vida rocketed out of her chair, heading toward me like a running back sniffing the end zone.

"Well? What was that all about? And my, but you look much improved. You should, however, put on some lipstick. You're very pale."

"Would you mind if I get something to eat? Then I'll unload, okay?"

Vida stalked me over to the pastry tray. Luckily, one croissant remained. I filled my coffee mug while she nudged me out of the way. "Those are very tasty," Vida remarked. "I don't suppose it'd hurt my diet if I sampled the petit fours. They are, after all, petite."

"Go for it," I said.

She took the last two and followed me back to my office. After a bite of croissant, I gave her the brief version of Tanya's emotional status. As expected, Vida had little sympathy.

"No spunk," she declared. "Tricia probably had some very modern and very silly theories about child rearing. I can't imagine that her philandering second husband was an adequate stepfather. I know Milo wasn't around his children as much as he might've been, but that was because of his job. Goodness, you couldn't expect him to keep going to Bellevue! All those people and traffic would've made him very grumpy. Why, even Bellingham is getting too big. It's hard to find a parking place, especially in the section they call Fairfield or Fairfax or —"

"Fairhaven," I put in. "It's a nice historic part of town, though."

"No more so than Alpine," Vida asserted. "I was in Pioneer Square once in Seattle. Why do they call it that? The pioneers arrived forty years before it was built."

"The first mill was there," I explained. "The logs were sent down what was called Skid Row to —"

"Oh, twaddle! We had a first mill and we had logs. So what? But to get back to Tanya, she's clearly mental. She needs to go back to work."

"I don't think she can do that right now. As I told you, Doc's going to talk to her this morning."

"I hold Gerry in high regard, but he is, after all, a man." She paused. "I'll pay Tanya a call to see for myself what's going on with her."

That struck me as a good idea for more than one reason. "Do it. I'd like to get your reaction. If you go today, would you mind seeing her around six-thirty?"

Vida looked shocked. "Are you crazy, too? I have to be at KSKY for my program. I can drop by afterwards, say around seven-thirty."

"That's fine," I said hastily. "Milo is going to . . . um . . ." I winced.

Vida heaved an exasperated sigh. "Yes, yes, I'm sure you're both very lonesome. Really, I had so hoped that once you got engaged, you'd act like adults. I'm beginning to think neither of you went through adolescence. My memory must be hazy. I could've sworn Milo did. He seemed normal — if extremely gawky — back then."

I changed the subject, if only to remind my House & Home editor that I was the boss. "Are you caught up on everything?"

"Of course, except trying to make sense of Clarence Munn's ramblings. Maybe we should hold off on those for now. I confess, I was stumped over the letter from the wife who was put off by her husband's reading matter. I assume she meant magazines like *Playboy*."

"Probably. Didn't they make her feel inadequate?"

"Yes. But the response didn't get into this issue even though the letter was written at least a week ago. Then I got another one from her yesterday saying not to bother. They'd taken care of the problem. I assume they cancelled his subscription. Naturally, I've been trying to figure out who she is. Not that I'd pry, but it's always easier to respond if you know the person. It was an Alpine postmark," Vida added, as if that would identify the writer. Of course, it often did.

"Shall we pull your answer?"

"Well . . . maybe. Though my advice might serve wives in similar situations. I said she should worry less about her husband's reading material and concentrate more on her personal grooming while making sure that he knew she loved him. I added that flattery was always a woman's best secret weapon, men being so vain and full of themselves."

"Your call about running it," I said.

Vida nodded. "When are you and Milo getting married?"

Even Vida couldn't listen at my office door keyhole. It was in the doorknob. Nobody's hearing was that acute. "What do you mean?"

She shrugged. "You have a license application. You were glum earlier, but you had on lipstick. To convince Tricia you're serious, marry and be done with it. Do it before deadline so I can put it on my page."

I gaped at Vida. "You are amazing. But don't tell anybody. Who's the local justice of the peace since Harold Krogstad retired? I don't know enough about Diane Proxmire's full range of duties. In fact, I don't know her at all."

"Don't you remember my story on Simon

and Cecelia Doukas last year? They went to China after his semiretirement. He was sick of divorce cases and got a J.P. license to deal with happy couples for a change."

"Simon Doukas?" I exclaimed. "I haven't spoken to him in fifteen years! I sure don't want him marrying us. He'll ask Milo if he wants to take this trollop as his lawful wedded wife."

"No, he won't," Vida said. "If he did, Milo would have to hit him. That would spoil everything."

"Let's hope Judge Proxmire can do it." I meant it. Just looking at Simon would make me want to hit him first.

"She probably can. If not, you could go to Sultan or Monroe. Unless it's pub day, of course." She rose from the chair. "Now don't forget my program tonight. I'm hosting Jennifer Hood from RestHaven. We'll discuss their volunteer program. I'm sure Roger's name will come up. I asked Rosalie Reed first, but she demurred. So busy, she said. My show is after hours. Dr. Reed has a great deal to learn about life in Alpine. I understand she's from the Bellevue area, too."

With that parting sally, Vida left. Only later would I remember a passing remark she'd made that would help finger a killer.

FIFTEEN

The rest of the morning moved along briskly. Fuzzy called to tell me that several of our fine citizens agreed with my editorial. I told him I was pleased, but didn't add that I'd gotten two letters, three phone calls, and four emails from irate readers stating they didn't want any taxes or levies or bond issues that would cost them money. Two called me an idiot, three said I was stupid, and one addressed me as Erma.

Mitch handed in his storm article before lunch. Except for the power outage, a minor washout on Highway 187 near the ranger station, and Carroll Creek sweeping away a chicken coop, there were no injuries or loss of life, not even for the chickens. They'd flown the coop years ago.

"By the way," I asked Mitch after telling him his copy looked fine, "was Deputy Gould back on the job today?"

"I didn't see him," Mitch replied. "And I

didn't ask." He looked sheepish. "Now that I know about you and the sheriff, I assumed you'd hear that sort of thing before I did."

"Guess again," I said. "Milo and I try to keep our jobs separate."

"Smart," Mitch said.

I smiled halfheartedly before going back to my office. If it hadn't been for Kay's concern about Dwight, I wouldn't have been curious. I dialed the sheriff's office. Lori Cobb answered.

"Dwight is back," she said. "Do you want to talk to him?"

"No," I replied. "I'd heard somebody say he might be sick." A small fib, but I couldn't reveal my source.

"He's fine," Lori said. "For Dwight. He's not here right now, though. He took a call about something on Second Hill."

I thanked her and hung up. I assumed Milo would be lunching with Tanya to hear how her appointment with Doc Dewey had turned out. I realized it was ten after twelve. The newsroom was empty. I contemplated getting a sandwich from Pie-in-the-Sky, but the croissants had spoiled my appetite. Maybe I could use the time to research other forms of local government. Or go back through old copies of the *Advocate* to find articles about Sheriff Moroni closing dens of iniquity. I was still mulling when Kip came in from the back shop.

"Don't get mad at me," he began, "but I turned on KSKY to see if the weather was really going to clear up. Chili and I want to drive over to Leavenworth for dinner tomorrow night."

"How could I ban KSKY when I have to listen to Vida's show?"

Kip nodded. "Required by all Alpiners. Anyway, a patient got loose at RestHaven a little while ago. Spence had it on the noon news."

"Got loose? You mean somebody from the psych ward?"

"Yeah, no name, but it's a man, fifty-six years old, and he could be dangerous. Description is five-eleven, a hundred and sixty pounds, balding, with gray hair and matching goatee. He's wearing regular clothes, probably dark slacks, corduroy jacket, and maybe a baseball cap."

"Great," I said, having scribbled down the description. "I assume Spence has confirmed this? If we put it on our site, I don't want to alarm the public unnecessarily."

"He did the broadcast," Kip said. "He sounded grim."

"Okay, I trust him, but I'll call first. Are you going to lunch?"

Kip said he'd wait until after one. He often did. His wife made him a big breakfast every morning. She was a far better mate than I was to Milo when it came to feeding him in the morning. At seven a.m., my future husband could go out in the backyard and graze, for all I cared. I called Spence to request confirmation of the escapee.

"You heard it?" he asked in less than his usual mellow style.

"Kip did." I repeated what I'd been told. "Anything else?"

"That's it."

"Do you know who it was?"

"Why do you want to know? We can't release a name."

"Hey, I just wondered. You don't have to get snarky."

"You've got everything you need. Got to run." He hung up on me. I might as well have been talking to the sheriff. Which made me wonder if Milo knew about the Rest-Haven breakout. Maybe not, if he was lunching with Tanya. I called his office and this time Doe Jamison answered.

"The boss is at the ski lodge coffee shop with his daughter," Doe said. "Jack Mullins and Dustin Fong are on patrol. Dodge doesn't need to know until he gets back."

"How's it going with Tanya on the premises?" I asked.

"It's okay," Doe replied. "Her dad put her to work this morning checking out license plates. She seems sort of sad, but otherwise it's not a problem. Bill Blatt's been helping her."

"Say," I said suddenly, "I just realized Mitch didn't come back with the Eriks autopsy report. Is it in yet?"

"Not until this afternoon," Doe said.

I thanked her and disconnected. After typing up my notes, I took the online version to Kip. "Spence verified it," I told him, "so it's a go. He sounded odd. Maybe he's coming down with something."

"It's still February," Kip said. "Cold and flu season."

"True." I took the long way to my office and looked outside. The clouds had lifted and a weak sun shone on Front Street. Good weather for the escapee. Not so good for everyone else if he was dangerous.

Vida returned just before one. "Well now!" she exclaimed, smoothing the pheasant feather on her hat. "I hear there's a crazy person on the loose. Who's in charge of security at RestHaven?"

"I'd have to look it up. Why don't you ask Roger?"

"He isn't back from Bellingham," Vida

replied, removing her coat. "Davin wants him to stay another night. The dorm students often entertain. Some wholesome fun will show Roger that college isn't all work and no play. If it's nice, perhaps they can have a wienie roast outside."

I couldn't look at Vida and keep a straight face. Visions of beer kegs or worse danced in my head. There were times when Vida's ability to deceive herself stretched my credulity.

When the rest of my staff had returned to the office ten minutes later, I brought them up to speed on what little we knew about the escapee. Mitch was the point man.

"Talk to Kay Burns and keep tabs on the sheriff's office," I said. Hearing the phones ringing on all three lines, I told Amanda we'd get calls from panicky residents, especially older people and parents of young children. Updates would be posted when we learned anything new.

"All this patient privacy," Vida fumed after Mitch and Amanda left us. "It's absurd. How can we cover news without names?"

"We have to, unless Milo can pry more out of them."

Vida harrumphed and stalked to her desk. I assumed she was still mad at the sheriff. She hadn't asked about witnessing our marriage with whatever J.P. I could find who wasn't Simon Doukas.

Back in my office, I wondered if I'd overburdened Mitch. He'd be leaving for Pittsburgh in less than twenty-four hours. If there was more breaking news, including the revised autopsy report, he might feel rushed. But he was touchy about my interference. Reminding myself I was his editor and not his handmaiden, I called the one RestHaven employee I'd gotten to know best — Jennifer Hood, R.N. She owed me for being discreet about the Tiffany sighting in Kay Burns's office.

My call was transferred to the medical rehab unit. Jennifer answered on the third ring. "I just got back from making rounds," she said breathlessly. "Are you inquiring about a patient?"

"Yes, but not one of yours," I admitted. "We need to know everything we can about the psych ward patient who left the premises. Our nervous readers are calling for updates."

Jennifer didn't respond right away. "I don't know much about him," she finally said. "I've seen him only once, when he had a sinus infection and I was the only nurse available. He was calm but suspicious, probably because he didn't know me."

"What's his condition?"

Another pause. "I can't tell you. Maybe you can guess."

I reflected on her earlier words. "Suspicion indicates paranoia."

"It could. I will say," she continued speaking more quickly, "that he seems very intelligent. I'd guess him to be some kind of professional. He certainly has never done any hard labor."

"Is he really dangerous?"

"Maybe. I'm sure Dr. Woo approved the announcement."

"The announcement?" I repeated in surprise.

"Yes," Jennifer said. "Isn't that what it's called when a statement is given to the media?"

"This part of the media had to hear it over the radio," I retorted. "Did Kay Burns release it?"

"I suppose," Jennifer replied. "That'd be her job, right?"

"Yes," I said in disgust. "By the way, who heads up security?"

"That position hasn't been filled. They've been interviewing, but the two most qualified candidates decided they wanted to move to a more metropolitan area. Dr. Farrell has assumed the role until an applicant is found to fill the job. Some people don't want to live in a small town. It was like that in Dunsmuir." Jennifer sounded as if she was trying to appease me.

"True. I'm sorry to press you, but it's my job."

"I know," Jennifer said. "I wish I could be more help."

We rang off on that conciliatory note. I wanted to throttle Spence and Kay Burns. This wasn't just a leak, but a major insult. I closed my door and dialed my rival's number to give him hell. When he answered, the first words out of my mouth were a threat. "I'm ordering Vida to cancel her show tonight," I said. "You and Ms. Burns have gone too damned far. It's one thing to get beat on some pissant information out of RestHaven, but this nut case breakout is big news involving the whole damned county. If Vida doesn't agree with me, I'll can her ass."

"God, Emma, are *you* crazy? It's not my fault you weren't notified."

"Then whose freaking fault was it?" I demanded.

Spence didn't answer right away. "The RestHaven people panicked. This guy's paranoid, and having this happen so soon after the grand opening is terrible P.R. If he does something reprehensible, they're liable and their reputation is trashed before the first month of operation is over. Cut them some slack."

"No. Reacting with panic doesn't befit pros who deal with the mentally ill. I'll inform Vida while you fill your empty airtime. I just talked to Jennifer Hood. Now you can tell her the interview's off."

"Wait, you mean you already told her she wasn't going to be on —"

I banged down the phone. Spence could deal with Jennifer. I stormed out of my office — and stopped. The newsroom was empty. Vida's coat wasn't there, either. I asked Amanda where Vida had gone.

"She's taking pictures of a triple birthday party at the retirement home," Amanda said. "She also mentioned seeing Mrs. Parker. Maybe there's news about Tiffany."

"Let's hope it's good news," I said as the phone rang. I started for my office, but Amanda called out that Rosemary was on line one.

"Don't tell me," I said after hurrying to take the call at my desk, "you're being menaced by the RestHaven loony."

Rosemary laughed. "Nothing so exciting, though I might not mind. I haven't been on a date in six months. This town's short of eligible men."

"Tell me about it," I said.

"You got yours," Rosemary said. "Maybe that's my problem — I've overlooked someone who's right in front of me. I tried to get Vida earlier, but she was on the phone and now she's out. Holly Gross came to see me after lunch. She's leaving town."

"How come?"

"Let's face it, she's sort of ADD. Her other two kids are still in Sultan and the foster parents were getting impatient for her to collect them. Holly's headed for Centralia, but she's not giving up — Esther Brant won't let her — so I suppose a legal hassle will follow. I called Amy Hibbert first, but she's not home. Where's Roger, by the way?"

I told her about his Bellingham visit. Rosemary speculated as I did, that Diddy or Dippy — or maybe the poor tyke was using an alias by now — was probably stashed with Roger's aunt and uncle.

"Can you tell Vida?" Rosemary asked. "Impress upon her that Roger has to prove paternity or they'll never see Dippy again."

"I will. Oh — you're on Vida's evil list with Milo and Proxmire."

"Holy Mother," Rosemary said softly. "Why can't Vida admit . . . forget it. I don't mind, but she's basically so sensible. I'd hoped she'd put her rose-colored glasses in the back of the drawer."

"It's her blind spot," I said. "Say, is Proxmire a J.P.?"

"I'm sure she is," Rosemary said. "I can check. Why do you . . . are you going to make it legal before you get the annulment?"

"We might," I hedged. "It's probably the thing to do. We wouldn't want to set a bad example for the younger set. Like Roger."

"Right," Rosemary said dryly. "I'll double-check on the judge."

I thanked her and rang off just as Mitch appeared in the doorway. "No autopsy report yet, and Dr. Reed isn't seeing anybody. In fact, neither are Woo and Farrell. They've gone to ground."

"It figures," I said, and recounted my exchange with Fleetwood.

Mitch looked surprised. "You really won't let Vida do her show?"

"That's right. Spence should've given us a heads-up, and Kay Burns has to learn she can't play favorites."

My reporter frowned. "It wasn't Kay. She called in sick today."

I was flummoxed. "Do you know who it was?"

"No. Woo, maybe. He might not know the protocol."

"Damn. Spence still should have told us."

Mitch grimaced. "Do you really want Vida to have another snit?"

I began to weaken. "I'll think on it. Did the sheriff's office have anything new about the escapee?"

"They're looking for him. So are the park rangers and the state patrol. No reports of stolen vehicles, so he's either on foot or hitch-hiking."

"He might've hopped a freight. Put an update online. It'll reassure people that something's being done. Is there a photo or a sketch?"

"Fong said there's no photo and they don't want a sketch. More patient privacy. That's wrong in this situation."

I agreed. Vida arrived half an hour later but immediately began returning calls that had piled up in her absence. She came into my office around three and declared that she was wild. "Jennifer Hood cancelled. Doesn't that beat all? I didn't intend to ask about the runaway lunatic, but to focus on her move here. She still refused, saying that Dr. Woo felt it was in poor taste, given the situation. Now what does the *situation* have to do with making a new life in Alpine?"

I relented about Vida staying off the air. "What will you do now?"

"It's short notice," she said, plucking at her yellow blouse's pussycat bow. "I'll find someone." She started to walk away, but paused. "What about Edna Mae Dalrymple? She was very nervous last year when I interviewed her and made a jumble of things, but literacy is in crisis."

"Give her a call. I just talked to her recently about my censorship editorial regarding *Tom Sawyer.* You could tie that in, too."

"Indeed. I'll ring her at once."

Mitch reappeared with his notebook in hand. "I had Kip post the sheriff's update about the escapee search, but something's odd."

"Besides the escapee?" I asked.

Mitch shook his head. "Fong was the only deputy there. He said they were on full alert — Jamison, Mullins, Heppner, Blatt. Dodge, too. He took his daughter with him. No Gould. I thought he was back to work."

"Dwight was there earlier," I said. "He was on a call."

Mitch shrugged. "Maybe he's still on it."

I didn't want to pass along Kay's alleged concern about her ex. "Dwight's probably on highway duty."

Ten minutes later Tanya showed up. "Hi, Emma," she said, still wearing her waif-like air. "Dad thought you might need some help."

"Can't he use you at his office?" I blurted out. "I mean, he must be shorthanded with just Lori and Dustin there."

She slumped into a chair. "Sam Heppner made some crack about me tagging along on the search. Dad didn't hear it, but it upset me. I'd just as soon not go back there right now."

"Sam's a jerk," I said. "I've got a project for both of us. Let's get some old copies of the *Advocate.* We're on a mission dating back to the era of your father's predecessor. Did you know Eeeny Moroni?"

Tanya followed me to the newsroom. "Sort of. Wasn't he a crook?"

"He turned out to be later." I pulled four bound volumes from the mid-1950s and gave half of them to Tanya. I cleared my desk enough to give Tanya some space and explained the seamy background Clarence Munn had related to Vida. "We only need to look at the front page and the editorials. Just be thankful the *Advocate*'s always been a weekly."

"Dad never mentioned hookers or other vice around here," Tanya said, beginning to flip through the 1958 editions.

"He hasn't told me, either. But remember,

he was a little kid during Moroni's early years as sheriff."

Tanya smiled slightly. "It's hard to think of Dad as a little kid."

I laughed. "It is for me, too."

We worked in silence for the next ten minutes. Finally I found something in a September 1960 issue. "Here's an article about the county auditor being investigated for embezzlement. Hector Thoreson allegedly stole twenty grand from SkyCo's road fund. There must be a follow-up." The first *Advocate* in October had a big headline: "Auditor Indicted on Graft Charges." I read the story aloud. Thoreson not only had used county money for gambling, but had taken payoffs from Rupert Grimsby, Tyee Café owner. Rupe, as he was known, had action beyond the kitchen — a high-stakes poker room and illegal betting. The café had been located on the site now occupied by Francine's Fine Apparel.

"Interesting timing," I murmured. "The story broke just before the 1960 presidential election." I scanned the rest of the page below the fold. Sure enough, a young and almost unrecognizable Eeeny Moroni was glad-handing Kiwanis members at a breakfast meeting.

"My, my," Vida said, coming up behind

Tanya and giving her a start, "look who's here! How nice." She patted the young woman's shoulder and sat down beside her. "You're doing research. Oh!" she gasped, pointing to the two-column photo of the late sheriff, "there's that idiot in his first election after being appointed to replace Seth Meyers. We thought Eeeny was an improvement! Seth shot himself, you know."

"I didn't," I admitted. "I never heard of him."

"Really, Emma, you should've done more history homework."

Tanya appeared to be trying not to smile.

"When I went to work in Portland," I said, "I never researched the Oregon Territory's history. Knowing about Lewis and Clark was enough."

"That's different," Vida declared. "The Oregon Territory was so big. Why, it included what would become Alpine."

Amanda was heading our way. "Mrs. Runkel," she said, "Spencer Fleetwood's been trying to reach you. I was in the restroom when you arrived."

"Oh, yes," Vida said. "He called on my cell, but I didn't want to interrupt my visit with Dot Parker." She turned away, but I stopped her.

"Wait," I practically shouted. "Let me talk

to him first."

Vida peered at me. "Why? The call's for me."

"Please," I said. "Then I'll have Amanda transfer him."

"Bother," Vida muttered, but trudged off to her desk.

"I changed my mind," I said, after Amanda put Spence on my line. "I was wrong, okay? But I'm still mad."

"I thought you might, so I haven't notified her sponsors. I expected she might put up a fight."

"She doesn't know about my threat. Can you keep your mellifluous mouth shut for once?"

"For the sake of media peace, I'll try," Spence conceded. "You are often a very difficult woman. It's a wonder Dodge hasn't strangled you. If nothing else, he's indulgent."

"He's not unethical — like you," I said, and rang off.

Tanya was looking bemused. "I had no idea about how a newspaper operates. Is this typical?"

"Yes. No. It depends." I ran my fingers through my unruly hair, which should have been cut back in January. "Let's see if there's anything else in this bunch of issues.

369

Then we'll move into the rest of the sixties."

The only other item of interest was Marius's editorial applauding Moroni's rout of his opponent, a long-gone Gustavson whose first name I didn't recognize. Back in the newsroom Vida was explaining to Spence that Edna Mae couldn't sub because she'd come down with the flu, but Effie Trews, the high school librarian, would take her place. That was fitting, given that Effie was retiring at the end of the school year.

By the time Tanya and I got to 1963 without finding any vice-related stories, it was after four. She was looking bored, a feeling I shared. "Let's quit," I said. "These headlines are blurring."

"I'll go to Dad's office," she said. "You must have work to do."

"We're on hold with the RestHaven breakout and the Eriks autopsy. I'm not inspired to start my next editorial." I saw Mitch coming toward us. "Maybe we've got some news. I'll introduce my reporter."

"I met him this morning," Tanya said. "Hi, Mitch."

"Hi. Are you here to replace me?" His expression was wry.

"No," she replied. "But it's kind of interesting."

"It can be," Mitch allowed. He looked at me. "Here's the autopsy report. It's a shocker. You better see it before I put a summary online."

I almost blew it by saying I already knew the final result, but I caught myself in time. "Wow. Make a copy for me, please?"

"Sure." The grimace stayed in place. "They can't find Gould."

Tanya and I both looked startled. "What do you mean, they can't find him?" I asked.

Mitch held up his hands in a helpless gesture. "He never came back from Second Hill. They can't reach him. No sign of his cruiser, either. Now the searchers are looking for him, too, but Dodge . . ." He paused to glance at Tanya as if in apology. "Dodge is keeping a lid on this one for now, but Fong told me it was okay to tell you. Maybe the RestHaven escapee got to him. That'd be a hell of a thing, wouldn't it?"

All I could do was nod in agreement. And wonder if Alpine was in the grip of a psychotic plague.

SIXTEEN

Tanya spoke first. "Something's happened to Dad's deputy?"

Mitch grimaced. "I don't know, but Gould's reliable. Journalists think the worst because it makes bigger headlines." He shrugged.

I was about to suggest that maybe Dwight had caught the rampant flu bug, but it wouldn't explain what had happened to his cruiser.

Tanya stood up. "Is Dad back at his office?" she asked Mitch.

"I didn't see him," Mitch said. "I talked to Fong."

"Maybe I should go down there," she said, looking at me. "Do you think I'd cause more harm than good?"

"No," I said, "but can you wait? I'll walk partway with you. I want to stop by Parker's Pharmacy, but I have to go over the autopsy report."

"Sure. I'll put these old issues back and talk to Mrs. Runkel."

I thanked her and began scanning the report while Mitch stood by. "It's a poisoning first for me," I said. "Condense it and put it online."

My reporter went off while I grabbed my purse and jacket. When I got to Vida's desk, Tanya was being subjected to an account of Roger's renewed interest in higher education. I interrupted before my House & Home editor could start in on a fantasy about her grandson sitting around a campfire singing "The Whiffenpoof Song" while sipping hot cocoa.

"Speaking of Roger," I said to Vida in my most chipper voice, "Holly Gross has left town. If you want details, call Rosemary Bourgette." Ignoring her aghast expression, I beckoned to Tanya to follow me out of the newsroom. I could hear Vida's squawks all the way out the door.

"What was that about?" Tanya inquired.

I asked if her father had told her about Roger's unfortunate saga. He had, but only the original version dating back to the trailer park incident. "Have him fill you in," I said as we crossed Fourth and passed the hobby and toy shop. "Now I have to buy toothpaste and shampoo." I didn't add that except for his shaving gear, the sheriff hadn't brought his own toiletries and I was running low on supplies.

Waving Tanya off, I almost collided with the pharmacy's original owner, Durwood Parker. At least he was walking and not driving a car.

"Emma dear!" he exclaimed, his round pink face showing genuine pleasure. "I haven't seen you in some time. Congratulations on your engagement to Sheriff Dodge." He paused, tugging his kidskin gloves and grappling with the shopping bag that had been jostled in our near collision. "You two make a fine-looking couple. I don't suppose you might sweet-talk him into letting me have my driver's license back, would you?"

I feigned regret. "Probably not. He doesn't want you to hurt yourself. You are, after all, an institution around here."

Durwood grimaced. "Sometimes I've felt that Milo thought I should be *in* an institution. But even when he had to arrest me, he was always kind about it. Speaking of institutions, I understand there's a madman on the loose. I hope he doesn't harm himself or anyone else. In fact, I'd better head home. I don't like leaving Dot alone with . . . without me." He gestured at a bicycle secured to a small rack by the hobby shop. "That's what I'm driving these days. Take care, Emma."

I thought it best not to wait to see if Milo was right about Durwood not riding a bike any better than he drove a car. But I did wonder why he'd stumbled over his words about Dot. I was even more curious why he had Pampers in his shopping bag. I'd noticed they were a toddler size.

Going into the pharmacy, I was disappointed to see that neither of the current owners, Garth or Tara Wesley, was on the premises. I'd intended to ask them about Durwood's purchase. I didn't know the young man who was behind the counter. He looked like a college student. I got what I needed and left, but noticed Milo's Yukon now in its usual spot. I decided to pay the sheriff an official visit.

Dustin, Lori, Tanya, and Beth Rafferty, the 911 operator and Tim's sister, stood at attention as Milo held court. "I don't give a rat's ass if somebody stabbed Blackwell," he bellowed, ignoring my arrival. "The priority is Gould. The nut job is secondary. You all got that?"

They nodded, including Tanya. Beth was holding her earpiece in place. Maybe she was afraid Milo's voice had shaken it loose.

Lori seemed dazed, and even Dustin wasn't quite his usual stolid self. The sheriff wheeled around and headed for his office.

"Hi," I said to nobody in particular. "I guess I won't bother your boss right now. Dare I ask what happened to Blackwell?"

Dustin rallied first. "It's weird. You know about Patti Marsh's accident, right?" He saw me nod. "She didn't have to stay in the hospital, so she went home. Last night Blackwell came to see her. He was sick, so Patti thought he had the flu and told him she'd take care of him. By this afternoon he was delirious, so she called Doc Dewey and said that if she could manage it, she'd put him in her car to bring him to the clinic. Doc told her he'd have an ambulance sent, but no siren, because it might scare people who thought it had to do with the Rest-Haven escapee. They got to the hospital an hour ago and it turned out Jack had been stabbed. The wound festered because he hadn't had it treated. Strange, huh?"

By the time Dustin finished, I'd leaned both elbows on the counter. "He didn't stab himself to file another complaint?"

"In the back?" Dustin said. "That'd be hard to do."

"Did he say who did it?" I asked.

The deputy shook his head. "He's still out

of it. He never mentioned it to Patti. She didn't find out until Doc checked Jack."

"Has your boss any ideas or is he too upset about Dwight to care?"

Before Dustin could answer, Beth Rafferty spoke up. "It'd be a help if somebody could find Tiff. I've taken half a dozen calls from fools who think they've spotted my lame-brained sister-in-law. They were all duds. What's wrong with people?"

"Good question," I murmured before gesturing at Milo's closed door. "Dare I?"

"I wouldn't," Beth said, heading back to her 911 inner sanctum.

"He's pretty grumpy," Lori murmured.

"I think he's on the phone," Dustin said in his usual polite manner.

"Do it," Tanya said, much to my surprise.

I smiled at her and opened the swinging door in the counter. "I will." Marching to the door, I didn't bother to knock.

Milo was hanging up the phone. "Beat it, Emma."

I closed the door behind me. "I will not. This is my business, too." I plopped down in a chair and set my drugstore purchases on the floor. "Mitch is on overload because he's leaving for Pittsburgh tomorrow. I need some updates before I go home."

"Jesus." Milo put a hand to his forehead.

"I don't know any more than what you probably heard from that bunch out front. No sign of Gould, no sign of the lunatic, no idea how Blackwell got stabbed. That's it. Go ahead, tell your readers the sheriff is baffled. I don't give a damn."

"Yes, you do."

Milo's hazel eyes finally met mine. He leaned back in the chair and sighed. "I was on the phone with Doc. Blackwell's wound isn't deep, but the dumb shit didn't have it checked and it got infected. He'll be fine."

"Is he lucid?"

"Was he ever?"

"He's always been lucid — for an asshole."

I could always tell when the sheriff relaxed even slightly. "It's Dwight that worries me," he said. "You know him — dependable as snow on Baldy. It's possible that he went after somebody on one of the old logging roads and had a wreck. The state patrol is bringing a helicopter to look for him and the nut. He doesn't answer from the cruiser or his cell." Milo glanced at his watch. "They should be overhead just after five."

"Maybe I should stick around," I said. "I mean, at my office."

The sheriff shrugged. "You do your job, I'll do mine."

I stood up. "Then I'll go away and stop bothering you."

Milo was staring at his wall map of Skykomish County as if he were trying to figure out where Dwight might be found. "Okay," he said.

I picked up the Parker's Pharmacy bag and left, closing the door behind me. "I survived," I announced, going through the reception area. "There were no injuries."

I headed back to my office. I'd gone only about ten feet when a SkyCo cruiser pulled up. I gasped when Dwight Gould got out. He saw me, mumbled something, and walked calmly into headquarters. I froze in place, wondering if I should go back to see what kind of welcome he'd get. Deciding that was the worst idea I'd had since I'd let Ed Bronsky talk me into editing his autobiography, I kept on going to the *Advocate.*

It was ten to five when I reached the newsroom. Amanda was on the phone, Leo was coming from the back shop, and Mitch was at his desk. Vida was putting on her coat.

"I didn't realize you'd gone shopping," she said, looking at my Parker's Pharmacy bag. "I'm leaving a bit early so I can prepare for the interview with Effie Trews. I haven't chatted with her in some time."

"Fine," I said. "The prodigal deputy has returned."

Vida's jaw dropped, Mitch looked up from his monitor, and Leo stopped in mid-step before reaching his desk. They all responded in some way, but it was my House & Home editor's voice that dominated. "Where on earth has that ninny been?" she shrieked.

I admitted I didn't know. "He arrived in his cruiser and in uniform. I decided to skip the fireworks. The sheriff was already steamed." I held up a hand to ward off a barrage from Vida. "Meanwhile, somebody stabbed Blackwell in the back. He's in the hospital."

More shrieks ensued from Vida, along with shocked expressions from my staff, which now included Kip and Amanda. I waited for everybody to shut up, though Vida was dialing her phone. "I should've known that Marje called me about something other than my eye exam reminder. She's still at the clinic. It doesn't close. . . . Marje, dear, I'm so sorry I was on the other line when . . ."

I backed away in order to be heard. "Mitch, go home. You've got to get ready for your trip. Leo, Amanda, feel free to do whatever, including leave for the day." I turned to Kip. "I'm not sure what we can put online, but we should do something."

"Can we say Gould's safe?" he asked, looking justifiably confused.

"We never said he wasn't," I replied. "That was strictly internal. Milo would explode if we reveal a lost deputy while a head case is loose. As for Jack, let's wait. He was too loopy to say anything coherent."

Kip fingered his bearded chin. "Maybe Jack did have the flu and then Patti stabbed him."

"Rethink that one," I said. "Though with that pair, anything's possible. We'll hold off until Doc reports to Milo and we get a formal statement. That could take time if they wait for Jack to make sense."

Amanda had already left. Mitch and Leo departed together. Vida had finished her call. "Well! A fine kettle of fish this is! Marje doesn't know any more than you do, Emma. Now I must dash to prepare for my program." She picked up her purse, but paused. "Maybe I should first call my nephew Billy."

"He may still be in the middle of the Dwight Gould reprisal."

"Fiddlesticks. Unless Milo is beating up his entire staff, Billy can still talk to his aunt."

Feeling a headache coming on, I got two Excedrin out of my little pill case and grabbed some bottled water from under the coffee table. Kip returned to the back shop; I went into my office. I could still hear Vida talking — and listening. Bill Blatt must be on the other end of the line.

Three minutes later, she tromped into my office. "If that doesn't beat all!" she exclaimed, the feather on her hat drooping over her forehead. I felt kind of droopy, too. "You won't believe this," she declared, flopping into a chair. "Dwight spent the afternoon with Kay Burns. He said if Milo could take the afternoon off to be with a woman, so could he, especially when he hadn't seen her in almost thirty years."

"D-D-Dwight was in b-b-bed with a w-w-woman?" I sputtered.

"Kay used to be his wife. I must assume the woman Milo was with was you. Did that happen when I was out of town for Christmas?"

I rubbed my forehead. "It was after he returned from nursing Tanya back to health. We were engaged. Well, almost engaged. But Dwight hasn't seen Kay in three decades. I thought she had the flu."

"Apparently she recovered," Vida retorted. "I wonder if Milo will suspend him again. That doesn't seem right, does it?"

"I don't know what's right anymore," I

admitted. "For all I know, Dwight stabbed Blackwell and then made off with Kay. They were both married to her. If that's the case, Milo may give Dwight a medal."

Vida turned thoughtful. "I don't suppose I could use that in 'Scene.' Delicately phrased, of course."

"Of course," I murmured.

She bolted out of the chair. "I really must run. I'm ill prepared."

I was still holding my head after Vida left. It could be a long time before we got official word about Jack. Kip and I might as well go home. I went into the back shop to tell him. I also related Dwight's amorous defection. Kip couldn't stop laughing. I tried to share his mirth, but I was dog-tired. Shortchanged on sleep, putting in a wild workday, and uncertain when I'd see Milo again, I drove home in the same befogged condition in which I'd arrived that morning.

It wasn't until I got inside my little log house that I realized I was starving. I hadn't eaten lunch. I'd also forgotten Vida had said that she was going to see Tanya after her program. I wondered if she still planned to do that, given that they had visited in the office. Searching the freezer, I found some tiger prawns. I thawed them in the microwave and started boiling water for udon noodles. After changing into my bathrobe, I realized the Excedrin was kicking in. I was munching raw carrots when the phone rang. It was my nice neighbor, Viv Marsden. "Emma," she began, sounding tense, "have you seen anybody near your house?"

"Like who?" I asked.

"A man was in our backyard about ten minutes ago when Val took out the garbage. It was already dark, but he seemed to fit the description of that crazy person. He appears to be gone now, but I didn't see Dodge's car, so I thought you must be alone. Should we call the sheriff?"

I almost choked on another carrot. "Yes," I gulped. "The Nelson house is still vacant on the other side of my place. He might be holed up in there. If it's him, I mean."

"I will," Viv said. "Make sure your doors are locked."

Just what I need, I thought, leaning back on the sofa. Mr. Paranoia showing up would be a fitting end to my day. Or the end of me. I got up to double-check the doors. They were secure, but I still felt nervous. My appetite had dwindled, though I kept eating. I needed my strength in case the latest menace broke a window to gain entry. Maybe I should get out the gun I kept in the closet. I'd never fired the thing and wasn't sure if I had any bullets. Milo had told me if I ever tried to use it, I'd shoot myself instead.

I had started for the kitchen with my empty bowl when I heard someone call my name at the carport door. It didn't sound like Milo. I paused by the sink, wondering if I should grab a knife. But whoever it was knew me. I moved cautiously and looked through the window. Jack Mullins looked back.

I opened the door. "Where's Milo?" I asked.

"Up at the ranger station," Jack said, taking off his hat and trying to tame his wild red hair. "Some guy in a snowmobile ran out of snow and hit a tree. The poor bastard's been lying up there since four-thirty. His cell was dead and he's damned lucky to be alive."

"A local?" I asked.

"No. A local would know better. He's from Kent. Where's the nut?"

"I haven't seen him. He might be at the Nelson house. It's been empty since you guys arrested most of the family last December."

"I'll check it out. You got any coffee?"

"No, but I can make some."

Jack shook his head. "Don't bother. I should get going."

"What happened with Dwight? I heard he was with Kay."

Jack grinned. "Can you believe it? I can't. I think he went fishing."

"Dwight wouldn't do that. I mean, not on the job, especially after he'd just been suspended."

Jack sighed. "It's more believable than Dwight making love to his ex-wife. But maybe he's human after all. Dodge let him off the hook for now, if only because we need everybody aboard until the nut's found. I wonder if the guy offed himself. I'd better go."

"Hey — where's Tanya? She could come here and stay with me instead of hanging out at headquarters."

Jack gave me his puckish grin. "Bill Blatt offered to stay with her at Dodge's house. Did you know he had a crush on her in high school?"

"You're kidding!"

"He did. And his own romance blew up just a little while ago."

"An interesting turn of events," I remarked.

Jack put his hat back on. "If Tanya wants a guy who's steady as a rock, that's Bill.

Keep yourself locked in, Emma."

As soon as the deputy left, I looked at the clock on the stove. It was five to seven. I hurried into the living room to turn on the radio. The hour-turn news always came on at five minutes to when it was Vida's night to howl. I caught all but the introduction — and realized that the voice I heard belonged not to Spence but to Bree Kendall, his part-time on-air person. She led off with the escapee still being at large, followed by the banged-up snowmobiler. I'd call Kip after Vida's show to have him get an update from the hospital. There was nothing about Blackwell. The rest was a quick take on regional and national news with the weather forecast — partial clouds with a high of forty-six and a low of thirty-five. To my further surprise, Bree began to introduce Vida's program. I wondered if Spence had fallen victim to the flu. The phone rang and I jumped, but quickly grabbed the receiver.

"All clear at the Nelsons' house," Jack Mullins said. "No sign of anybody trying to get in."

I thanked him and rang off just as Vida wound up her usual greeting before talking about the decline of literacy and decrease in readership. "Subjects," she said, "with which my guest is very familiar. Effie Trews has been the librarian at Alpine High School since 1965 and will be retiring in June. Effie, tell us why reading has declined in the . . ."

I drifted while Effie listed dry statistics. Vida pointed out the danger of ignorance and the pleasure of reading. Effie noted that books provided escape from the dreary everyday world. She sounded dreary, too. I missed Edna Mae's bird-like chatter, even when she got rattled and referred to Charles Dickens as Slim Pickens and Elmore Leonard as Len Elmore. The commercial break was for Alpine Auto Supply and Swanson's Toyota, both ads taped by Spence. When Vida returned, she asked Effie about the attempt to ban *Tom Sawyer* from the high school.

"That," Effie declared, her voice suddenly springing to life, "was an insult to one of America's greatest writers and to the intelligence of any age group, including teens. I'm opposed to all forms of censorship. Children grow up faster these days. Parents complain about smut on the Internet. If they really knew what their children read and see, their eyes would pop out. Some call it pornography, but that's for the courts to decide. If you put a classic such as *Tom Sawyer* in the same category with what we sometimes find in student lockers, those foolish parents would think twice before making their silly protests."

A slight pause ensued. I guessed Vida hadn't expected such a heated response. "Do you mean there's pornography at the high school?"

"I believe I just said that," Effie huffed. "What I'd like to know is where it's coming from. From what I've seen, it's local."

"You mean," Vida asked, unable to keep the shock out of her voice, "someone in Alpine is distributing porn?"

"Yes. I recognized some of the subjects in the photos."

"This is quite shocking," Vida asserted, seemingly having regained her aplomb. "Has it been reported to the authorities?"

"Not to my knowledge," Effie replied. "But it should be."

"I agree," Vida said. "Is Principal Freeman investigating?"

"You'd have to ask him. He's opted for discretion among the faculty. I had no knowledge of this until shortly before Christmas break."

I glanced at my watch. Vida was about to close her cupboard. "Effie," she said, "you've not only pointed out the sad state of literacy along with the decline in reading, but revealed an alarming situation within the walls of our beloved high school. Congratulations on your long and tireless service to our youth. I wish you all the best in retirement."

"Thank you," Effie replied. "It has been a joy. For the most part."

The door creaked closed, signaling the end of the program. Bree came back on, announcing that following a break for Sky-Co's fine sponsors, the remainder of the hour would include the top ten hits from 1975. My phone was ringing before the first commercial started.

"Who's in the most trouble?" Kip asked. "Vida's not supposed to put real news on the radio. And will Miss Trews be able to work long enough to have a retirement party?"

"I have to give Vida a pass on this one. She was clearly stunned. As for Effie, I don't think she's in as much trouble as Karl Freeman. The school board will pitch a fit. I've heard rumors about porn among the students, but Freeman stonewalled Mitch."

"I didn't know that," Kip said.

"We'll sit on this for now," I told him, but added I'd check on the snowmobiler and get back to him. I immediately called the hospital. Luckily I was transferred to Julie

Canby, one of the few nurses I hadn't antagonized over the years. She gave me the accident victim's name and verified that he lived in Kent, a Seattle suburb. The snow-mobiler was still in the ER but wasn't seriously injured.

"Maybe a broken arm," she said. "Contusions and shock along with one wrecked snowmobile. People should do those things in pairs."

"That's good news," I responded. "Can we say minor injuries?"

"Wait until I get official word. I'll call you back. It shouldn't take too long before he's up here in a room."

"Okay. By the way, did you know Vida interviewed your uncle Clarence yesterday?"

"No," Julie said. "Did he make sense?"

"He seemed to," I replied, "at least as long as he kept to the past. Has he ever talked to you about what things were like back then?"

"Not really," Julie admitted. "I moved to Maltby when I was twenty and didn't return until I married Spike. Excuse me, Emma, I've got a patient calling me." She lowered her voice. "It's Jack Blackwell. He must be conscious." She rang off, leaving me with some unasked questions.

Shortly before eight, Vida called. "You must be as flabbergasted as I was," she said.

"I wanted Effie to elaborate after the show, but she felt she'd already had her say. Such a box of bees!"

"Did you light up KSKY's three phone lines?"

"I have no idea. I left right away. I do not enjoy Bree Kendall's company any more than you do. She's working full-time there, which I didn't know. I wondered why I hadn't seen her lately at the hospital reception desk. I shall take Spencer to task for not telling me."

"Where was Mr. Radio?"

"According to Bree, he had a previous engagement he couldn't cancel," Vida said in an indignant tone. "I'm quite vexed with him."

"I thought maybe he had the flu."

"Apparently not. I must call Harvey Adcock. He's the new president of the school board. Are you alone?"

"Yes," I said, and told Vida that Val Marsden thought he'd spotted the escapee in his backyard. "Jack Mullins stopped by to make sure I was okay. Did you know your nephew Bill's staying with Tanya?"

"What?" Vida screeched.

I heard a sound outside. "I'll let you sort that one out. I think Mullins may be back. Bye, Vida."

I hung up but took the phone with me to the kitchen door. It swung open before I could get past the sink.

Milo walked in, took off his hat, and let out a weary sigh. "Jesus, I'm beat. I've got to make this quick. How about if I bring Tanya over here tonight? I can't leave either of you alone, and Bill's been on the job for over twenty-four hours. The poor guy's probably about to pass out."

"That's fine," I said. "I take it you'll stay here, too?"

"Hell, yes, but don't expect any thrills and excitement. I might pass out before Bill does."

I smiled. "I won't. I want to crash, too. Is the nut still loose?"

Milo put his hat back on. "Yeah. I figure he headed for the woods. No reports of a hitchhiker out on Highway 2 or anybody picking him up. The state patrol expanded the bulletin to Snohomish, King, and Chelan counties. We did find out that the guy's last known address was in Issaquah. Maybe he thought he could hike through the mountains and end up on I-90 close to his old home on the Eastside. Hell, if he lived in Issaquah, maybe he'll surface at Mulehide's house in Bellevue and end up as husband number three." Shaking his head, he turned to the door. "See you in an hour or so. Stay safe until I get back."

After I heard him test the knob outside to make sure the door was locked, I went into Adam's room, which was crowded with my old bed and some of Milo's belongings. The twin bed was made up and accessible. I was in the living room when Julie called back. The snowmobiler had a simple fracture in his right arm and multiple bruises but was stable. I passed the information on to Kip, who wondered if we should put the story online, given that the injured man wasn't local. I'd had my own qualms but felt that our already nervous populace would wonder what the emergency vehicles had been doing on the Icicle Creek Road. They might fret that the escapee was in their midst. Kip agreed that was sufficient reason to go online. Thus are great news decisions made in small towns.

Just before nine I realized Milo probably hadn't eaten dinner. I had chicken breasts, hamburger, and the leftover crab in the freezer. Fifteen minutes later the sheriff and his daughter arrived. Tanya looked more chipper than her father. I assumed Bill hadn't passed out on her. In fact, she informed me, Vida's nephew had taken her to dinner at the ski lodge. Milo, however, hadn't eaten since lunch. He told me to fix whatever was easiest and poured himself a drink.

"You want one?" he asked as an afterthought.

I told him I did, having passed on liquor earlier. The hamburger was enough for a steak-sized serving, so I defrosted it and started frying potatoes in chopped onion. Tanya had gone into the living room and turned on the TV while her father sank into a kitchen chair. He was not in a talkative mood. In fact, he didn't speak until after the hamburger was frying and some canned peas were starting to boil.

"Thanks," he said.

I turned the peas down to a simmer and looked at him. "For what?"

"For not asking a lot of dumb questions like you usually do."

I picked up my drink and sat down. "You're tired. So am I."

He put his hand on my arm. "How'd I get so lucky?"

"You earned it after fifteen years. You're a very patient man."

He shrugged. "Not always, but I was when it came to you. You're the most contrary woman I ever met."

"I prefer perverse."

"That works, too." He squeezed my arm before lighting a cigarette and offering me one. I took it. "You heard about Gould?" he asked.

"Oh, yes. Is it really true?"

Milo laughed. "Dwight has no imagination. He couldn't make that up. The call he answered was from Kay's place. She's buying Denise Petersen's former town house on Second Hill. Kay claimed someone tried to break in. One thing led to another, and . . . yeah, it *is* hard to believe. His cruiser was in her garage. From what I remember, Kay can't survive long without a man. Widowhood doesn't suit her."

I laughed, too. "So what will you do about Dwight going AWOL?"

"I'll dock his pay for the time off. It's so damned funny that I can't get too pissed. Besides, he's right — I did the same thing with you. I probably should've docked my own pay, but I never thought about it."

"Too late now," I said, getting up to turn the hamburger and potatoes. "By the way, Julie Canby says Blackwell's conscious."

"Shit. I should . . . to hell with it. He may be awake, but he's not lucid. He stabbed me in the back often enough. Now it really happened to him."

"You look smug."

"I am. You look like you want to ask me a question. Don't. I have no idea who stabbed him. If I did, I'd shake his — or her — hand."

"No, you wouldn't," I said, getting up. "You go by the book."

"So I do. Dinner ready?"

"Yes," I said, and proceeded to dish it up. "Go ahead and eat in peace. I'm going to talk to Tanya."

The sheriff's daughter was watching *CSI,* which seemed appropriate. I asked if I could get her some wine or another kind of beverage. She said no, muted the TV, and asked how her dad was doing. I told her he was eating and would probably survive.

"Are you mad at me?" she asked.

I sat down on the arm of the sofa. "No. Why would I be?"

"Well . . ." She frowned, and when she spoke again, it was almost in a whisper. "I didn't think much about you as a couple when I was here the first time. Maybe, like Mom, I didn't take your . . . relationship seriously. I never really got to know you, not even when you and Dad were dating years ago. He's changed. I noticed that when he stayed with me while I was recovering. But it didn't sink in until tonight, when he told me we were coming here. What he said was he had to go home. I don't think he realized how he put it. Then it hit me on the way here. You make him happy. I don't remember Dad being happy since I was a little kid."

"Oh," I said, touching her arm, "that makes me want to cry!"

"Me too," she said, sniffling to prove it. "But I'm not helping."

I smiled. "Let's put it this way. Your father and I haven't had a lot of time together since we got engaged. But we're not a young couple just starting out. We've been friends for going on sixteen years and lovers off and on for over half that time. We've always had other responsibilities. The difference now is we face them together. Your dad already has had to put up with my brother causing a problem, but we worked through it. The main thing for you is to deal with your crisis and heal. I'll do what I can to help both of you. When it comes to coping with adversity, we're seasoned veterans. We may bitch, we may bend, but we don't break."

Tanya put her hand over mine but didn't say anything. The twin tears that trickled down her cheeks were thanks enough. Except for the rare occasions when I'd seen Milo's children on their visits to Alpine, I'd never thought much about his role as a father. To me, he was always the sheriff, my friend, and my lover. Now I was seeing him in a role he'd assumed long before we met. Maybe I wouldn't turn into an evil stepmother. I might even become a good wife.

Milo and I both slept like bricks that night. Tanya apparently was nightmare-free. She had gone to bed after we did, having stayed up to watch Jay Leno. The sheriff got up at his usual time while I dozed until a few minutes after seven. He was in the kitchen when I stumbled into the bathroom. After I finished showering, I couldn't find my hair dryer. Tanya's door was closed, so I assumed she hadn't gotten up yet. I found Milo dishing up ham and eggs.

"Did you use my hair dryer?" I asked.

He scowled at me. "I dry my hair with a towel."

"I can't find it," I said.

He sat down. "Oh — I forgot. It's in the carport."

"The carport?" I yipped. "What the hell is it doing there?"

"You don't own a blowtorch," he said complacently as he buttered the toast. "It dropped to thirty-one last night. I thought maybe the pipes had frozen. Turns out they were okay."

"You were going to use my hair dryer to . . ." Of course he was. I supposed it made sense in some weird male way. I went out to the carport and found the hair dryer on top of the woodpile.

"Jerk," I said, brushing by him on the way back to the bathroom.

He was gone by the time I was dressed and back in the kitchen. Tanya was still sleeping. I ate cornflakes and drank some coffee — which tasted like sawmill sludge. Was Milo's mere presence near a coffee-maker sufficient to turn my good brew into whatever they drank at his office?

I was going to pour the rest of it down the sink when I saw a note he'd left under my flour canister. My irritation fled as I picked up the small sheet of notepaper, which read: "Your coffee tastes like you made it in the bathtub." I ripped up the note and threw it in the garbage. And realized I'd been so tired that I'd forgotten to make a fresh pot before I fell into bed. Sure enough, the pot was almost dry. I unplugged it and headed for work. Tanya was on her own.

Amanda, Mitch, and Kip had already arrived. Leo had the bakery run. "Anything new?" I asked, sounding more like a cub reporter than the editor and publisher. In my usual perverse way, I hadn't turned on

400

KSKY for Spence's morning update.

"Nut's still loose," Kip said. "I suppose Dodge told you that."

I didn't comment. "Any word on Blackwell?"

My three staffers stared at me blankly. "Okay," I said, "I'm out of the loop this morning. I'm still reeling from Vida's show last night." I turned to Mitch, aware of the flight bag sitting by his desk. "You'll have to talk to Karl Freeman this morning. He'll probably give you a 'no comment,' but we've got to have something."

"Shouldn't Vida handle that?" Mitch asked.

He had a point. Vida, after all, had known the principal since he'd arrived in Alpine, shortly before I had. "You're right. That story shouldn't have broken on her program, but that isn't her fault. You can check on Blackwell. He regained consciousness last night, but wait until the sheriff talks to him."

Mitch looked puzzled. "Hasn't Dodge done that already?"

"No. He wanted to wait until he had a good night's sleep. Blackwell, I mean." That wasn't what I meant, but it sounded better. "He might've been incoherent last night." This time I did mean Jack, although it could have gone either way by ten-thirty, when Milo was reduced to muttering something that sounded like "good night."

Luckily, Vida entered in a flurry of sparkling rhinestone snowflakes on a black cloche. "My phone never stopped ringing last night! Everyone from Harvey Adcock to Grace Grundle. Grace, of course, thought kiddy porn was actually kitty porn and had something to do with her cats! She wanted to know if there were lewd pictures of Tiddlywinks or Crosspatch or whichever other wretched felines she keeps in her menagerie."

"Poor Grace," Amanda murmured, trying not to giggle.

"What," I inquired, "is Harvey going to do with the school board?"

"He's calling a closed emergency meeting tonight," Vida replied.

"I assumed he would," I said, seeing Leo make his entrance. "Did Harvey have any idea about what was going on at the high school?"

"If he did, he wouldn't admit it," Vida said, unwinding a long angora scarf from around her neck. I wondered if she'd had it made out of one of Grace's cats. "The only thing of interest he told me was that Effie Trews would be on hand. And Karl Freeman, of course. We should put that online," she added, looking at Kip.

"Got it," Kip said, his gaze straying to Leo and the bakery box.

"Porn City," Leo said. "I tried to find some indecent pastries, but the closest I could come was cinnamon twists."

"Leo!" Vida cried. "Don't make things worse!"

I heard my phone ring. "Amanda," I said, heading for the coffee table, "can you get that and put it on hold? I need real coffee."

Leo was setting out the pastries. I grabbed a cinnamon twist, filled my mug, and hurried to grab my phone before sitting down.

"Guess I beat you again," Spence said, sounding slightly apologetic. "Hey, I had no idea what Vida was doing. Forget I complained about her program getting bland."

"You'd better treat her like an empress," I declared. "Where were you last night? She's not happy with your absence."

"Damn. Trust me, I had a crisis of my own. I *do* have a life."

"Want to tell me about it? It could be *news*. You owe us."

"No, I don't. Advantage, *Advocate*. Vida's probably hightailing it up to Alpine High. When did I ever pry into your private life?"

"How about when Milo broke your nose

for defending my honor?"

"That was different. I thought Dodge was interested in other things about you than your honor. Macho mistake, okay? Let's drop it."

Spence sounded unusually grim. I saw I had another call waiting. "Just make sure you grovel when you talk to Vida. I've got breaking news. Ha-ha." I hung up on him.

I'd lied, of course, but when I picked up the other call, the urgency in Beth Rafferty's voice got my attention.

"Emma," she said, speaking rapidly, "I can't stay on the line very long in case I get a 911 call, but can we meet for lunch at the ski lodge?"

"Yes, sure. Noon?"

"A little after. Evan Singer is filling in for me. See you there."

Vida was also tied up on the phone, but growing impatient, tapping her pencil on the desk until it finally broke. "Such ninnies!" she declared when I went for a coffee refill just after nine. "Most of these callers aren't high school parents, they're voyeurs. They ask such prurient questions."

"Are you going to arrive unannounced at the high school?" I asked.

Vida stared at me over the rims of her big glasses before pushing them back up on her nose. "Certainly. A surprise attack is always best."

Leo looked up from his monitor. "Why not a blare of trumpets, Duchess? That might get the attention of the kids who're ogling porn."

Vida sniffed disdainfully as she wound the angora scarf around her neck. "I would certainly like to find out where this filth is coming from. Has either of you heard anything but vague rumors?"

Leo and I both looked blank, though he did respond. "I haven't even heard the rumors. First you have to define what porn is."

"It's repellent," Vida asserted, putting on her coat. "I shall return." She swept out of the newsroom.

"Maybe I should start calling her General MacArthur," Leo murmured. "Why are we assuming the purveyor is local?"

"Good question," I said, sitting on the edge of his desk. "Effie thought it had shown up before Christmas. Some families go out of town for Thanksgiving to visit other relatives. Maybe somebody brought it back with them. A half dozen photos could be considered an epidemic."

"True enough," Leo conceded, lighting a cigarette.

Amanda called my name. "Emma, Donna Wickstrom on line one."

Hurrying back to my office, I'd realized I'd forgotten that Craig Laurentis was supposed to be sending her a new painting. I eagerly picked up the receiver. "Hi, Donna. Have you got the new masterpiece?"

"Not yet," Donna said. "Next week, maybe. But Craig did contact me. He found the man who escaped from RestHaven. He insisted I tell you, rather than calling the sheriff."

"Where is he? The escapee, I mean."

"He's off that old abandoned road on Tonga Ridge near Carroll Creek. I couldn't get Craig to give me an exact location. He identifies things by trees and rocks and . . . anyway, it doesn't matter in terms of finding him fast. He's dead."

SEVENTEEN

Donna couldn't tell me anything further. She was in full swing with the day care, and a toddler named Wisteria had fallen off a footstool and landed on another kid named Joe. Or Jo. I didn't get a chance to ask that, either. And while Craig might trust me but not the sheriff or any other representative of a government agency, I did. I dialed Milo at once.

"The jerk's dead?" my beloved barked at me. "Great. 'Somewhere near the end of the abandoned road by Carroll Creek' doesn't pinpoint where he is. There are two of those roads in that area."

"I'm just the messenger. He's not going to get any deader. Will you notify Rest-Haven?"

"I'll let Heppner do it. He's got no tact. It'll serve them right for letting the guy get out in the first place. And just when I was going to pay a call on Blackwell."

"Hey," I said. "I left Tanya still sleeping. Should I check on her?"

"I already talked to her," Milo said impatiently. "She's fine. Bill's got the day off after serving two shifts. Later on he's taking her for a ride. Leavenworth, maybe, or Lake Chelan. Hang up, Emma."

Mitch returned before I could decide what to do next. I met him in the newsroom.

"Not much new at the sher—" he began.

"There is now," I broke in, but seeing his look of dismay, I changed tactics. "Are you caught up?"

"I will be, as soon as I write up what's in the log. It's not very exciting, but it's long because half the town reported seeing the escapee or somebody trying to break into their houses. The snowmobiler accident, Blackwell's stabbing — that's either old or no news."

"Okay," I said. "Then follow up on Blackwell and I'll take the escapee story. That should be it for you. The head case is dead, by the way. I'll have Kip put it online now."

"Jesus," Mitch murmured. "Now I feel left out."

I smiled. "You can't have it both ways." I hurried to the back shop.

Kip was stunned by my latest bulletin. "How'd he die? Exposure?"

408

"I don't know," I said, "but Heppner's going to tell the RestHaven people, so it's official — or will be in a few minutes. Go with it, and say that his body was found by a local resident."

"Who? We should have a name."

"Not this time. It was Craig Laurentis, the recluse artist. He doesn't want publicity, and I'm honoring that."

"Your call," Kip said, though he didn't seem too pleased.

The phone rang just as I got back to my desk.

"This is Kay Burns," the voice at the other end said in a strained tone. "You don't intend to announce the supposed death of our patient, do you? There's no official confirmation of identification."

It occurred to me that technically she was right. "Wouldn't he have some ID on him?" I asked.

"No. Psych patients aren't allowed access to their ID. It's for their own good, of course."

"Then since we never knew his name, why shouldn't we go with the news so that everybody can relax?"

"Please. Wait for Dr. Woo to make the announcement. We heard about it less than five minutes ago. If it's true, the body may not be recovered until later today."

I paused. "How about this? We say, 'The body of an unidentified man who may be the patient . . .' and so on. This would quiet everybody's fears. It's our duty as a newspaper to keep our readers informed when it comes to public safety. I'm sure Spencer Fleetwood will agree."

It was Kay's turn to hesitate. "Let me ask Dr. Woo. I'll get right back to you."

I thanked her and rang off. For the first time since KSKY went on the air, I called Spence to share a story. I needed him as a media ally. His reaction wasn't what I expected.

"I don't know, Emma," he said slowly. "This is a delicate matter. Patient privacy, the poor guy's family . . . let's sit on it for a while."

"You're nuts. This isn't just a news item, it's in the public interest."

"Have you cleared it with RestHaven?"

I winced and was glad Spence couldn't see me. "I'm waiting for a green light from Dr. Woo."

"Okay, when you get it, call me back. Talk to you later."

Setting the receiver down, I pondered Spence's attitude. Was he putting me on about Kay Burns coming on to him? That didn't add up, given that Kay had ended up in bed the next day with Dwight Gould. Or was Kay a nymphomaniac? "Something's off," I said as Mitch came to see me.

"What?" he asked, handing me a printout of the sheriff's log.

"May I ask an impertinent question?"

He shrugged. "You're the boss."

"Has Kay Burns made a pass at you?"

Mitch laughed. "No. I mean, not overtly. She did strike me as probably not the kind who needed much encouragement, though."

I considered telling my reporter about Dwight's defection but figured that Milo must be keeping the matter internal. If he wasn't, one of the deputies — especially Jack Mullins — might have mentioned it. Maybe they'd stick with the sheriff's earlier speculation that Dwight had gotten stranded chasing somebody on a logging road.

"Forget I asked," I said. "I'm still trying to figure out how Fleetwood keeps beating us. By the way, Dodge was going to see Blackwell. Give him a call in a few minutes and then you're good to go."

"Should I ask if they're searching for the escapee's body?"

"Yes. If Dodge says they are, then I'm posting it online."

A few minutes later, Amanda brought the

mail. There were more letters about my editorial, mostly against it. Fuzzy's plan was going to be a hard sell until I got to specifics pointing out that reorganization would save taxpayers money — at least in theory.

I'd just finished reading the last letter when Mitch showed up again. "Dodge wasn't back from the hospital yet, but Doe Jamison and Dustin Fong had taken off to look for the dead guy by Carroll Creek."

"Good. It's official." I quickly typed up the bulletin and took it to Kip in the back shop. If RestHaven complained, I had the sheriff to fall back on. Milo had always had my back. And vice versa.

By coincidence, he phoned me five minutes later. "Don't ask me any questions about Blackwell."

"Uh . . . I think *you* just called *me.*"

"You bet I did. I figured either Laskey or you would be after me as soon as I got back from the hospital. Fleetwood too. I'm not giving out anything until I sort through this frigging mess. I don't suppose your in-house spy has any idea where Tiffany is?"

"If she does, she hasn't told me," I said. "She's up at the high school, grilling Karl Freeman about the porn."

"What porn?"

"You haven't heard?"

"No, and I don't want to. I've got enough on my plate." The sheriff clicked off.

I went to tell Mitch he was off the hook. "Go ahead, get an early start to the airport," I said. "It's Friday traffic."

Mitch's smile was grateful. "Thanks, Emma. I don't want to get stuck on one of those floating bridges. Or should I go around the lake?"

"I would. Take I-405 to the Burien Freeway. You'll end up right by the Sea-Tac turnoff. Good luck." I kissed his cheek, my version of an employee attaboy.

It was going on eleven when Mitch left. Vida had been gone for two hours. She must be doing more than applying thumbscrews to Principal Freeman. I was beginning to worry when she finally showed up fifteen minutes later.

"Karl," she began, sitting down across from my desk and removing her scarf, "is a dreadful prig. And far too secretive. He's as bad as those people up at RestHaven and their patient privacy. Has everybody forgotten the public's right to know?"

"Freedom of speech is being trashed," I said. "Why not all the rest of our freedoms? Did the principal have anything to say?"

"He allowed there's porn at the high school," she replied, taking off her coat, "but he wouldn't go any further until he's met with the school board. A lot of good that does us, given that it's a closed meeting. The other members besides Harvey Adcock are Jim Medved, Henry Bardeen, Arnie Nyquist, Stella Magruder, Lois Hutchins, and Duane Gustavson. Scratch Arnie — he's impossible. As a veterinarian, Jim may be closemouthed, believing in privacy for Grace Grundle's cats or other animals he treats. Lois is Doc Dewey's sister, and very discreet, like all those Episcopalians. Henry is Buck's brother, but he's another one who won't talk, being so considerate of his ski lodge guests. Stella talks too much, as hairdressers often do, but they can keep secrets. That leaves Duane Gustavson." She nodded more to herself than to me. "Yes, definitely Duane," she said in triumph. "He may not reveal anything, but his wife, Anita, will. She's my niece on the Runkel side."

I had become so fascinated with Vida's mental gyrations about sources that I'd almost forgotten what she was trying to find out. "Wouldn't it be easier to bug the meeting room?" I asked.

Vida tipped her head to one side. "That's an inspired idea. Kip would know how to do that. Is it legal?"

"Probably not," I said. "Let's stick with Anita."

"Yes," she agreed. "Perhaps I'll invite Duane and Anita to supper tomorrow night. I have what sounds like a tasty new recipe for a cheesy ham and potato casserole. It came in this morning's mail."

I wished they'd mailed Vida the casserole — or an antidote that could be given to the Gustavsons. I asked how much time Freeman had spent with her.

"Less than twenty minutes," she replied indignantly. "That's not counting the first ten, where I tried to show interest in his wife, Molly, and their daughter, Katie." She grimaced. "I even asked about their wretched Pekingese, Bandersnatch. An apt name for that little beast."

"I wondered," I said. "I was starting to worry about you."

"You were?" She looked faintly puzzled. "Oh — I called on the Parkers. They're still upset about Wayne's death — and Tiffany, too."

"I always thought Dot and Durwood were pretty well grounded. And I'm not referring to Durwood being grounded by Milo because of his terrible driving record."

Vida had stood up. "Well . . . they are usually, but this is a double dose of woe.

415

They're not as young as they used to be, you know."

"True," I allowed.

Vida gathered up her coat, scarf, and purse before heading to the newsroom. I checked my watch. It was just after eleven-thirty. I had a sudden urge to visit the Parkers, too. Their home was on the way to the ski lodge. If I didn't have to meet Beth Rafferty until after twelve, I'd have time to do a little sleuthing of my own.

It was still chilly, but the sun was trying to peek out above Cowboy Mountain to the east. I turned right, making it unnecessary to get out my sunglasses. Seattle natives like me react to February sun like moles. It's no wonder we buy more shades than anyone else in the nation. They're needed so seldom that we can't remember where we put them.

The Parkers' white two-story house with its half-wraparound porch looked as tidy as ever. The only oddity was that Durwood's battered Chrysler was parked on the verge instead of in the empty garage. That seemed odd, given that both Parkers no longer drove.

Dot came to the door. "Emma, dear!!" she exclaimed. "Are you lost? I haven't seen you in months."

I laughed. "I know. I've been really busy

these last couple of months. But I'm on my way to the ski lodge and thought I'd stop by to say hello. I did see Durwood yesterday outside the drugstore."

"Oh," Dot said, leaning against the door, "I'm so sorry, but Durwood's taking a nap. Why don't you stop by later and have tea?"

I grimaced. "That might work, but . . . I hate to say this . . . I have to use your bathroom. Ours was occupied and I don't think I can make it to the ski lodge in time." I gently nudged past Dot. "Sorry," I said over my shoulder, moving into the entry hall. "Which way . . ." I stopped, looking into the living room. A young child sat on the floor. I'd gotten a close-up look at Holly's youngest boy last October. In shock, I turned to Dot. "That's not Tiffany's kid," I blurted.

Dot put her hands to her flushed cheeks just as Durwood came down the hall. "No," he said, not sounding like his usual cheerful self. "Please, Emma, try to understand."

I put my arm around Dot, who was crying. "I think I do. It's the old switcheroo, right?"

Durwood nodded. "Come, sit down, we'll try to explain."

I nodded, still hanging on to Dot. The round-faced toddler eyed me curiously

417

before taking a plastic hammer and whacking some big-eyed bugs on a sturdy blue stand. A saucy little tune played with each blow.

"I think I get it," I said, sitting next to Dot on the red and blue plaid sofa. "This is Vida's great-grandson Dippy. Tiffany's child is in Bellingham."

Durwood was bending down, apparently to turn off the toy's music. "Vida's idea, of course. Very clever." He stood up and beamed at me. "You have to get up pretty early in the morning to beat her, eh?"

I nodded. "I knew something was up, but I couldn't figure out what." I pointed at Durwood, who was sitting down in a recliner. "It was those toddler diapers in your shopping bag. Your granddaughter isn't quite old enough for those. That and Vida spending so much time here."

Dot had composed herself. "You won't tell anyone? Not even Milo?"

"Of course not," I said. "You think I'd cross Vida? Besides, who could compete with this kind of cunning? It's sheer genius."

"I suppose it is," Dot said, "but we miss Ashley. Hopefully she'll be back this weekend. Roger's supposed to bring her down Sunday. Or his parents will go get her. Vida was so afraid Holly might go to Bellingham, you see. But I hear she's left for Centralia."

"She has." I was trying to see if Dippy resembled Roger. Except for his round face and his coloring, I couldn't see much of his father. But those curious eyes were sheer Vida. "Where *is* Tiffany?"

Durwood adjusted his recliner, which seemed to have enough controls for a car. Maybe that was safe for him to drive as long as it didn't have wheels. "She's visiting a friend in Skykomish," he said, keeping an eye on Dippy. "They may go to Monroe for some event at the fairgrounds this weekend. Her dad's passing made her a bit gloomy."

I wondered if Tiff still had Jack's Rover. That might explain the empty garage. "Has the burial service been set?" I inquired. "We haven't heard anything since the revised autopsy came in yesterday."

The Parkers exchanged quick glances. "We're not sure," Dot said.

"Heck of a thing," Durwood declared. "A poison I never knew about. Just as well I unofficially retired. Hard to keep up."

Dot suddenly swerved to look at me. "Emma! Do you really have to go to the bathroom?"

"I lied," I admitted. "Working with Vida has made me cunning, too."

Dot poked me in the arm. "You should be

ashamed of yourself!" But she laughed.

I left a couple of minutes later, still amazed at my House & Home editor's duplicity. I wondered if I should let on that I'd uncovered her deception. But as I pulled into the ski lodge parking lot, I figured she knew. Vida always knew everything.

I got to the ski lodge before Beth Rafferty arrived. The coffee shop was filling up, so I waited for her in the lobby. The urgency in her voice had suggested she might want privacy. Two minutes later she hurried through the front door. Beth looked younger — and prettier — than she had even before the tragic death of her brother, Tim. I guessed that was due to her new beau, the man I'd seen with her at Delia Rafferty's funeral.

"Thanks for coming," Beth said as we exchanged a quick hug. "Is the dining room okay with you?"

I assured her it was. Henry's daughter, Heather Bardeen Bavich, was on hostess duty. She led us to a relatively private table away from the bar. We both declined any beverages except ice water.

"Nobody," Beth remarked after Heather moved on, "wants a sloshed 911 operator, though I'll admit I wouldn't mind having a drink."

"In days of old, everybody expected a sloshed newspaper editor," I said, "but times have changed. You look great, Beth. How's Keith?"

"He's fine." She grimaced. "I just hope he doesn't decide to take a job somewhere else now that the RestHaven project's finished."

"Is Nyquist running out of work or doesn't Keith like small towns?"

"Arnie's starting an addition to the college dorms next month," Beth said. "At least the state has a few spare dollars. But Keith doesn't get along very well with his boss. Nyquist can be a jerk."

"Yes, he can," I agreed. "At least Keith seems to like you."

Beth revealed her dimples in a smile. "I like him. If you and Dodge can find love in middle age, maybe I can, too."

"We found it a long time ago. I just didn't know what it was." I glanced at the menu, wondering if Beth had come to discuss her romance. But I didn't think so. "You sounded upset on the phone. If you need advice, write to Vida."

"I'm not that desperate," Beth said. "You're right, though." She paused. "Here comes our blond waitress du jour. Brittany or Brianna?"

"Brandy," I said out loud, seeing the

server's name tag. "I'll have the tuna salad on limpa toast."

Beth quickly scanned the lunch options. "The Reubenssen," she said, handing the menu to Brandy. "Thanks." As the young, buxom blonde left us, Beth shook her head. "How does Henry Bardeen find so many of these fair-haired girls whose names begin with B? I'm blond. Maybe I should have tried to get a job here when I got out of high school."

"You also have a brain." I shrugged. "I shouldn't say that. It makes me sound like a snarky aging brunette. You were saying . . . ?"

Beth leaned closer. "You remember that after Tim died, Toni Andreas moved to Alaska. She gave you a carton of Tim's baseball memorabilia that you turned over to me."

"Of course," I said, my mind drifting back a year and a half to Tim's tragic death. Milo's former receptionist had been in love with Beth's brother. The affair had been triggered in part by Tiffany's shrewish, selfish behavior after she got pregnant. "Tim gave the sports items to Toni because Tiff thought they were junk."

Beth nodded. "Typical. Unlike the items that were burned in the fire, the ones in the carton had some real value. I checked them out. The Ken Griffey Jr. autographed rookie card is worth at least three hundred and fifty dollars. Alex Rodriguez's is two hundred and fifty. There's Randy Johnson, Edgar Martinez, Jay Buhner, and Jamie Moyer, along with some other big names from different teams. I've no idea how much it's all worth, but probably three, four grand."

I wasn't surprised. "I recall seeing Edgar's signed bat. If he isn't voted into Cooperstown because he was mainly a designated hitter, it'll be a terrible injustice. What are the sportswriters thinking? His career numbers hitting for average, RBIs, and home runs are —"

Beth held up a hand. "Stop, Emma. You're getting kind of heated. I'm not a huge baseball fan, but I recognized those players' names. I never gave the carton to Tiffany. Yes, they belong to her as Tim's widow. I just couldn't do it. But at Mom's funeral, my conscience got the better of me." Her expression was grim. "The problem is, I can't find them."

I didn't respond right away. Brandy had brought our orders. I waited until she left to ask the obvious: "What do you mean?"

"I had them stored in Mom's old bedroom closet. I hosted a family gathering after her funeral. Tiffany was there with Jack Black-well, of course. I wonder if she stole them."

"Oh, no! Why would she do that?"

"To sell them, I suppose." Beth paused to eat a bite of corned beef. "Actually, I see what you mean. Maybe she told Jack about them. I wonder if he realized they might be valuable and took the carton."

"He's slippery but not a thief. Any idea who stabbed him?"

"No." Beth wound some sauerkraut on her fork. "I've heard rumors that somebody's been trying to kill him, though. Has Milo got a suspect?"

"He didn't believe Jack — until now, I guess."

Beth chewed and swallowed before responding. "I wish I knew where Tiff and Ashley are. Not that I ever see much of my niece. I babysat her a couple of times when she was still an infant, but since then, the two or three times I've gone to the Erikses' house, either Cookie or Tiff told me Ashley was napping or had a cold. I was hoping they'd bring her to Mom's funeral, but they left her with Donna Wickstrom."

I told Beth what the Parkers had said about Tiffany's visit to a friend in Skyko-mish. "She'll be back," I added. "She has free babysitters with her mother and her grandparents. What I don't get is why she ever hooked up with Blackwell in the first place. Maybe it seemed like a young widow's dream at the time, but Jack's abusive."

Beth scowled. "So's Tiff. Did you forget how she treated Tim?"

"But only verbal and emotional abuse, right?"

"I think she got rough sometimes. Tim never admitted it, but he had bruises that he laughed off as weird accidents."

I recalled rumors. "Do you think she stabbed Jack?"

Beth looked pained. "I wouldn't put it past her. When did it happen? I thought it was after Tiff took off. Maybe there's a dark horse lurking somewhere. What did Milo say?"

I shrugged. "My fiancé is still the sheriff. He doesn't tell me all."

"Darn," Beth said with a wry smile. "I figured he'd dump all his work worries on you."

"Guess again," I replied.

And with that, we began to speak of other, less annoying things.

The meal was good, but Beth had given me something else to chew on. Tiffany Eriks Rafferty had been seeing Jack Blackwell before Delia Rafferty's funeral. Maybe she'd already moved in with him. Then her father was killed and Tiff took off not long after that. Jack got stabbed but apparently didn't think he was seriously injured until the wound became infected. Was there a connection between his stabbing and Tiffany's erratic behavior? I pondered all these things as I drove down Tonga Road under intermittent sun.

By the time I got back to the office, I was bursting with questions for Vida but thought it best to keep mum about Dippy. She was the only staffer in the newsroom. Mitch had left and Leo was on his ad rounds.

"It seems quite simple to me," she said after I'd unloaded on her. "I'll call on Cookie to ask when Tiffany's coming home so I can use the visit to Skykomish for 'Scene.' I didn't know Tiffany had girlfriends. She was always glued to Tim's side before they finally married."

I went into my office, where the phone was ringing. "Get your butt to the courthouse," Milo said. "We're filling out the marriage license."

"Right now?" I gasped.

"You deaf? I'm on my way. Move, woman."

Mr. Romance hung up on me.

I assumed Vida was talking to Cookie when I left. I was just as glad. I didn't want to have to explain where I was going. I told Amanda I had an errand to run, knowing she wouldn't grill me. By the time I walked the two blocks to the courthouse and crossed Front Street, I realized I was shaking. I paused at the bottom of the stone steps to catch my breath. *Relax,* I told myself. *You're not going to the guillotine. You're merely filling out an official form. Just because you've never done this before, it shouldn't scare you. Lots of people do it all the time.*

Like a complete idiot, I couldn't seem to move. Finally I looked up. Milo was standing at the top of the ten steps. "Do I have to carry you inside, you little twit?" he bellowed.

I squared my shoulders. "No," I called up to him. I walked purposefully — if unsteadily — up to meet him.

"Damn," he said, putting his arm around me, "you are so . . . perverse." He stopped at the door. "Do you love me or not?"

I craned my neck to look at him. "Of course I do. I love you more than . . ." I couldn't get the words out.

He gave me a little shake. "Say it."

I lowered my eyes and swallowed. "I love

you more than I ever loved Tom." Defiantly, I finally met his hard hazel gaze. "Are you satisfied?"

"You bet." He leaned down to kiss my forehead. "Let's do it. I got a waiver on the license. We're getting married."

"What?" I shrieked as he opened the door.

"Pipe down. You want everybody staring at us?"

"No," I squeaked, aware of a half-dozen people who were doing just that as we moved toward the judge's chambers. "Who's marrying us?"

"The new judge, Proxmire. She can squeeze us in just before traffic court. Rosemary Bourgette and the bailiff, Gus Tolberg, are witnesses."

I started to giggle as we entered the courtroom. I'd only glimpsed the fair-haired Amazonian Diane Proxmire from a distance. She was standing in front of her bench between Rosemary and the always grumpy Gus. Her Honor shook my hand as Milo introduced us. I nodded to Rosemary, who was all genuine smiles. Gus, of course, looked as if we'd come to be buried, not married. I barely heard the words of the standard civil service, though apparently I made the correct responses. At least Milo didn't have to kick me into speaking up. It was only when the judge asked if Milo had a ring for the bride that I became fully aware of what was happening. He took my hand and slipped an antique gold band with twin circlets of tiny diamonds onto my finger. We were married. Milo kissed me, more decorously than usual, and said, "Come on, Mrs. Dodge, we have papers to sign. Then I've got some news for you."

As if he hadn't done that already.

EIGHTEEN

"Where," I asked as we went down the courthouse steps, "did you get this beautiful ring?"

"Out of a drawer at my house," Milo replied, holding my hand. "It belonged to my grandmother. Mulehide didn't like it. We can replace it."

"No! I love it! And it fits."

"I don't remember much about Grandma Dodge," Milo said as we crossed the street. "She died when I was about six. But she was little, like you. I thought it might be the right size." He paused at the corner of Second and Front. "Well? Are you through being terrified?"

I leaned against him. "Yes! I . . . I'm sort of speechless."

"Hunh. Like that'd ever happen." He led me across the street. "I suppose you'll have to tell Vida. Is she still mad at me?"

"I think so. All three of the people she isn't

speaking to were in the courtroom. She never liked Gus Tolberg anyway."

"Who does? But he's a decent bailiff."

We'd reached the sheriff's headquarters. "Are you going to tell your staff we got married?"

Milo shook his head. "Not now. I don't need distractions. We're back to business. If we weren't, you'd be going to your own office."

Lori and Dwight were the only people out front. Beth had returned to her 911 post in the rear of the building. Lori greeted me with a cheery smile. Dwight looked as if he'd rather eat a bug than say hello — but he did, probably in deference to his boss, who was leading me into his office.

"Okay," Milo said, sitting at his desk after taking off his hat and jacket. "Let's start with Blackwell. I can't figure that guy out. His wound was fairly superficial. According to Doc, a steak or kitchen knife. If it hadn't gotten infected, it would've healed in two, three days. Blackwell claims he doesn't remember being stabbed. I almost believe him. Which means he must've been asleep." The sheriff had been looking at his notes, but he finally raised his eyes. "He swears he was alone."

"Tiffany comes to mind. Did she have a

key to his house?"

Milo made a face. "Jack doesn't always lock up at night. He's so damned arrogant that he figures nobody would dare break in."

"Typical." I rested my chin on my hand. "Patti's a possibility, even if she took him in and got him hospitalized. She loves the guy, so she'd feel remorse. Does this mean you believe the earlier threats were real?"

"Hell, no. This doesn't prove any of the others."

"Have you found the weapon?"

"Heppner found eight of them — all wiped clean." Milo offered me a cigarette, which I accepted. He was lighting it for me when his phone rang. "Screw it," he murmured, leaning back in his chair. "Lori can take it. The knives will go to the SnoCo lab as soon as I can free somebody up to take them over there. For all I know, whoever stabbed Blackwell might've tossed the thing."

I was about to ask if the sheriff was going public with any of this when Lori interrupted. "Doe called to say they found the body on Tonga Ridge. They're taking it to the hospital morgue. Is that okay with you?"

"Fine," Milo said. "Call RestHaven and tell them to send somebody to ID Mr. Nut.

We need a name this time. And make sure Doc knows he's got a stiff coming in."

Lori nodded and scurried off. I posed my question to the sheriff.

"Hell, Emma," Milo said, "you can't do anything on Mr. Nut until we get an ID, right? But I wanted to give you background on Blackwell to see if . . ." He stopped, took a drag on his cigarette, and shook his head. "Damn it, maybe I just wanted to spend some time with my wife."

I smiled. "That's incredibly sweet. But I don't believe you."

Milo scowled at me. "Okay, it's partly true. Knowing you, I suspect some ideas are dancing around in your funny little head."

I tapped my cigarette into the sheriff's NRA ashtray. "As a matter of fact, I was thinking about that sort of thing on the way back from lunch with Beth." Given that Milo had left the door open, I lowered my voice and told him about the missing box of sports memorabilia. "I gather," I concluded, "she hasn't mentioned it to you."

He shook his head. "I hardly ever see her. She stays holed up in back and works until six. You think Blackwell took the stuff?"

"Well . . . Tiff wouldn't know the value. She apparently never asked Beth about it after Tim died. But if she knew it existed, she might've mentioned it and then he decided to check it out."

Milo stroked his chin. "No. That doesn't sound like Blackwell. Even for a few grand, I doubt he'd pull a stunt like that. How about Wayne? He was a baseball fan. The few times I talked to the guy he'd always yap about the latest game he'd watched."

"I never thought of him," I admitted. A thought flashed through my mind. "Don't think I'm crazy, but Jennifer Hood told me something was burned by the road where Wayne was killed. Did you notice that when you were at the crime scene?"

"Yeah. It looked like some paper. Not much of it, either."

The sheriff was probably right, but I persevered. "Kip lives next to Mel and April Eriks's house. He told me Mel was burning something in his backyard right after Wayne died. I happened to run into him at the Grocery Basket and I alluded to that. Mel seemed . . . evasive."

Milo leaned back so far in his chair that I thought he'd tip over. "Mel's a baseball fan, too. Hell, Emma, do you think he'd set fire to Ken Griffey Jr.'s rookie card? He's not nuts."

"Okay," I said, sounding humble. "But if

you're right and Wayne took the carton, then Tiff probably has it. Unless it's still at Cookie's."

The sheriff shrugged. "So? That's where it belongs — legally." He sat up. "I don't see where this stuff has anything to do with Wayne's murder. Or Blackwell's stabbing. Tiff will show up sooner or later. We'll talk to her. In fact, when Doe gets back, I'll send her to talk to Patti." He paused. "We should talk to Kay, too. Maybe Dwight wasn't the only ex she decided to bang for old times' sake."

His phone rang again. He stared at it as if he could make it explode. "Damn, it must be important or Lori . . ." He picked up the receiver. "Dodge," he barked. I watched his jaw set as he listened, obviously trying to remain patient. "Okay, Doe, here's what you do. Tell Dr. Reed to get her ass down to the morgue pronto and ID the stiff or we'll take a picture of him and post it on every utility pole in SkyCo until somebody comes up with a frigging name." He banged the phone down. "Those dinks at RestHaven are going to drive *me* nuts. Woo's having emergency dental surgery at Dr. Starr's office and, according to Dr. Reed, he's the only one with authority to ID the dead guy. That's bullshit. Isn't he Reed's patient if she's in charge of the nut jobs?"

"I'd think so," I said. "That sounds a little too weird." I stood up. "Maybe I'll go up to RestHaven."

"Hold it." Milo had gotten out of his chair. "I'll do that. You keep out of the way. I'll let you know what happens."

"No, you won't!" I actually stamped my foot. "This is news, you big jerk! I'll take my own car. If Mitch were here, I'd send him."

Milo took his jacket off the hook on the wall and slung it over his shoulder before looking down at me with bemused hazel eyes. "I can't win. I had one wife who hated my job and didn't want to hear about it. Now I've got one who can't keep her nose out of it. You're on your own." He pushed me out of sight from the outer office, wrapped his free arm around my neck, and rested his chin on the top of my head. "Happy?"

"Yes." I rubbed my cheek against his chest. "I hate you, though."

"I know. You often do." He kissed my nose and let me go.

Milo was just ahead of me a couple of blocks from the River Road arterial when, instead of crossing the tracks, he made an abrupt U-turn onto Seventh Street. I didn't dare attempt that maneuver, so I reversed in Swanson Toyota's parking lot and tried to spot the Yukon. I had to wait for the stop sign at Front Street. Up the hill, Milo turned onto Pine. I guessed he was going to the hospital. After I hooked a right off Seventh and passed the Presbyterian church, I saw him walking into the main entrance. The Yukon was parked in a loading zone. There was just room enough behind it for my Honda. As Mrs. Sheriff, surely I had *some* perks.

Milo had disappeared by the time I got inside. Jenny Bjornson was on duty again. "Are you looking for Sheriff Dodge?" she asked.

"Yes. Where did he go?"

"To the morgue in the basement." She grimaced. "Do you really want to go there? Just seeing the sign creeps me out."

I assumed my callous reporter's air. "Yes. Which way do I turn when I get down there?"

"To your left. Oh! Here's Mr. Fleetwood. I'll bet he wants to go to the morgue, too. Hi," she said with a big smile for Mr. Radio.

"The charming Jenny," Spence said, blowing her a kiss. "Did you say the magic word 'morgue'? I'm headed there with Ms. Lord."

He practically pushed me to the elevator. "Surprised to see me?" he asked through gritted teeth. "Who's getting news leaks now?"

"I happened to run into Dodge at the courthouse," I replied as the elevator doors slid open. "I'm filling in for Mitch. He's gone out of town."

"Good timing on your part? Or were you letting the resident bear maul you during working hours?"

"Hey," I said as the elevator stopped, "don't get nasty. By chance I was there when the call came through about finding the escapee's body."

Spence stopped at the morgue's door. "You ever done this before?"

"No," I admitted. "Milo's always spared me."

"Then why don't you turn around and go back to your office?"

It wasn't the worst suggestion I'd ever heard, but I refused to let my rival intimidate me. "It's my job. Open the damned door."

"We have to be buzzed in," he said, but before he hit the button, a female voice called his name.

We turned. Rosalie Reed was coming from the doctors' parking area. "Spencer!" she cried before falling into his arms. "Help me!"

I stared at them. Spence was holding her close, speaking soothing words and patting her back. "It's okay. I'm so sorry."

Stupefied, I hit the buzzer. I heard Doc Dewey ask who it was. I told him it was me — along with Dr. Reed and Fleetwood. Doc said to wait until I heard a click before turning the knob. A moment later all three of us entered a small office where Doc and Milo were standing by a large wooden filing cabinet. They both looked faintly dismayed.

"Is this a media tour?" the sheriff demanded.

Doc pulled out a chair for Rosalie, who was still sobbing. "Sit, please. Are you ill, Dr. Reed?"

Spence eased her into the chair. "Dr. Reed," he said softly, "gets emotionally involved with her patients. She's very upset. Is there some way to prevent her from having to make the ID?"

"We can't wait for Dr. Woo," Doc replied. "What about Farrell?"

"He didn't know the patient," Spence said, his hand on Rosalie's shoulder. He cleared his golden throat. "Would you trust me to do it?"

Doc removed his glasses to stare at

Spence. Milo shot Mr. Radio a sharp glance. "You know the man?" Doc finally asked.

"I've known him for six years," Spence replied solemnly. His dark eyes flicked in Milo's direction. "Do you need a sworn statement?"

"No," the sheriff said. "You'll sign the death certificate. If you're lying, criminal charges will be brought."

"I'm not lying," Spence declared with dignity.

"Then let's do it," Milo said. "Come on, Doc, Fleetwood." He turned at the heavy steel door and pointed to me. "You stay put with Dr. Reed. You got that, Ms. Lord?"

"Yes, sir," I replied. Grim as the circumstances were, I could have sworn that Milo's eyes sparked.

I pulled the only other chair up next to Rosalie, who seemed to be getting a grip on her emotions. "Could I get you some water?" I asked.

She shook her head and sniffled into a tissue she'd taken from her hobo bag. "No. No, I'll be fine. Thank you." She sniffed some more and dabbed at her eyes. "It may seem unprofessional for a psychiatrist to become so emotional, but I care deeply about my patients. I personally had the deceased transferred here. He'd been under my care for some time in my former practice. I didn't think a change would benefit him."

I refrained — barely — from saying, *You're the doctor.* Instead I said I could understand her attachment. "It's very human," I added.

"Some may think it unwise, though," she said. "Oh! What a lovely ring. It looks like an heirloom. Did you have that when we first met? I'm very fond of antique jewelry."

"I wasn't wearing it that day," I replied, doing some quick mathematical calculations. "Yes, it's quite old. At least a hundred years."

Milo, Doc, and Spence returned to the room. "We're done here," the sheriff announced. "Show Emma your statement, Fleetwood. She gets equal time."

Spence handed me the form. "Philip Randall Curry, age fifty-six, last permanent address, Issaquah, Washington. Got it." I gave the form back to Mr. Radio and hurriedly wrote the information down in the notebook I kept in my purse. "Thanks." I turned to Doc. "Will you let me know about cause of death?"

"When I find out, I'll pass it on to the sheriff, Emma. He can take it from there. I will say that as far as I can tell, there was no obvious evidence of foul play." The last words seemed intended for Rosalie. "But don't quote me." He glanced first at Spence and then at me.

Milo slapped Doc on the shoulder. "I'm done here, Gerry." He loped out of the room.

"I should go, too," I said. "Thanks, Doc." I looked at Rosalie. "Take care." My gaze took in Spence, conveying I knew he'd be of comfort to her. But I didn't know exactly how. Or why.

Closing the door behind me, I raced down the hall to where Milo was getting into the elevator. "Stop!" I yelled.

"God," he said, holding the door. "I can't escape my nagging wife."

"I'm not nagging. I don't like it down here. Jenny's right. It's not only creepy, but it smells like formaldehyde. Are you and Tanya coming to dinner?" I asked as the car stopped on the main floor.

"Yeah, unless she eloped with Bill," he said, nodding to Jenny as we passed the reception desk. "I should be so lucky. So should Tanya."

"Did she like him in high school?" I asked after we were outside.

"No. She thought he was a dweeb. She was only a sophomore back then. The next year, she was in Bellevue." He nodded at my car. "You got a ticket. Why the hell did you park in a loading zone?"

I gaped at my windshield. "Damn! Who's on patrol in town?"

"Heppner," Milo said.

"Sam knows my Honda. He's being mean. Can you fix it?"

"No. Are you nuts? You know better than to pull a stunt like that."

"Milo . . ." I sounded like a whiny six-year-old. "We're married. . . ."

He shook his head. "That doesn't change the law. Hey, it's only thirty bucks. Go pay it now. Otherwise you'll forget."

"I don't have thirty bucks on me."

"We take checks," he said with a straight face.

"Ohhh . . ." I whirled around — and bumped into the loading zone sign. "I really do hate you!" I yelled as I staggered to my car.

"Salmon sounds good," the sheriff called to me.

I made an obscene gesture and got into the Honda. I'd hurt my knee on the blasted sign. I ignored the pain, trying to start the car so I could cut off the sheriff before he pulled out, but I dropped my keys on the floor. By the time I'd retrieved them, the Yukon was turning onto Second. The big jackass driving the big SUV managed to avoid having to stop for any traffic on Front Street, but I had to wait for a Blackwell Mill eighteen-wheeler to pass. When I finally pulled into a legal parking place by the sheriff's office, Milo was already inside. I was still seething when I made my entrance. "Where'd he go?" I asked Lori.

"The men's room, I guess," Lori said. "Are you okay? You look upset. Would you like some coffee?"

"No!" I winced. The coffee in the sheriff's office tasted like swill, no matter who made it. "I mean, no thanks," I said, lowering my voice. Luckily, Lori was the only one in the reception area. "I have to pay a parking ticket."

Lori's eyes widened. "You do? Gosh, Emma, I don't think you've ever gotten a ticket before, at least not since I worked here."

"There's a first for everything," I said, trying to remain calm as I handed over the citation. "You take checks?"

"Yes, local ones." She frowned at the ticket. "Sam did this?"

I'd already gotten out my checkbook. "Sam, like his boss, goes by the book. Do I make it out to SkyCo? Or for Sam's new fishing license?"

444

"Skykomish County Treasurer," Lori said, still looking puzzled.

I paused at the space for the payment description.

"Just put in 'dumb shit,' " the sheriff said. I'd been so focused on the check that I hadn't noticed he'd come into the open area behind the counter. "Gee — just when I was trying to figure out how to spell 'deputy assholery.' "

"Which one?" Milo asked. " 'Deputy' or . . ."

I tore off the check and threw it at the sheriff. "I hope you're having fun at my expense," I snarled.

"Actually, it's community . . . service," he amended.

"What?" It dawned on me that he was going to say "community property," given that we were now jackass and wife. "Yeah, right," I mumbled. "Why don't you tell Heppner that, as a member of the press, I have rights, too?"

"Then you should get a permit," Milo said reasonably. "Why didn't you do that years ago?"

"I never thought I'd have to use it," I said sulkily.

He sighed. "Sounds like you. Come on into my office. I've got a couple of questions." He opened the gate to let me pass through.

"What? About parking regulations?" I asked before we sat down.

Milo was chuckling. "You're so damned ornery. Change gears. What did you make of the Fleetwood and Reed interaction?"

I took a deep breath. *Damn,* I thought, *why didn't I marry a man I could manipulate, at least a little?* "If Spence knows the dead guy from six years ago, I'll bet he's known Rosalie for that long. Brother, maybe?"

"At least," Milo said. "Want to find out?"

"Sure," I said. "Are you humoring me?"

He shook his head. "No, but I knew you were thinking the same thing. It's easier for me to check public records than it is for you. Sometimes you have to pay twenty-five or thirty bucks to access them online. I thought I'd save you some money."

I laughed. "Oh, Milo, why can't I stay mad at you?"

"Damned if I know. Mulehide sure could." He swung around in his chair to look at his monitor. "Want to sit on my lap?"

"I can't do that here."

He shrugged. "Just thought I'd give it a shot. Rosalie Reed, M.D. . . . Four of them? Where did this one come from?"

"Didn't you read our special section on

the RestHaven staff? Never mind. She had her practice in Bellevue."

"It's a wonder Tanya didn't run into her. . . . Ah, right. Started there eight years ago after moving from Santa Monica, California. One son, Clifford. Married, but it doesn't say to who." Milo looked at me. "Did you interview her?" He saw me nod. "Did she talk about her husband? Is Reed her married or maiden name?"

"She gave me very little personal information," I said. "In fact, it was an annoyingly short interview, though not as aggravating as the one with Iain Farrell. I did ask about her husband. She said he was retired. The son's at UCLA."

Milo stared at the monitor. "Okay, let's put in the stiff's name and see what happens. He glanced at the form Spence had filled out. "Philip Randall Curry. Sounds pretentious. No wonder he went nuts." Milo grinned. "See for yourself."

I got up and went to stand by Milo's chair, trying to ignore the big hand that caressed my rear. "Psychiatrist in Beverly Hills, residence in Santa Monica as of 1997. No other information except his education and other professional achievements, all in the Los Angeles area. Could he be Rosalie's husband?"

"One way to find out." The sheriff stopped pawing me and picked up the phone. "Lori, connect me to student information at UCLA in Westwood, California."

"How do you know where UCLA is?" I asked, sitting back down.

Milo looked at me as if I were the dumb cluck. "John Wooden, the Wizard of Westwood. What college basketball fan doesn't know that? I was in high school when Alcindor — sorry, Kareem — and the rest of that gang started their big run to all those NCAA . . ." He held up a hand. "Yes, I'd like the phone number of a student named Clifford Curry. Or he may use Reed-Curry." There was a brief pause. "I see. No, that's fine. I'll call his mother to get the number. Thanks." Milo set the phone down. "Clifford Reed-Curry lives off campus. I'm glad I don't have to tell him his dad croaked. Maybe Spence can do that to help Rosalie out. I wonder what else he's doing for her? Or is he just doing her?"

"Well . . . it might explain why he often has spent long weekends in the Seattle area. And why he's never mentioned having a girlfriend." I slammed my hand against the desk. "Damn! That's the leak! Not Kay Burns — it's Rosalie!"

"Does that make you feel any better?"

"No, but at least I know where it's coming from. Oh, my gosh — how's Rosalie going to put together an obituary? No wonder we haven't seen her husband around here. Maybe she won't go public in Alpine. She might have his death run only in the L.A.-area papers. Or is there just one paper there now? I forget. He sounds fairly prominent in his field. Before he got goofy, anyway."

"You through speculating?" Milo inquired.

"My ears are falling off."

I stood up. "Then I'm leaving."

"Good. I've got work to do. You're a distraction."

I picked up my purse and started out of Milo's office.

"Don't forget the salmon," he called after me.

I kept going.

As soon as I stepped into the newsroom, Vida demanded to know where I'd been. "It's after three," she declared. "Don't tell me you took a long lunch. I know better. Let me see your hand."

Leo stopped on his way from the back shop. "What's wrong, babe? Did you hurt yourself?"

"No," I said, annoyed by Vida's omniscience. I realized that the county auditor,

Eleanor Runkel Jessup, had undoubtedly called her aunt as soon as Milo and I left the courthouse. "Here," I said, holding my left hand out to her.

"Hmm. Rather nice. Olive Dodge's ring, if memory serves."

"Yes." I showed the ring to Leo.

"You mean . . . ?" he said, his jaw dropping.

"Yes."

Amanda had come into the newsroom. "What's going on?"

"I had nothing better to do this afternoon, so I got married," I said — and immediately felt contrite for my waspish tone.

Vida stood up. "You should have stayed in the office. I regret that under the circumstances, I can't offer you my congratulations." Head held high, she stalked off to the back shop.

Leo put his arm around me. "Damn it, I thought maybe she'd gotten over her snit. Don't let the Duchess get you down."

I was on the verge of tears. "She's a mule," I whispered.

Amanda patted my arm. "I think it's terrific. Can I see the ring?"

I sniffed a couple of times. "Sure." Leo let go of me so Amanda could take my hand.

"It's lovely," she said.

I nodded. "It belonged to Milo's grand-mother. I love it."

Leo hugged me. "I should buy you a drink. Now. How about it?"

I had to smile. "I get married and then hang out in a bar with another guy? Somehow that fits with the rest of the day. Why not?"

Leo picked up his jacket. "If anybody asks," he said to Amanda, "tell them Emma and I eloped. That'll confuse the grapevine."

Amanda was giggling when we left. I was getting to like her more every day, despite almost firing her after she first came to work for us as Ginny Erlandson's maternity leave fill-in.

"This is decadent," I said to Leo as we approached the Venison Inn.

"Hey, it's your wedding day. When's the honeymoon?"

"Ha. I suspect that we'll have Tanya staying overnight with us again," I said as Leo opened the V.I.'s door for me. "Unless Milo has to babysit her at his own house."

"How long will that go on?" he asked as we walked through the almost-empty restaurant section.

"I don't know," I replied. "I'm afraid we're in for the long haul."

The bar wasn't busy, either. In fact, Oren

Rhodes, the usual bartender, wasn't on hand yet. The fair-haired, ponytailed young man who took our orders looked faintly familiar, but I couldn't place him. Leo, with his ad man's memory for faces and names, came to the rescue. "Hi, Eric. Ms. Lord and I are taking an unusual afternoon break to celebrate my five hundredth edition of the *Advocate*. Emma?"

"A screwdriver, please," I said.

"Short Scotch for me," Leo told the young man.

"Who is that?" I asked after the lanky Eric headed back to the bar.

"Lori Cobb's kid brother. He's taking a semester off from WSU to think about changing his major. Vida had a snippet about that on her page while you were recovering from your near-death experience."

"Vida," I said on a sigh. "What will I do with her?"

"Nothing. She has to come around. Uh-oh. Here comes trouble, still limping from her alleged fall."

I followed Leo's glance toward the darker reaches of the bar. "Patti Marsh. Was she drinking alone?"

"Not anymore," Leo murmured as Patti stumbled a bit before sliding next to Leo on the banquette.

"Hey, handsome, how are ya?" Patti asked, ignoring me.

"Not as handsome as I used to be," Leo replied as Eric came to deliver our drinks.

Patti pointed to Leo's glass. "I'll have one of those, too."

Eric, looking stoic, nodded and left us.

"Gotta pick up Jack," she said, taking a pack of cigarettes out of her shiny silver shoulder bag. "Light me up, hon."

Leo complied, offering me the pack. I accepted, letting him light me up, too. I recalled being sixteen and perusing bridal magazines with their elegant photos of post-wedding festivities in handsome hotel dining rooms and under canopies in lush English gardens. At least I wasn't at the Icicle Creek Tavern with Ed Bronsky. Yet.

"So Jack's being discharged?" Leo asked.

Patti nodded. "At five. That's when his IV annybotics are finished. I take over from there. Hell, I can nurse him better than a pro. I know the kind of treatment he needs." She nodded at least three times.

Eric seemed a bit uncertain when he brought Patti's drink. I wondered if he was having doubts about serving her, but he went off without a word.

I decided to prove I existed. "Do you

453

know who stabbed him?"

"Not me," Patti said, trying to focus across the table. "Maybe Tiff. Prob'ly pissed off 'cause he dumped her. She stole his money and ran off." She paused, rubbing her bruised forearm. "I dunno — don't think she'd bother coming back to stab him. Too lazy." Patti finally zeroed in on me. "Always a dark horse, right? Your big stud got an idea? Or doesn't he give a shit because he wishes he'd done it himself?"

I stiffened in my chair. "If you mean the sheriff, he questioned Jack earlier today. Your not-so-big stud drew a blank."

"Hey! Don't talk that way 'bout my guy!" She gave me a defiant look before tossing back half of her drink in one gulp. "And he still *is* my guy. You got that? The only nurse he needs is me." Polishing off her Scotch and sticking the cigarette between her smudged lips, Patti awkwardly got up from the banquette and limped toward the ladies' room.

"Good God," Leo groaned. "With any luck, when she drives Blackwell from the hospital, they'll end up in the river."

I couldn't see my watch in the bar's dim lighting. "What time is it?"

Leo glanced at his wrist. "Four. She has an hour to sober up."

"She hasn't left the bar yet," I said after taking a sip from my screwdriver. "Make sure she doesn't stiff us for her tab."

"This," Leo said, finishing his own Scotch, "was not one of my more brilliant ideas. Let's go. My treat. It's the least I can do after Patti."

"Thanks." I couldn't quite finish my own drink. "I'm low on cash."

Leo paused to give Eric a thumbs-up sign before putting a hand on my back to steer me out of the bar and to the exit. "What," I asked, "will Vida say when we show up reeking of liquor?"

"Let her stew. She'll be dying of curiosity to know where we went, what we did, who we met, and who else was drinking in the afternoon."

When we returned, Amanda informed us that Vida had left early. "A family situation," she said wryly. "Roger?"

"I'll bet she's collecting him in Bellingham," I said. "Holly's taken off, so . . ." I paused, not wanting to squeal on the Parkers and their role in Vida's devious plot. "The coast is clear for now."

At my desk, I tried to focus on my next editorial. The phone rang before I could gather my thoughts.

"Okay," Mavis said, "you're not dead, Ms.

Lord. You must be mad."

"I'm not mad," I replied. "I'm Mrs. Dodge."

I had to hold the phone away from my ear to avoid being deafened by Mavis's shriek. "You're mad, all right," she finally declared. "Mad as a hatter. Emma, I can't believe it."

"You'd better. I'm happy, happy, happy."

"I don't know what to say."

"How about 'congratulations'?"

She sighed loudly. "I . . . what am I missing here? You always made Dodge sound like some hick whose only talent was explaining the infield fly rule."

"I guess I never told you the part about what he was doing when he explained it. Would you like to hear it now or should I just purr?"

"Oh, no!" She sighed again. "Do you want to make me jealous?"

"Someday when we both get very drunk I'll tell you. I'm not mad. But here's something you *can* understand. It's going on five and I've got to write an editorial before I go home to make dinner for my husband. I may get off a letter to you this weekend — if I have time." I made a purring sound just to annoy her.

Mavis hung up on me. Three minutes later, an email from her showed up. "I think

I just figured out how to cheer up the Resident Grump. Why didn't you tell me this sooner? Congratulations — to me."

Alpine had been founded as a company town by Carl Clemans. He had been impressed by the cooperative philosophy of his alma mater's president, Leland Stanford, but he hadn't embraced that concept in his logging community. Money never changed hands, as workers were paid in scrip to buy goods at the company store. Many early Alpiners saved some of their earnings, a boon when they were forced to move on after the original mill's closure. I had historical grounds for my editorial. There was more than one way to fund a town or a county. That was a start toward changing local minds.

What I didn't know was that someone would soon change my mind about murder.

NINETEEN

The Grocery Basket had only previously frozen Alaskan king salmon filets. I bought enough for three, assuming Tanya would join us. It had been a long day — a long week — and I was tired. Having gone to the ATM, I splurged on Betsy's Bakers, potatoes that were ready to serve and came with a variety of toppings, none of which Milo liked, but I do. As with most things in life, he kept his food simple. Butter suited him just fine.

He arrived at ten to six — alone. "Where's Tanya?" I asked.

"Blatt's car broke down," Milo said, hanging his hat and jacket on its usual peg. "There was nobody around to fix it after four in Lake Chelan. Nobody to tow it this far, either. They're spending the night at Kelly's Resort. They may stay until Sunday. And no, I didn't sabotage Bill's car. I told him last week it sounded like a washing machine."

"They're spending *our* wedding night at a resort?"

Milo laughed — sort of. "Sounds about right." He cradled my face in his hands and kissed me. "How's my wife?"

"Tired, but . . ." I looked up at him. "You want to eat or . . . ?"

He kissed me again before heading to the kitchen. "I'm unwinding. I spent two hours interrogating the three witches from *Macbeth.*"

I followed him. "I didn't know you'd ever seen *Macbeth.*"

"Seen it?" he said, hauling out the liquor bottles. "I was in it in high school. It was an English project. I was Birnam Wood."

"You weren't!"

"No, I was Banquo. Being so damned tall was good for a ghost. I didn't have to memorize as many lines as the other kids did."

"You have hidden depths," I said. "Who played the Macbeths?"

Milo frowned in an apparent effort at remembering. "Jim Carlson, Norm's kid brother, and . . ." He laughed. "Cookie Parker."

"Cookie? The meek Mrs. Eriks? How'd she do that?"

"Badly. She subbed for Ellen Vickers, who got mono."

"Not a role for Cookie," I said. "What three witches?"

"Patti, Kay, and Tiffany," he replied, putting ice into our drinks.

"Tiffany? Where is she?"

"With Cookie." Milo looked at the stove. "How come the oven's not on?"

"I didn't know when you'd get here," I said, opening the fridge to take out the salmon. "Can you eat all this? I got enough for Tanya too."

"Sure. I never had lunch. I was too busy getting us married."

I turned the oven on and put the fish in a baking dish. "How was Tiff? Did she reveal all about her brief encounter with Blackwell?"

"She clammed up, insisting she just wanted to get away for a few days. Hated her job, needed a break, tired of winter, thought Jack was taking her to Palm Desert for a few days. When she found out he couldn't get away because of his business, she split."

I opened a can of string beans. "Do you believe her?"

"I wouldn't believe her if she told me you

460

were dumb enough to park in a loading zone."

I shot him a flinty look. "What about Kay?"

Milo leaned against the sink. "I haven't seen her in almost thirty years. She looks good, considering all the husbands she's had. The exes haven't held up so well, two of them being dead. The one before Burns died in a car wreck. Kay admitted she'd gotten it on with Dwight — because he was her first husband, she'd always had a soft spot for him, especially with Jack being a womanizer. Nobody could ever accuse Gould of that."

I started the potatoes and the beans. "Let's sit. Tell me what she said about not stabbing Jack. Or did she confess?"

Milo didn't answer until we were in our usual living room places. "Kay admitted she'd seen Jack at RestHaven, including the open house. She called the exchanges 'brief and frosty.' She said if she wanted to stab him, she'd have done it when he dumped her for Anne Marie Olson."

"Was that wife number two?"

"More like number four, but the second wife here. There'd been a couple of others in Oregon or Idaho. Or maybe California."

"No wonder he never bothered marrying

Patti. Was she sober?"

"Is she ever?" Milo paused to sip his drink and light a cigarette. "She wouldn't let me in. I got to her place a little before five and she was on her way to pick up Jack at the hospital. After she got through calling me every name in the book, she denied stabbing him. Hell, maybe all those women are telling the truth. I'll wait to see what the lab turns up on the sheets we took out of Blackwell's house."

"What?" I shrieked, almost falling off the sofa. "You didn't tell me about any sheets!"

"Hell, Emma, I don't have to tell you everything until it's official. You think we wouldn't process the place after Blackwell got stabbed?"

"When will you get the results back? Are you looking for DNA?"

"Right. We'll have to get samples from the three witches."

"Can you do that without them knowing it?"

Milo had put down his drink and stubbed out his cigarette. "Doe can. She's crafty. Have I got time to change?"

"Yes. Eight minutes."

The sheriff loped off to the bedroom. I tended to my cooking and set the table. When he entered the kitchen I was about to dish up. I asked if Blackwell had any kids by his ex-wives.

"Not that I know of," Milo said, sitting down. "If he did, maybe that's why he kept moving north and ended up here — he was fleeing child support. Too late now to nail him for that."

"What happened to the wife after Kay? Anne Marie . . . Olson?"

"Right — Olson with an 'o.' " Milo paused to admire the salmon. "Looks good. She married somebody from Monroe and moved there. I dated her for a while. Nice girl. Not too bright, though."

"Were you jealous when she married Jack?"

"Hell, no," he replied, putting a chunk of butter on a Betsy's Baker. "I was dating Mulehide then. Jack bragged about stealing her, but Anne Marie was up for grabs." He eyed me curiously. "Why this past history?"

I sighed. "Somebody told me your history with Jack went back further than the Cody Graff case. I thought if that was true, maybe it was over Anne Marie."

Milo shook his head. "Face it, Blackwell's an arrogant S.O.B. He came here right after I started as a deputy. He sucked up to Eeeny, but wanted to make sure I knew my place — under his heel. Even back then I didn't take well to that kind of thing. Basic personality clash, maybe."

I smiled at him. "You wouldn't, big guy. But I'm asking about some of the history because of tales Clarence Munn's been telling about corruption in years gone by." As we began to eat, I told Milo about the research Tanya and I had done.

"Oh, yeah," he said when I finished. "But let it lie for now, with Fuzzy's brainstorm bubbling on the back burner. You might want to save that kind of stuff for later to show what happened under the old regime."

"Good point," I conceded. "But am I missing something?"

Milo looked puzzled. "About what?"

"I've heard a couple of references to a dark horse lately. I don't know if it's about Wayne or Blackwell or . . . Go ahead, tell me I'm crazy."

"Why repeat myself? Decent salmon, even if it was frozen."

I touched his hand. "Why don't I feel different being married?"

"What did you expect? Shooting stars and comets?" He put his hand over mine. "We've known each other for over fifteen years. We went through a civil process lasting five minutes today. It took you almost that long to pay your parking ticket. Despite you being in denial and me telling myself there had to be somebody besides you, we knew we belonged together from the first time you stumbled into my office."

My eyes widened. "You noticed that? You remembered it?"

He took his hand away. "You bet. I'd seen you around town, but you waited two weeks to introduce yourself. I'd run you through the system, grilled Vandeventer, and heard the rumors about your tainted past. I didn't want the *Advocate* falling into the hands of some city tart who didn't know a Swede saw from a Swedish meatball. You drove a Jag and your clothes were too classy for Alpine. But you were damned cute. I could see that from a block away. I waited for you to come to me. And when you did, you tripped over your own feet and gave me a big doe-eyed look, pretending nothing had happened. I figured maybe you were okay."

"I was nervous. *I'd* seen *you*. I worried you'd be as daunting and grim as you looked. But you weren't. You bought me a drink."

"It was all I could do then. I was still screwed up from the divorce."

"You sure were. When you finally asked me out on a real date, you didn't seem to notice I was a girl. I was damned disap-

465

pointed, big guy. I felt there was zero chemistry between us."

Milo didn't answer until he'd finished chewing and swallowing some green beans. "Good God, Emma, you showed up in a white blouse and a black skirt looking like one of those nuns from your church. I knew your brother was a priest. I figured maybe you'd planned to be a nun but got knocked up and tossed out of the convent. You might be some religious wacko. That outfit scared the hell out of me."

"I thought I looked nice. You knew by then I wasn't wacky, you jerk. What about the green dress I spent three hundred bucks on when you took me to dinner at the ski lodge a year later?"

Milo leaned back in the chair. "I was going with Honoria then."

"You held my hand in the sleigh going up to the lodge before it got tipped over and we fell in a snowbank."

He sighed. "Okay, so I wanted to make a move on you. But that sleigh accident made me think it'd be a bad idea. It wasn't my style to cheat on Honoria. I had to fight myself to keep from jumping you during dinner. I've never seen you wear that dress since. It's still in your closet."

"I wore it once for Tom," I said bitterly.

"Let's go to that French place tomorrow night. Wear the dress and you can try your luck with me again." He stood up.

I stared at him. "We're not done eating," I said.

"Yes, we are." He lifted me out of the chair into his arms. "Let's go act like married people. You don't need a damned dress for me."

I nestled against him. "It's about time. I thought you'd never ask."

Milo was on his cell when I staggered into the kitchen the next morning. "I owe you," he was saying. "Thanks." He clicked off and looked at me. "Bill has to have the car towed here. The Chelan County sheriff is having a deputy drive him and Tanya back to Alpine on Sunday."

"Did you talk to Bill or Tanya?"

"Bill. They're staying over there because the weather's better."

I paused in the act of pouring coffee. "It usually is. You mean they're having a good time together?"

Milo rubbed the back of his head. "I guess so. It's almost too good to be true. They've both had romances go sour. Maybe they need each other. Hell, why not?"

I sat down. "What are you doing today?"

"I should start cleaning up at my place. I'm serious about putting the house on the market in early March. You can come along and figure out what — if any — of the furniture we should keep."

"We don't have room for much more stuff," I said, still feeling a bit foggy. "Your sofa's newer, but it's bigger and wouldn't fit here."

"I could put it in my workshop if I wanted to take a nap."

"Milo! How big is your workshop going to be?"

He laughed. "Not that big. Relax. I'm kidding."

"Oh." I sipped some coffee. "I'll tag along. I've never really seen all the furnishings in your house."

We arrived at the sheriff's split-level a little after ten. "You'll have to hire somebody to clean up the yard," I told him, gazing at what once was probably a decent, if modest, garden. "This is a jungle."

"Mulehide and the kids handled that stuff," he said. "I only did the heavy lifting. When do I have time for anything but basic maintenance?"

"I like to work in my garden," I said. "It's good exercise. Jeez, Milo, you've got wild berry vines and small cedars and just plain junk in the flower beds. You could have snakes for all I know."

He shrugged. "Only garter snakes. They're harmless."

"I can't stand it," I declared. "Since it's not raining, I'll start here."

"Go for it. I'll see you inside."

I spent the next twenty minutes pulling weeds, saplings, four kinds of vines, and what looked like a trail of Marlowe Whipp's careless mail deliveries. At least there was no wind or my pile of debris would have blown all over the other houses in the Icicle Creek development. I was wishing the sheriff could arrest himself for littering when I picked up a bedraggled photo that had caught on a small holly bush — and dropped it. Running up the steps into the house, I called Milo's name.

"What?" he asked, coming from downstairs. "You found a snake?"

"No. It's much worse. Come see for yourself."

With an impatient sigh he followed me outside.

The photo was filthy in more ways than the obvious. Milo didn't pick it up. "Jesus," he said softly. "It's kiddy porn. Did you touch it?"

"Briefly," I admitted. "I didn't know what it was."

"Don't move," he said. "I'll get some gloves and bag it. No fingerprints in this weather, though."

I kept my distance from the blasted picture, wondering where it had come from. Not Marlowe — he was an odd duck in his way, but he wouldn't leave a porn trail behind him. I was deadheading a rhododendron when Milo came back outside. He made short work of his task before joining me.

"Okay, tell me I should've busted into Freeman's closed meeting last night about the porn problem."

"I should have, too," I said. "But the press wouldn't qualify."

"He might have barred *me* — or moved the venue." Milo sighed. "Okay, so who's the porn perp?" He looked up at the overcast sky. "Or who *was* the porn perp?"

"Are you thinking what I'm thinking?"

He took off his gloves before tipping up my chin. "It has to be somebody around here. I could be wrong."

"So could I. What are you going to do?"

"Get to work," he said, his hand falling away. "You can't come with me. I'll drive you back home."

It was useless to argue. Besides, I had an agenda of my own. "The furniture can wait," I said. "Are you going to talk to Freeman?"

"Not yet. Hang on while I lock up." I waited while he secured the house. "I figure he's clueless about the source," Milo went on after we got in the SUV. "That kind of meeting is to rally the troops and bring them up to speed. If any staff or faculty know where the junk's coming from, they won't admit it. My guess is that they don't. The kids bring it in."

We left the Icicle Creek development, heading up to Fir Street. "You processed Wayne's PUD van, right?"

The sheriff shot me a reproachful glance. "It *was* a murder site, even though we weren't sure at first. But I kept it in impound anyway. Early on, my first concern was for the safety gear in case it was faulty or someone had tampered with it. But there was no sign of anything else suspicious."

"What about the little fire by the road?"

Milo frowned. "You're right. That might mean something. Now."

I patted his arm. "Gosh, now that we're married, you listen to me?"

"I don't have much choice. I'm stuck doing that for the rest of my life. Just don't get bigheaded about it, okay?"

"You really are a beast," I said as we passed the high school football field. "I wonder how often Wayne worked on the lines around here, whether they needed it or not."

"Don't rush to judgment," Milo advised. "If Wayne's truck was the pornmobile, every teacher and parent in town could be a suspect."

"Why kill him? Why not report him to you?"

"You expect people to be rational? You know better."

We went by Edna Mae's house. "She mentioned the porn to me."

"Edna Mae looks at porn? Maybe that's how she gets her thrills."

"No. She said it was found in two basketball players' lockers."

"I'm surprised. Those kids can't find a loose ball on the court." Milo pulled into my drive. "You stay put, okay?"

"I might run some errands," I said.

"Emma . . ." His hazel eyes were stern.

"Hey, I'm not an idiot. Really."

"Yes, you are." He mussed my hair. "I mean it."

"I know," I said, getting out of the Yukon. "You be careful, too."

To justify my presence at home, I put in a load of laundry. Milo had never gotten over his habit of leaving his clothes on the bedroom floor, a trait I'd tried to overlook when we'd been together the first time. It didn't bother me anymore. At least not much.

Then I followed up on my hunch. Journalists get them, and sometimes they're right. In all my years of reporting, I was batting .300 — not bad for a ballplayer, but not good enough to win a Pulitzer Prize for turning the hunch into an award-winning story. Milo was right about a fee for public records, but I knew from experience that there were sites you could access for free or on a trial basis. The first one I found for the state of California offered three introductory hits. I typed in Jack Blackwell's name. Nothing. Maybe his first name was John. I tried that — and got zip. I only had one freebie left. Jack might be a nickname. His dark coloring might indicate he was part French. Without much hope, I typed in "Jacques." The screen informed me there were three documents on file that were included in the introductory offer. The first was his birth certificate, June 4, 1947, Redding, California. The second was a marriage license for Jacques Eugene Blackwell and

Jennifer Ann Hood, May 10, 1973, Dunsmuir. I was shocked, not because my hunch had paid off but because Jennifer didn't look much over forty. Even if I added a few years, she must have been a child bride. Jack would have been twenty-five. I went for the third document — a no-fault divorce decree granted on September 24, 1974, in Redding. Maybe I'd found my dark horse.

But had I found Wayne Eriks's killer? I closed the site and tried to come up with a link between Jennifer and Wayne. Nothing, except for the mention of some smoke near the PUD van not long before she heard sirens. Why had she brought up the subject in the first place? As I recalled, we hadn't been talking about Wayne's death.

I dialed RestHaven's number and asked whoever answered if Jennifer was at work. She wasn't, the brisk female voice informed me. Could I get her home phone number? No, RestHaven didn't give out the staff's personal information. I identified myself, adding I'd planned to invite Jennifer for dinner tonight but had to postpone. The voice softened, saying she'd take my number and have Jennifer call me.

There was nothing I could do except wait. Meanwhile, I called Harvey Adcock to ask him about the school board meeting. If Vida or Mitch had been in town, I would have let one of them do it, but I was the designated inquirer. Fortunately, Harvey was home and not at his hardware store.

"I can't help much," he said. "Karl was candid, telling us about the filth found in some of the students' possession. He did show us a couple of photos, and yes, they were porn."

"Adult or kiddy?"

"Adult. Women undressing, probably taken through windows. Oh, my, I don't want to think of anything involving children! That's worse."

"You never know these days. Did Freeman or anybody else find out where the kids were getting it?"

"A few students have been asked, but they claim to have gotten it from someone else or found it by accident. We're holding another meeting next week, but no date or time's been set."

"May I go public with that?"

"No, please don't. It's an internal matter involving children — most students are under eighteen. It's embarrassing faculty, parents, the youngsters, and the school board, too. I shouldn't have told you this much."

"Harvey," I said sternly, "surely you're

reporting this to the sheriff?"

"Not yet," he replied, sounding shocked. "We have to discuss it."

"You did that. What next? Torture the kids until they come clean?"

"Certainly not!" Harvey sounded as upset as if Durwood had driven his car right through the hardware store. "Please try to understand."

"I do. So does Dodge," I said. "In fact, he's on the case right now."

"He is?"

"Yes, which is why I'll be putting your information online as soon as Dodge gets back to me." Unless, of course, Milo told me to stick it in my ear for now. "I doubt Effie Trews will object. She already went public."

Harvey didn't speak for a long moment. "Don't quote me. Please."

"Fine. You're an unidentified source. Good-bye, Harvey."

To work off my anger, I finished cleaning Adam's closet. I'd gotten everything off the floor by eleven-thirty, when the doorbell rang. Maybe Harvey wanted to plead his case in person. Opening the door, I found a distraught Cookie Eriks almost falling across the threshold.

"Oh, Emma!" she cried. "You've got to

help me!"

I grabbed her arm and gently pushed her into the easy chair. It seemed to swallow her up. I hovered over her, noting the red eyes that indicated she'd been crying. I asked if I could get her something to drink.

"Water," she said.

I went to the kitchen, poured a glass of water, added some ice, and went back to the living room. "Take your time," I said, sitting on the sofa.

Cookie sipped from the glass, took a rumpled tissue out of her rain jacket, dabbed at her eyes, blew her nose, and stared into space before speaking. "The sheriff's at our house with a warrant. He said it was for evidence about Wayne's death. I couldn't stand it. I left. You were kind to me when Wayne was suspected of killing Tim. I don't know where else to turn. Are you and Dodge engaged?"

I involuntarily fingered my wedding ring. "We're married. That doesn't mean I know everything about what he does on the job."

"You're . . . ?" Cookie dropped the tissue. "Oh! Maybe I shouldn't have come. Now Tiff has to deal with . . . the sheriff." She jumped out of the chair. "I should go."

I stood up, too. "No." I spoke quietly. "You wanted to talk to me. My marital status hasn't changed who I am. I gather you trust me. Sit and try to pull yourself together. If nothing else, I can listen."

Cookie was clearly at war with herself, which was better than being at war with me. Finally she collapsed back into the easy chair. "You don't know what I've been through."

"I can guess," I said, also sitting back down. "It's about Wayne, isn't it? He wasn't a very good husband."

She nodded. "That's not the worst part. He wasn't a good father, either. He . . ." Cookie had taken out another tissue and was shredding it. "This is so hard. . . . I tried to put it in a letter to Vida, but . . . I couldn't."

A vague memory came back to me. "Did you write to her twice?"

Cookie's eyes widened. "How did you know?"

"I read your first letter while Vida was gone. Another letter followed saying the problem was solved. You described yourself and it fit you."

"Does Vida know?" Cookie asked, her voice verging on panic.

"I doubt it. Vida's had her own problems. Sexy magazine photos weren't the real issue, right? Were the pictures taken by

Wayne?"

Cookie drooped in the chair. "Yes. Not just women — children, too. But that's not the worst part." She winced. "He abused Tiff when she was younger. That's why she glommed on to Tim right out of high school. She ran away from home a few times, but never got very far."

I tried to hide my shock. I'd expected porn, but maybe I was naïve. As a longtime observer of human depravity, I should've guessed. I phrased my next question so it wouldn't make Cookie defensive. "You must've been afraid to tell anyone. Is that the reason you were so upset when Wayne was arrested for Tim's murder? Did you think Tim knew what had gone on with Tiffany?"

Cookie nodded. "He did. When Tiff got pregnant, she started taking out her anger on Tim and told him about her dad. Tim confronted Wayne, who denied it, of course. When Tim was killed, she blamed her dad and felt responsible. Tiff thought she'd ruined everything she and Tim had together."

Tiffany's self-absorption after moving home was explained. Back then I'd thought she was just a spoiled brat. She *was* spoiled, but not in the way we'd thought. "Did

Wayne molest Tiffany after she came home?"

"No. I think he knew that if he did, she'd report it. She was terrified what he'd do when Ashley got older. That's why she moved in with Jack."

"But that didn't work out," I said. "Was Jack abusive? Physically, I mean. He has a reputation for it."

Cookie sighed heavily. "He threatened her. She borrowed some money from him to buy clothes. He got mad. That's when she left him."

"That was probably smart of her." I paused, realizing I still wasn't sure why Cookie was sitting in my living room and shredding yet another tissue. "Given everything you've told me and that the authorities should have been notified long ago, why are you so upset now that the sheriff's searching your house for Wayne's porn?"

Cookie squeezed her eyes together. "He won't find any. We burned it. Mel hauled most of it away."

"I don't understand."

She opened her eyes, but looked at the floor. "Because I think Tiff's still on the edge after everything that's happened. In fact, I'm afraid she may confess that she killed Wayne."

480

TWENTY

Cookie Eriks, who I had thought to be not much more than a cipher in the Eriks-Rafferty lash-up, had dumbfounded me with one shocking revelation after another.

"Why would Tiffany do that?" I asked, it being the only question I could think of after her latest bombshell.

"Because she did," Cookie replied with artless candor. "I went to see Marisa Foxx for advice, but she told me I needed another kind of lawyer. I didn't know what to do next."

I'd managed to kick my brain into working order. "You mean she killed him? How?"

"Well . . ." Cookie crossed her legs and swung one foot in a nervous manner. "She'd found some awful pictures he'd taken of her in the bathroom. Tiff got so mad she rushed out of the house. She knew he might still be working at RestHaven or somewhere close by. It turned out he'd gotten soaked by the rain and was changing into dry clothes. She showed him the pictures. He laughed." Cookie paused, though her leg was swinging even faster. "Tiff said she was taking the pictures to the sheriff. He grabbed her and she fought him, and then she got hold of the wire — she knew enough to wrap it in his undershirt, which was on the floor — and she stabbed him. He fell. Despite the undershirt, she burned her hands — not badly, just enough to hurt, but she threw the wire and the shirt into the river. Then she got out of the van."

I recalled what had looked like a rag hanging on a branch over the Sky. I waited for Cookie to continue, but her leg had stopped swinging and she had started to cry. "Did she come home?" I asked.

"No," she gulped, wiping her eyes. "She just stopped by to get some of her things. She went to Jack's house. Ashley was with me."

"She could drive with burned hands?"

"I guess." Cookie had stopped crying, but she looked even worse than when she'd arrived.

And I was confused. "I'm sorry," I said. "The second autopsy revealed Wayne had been poisoned."

"I don't know anything about that,"

Cookie declared, suddenly showing a spark of defiance. "It was self-defense, really. Dodge will understand. You can explain it better to him than I can."

"That's not up to me," I said. "I'm his wife, not Tiff's lawyer."

"Oh. Yes. I suppose she needs a lawyer. I wonder if Mr. Doukas would represent her, even though he's sort of retired."

I refrained from commenting on Simon Doukas. "You might want to call him when you get home," I said, hoping she'd take the hint.

Cookie mulled my suggestion. "I will. But I won't mention Dad."

"Your dad?" I said.

We had both stood up. "Yes. He helped Tiff when she needed him."

I nodded. "Durwood's a fine man," I remarked as she moved slowly to the door. *Except when he drives,* I thought.

"Thank you, Emma," she said. "Goodbye."

After closing the door, I leaned against it. What was Cookie trying to tell me? Did she even know what she was talking about? I paced the living room for a few minutes, wishing I could talk to Milo. Maybe he was in his office. I picked up the phone and called him.

Dwight answered. "Sorry," he said, not sounding at all contrite. "Dodge is interrogating someone. Talk to him when he's not working." He hung up.

Despite Vida's attitude, I wished she were home. It occurred to me that she might come back this morning. I dialed her number, but got the usual message to leave every detail except my shoe size. Disappointed but undaunted, I headed off along Fir Street under a pale winter sky almost directly overhead. The Parker home looked as it usually did — comfortable and welcoming. But I wasn't sure their hospitality would last very long. I was on a mission I wished I could avoid.

Dot greeted me with a surprised smile. "I thought it might be Vida," she said, ushering me inside. "She said she'd come back early if Meg and her husband had dinner plans."

"Is Durwood home?" I asked.

"Yes, he's giving Dippy his lunch. We're going to miss the little fellow. But at least we hope to see more of Ashley." She led me down the hall and into the kitchen. "You have a visitor," she said to Durwood, who was scooping what looked like banana off Dippy's chin.

"Almost finished," he said, offering

Roger's child a last bite of chicken. "This little guy likes his chow. Not fussy like our girls were."

Dot lifted Dippy from the high chair, which he'd almost outgrown. He protested loudly and kicked his feet, but she whisked him away from the kitchen. "Nap time," she called over her shoulder.

"Should I put the teakettle on?" Durwood asked.

"No, thanks," I said. "I'm fine. Am I interrupting your lunch?"

"Not at all," he replied, leading me into the living room. "Dot will read to Dippy until he settles down. We don't have lunch until after one anyway. When I retired from the pharmacy we changed our routine a bit."

I again sat down on the plaid sofa; Durwood eased himself into the recliner. "Cookie came to see me a little while ago," I began. "She was very upset. Maybe confused, too. She told me quite a tale."

Durwood looked at me over the top of his half-glasses before lighting his pipe. "Did she now? Cookie's not very imaginative."

"Do you mean she wouldn't make things up?"

He smiled, his round face cherubic. "She's not a liar. Why don't you tell me about her story?"

"It's about you helping Tiff, but Cookie didn't say how you did it."

"Ah." He leaned back in the recliner. "Poor little Tiff. She hasn't had an easy time of it. Tell me, Emma, what would you have done in my place?"

"That depends on the situation," I said, feeling inadequate.

Durwood puffed on his pipe and nodded. "Yes. I hope you never face such a dilemma. Your son's a priest. Being Episcopalian, I know more about that vocation than your average non-Catholic. He's no doubt very levelheaded. But Tiff isn't. Never was." He fingered the furrows in his forehead. "We never knew, not until she moved back home. Dot and I felt so guilty. Why hadn't we been able to sense what was happening?"

"There are some things we don't want to know," I said lamely.

"Turning a blind eye." He stared at the deep blue carpet. "Trying to think the best of Wayne. Not that Dot and I were happy about Cookie's choice, but it was her life."

"Yet you finally stepped in," I said.

Durwood looked rueful. "Thirty-odd years too late. Tiff called me in a panic. She thought she'd killed her dad. I asked if he had a pulse. She couldn't tell. Too distraught. He was still in the van. I told her to

486

stay put. I bicycled down there in the rain. Almost crashed the bike into a gatepost." He chuckled, a hollow, dry sound. "I told her I'd give him an injection. And I did." He folded his hands in his lap and stared at me. "It didn't help Wayne. But it helped Tiff."

I didn't know what to say, but I finally found my voice. "What did you do then?"

He shrugged. "We put his shirt back on. I had matches and burned a hole in it. Not sure why, really, but I thought it might muddle things. All this took less than five minutes. I asked Tiff if she could drive. She said yes. She'd left Jack's Rover in the drive at RestHaven. As soon as she was out of sight, I gave Wayne a swift kick out of the van and he landed on the ground. I should've done that thirty years ago. Then I got on my bike — I'd put it in the van — and came home."

"As a pharmacist, do you know anything about sux?" I inquired.

"Sux?" Durwood looked puzzled. "You don't mean sex? I do remember a little about that." He winked. "Oh — come to think of it, I do recall something about the Dithers sisters having to put down one of their horses with something that sounded like that. A shame — those poor women dote on their four-legged friends. But then animals are often better creatures than some human beings."

"Like Wayne?" I remarked quietly.

Durwood shrugged. "I did what I could. I gave him a heart stimulant. He was on his own after that." He puffed again on his pipe. "I hear Dot going into the kitchen. You sure you won't stay for lunch?"

I stood up, trying to smile. "Thanks, Durwood, but no. Some other time. I can see myself out."

"Come again," he called. "You can meet Ashley. She's a cutie-pie."

Feeling numb, I drove to the sheriff's office. The clouds seemed darker. The sun had disappeared somewhere over the Valley of the Sky. I saw the Yukon in its usual place. Dwight Gould was still on duty.

"What now?" he asked. "Isn't this a Saturday?"

"I don't know," I said, leaning on the counter. "Where's Milo?"

"He went to the Burger Barn. Leave him alone. He's got Beth Rafferty with him."

"Beth?" I said stupidly. "You mean Tiffany?"

Dwight scowled. "Did I say Tiffany?"

"Is she here?"

He shook his head. "Mel Eriks took her home."

"I'll wait." I parked myself in a chair near the door. Dwight went back to whatever he'd been doing before my arrival.

For the next fifteen minutes, phones rang, people came in to report incidents that might or might not make the daily log, and a tourist with a ferret on a leash asked for directions to Snoqualmie Falls. Dwight told him he was on the wrong highway — he had to go south eighty miles and take I-90. "Damned Californians," he muttered, not looking at me. Why he thought the guy was from California, I didn't know. It was as good a guess as any.

Milo finally showed up — without Beth Rafferty. "What are you doing here?" he asked in less-than-husbandly fashion.

"I heard you were seeing another woman," I snapped. "I want a divorce." I ignored Dwight's stare and headed for the sheriff's office.

By the time we both sat down, Milo seemed to decompress. "I had to talk to Beth to find out what she knew about Tiff and this frigging Eriks mess. It appears you stayed out of trouble. I'm amazed."

I got up and closed the door. "I did and I didn't. Before I unload, tell me what happened with Tiff."

Milo leaned back in his chair and looked at the ceiling. "Oh, God! It was a freaking zoo. Why do people keep secrets? And on my watch."

"You couldn't help it if you didn't know about it," I said.

Milo regarded me with curiosity. "*You* know?"

"Yes, Cookie came to call. But I had no idea, either. I was shocked."

"I wondered where she went," he remarked. "I should've guessed. I'd forgotten how you propped her up when I busted Wayne. That family is about as screwed up as any bunch I've ever run into."

"You didn't arrest Tiff, though. Why not?"

Milo shrugged. "Self-defense. I brought her down here to see if she'd be more coherent outside the house. That place is contaminated. At least I gave her time to collect whatever brains she has. She said Durwood tried to save Wayne. Or do you know about that, too?"

I hesitated. "You mean by trying to start his heart?"

"Right. CPR didn't do it. What I don't get is . . ." He narrowed his eyes at me. "Emma, you can't lie to me. You never could. What the hell are you *not* telling me?"

If I'd flunked lying to Milo when we were friends and even lovers, I couldn't do it now that we were married. But I felt miserable. I wasn't certain I could translate what I thought Durwood had meant.

"After Cookie left, I went to see the Parkers," I said. I paused again, trying to recall what Durwood had told me, word for word. "Does that sound like a murder confession?" I asked when I'd conluded my recital.

"Shit," Milo muttered, holding his head. "Is the old coot addled?"

"I don't know," I admitted.

Neither of us spoke for what seemed like a long time. It was the sheriff who broke the silence. "This reminds me of what happened years ago when Cody Graff was poisoned. The wrong person doing the right thing. Or is it the other way around?"

"Both, I guess."

He turned in his chair, staring at his wall map of SkyCo. "I could get a warrant," he said, "but any evidence is probably gone. Interrogating Durwood is another matter. He'd play the senile card." Milo laughed and looked at me. "Hell, he could prove it by pointing out all the times I had to bust him for driving his car through store windows and over Fuzzy's petunia planters on Front Street."

I smiled, surprising myself. "I'd hate to see anybody try to depose Tiff — or Cookie."

Milo had sobered. "I don't like it, though."

I understood. "You've already considered the alternative. It sounds impossible." I played my own hole card. "Think of all the paperwork."

"Emma," he said, "that's a cheap shot. But I like it."

I left Milo to do whatever he had to do regarding the Eriks-Rafferty case. It didn't make me feel any better to learn from him that Beth had never suspected her sister-in-law had been a victim of molestation. Having taken calls of such nature over the years, Beth was more angry than guilt-ridden. Tim had never had a chance to convey his knowledge to his sister before he was killed. The circumstances of his death only made Beth more upset about the tragedies the two families had shared.

If Milo had work to do, so did I, and it wasn't for the *Advocate.* I couldn't ask Kip to put anything online until the sheriff made an official announcement. Getting in my Honda, I drove up to Second Hill and the town house where Kay Burns lived. The trio of homes were on the southeastern edge of the forest, under the shadow of Spark Plug

Mountain. To the north, Mount Baldy and Windy Mountain were obscured by clouds. As I got out of the car, I could barely see the Tye River before it joined the Skykomish just above the turnoff to Alpine.

Kay came to the door wearing overalls and a kerchief tied around her head. Obviously, she'd been cleaning. "Emma?" she said, as surprised as Dot Parker had been when I'd called at her house. "Come in. I'm getting this place in order. The previous owner was no housekeeper."

"Denise Petersen also had a big dog," I said, stepping inside. "It actually belonged to her ex."

"So I was told," Kay said, indicating a sleek dark green sofa where I should sit. "Why do I think this isn't a social call?"

"Because I'm a professional snoop. I want your opinion."

Kay sat down in a matching armchair. "Is this a poll?"

"In a way. What do you think of Jack's claims that someone's trying to kill him?"

Kay looked pained. "I only heard vague rumors until Jack came into my office the day before the grand opening. Typical Jack — all bravado, as if nothing had ever happened between us." Her hand touched her jaw as if she could still feel a blow from decades past. "Dr. Woo insisted I look at Jack's speech. It needed only minor tweaking. Jack's smart. Then, to gain my sympathy, he mentioned his close calls. My first reaction was that he thought I might be responsible. But I don't really think he did. I commiserated briefly and that was that."

"Did you believe him?"

"I don't know. Jack's lucky somebody didn't do him in a long time ago. Frankly, I wondered about Dwight. But why wait this long? It didn't make sense." Suddenly she flushed. "I do have a confession to make. I went through Dr. Woo's files during the open house."

I knew I looked startled. "The patient files? Why?"

Kay shook her head. "A ruse. I wanted to see the staff files. I knew Jack had been married to a girl from Dunsmuir before marrying me. Yes, it was Jennifer Hood. She'd had to list the marriage in her personnel file. If anybody has a grudge against Jack, I'm guessing it's Jennifer."

"I wondered, too," I said. "I did my own digging. Jack's complaints didn't start until after everyone was in place at RestHaven. That's why I was surprised when I thought it was only patient files that were rifled."

Kay shrugged. "That's what I wanted

people to think. I suppose you're going to rat me out to Dodge."

"Why? You're an employee. You have a right to see the files."

"No, I don't. Nobody does without permission from Dr. Woo. He's extremely strict about confidentiality for patients and staff. It's a mania with him." Kay's shoulders slumped. "I violated an internal rule."

"That's none of the sheriff's business. He and I and everyone else dealing with Rest-Haven have been frustrated by the insistence on privacy. It's like a fiefdom. Milo wasn't happy with Dr. Woo about the so-called break-in and told him so."

Kay smiled. "Good for him. Don't get me wrong," she added hastily, "I like my job. Woo's a fine practitioner and administrator. But he does have his quirks."

"Corner office mentality," I murmured, getting up. "I feel kind of dumb coming here and asking you these questions. But I want to make sure the sheriff hasn't . . ." I couldn't find the right words.

Kay had also gotten to her feet. "Let his feelings about Jack get in the way? Easy to do. What I wonder is if Jennifer still loves the jerk."

"You mean enough to sleep with him?"

Kay shrugged. "That's one way to put it.

What's the quote — 'I kissed thee ere I killed thee'?"

"*Othello*," I said.

Kay smiled. "Yes. I was Desdemona in a reading we did in our high school English class. Cal Vickers was Othello and Warren Wells was Iago. Not exactly type-casting."

I smiled back. "Maybe your English teacher had a sense of humor."

"Not really," Kay said. "It was Vida Runkel's future sister-in-law, Miss Hinshaw, who later became Mary Lou Blatt. Very strong-minded and opinionated, with a tongue that could cut steel."

I didn't comment that Vida and Mary Lou had a lot in common. That was probably why they couldn't stand each other. I put my hand on the doorknob. "By the way," I said, "I saw Dwight earlier. He's on duty today at the desk."

"Oh?" She looked intrigued. "Maybe I should call to say hi."

"Good idea," I said, and left Kay to her cleaning duties.

It was raining when I got home at three o'clock. I checked my voicemail, but Jennifer hadn't called me. Ben, however, had left a message.

"Hey, Sluggly," he said, "you should have the annulment stuff by now. Maybe Dodge took a look at it and fled the county. Don't call me — I'm off on the mission circuit for evening Masses. Go with God."

I hadn't checked the mailbox. Sure enough, there was a huge packet stuffed inside. It was addressed to Milo in care of me, but of course I'd let him open it. Maybe not today, though. We'd both been through enough already.

The phone rang as I put the mail on the coffee table. "Can you keep your mouth shut?" Spencer Fleetwood asked.

"About what?"

"Rosalie — and me," he said, sounding subdued. "Hear me out. I met her at a PBS fund-raiser just after her husband had to be institutionalized. She impressed me in a lot of ways. I decided that maybe she could help me out of my funk over losing the love of my life. I'd never seen a shrink before. In the process, she became the new love of my life. But she had a husband. You know how that goes when it comes to the case of the crazy spouse. Maybe now, down the road, we have a real future. But in the meantime, I'd appreciate your discretion. And that of your favorite bear."

"I'm shaking my head," I admitted. "Not a negative response. Naturally, Milo and I wondered. Don't worry, Spence. We can both keep a secret."

"Good. Then I won't worry about him making some crack and having to break *his* nose."

"Will you tell Vida?"

I heard him heave a sigh. "Hell, I won't have to. She probably already knows. Doesn't she always?"

I agreed, and we rang off on a conciliatory note.

Along about four-thirty, I wondered if Milo seriously planned on going out to dinner at Le Gourmand. More to the point, I doubted we could get a reservation at this late date. The restaurant drew diners from all over the region, especially on weekends. I had chicken breasts, more hamburger and tiger prawns in the freezer. We wouldn't starve. Maybe Tanya would be back with us. Feeling unsettled, I resumed cleaning out not only Adam's closet, but two of his bureau drawers.

It was almost six when Milo arrived, looking weary. "Sit," I said, pushing him to the easy chair. "Let me get you a drink."

"Make it a stiff one," he said, handing me his wet jacket. "God, Emma, sometimes I hate my job."

"What else happened?" I asked.

"Just get the drinks," he said, collapsing

in the chair.

I pulled the chicken from the freezer and got out more ice. Obviously, we were going to eat chez Dodge.

After making drinks, I sat on the floor next to the easy chair. "Tell your wife all about it," I said, looking up at Milo.

He reached out to ruffle my hair. "Mel burned all the photos they could find, but we confiscated Wayne's computer. He'd used a program that allegedly wipes stuff out, but it's still there. It just takes some guru to find it, and we will. Even if he's dead, he may have had customers outside the area. At least he can't peddle that junk anymore to high school kids or anybody else in SkyCo."

"You might have gotten on top of that sooner if Freeman hadn't put the lid on things at the high school."

"That's the trouble," Milo said, lighting cigarettes for both of us and handing me mine. "All this damned secrecy — Cookie and Tiff, Freeman, Woo. Sure, I respect people's right of privacy, but it impedes justice and causes bad things to happen. Damn it, I'm still not sure what to do about Durwood. Am I getting soft?"

"You've had to face this sort of impossible situation before," I pointed out. "Did you lose any sleep over it?"

"It was different back then. The guilty parties were on their way out. Durwood's in good shape for his age. Physically, anyway."

"That's my point. Deep down, do you feel he should be punished?"

"Hell, no." Milo sipped his drink and looked thoughtful. "I publicly stated it was a possible homicide. If I retract that statement, how do I look? Like a dope? How does that make the SnoCo lab guys look?"

"Confused. *I'm* confused. Maybe Wayne was almost dead after Tiff jabbed him. Maybe Durwood *was* confused. Have Tiff make a formal statement about why she stabbed her dad in the first place. Eventually the whole town is going to find out what happened to her."

Milo frowned at me. "How?"

I rested my arm on his leg and smiled. "Vida. How else? You let her broadcast that on her program and she may start speaking to you again."

"Is that good news or bad news?"

I punched him. Gently. "You know what it is. And it *is* news."

"For you, too," he murmured.

I grimaced. "I'm dumping this one on Mitch. I might let Vida and Spence scoop me. We can do a follow-up series on child molestation."

Milo held out his glass. "How about a refill?"

I polished off the rest of my bourbon. "Why not? The chicken's not thawed yet."

Milo followed me out to the kitchen. "I forgot to tell you Dwight got a tip today about Blackwell's stabbing."

"Oh?" My back was turned as I added more ice to our glasses. "What was it?"

"Not for publication. Yet." His gaze was steely. "That nurse at RestHaven, Jennifer Hood. You won't believe this, but Dwight told me she was Blackwell's first wife. Maybe she really did make those other so-called threats on his life. It galls me to think I might have to bust her. I wonder if she was afraid the S.O.B. would make trouble for . . ." He grabbed me by the shoulders. "Emma, you little twit! How'd you figure out that one?"

I fell against him and he put his arms around me. "You told me not to get into trouble, so I didn't. I just worked on some research."

I felt him groan. "I'm glad I married you. You're too dangerous to be let loose on your own."

I looked up into his eyes. "Are you sure we're married? You said you got a waiver, but I thought both parties had to sign the application."

"Right. You signed it."

"When?"

He chuckled. "When you thought you were signing the quote for Melville. You never looked at the thing. You were still half asleep."

I tried to pull away, but he held me fast. "You tricked me?"

He shrugged. "I lost you once. I wanted to make damned sure it wouldn't happen again. Are you sorry?"

I put my arms around his neck. "No. But it must be the only time you didn't go by the book, Sheriff."

"That's because I wanted to write my own book. You realize you're stuck here with me in Alpine for the rest of your life?"

A flood of memories came back to me, almost as if they were reflected in Milo's intense hazel eyes: my first day on the job, with Vida overwhelming me with names and places as foreign as if I'd landed in Outer Mongolia; the little town's cluster of nondescript commercial buildings and mostly modest houses clinging to the craggy terrain of Tonga Ridge; the smallness of it all, the relative isolation, the thick forest encroaching on a tiny patch of civilization. I'd spent my life in cities. I'd come face-to-face with culture shock. All I'd had was a college-bound son, a used Jaguar, and a will to strike out on my own. I hadn't thought about spending the rest of my life in Alpine. Getting from one deadline to the next and putting out a decent newspaper were my only goals. I never guessed that when I stumbled into the sheriff's office on a warm August afternoon, I'd met my future. I'd had no dream of finding my own little Eden, my snowcapped paradise, my Xanadu in the Valley of the Sky.

I looked up at Milo. "Maybe this is where I was always headed, even when I wasn't sure where I was going. I might belong here after all."

He nodded. "We both do. It's home, Mrs. Dodge."

I smiled. "And now it's *our* home."

ABOUT THE AUTHOR

Mary Richardson Daheim started spinning stories before she could spell. Daheim has been a journalist, an editor, a public relations consultant, and a freelance writer, but fiction was always her medium of choice. In 1982, she launched a career that is now distinguished by more than sixty published works. In 2000, she won the Literary Achievement Award from the Pacific Northwest Writers Association. In October 2008, she was inducted into the University of Washington's Communications Hall of Fame. Daheim lives in her hometown of Seattle and is a direct descendant of former residents of the real Alpine when it existed in the early part of the twentieth century until it was abandoned in 1929. The Alpine/Emma Lord series has created interest in the site, which was named a Washington State ghost town in July 2011.

www.authormarydaheim.com